THE
INNOCENT
GIRLS

BOOKS BY B.R. SPANGLER

Where Lost Girls Go

THE INNOCENT GIRLS

B.R. SPANGLER

bookouture

Published by Bookouture in 2020

An imprint of Storyfire Ltd.
Carmelite House
50 Victoria Embankment
London EC4Y 0DZ

www.bookouture.com

Copyright © B.R. Spangler, 2020

B.R. Spangler has asserted his right to be identified
as the author of this work.

All rights reserved. No part of this publication may be reproduced, stored in any retrieval system, or transmitted, in any form or by any means, electronic, mechanical, photocopying, recording or otherwise, without the prior written permission of the publishers.

ISBN: 978-1-83888-258-7
eBook ISBN: 978-1-83888-257-0

This book is a work of fiction. Names, characters, businesses, organizations, places and events other than those clearly in the public domain, are either the product of the author's imagination or are used fictitiously. Any resemblance to actual persons, living or dead, events or locales is entirely coincidental.

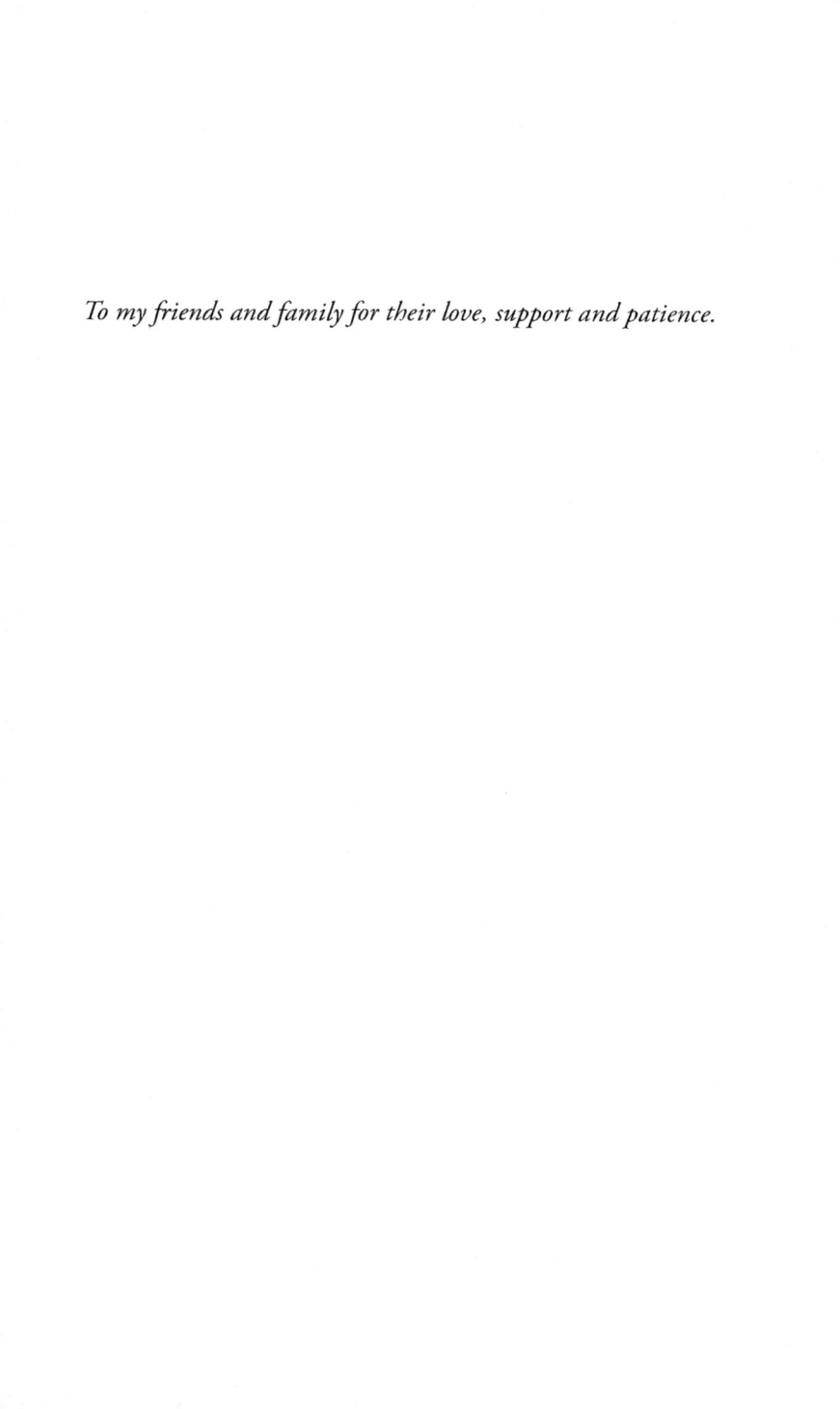

To my friends and family for their love, support and patience.

PROLOGUE

I imagined your first innocent kiss. Sixth grade. The end of a school dance. A cloudy gray day coming to an end, the night just starting to fall, and the moon slipping into the open.

You wore makeup for the first time. Nothing over the top. Just enough to put some color in your cheeks and a touch of the same on your lips. I added a tiny bit of eyeshadow over your eyes too. The same as mine, you'd insisted.

When the moment came, there was a gust of wind, tree branches black against the sky, clacking and spitting autumn foliage. You heard none of it though, your eyes on his. You smiled nervously, bashful and shy, the boy reaching for your hand.

I clutched your father's arm as we spied through the window. The tree let out a soft groan as though approving. The wind subsided as the moonlight shone on your faces. I held my breath when you leaned in and kissed him.

I miss you, Hannah.

CHAPTER ONE

It started with an argument. It ended with murder.

Lisa's chest went tight while she held her words inside and waited for what her parents would say next. Her plan was simple. She'd told them she'd hook up with friends at the boardwalk arcade, near the old change machine, the broken one that sometimes spat out five tokens for a dollar instead of four. So why were they making such a big deal out of it?

She peeked through the window to see the daylight retreating. She shifted restlessly. The sun had already dropped below the horizon, which meant she'd only have the moonlight to guide her. But the darkness and the late hour weren't the problem. Her parents were. *Could they know somehow? About him?* Maybe they were on to her. Maybe they knew she wasn't telling them everything. After all, the boardwalk wasn't the only place she was going tonight.

Daytime in the Outer Banks meant sun, sand and surf. It meant oiled bodies and beach towels. It meant ocean spray in your face, sand between your toes, and cool breezes on your wet skin. It meant all these things, and all this was why Lisa insisted they vacation there.

The night-time meant the boardwalk and adrenaline-pumping rides. It meant food and friends and crowding into a photo booth to take goofy photographs. It also meant boys, fleeting summer crushes, and evenings ending with a kiss. But this evening was for someone else, and not even boardwalk crushes could keep her away.

She heard a memory, heard *his* voice, *his* words. A flutter ticked inside her chest, and her heart swelled. There was a place she had to be. It was her secret: no beach, no boardwalk, and certainly no parents. *Eight twelve*, the time on the wall-clock read, the second hand sweeping around the top, the smooth motion needling her, urging her to leave. *I could do that. I could just leave.* She couldn't be late. Not to see him.

A nudge, cold and wet brushed against the back of her knee. Lisa reached for Tiny and ran her fingers behind his ears. The RV's space was already tight, but they couldn't have left their aging German shepherd with a boarder. Would they have known how frail he was? Or how to feed him properly? She left her seat, kneeling as parental voices droned on, their figures in Tiny's cloudy eyes. She took to rubbing the dog's legs, hoping it brought him relief, the joints stiff and swollen with arthritis.

"Are you even listening?" her mother barked, a crease forming in her brow, the wrinkles deeper since her weight gain.

"I'm listening," Lisa answered sharply. But it was a lie.

Her mother made the face then. It was a look Lisa knew to be a bad sign. They were far from home, having rented an RV, a first for their family, but the vacation had become a disaster, and her parents complained about it constantly.

It was their size that was the problem, the quarters too cramped, the space unusually tight. Lisa sat at the center of the RV, far enough to be safely out of the way, a narrow hall separating her from them. Out of nowhere, Lisa imagined them suddenly getting stuck, their bodies wedged between the kitchen counters. She imagined having to call the fire department, the firefighters coated in grime and sweat, their muscled arms taking to the RV's shell with clacking mechanical jaws to rip into it like a tin can and free her parents. A smile crept to her lips, but she hid it, knowing if she laughed now, that'd really get them going.

"You're just too young," her mother continued, her tone adamant.

"I'm thirteen," Lisa said, her voice sharp, tears standing in her eyes. Some of her reaction was born from emotion, and some of it was rehearsed, helping her get what she wanted. "I see a lot of kids out at night."

"It's *because* you're only thirteen," her mother explained, her voice pitchy, her neck and cheeks pinking. She fanned the air. "And why is it so damn hot?"

"I'm thirteen," Lisa repeated. She needed the time away from them. Now more than ever. "I just want to hang out with my friends!"

"For a week," her father objected, his voice booming. Lisa reeled back. He caught her reaction and said in a calmer voice, "Lisa, you've only been thirteen for a week. And who are these friends? We're on vacation. We're on an island that's hundreds of miles from our home."

A long pause. Tiny whimpered and nudged Lisa again, wanting to be petted. "For Christ's sake, be reasonable," her mother said, wiping sweat from her face.

"You be reasonable!" Lisa shouted, standing and smacking the table. The tone cut the air and a sting set in her palm. "They're just friends."

"Where did you meet these *friends*?" her mother asked, her voice hanging on the last word. Tiny followed the exchange, his head swaying back and forth. Her mother poured a glass of wine, the fruity smell pungent. "All your friends are home in Pennsylvania."

Lisa chewed nervously on her upper lip. "These are a different group of friends. I met them online."

Her father's eyes blazed as he traded looks with her mother. Lisa realized her mistake in her choice of words.

"But I've known them for almost a year."

"Online?" he asked, breathing hard, his face a ruddy color. He ran his fingers through his thinning hair, brushing it from his damp forehead. "Can you even hear yourself? What have we told you about people online? They're strangers."

"Dad," she began, her hand in the air, hoping he'd settle. She didn't like when he looked like that. Her best friend's father used to get that way, red in the face. And then he died. "Dad, they *are* real."

"Have you ever met any of them in person?" her mother asked, her lips on the wineglass, her voice a hollow echo.

"Sometimes we video chat."

"Oh, that's wonderful," her mother muttered. She shook her head and hastily tipped the bottle for a refill.

"Video chat?" her father asked, his tone shifting. He rubbed the back of his neck, thinking.

Tiny's ears perked up, as did Lisa's brow. She'd struck an interest.

"Yeah, we video chat all the time," she added, believing it would help. "Like you said, Dad, with the tech these days, the world is a much smaller place."

"I have an idea," he began, surprising them. "How about I drive Lisa to the boardwalk?"

Her mother tilted her head, a sign she was listening. But Tiny leaped onto all fours and gave a sudden bark, enormous in the RV, at a shuffling sound outside. The hairs on his nape rose as Lisa's mother pointed a finger, until he sat down.

"Come on, boy," Lisa said, coaxing Tiny to come closer to her.

When the outside was silent again, her father continued. "Tell you what. I'll drop Lisa at the boardwalk where I can see her friends. And if I'm comfortable with what I see, then I'll—"

The crash came without notice, her father's words lost amidst an explosion of metal and glass and particle board, the pieces flying inward like confetti at a parade. Lisa saw a foot and then a leg, a black leather boot, the heel thick and raised. Next, she saw a man, his face covered. She saw a wine glass shattering against the floor and her mother's round face frozen in a scream.

Lisa sunk down and scampered into the RV's bathroom, coaxing Tiny to follow, their motion hidden behind her father as they made their way inside.

The RV's bathroom was small, like the kind in an airplane. From behind the pleated door she saw her parents' legs. Commotion erupted, flesh pounding with grunts and yells. Through the panic, she had one thought: the police. She searched for her cell phone but found her pocket empty. Wide eyed, she peered through the opening and scanned the RV, finding the mess of white charging cables sprouting from a wall socket next to the wine bottle, a spaghetti strand plugged into her cell phone.

"What are you doing? What do you want?" her father yelled. Bodies crashed against the sides of the RV. His voice again, breathless, "Is it money? We have traveler's checks, maybe some—"

"Oh my God!" her mother screamed. "Oh please God no!"

A blade was revealed, a hard light glinting as the intruder raised it above his head and plunged it into her mother's neck. At once, her mother's screaming ceased. Lisa ducked inside, covering her ears, all of her senses feeding on the nightmare beyond the pleated doors. She felt a huge thud vibrate through her like a heavy sack hitting the floor. Lisa had to see, had to look, and wished she hadn't. Her mother was down, her legs kicking, her lips blue, her mouth a peculiar pucker, opening and closing as she desperately tried covering the gash in her neck.

Lisa's father was a large man, but softer than the muscly young suitor she'd often admired from the family's old photo albums when he was courting her mother. He took to the attacker with hands balled into fists like clubs, his knees lunging and overwhelming. Lisa held onto Tiny, his teeth bared with a menacing growl. She gripped the dog's coat as hard as she could, knowing it would hurt, but knowing he'd be killed if she didn't keep him inside the bathroom with her. Lisa tears were silent, her cries pinched by the terror gripping her.

She had to turn away again, wishing she could cover her ears, but having to hold Tiny as the fight was heard and felt, her father taking a stand. Lisa eyed the window above the toilet. An escape. She peered back into the RV, saw the bloodied knife on the floor, a hammer in the attacker's hand, swinging wildly. There was a whoosh and a sharp thwack as the head of the hammer struck her father. His body twitched and twisted as he fell to his knees, a fold of skin dangling from his forehead. He swiped errantly at the wound while trying to regain his balance.

For a moment, Lisa could see the attacker, she could see all of him—his head and shoulders and front were covered in black, like the boots and pants he was wearing. She recognized the gear then, padded, the kind she'd worn with her father during paintball tournaments.

Her father saw Lisa, and motioned curtly, the expression on his face horrifying. "Run," he mouthed. "Run now!"

Tears streamed down Lisa's cheeks, all emotion this time, her mother dying or already dead, her father in a battle for his life. With her father's focus on her, the attacker struck again, the blow dense, cracking, and sickening. Lisa saw her father's fingers flex erratically.

She swallowed her cries and slithered toward the window, dragging Tiny. Despite his age she could feel him gaining strength, his ancestral instincts telling him to fight, to defend. She blocked her dog, clutching the door's thin panels, her fingers frantically tracing the edges to secure it. The door's latch was broken, leaving a frightful sliver of light eking through. Her heart cramped with a nightmare, her pulse beating feverishly in her head.

She grabbed the trashcan, near full, and rummaged through the litter until her fingers found a spent toothpaste tube. She curled the plastic-aluminum in half, rolling the remains, and formed a makeshift doorstop. She pinched the end, shoving it beneath the door panel, fixing it in place. It worked, but wouldn't hold anyone trying to enter.

She struck at her doorstop once more, forcing it deeper as a scream from her father stopped her mid strike. The gruesome sound resonated throughout the RV, his voice cut short in a clotted and choking breath. The noise from the fight ended, the silence piercing. The killer had finished. Her eyes dried at once, the need to cry distant, her emotions replaced with a fear so dreadful her mind could barely comprehend it. She was going to die.

The window. She searched the inky black on the other side of the glass until her eyes adjusted. The faint shape of trees appeared, silhouetted, showing her the campground's wooded lot. The window was short, narrow. She was growing, the cold winter bringing curves to her middle like her friends. Would she fit through?

She heard footsteps. Tiny fidgeted, his ears perked, his hair standing, his teeth bared. He wanted out of the bathroom. Lisa took hold of him, laying his head across her lap and covered his nose and mouth, squeezing, desperate to keep him quiet.

"Please," she begged, whispering into his ear. She dared not wipe her tears. Dared not make another sound.

He answered with a whimper that crescendoed into a growl, a response to the activity beyond the door.

Her toothpaste doorstop held, but an edge of light remained, enough for her to dare a look. She saw her father's body lying next to her mother's—his eyes huge, round like saucers, lifeless. The killer stood over her father's body, his frame set in black, the knife back in his hand, the hammer in the other. He glanced over his shoulder as though he knew Lisa might be watching. She froze, squeezing

Tiny's head and holding her breath. She told herself to look away, but couldn't make herself move.

The killer kneeled as if to say a prayer. And like a painter preparing a fresh canvas, he brushed an area of her mother's skin, cleaning it, and then took the knife to it. He began to draw, he began to carve.

The dead don't bleed, Lisa remembered hearing in a movie once. It was true too. Her mother was dead, the cuts appearing like carvings in the mottled rind of a pumpkin.

Tiny barked, his voice monstrous and startling. His weight was too much as he squirmed free from her lap and jumped at the door, the signs of advanced arthritis gone, his front paws vaulting up in a push, revealing their hiding place. His barking came alive, saliva dripping from his lips. Lisa saw the killer stand to face them.

Terror struck her deeply. She yanked Tiny, his hair coming free, shedding into her palms. He stayed on all fours, panting, and charged the door again. A footstep.

Lisa was suddenly deaf, blood thrumming in her ears, her heart swelling in her throat, her bladder threatening to release. She took to the toilet, climbing atop the bowl's lid and gripped the window. The attacker's heavy footsteps rippled through the RV, the vibrations hitting her bare feet. He was coming for her. Tiny's growls were furious as he incessantly pawed at the door's corner. She glimpsed the makeshift doorstop, the rolled tubing saddled between the door and floor holding its place, but not for much longer.

The window opened in a rushing motion. Ocean sounds and smells filled the bathroom. Bells and whistles and joyful roars came from the boardwalk.

Jumping down, Lisa took hold of Tiny in a hug and pulled her companion toward the toilet, eager to push him through the window. She couldn't leave without him. But he cried, whimpered, and wrestled against the hug until slipping free.

"Please," she begged, trying again. But he was too bulky, too heavy. He let out a cry, baring his teeth, and then snapped at her face. Instantly she dropped him, scared of him. In all her years, he'd never growled at her, never once bared his teeth or shown any type of aggression.

It's his arthritis, she justified sadly. *I hurt him is all. I must have hurt him.*

As if agreeing, Tiny nosed her leg, his round eyes apologetic the way a dog's eyes sometimes are. He was seeing her again and she fell next to him. Her heart broke.

"I'm sorry. I can't take you with me," she whispered in his ear. Tiny lifted his paw, misunderstanding and playing an old trick he'd played a thousand times. "No, I don't have any treats. I have to go."

Lisa climbed through the window's tight opening, her arm catching on the metal frame, ripping open her skin. There was noise from the other side of the door, the killer's voice reciting strange words. Panic urged her to move faster, to ignore the pain. Tiny went back to the door, barking, scratching at the panel, his nails digging into the flimsy vinyl.

She got stuck then, her body stiff with fright, her waist latched sturdily onto the window's sill. Behind her, Tiny's feet scratched against the floor, his nails rapped on the toilet seat. He picked at her feet next, his teeth gently nipping at her toes, wanting to pull her inside the bathroom. Sweat covered her head and face, and with every muscle quaking, she lifted herself, shifting her body's weight until she fell through the window. The ground came rushing at her like a high drop from an amusement ride, stone and sand crushing her hands and head as she tumbled into a somersault.

Tiny's barks went silent as her vision clouded. She got to her knees, wobbling. Her stomach threatened to empty, a sour taste rising in her throat. It passed, her thoughts swinging to her dog, and to get help.

"Tiny," she mumbled, staring overhead, his nails hitting the toilet seat again, his voice a whimper as he tried to follow. He stopped briefly, and then started again, another whimper and bark coming as Lisa clutched her chest.

The night was dark. Without the city lights she could disappear within a few steps from the RV. With no shoes, no cell phone, Lisa knew she had to find help. But what if he was after her? She'd seen the killer. She'd seen what he'd done. Who could she trust?

His voice returned. And with it came calmness, a serenity. *He* would know what to do. Lisa could go to *him*.

Tiny's cries were louder as he tried to follow her. For thirteen, Lisa was tall, and she could reach the window with one leap. She eased herself up to the window's edge, but had no idea how this would work, how she would lift a dog weighing more than she did. She only knew she had to try.

When she peeked into the bathroom, the killer was there, the pleated door shoved open, her doorstop discarded to the other side of the small room. In his arms, the killer held Tiny, his gloved hand gripping her dog's face. A scream came. A vapid, empty sound, the horror cracking something fragile in her mind. Lisa dropped from the bathroom window, the air rushing past her, the stones and sand warm on her feet. And finally, she did what her father had told her to do. She ran.

CHAPTER TWO

I love the smell of freshly cut grass, of the walkways and roads after a spring rain, of gardens in bloom and of trees heavy with seasonal blossoms. My daughter loved this time of year too, her smile broad and dimpled, jumping excitedly from puddle to puddle like a butterfly working a row of flowers.

Her father was less pleased with what the season had to bring. He worked a tenth or eleventh pull on the mower's starter, cursing under his breath at the old oil guzzler, a junk heap held together by rusting bolts. The cutting blade had stuck, and the grass was still too wet from the brief thunderstorm.

A distant rumble interrupted the birds singing, growling harshly as it bounced across the neighborhood, warning of another dark storm. I searched for threatening clouds, but the sky was clear. Hannah jumped into another puddle, her laughter pealing and the water splashing while her father muddled over the mower's state. He disappeared behind our house then, leaving us alone, another thunderclap making me jump and consider going indoors.

"Don't get too wet," I warned, the sky remaining strangely blue, the blades of grass around me seeming to grow before my eyes.

Sunlight caught a charm from Hannah's bracelet as she spun playfully like a ballet dancer. That's when I saw the car at the top of our street: the color blazing red, its tires like claws chewing into the asphalt, the motor heaving with a thunderous boom.

Panic seized me when I saw the piercing eyes, their sparkle like diamonds gleaming from behind a black windshield. The woman's ice-blue stare instantly turned me cold, her face dead below the eyes, her skin stitched together in odd-shaped patches like a quilt. I knew the car, knew the woman inside too. And I knew she was here to steal my child. I screamed, "Hannah!"

Hannah ignored me, her eyes stolen by the sight and the booming roar. Ronald was gone, so were the trees, so was everything except the lawn and the road. The car raced to meet Hannah, but I'd stop it this time, I'd take my child inside where it was safe. The lawn stretched into two, and then into three, the length of it growing. The car door opened its ugly mouth, Hannah laughing with delight as she climbed inside.

"Hannah!" I screamed. I trudged through the tall grass, panting, toothless mouths sucking the shoes off my feet and leaving me to run barefoot. The blades climbed my legs and whipped the air, slicing my hands as I batted away their attack. I saw my girl's eyes then, saw her warm smile, her pudgy fingers waving me a goodbye as the car's door slammed shut. "Please don't take my baby!"

With a flash, the dream was gone. The woman and Hannah disappeared. I sat up in my bed, screaming, a coat of sweat sending a shiver through me. There were cries then, mine, as my heart broke just as it had so many times already. Like the woman's face in my dream, my heart was a patchwork of stitched wounds, the seams nearly bursting with sorrow.

All I could think was, I did this. I'd lost my child. I closed my mouth, silencing the nightmare and what came after, and checked the time. It was two in the morning. I was certain I'd never get back to sleep and cursed the dream for sentencing me to toss about until the day's first sunlight crept through my window.

I listened then for the woman's laughter, holding my breath and the cries that wanted to come. I only heard ocean noises, the tranquility that came with my new beachfront apartment. The rolling and crashing of the waves unexpectedly lulled me closer to sleep, my eyelids heavy, although I still knew sleep would elude me. I'd lost count of the number of nights I'd woken sweaty and shivering, of the nightmares and the days of dark circles beneath my eyes. Perhaps I should have seen a psychologist, but I didn't need a doctor to tell me what the dreams were about. They were about the guilt, about what I'd lost, and who should take the blame. The dreams were about losing Hannah.

My phone's ringer jolted me from wherever we go when falling asleep, stirring me to sit straight up in my bed, the clock showing it was already five in the morning. I rubbed the sleep from my eyes to check again, finding a small miracle of miracles. I'd actually slept a few hours.

Checking my text messages, I found there'd been another nightmare last night, only it hadn't been mine. It was born of reality rather than some dreamland. And it had ended in murder.

CHAPTER THREE

It's a new summer season in the Outer Banks of North Carolina. The temperatures are already sweltering, and the vacation town already teeming with tourists. This morning, there was a hurricane looming, early for the season, its breezy fingers stealing my hair and spinning it into a twirl. I'd let my hair grow out during the last year and was still getting used to the extra length on my shoulders. I stopped to study the scene of the crime when we reached the recreational vehicle. The first sight of the RV told me nothing out of the ordinary, except for the obvious: the door was almost destroyed, the handle and lock broken and the frame around it bent inward. What I couldn't see was hidden just beyond the light, the RV keeping it like some terrible secret. A double murder had been reported. Every murder scene is bad in so many ways, but we'd been told this one was particularly so.

Despite it being just before seven in the morning, a crowd had already formed—curiosity having no sense of time, just an itch needing to be scratched, a desire needing to be satisfied. I studied the blank faces, the gawking, the empty eyes, and neck craning, the husbands and wives trying to catch a glimpse of the scene, their lips moving as they exchanged opinions. I took note of every person, every feature—the murderer might have decided to watch us work.

The area was cordoned off by a hundred feet of crime-scene tape, the black-and-yellow ribbon slung taut from tree to tree and wrapped around lamp posts and a park bench to provide a barrier. The edges of the tape twisted and flapped noisily, teased by the hurricane's moist breath. A row of patrol officers stood at the ready, guarding the property as crime-scene technicians hurried toward the RV, talking amongst themselves, rattling off checklist items while waiting for me to give the okay to venture inside.

The early-morning light was dulled by a curtain of evergreens surrounding the campground, the RV and outdoor furniture beaded with dew. Another gust came, strong enough to force me into a lean as the tall trees groaned and swayed. Though we were a mile from the ocean surf, I could taste salt in the air.

The RV's broken door flung open with a loud clack of metal striking metal, releasing the scent of blood and death. Sally Majors, a senior technician, raced to tie it shut. I wouldn't know until we had measurements like body temperature, but from my experience, the death was a day ago, at most, possibly as recent as the previous evening.

The electricity leading to the RV had been cut when the call was made to the police, the manager of the campground pulling the powerline, citing the need as a safety concern. With no lights on the inside, the opening to the RV was as dark as midnight, reminding me of funhouses that were more horror than laughs—and the sight of it was enough to give me pause.

Two murders had been reported at the Neptune Campgrounds, located inland a couple of miles past the intersection off route 58 and 264. From Sally, I'd learned it was a popular campground, a touristy kind of place with families driving in from all parts of the country to call the Outer Banks town of Kitty Hawk their vacation home. A sticker on the RV's rear bumper had a name and logo: Trenton RV Rentals. I made a note of it.

A scurry across the tall evergreens caught my eye: a flash of feathered blue-and-white as jays called to each other, playing a game of chase before making their way deeper into the woods. I flipped through the screens in my notes, finding a recent report from narcotics about drug activities traveling from the south. There'd been gangs creeping across the bay to increase their territory while the Outer Banks summer vacation season was readying. With the campgrounds completely hidden from the road—the nearest highway a mile or more—it was a perfect place for dealers and buyers to meet and do their business. I'd keep the idea in mind but wouldn't make a call to the guys in narcotics just yet, not until I had more to work with.

Cameras, I thought, checking the telephone poles and trees, hoping for a security feed, even a still-photo camera like the kind used by rangers to capture wildlife and poachers. There was nothing, every pole and tree bare, which surprised me, given how cameras had sprung up everywhere. It was suspicious enough to make another note for the investigation—that left us with no record of traffic coming or going through the campground—and another point to mention to the narcotics team.

I could still smell death waiting in the dark as I mentally prepared to enter the RV.

"Got a flashlight?" I asked. I needed light. I saw the campground manager watching us from behind the yellow tape, his stout frame crooked, his hand resting on his hip. "Better yet, let's have the manager turn on the juice."

"Sir," Sally ordered. The manager straightened and offered a curt nod, eagerness on his round face. "Would you mind getting power to the RV? We need the light."

"Oh, certainly, ma'am," he shouted, his accent heavy. "I turn on for you now."

He circled round the taped area and went to the other side of the RV, disappearing from sight, his work boots scratching a path in the sand and stone. I heard him work the connections as plugs were plugged and switches were switched. A moment later, the interior lights flicked on and off and then came to life. With light came the sight of a veiny pale leg lying inside the entrance.

"We got light!" Sally Majors yelled. The manager circled back round to the yellow tape, and we moved over to him.

"Thank you," I said.

"Yes," he answered, carrying the word like a soft whistle. He dipped his chin, and asked, "I stay. To help?"

"That's appreciated," I told him. "We'll want to question anyone working earlier too."

"Just me," he answered, his fingers splayed across his chest. He pointed to the ground, adding, "My home, I manage."

"Should make for a quick interview," Sally said, looking at me.

Before the manager walked away, I asked, "Sir, can you supply the paperwork? The order for renting the site?"

"Yes," he answered, taking a fold of office papers from his pocket. "I bring, in case asked."

"Very efficient," I told him, appreciating the helpfulness. I unfurled the white and yellow pages, the office forms reminding me of a property lease. Across the bottom I found the names. "The site was rented to a Carl and Peggy Pearson."

"Carl and Peggy," Sally spoke the names slowly and lowered her camera. "Let's find out what happened to them."

With a nod to the manager, we moved back to the RV, observing the damage to the door. Someone had wanted to get inside, badly.

"Not much left of it, is there?" I said, indicating the door. From the impression of the outside, there was a lot of force used, the aluminum dented, kicked, possibly multiple blows. "Let's make sure we get some dusting, and check for any prints too."

"I'm on it."

As Sally Majors barked an order, the wind stealing her words, I inspected the point of entry. The RV had been forced open, the doorframe obliterated where the handle's latch locked with the latch plate. This suggested to me the killer had come to the site with intent. Then again, a neighboring camper could have been annoyed by loud music or the smell of bad cooking and gone off on the family.

"Any word on who secured the RV?" I asked, adding a new note, writing the details of the rope hanging from the broken handle. From the color and length, it was from a marina.

Sally flipped through the pages on her pad, answering, "The manager. He's also the one who called it in."

"He's already been inside?"

"Must have," she answered, pointing to the victim's leg. "Took a look inside and then called the police."

I motioned to the crowd and then to the RV, asking, "Was there mention of a commotion or a disturbance?"

She shook her head. Her hair pressed to one side, the storm blowing a hot wind. "The manager only mentioned noise, the wind catching the door."

"Okay. Let's get an interview with him," I said.

"Right," she agreed as the pages on her pad flipped violently until she closed the notebook's cover.

I heard a voice from behind us. "Detective Casey White."

Mayor Ashtole lifted the crime-scene tape and entered the scene, his expression telling me he was troubled. I raised my hand, stopping him. I already had enough work without having to eliminate any more foot traffic and fingerprints. His presence at the site said a lot more than my first impressions—there was money here, enough of it for the mayor to press the work, make for an urgent turn-around, a fast cleanup, *shuffle the ugly under the rug*, as my father liked to say before company arrived on weekend afternoons.

"Mayor Ashtole," I offered, approaching and taking his hand.

"Come on now, call me Daniel," he said, a breeze inflating his suit jacket. He offered a weary smile, his eyes shifting behind a pair of round spectacles as he surveyed the crime scene. When the stench hit him, he stopped as if he'd reached an imaginary line drawn in the sand. "That smells like a damn ugly one. I understand there are two victims?"

"Double homicide, but can't confirm until we go inside," I explained, holding up the paperwork. I motioned to the RV, adding, "Could be a husband and a wife. You're welcome to walk the scene with us. I'm about to go in and we've got plenty of gloves, booties, all the gear for an extra set of hands."

He checked his shoes, brown Oxfords, lifting one foot, his print in the thin sand. He glanced toward a crime-scene technician who was new on the job, her first task handling the issuance of gear, a box of masks, booties and gloves at her side. I'd asked as a joke, but saw he was contemplating the walk.

"It's been some time, but I still know my way around a crime scene," he answered, his tone as familiar as his attire. I'd never noticed until now, but he almost always wore the same thing: maybe not quite the same, but from Oxfords on his feet, the pleated slacks, the button-down collared shirt, tie and jacket. It didn't matter the time of year, the temperature or even the weather. "I think I'll leave it to you and the team."

"What's on your mind then?"

Closing the distance between us, his aftershave mixed with death. He spoke in a voice only I could hear. "There's a very real potential for the press to bite into this case. If that happens, they'll chew on it, if you know what I mean. We've got a double murder, the crime occurring at a popular location. With the season barely started, I wanted to give you a heads up on any questions they're apt to ask. Capeesh?"

"Oh, I do," I said. The idea to move this case along for any reason other than serving justice left a sour taste in my mouth, but that was politics. I couldn't blame Ashtole, he had people to report to too, just like I did. The game was the same no matter where I decided to play cop. It was the balance. It was the political hopscotch and the endless juggle of risk and danger. "Daniel, I understand plenty."

"Good," he said with a lilt in his voice and what looked like a touch of shame on his face. He knew the game. He'd played. He'd been a lawyer and a district attorney for as long as I'd been a cop. And from the looks of him, it had left a bad taste in his mouth too. "I'm glad we're on the same page."

"Same page," I assured him and motioned toward the RV. "If that's all?"

"Here, put this on," the technician carrying the protective gear offered, handing me a mask. "It might help some with the smell, and it'll filter the air and whatever else might be inside."

"Good idea," I told her, seeing her nose and mouth hidden beneath the fabric. For a second, she looked like the woman from my nightmare. The image stole my breath, but I shook it off and dressed the mask over my face, pinching the metal band until I felt it firm against the bridge of my nose. "If I'm right, we'll be inside a few hours too."

The technician handed me a pair of booties and gloves next, the mayor offering his arm while I covered my shoes and then sleeved my hands. Another wave drifted from the RV's opening, the stink reminding me of an animal struck dead and rotting along a roadside.

"Wow. I could never get used to that smell," Daniel said, shaking his head and retreating to the other side of the crime-scene tape.

As the mayor did his best to shield himself, I checked the ground. While there were no cameras, we still had a recording of the night's traffic. Tire treads cut into the sand, each speaking a unique language for us to decipher. We'd no idea how the killer, or killers arrived. But if they drove, there could be evidence beneath our feet.

"Listen," I said, catching the attention of the technician handling the box of gloves and booties. A hot gust teased her hair, the same color as mine, light brown with summer highlights. "Do you have your camera?"

"Yes ma'am," she answered, dimples appearing like round buttons. The smile turned then. She held up the box, adding, "I was told to stand here, make sure nobody goes in without a pair."

"Leave them at the entrance. I've got something else for you to do." The technician did as I told, leaving the box behind, her focus on me. I motioned to our feet, drawing Ashtole's attention to the ground, to the faint tread in the sand. "Get your camera and carefully photograph every tire tread."

The technician slowed her gaze, the count of possibilities high. "Geez, that's a lot of pictures, but I can do that."

"Some of them are from our vehicles," Daniel commented.

"Also get pictures of all the tires from the cars and trucks. Make sense?"

"To rule them out," she said, understanding.

As she tried to leave, I raised my hand. "I need the same for the shoes. The footprints." I saw the whites of her eyes then, and the sands littered in shoe prints. "We have to rule out everyone here."

"I'm on it," she assured me with a curt nod. "And after?"

I liked that she was already asking for more to do. "How about coming inside with me? A crime-scene technician should work a crime scene. Right?"

"Definitely," she answered excitedly, her words trailed as she turned to leave, "This is so much better than what I was doing."

"Mr. Mayor, it's time for me to get to work," I said flatly. But I hesitated to leave his side. I'm good at what I do, good at it without involving any feelings. That might sound cold, even uncaring or mechanical, but when it comes to seeing the worst in people, cold and mechanical are some of my best qualities. Today, however, I felt anxious.

"I'll leave you to it," Daniel said, handing me a card. On the face, I saw the embossed lettering spelling the "Office of Mayor", and then his name beneath. Why the card, the formality? When he caught the confusion, he flipped it over. On the back, he'd put a cell phone number along with a home number.

"A direct line?" I asked in a tone making light of the courtesy.

"It is," he said stoically. "I'm giving you direct access. Anything you need. This is my first summer season as mayor and I don't want to fuck it up. After the last year, the Outer Banks deserves better."

I plucked the card from his hand and tucked it into my pocket. It wasn't often an official at his level took an interest. That's one of the things I loved about the Outer Banks. The closeness.

"I'll probably take you up on the offer," I warned. "Hope you don't regret it."

He offered a grim smile before turning to leave, his Oxfords grating against the sand. "I'll take my chances," he said over his shoulder.

The technician reappeared and flashed her camera, not wanting to waste another minute. She snapped a picture to record every step we'd already made this morning. I moved to give her room as she centered her camera again, focused and continued, the camera's shutter fluttering with the strobe's light striking the RV's interior, unmasking the gruesome hidden details.

Wanting to go inside, and to make good on the offer for experience, I gestured to the technician to join me.

"I haven't finished with the—"

"—That's fine. We'll get someone else to finish." I asked the technician, "What's your name?"

"Tracy," she said, sunlight on her face. "Tracy Fields."

"Well, Tracy, are you ready?"

When Tracy motioned she was ready, we approached the RV, intent on going inside, intent on ignoring any additional interruptions. My tongue felt dry like the dirt. My heart raced too, and my breathing was hurried, which was normal considering what awaited us. We stopped at the RV's entrance and began the note taking and the photography.

The victim's foot was bare, a flip-flop hanging from a toe, the leg shaven and nails painted, some of them chipped. Female, presumably Peggy Pearson, heavyset, her skin already mottled by death, a web of purplish and green veins across the ankle, some of them bulging like corded rope.

It was the victim's toes that caught my attention. They'd already begun to turn, the round tips darker than the rest of the woman's leg. Some were a deep blue, and a few were closer to turning black. Soon, they'd all look like bits of coal. Toes are the furthest distance from the heart, and they are the first parts of the body to die. Tracy moved into position, taking a picture, capturing their current appearance, a timestamp marking the moment for our records. The state of the victim's toes would help us determine the timing of the attack. And while nothing could help the victims now, this was one of many clues we'd find, and we only needed the right one to catch the murderer.

CHAPTER FOUR

The inside of the RV was far worse than I'd imagined. With the lights back on came the sight of the second body, Carl Pearson—another presumption in advance of a positive identification. From outside, there was a short step leading into the RV just behind the high-back seats where the driver and a passenger faced the road, the panels of dashboard equipment dead with the exception of a few warning lights.

The woman's face was discolored, skin ashen, a thin web of purplish veins beginning to appear. Her mouth was frozen in a pucker as though she'd been giving someone a kiss. And there were her eyes, sunken into her head, the skin around them dark like a raccoon's.

"You see that?" Tracy asked, her lean figure like a fairy's as she tip-toed silently over the woman's body. She focused her camera on the victim's neck, a gash from the throat to her ear. The woman had only lived briefly after the attack, the amount of pooled blood significant, as was the spray and spatter on the walls and floor. Her heart had pumped violently in its final moments. "Knife wound?"

I stepped over the woman's body, taking care not to tread in the puddle of blood. By now, it was the consistency of molasses, and nearly the same color too. Stains on the woman's clothes were a dark red, some of it already a patchy black, lending to the timeline I'd surmised from the color of the victim's toes. The knife wound was three inches or more. It could have been simple chance the killer had struck the most vulnerable part of the neck, the carotid or jugular perhaps. Or it could be the killer knew exactly where to attack.

"Any other injuries?" I asked, kneeling to check the victim's hands for any defensive wounds. I checked her arms too, searching for the types of injuries sustained when fending off a knife assault. Tracy shook her head, her stare locked on the other victim's face. "We'll get to him in a moment."

"He fought back," she said without looking at me. Her voice broke then, as she continued. "I mean, he really tried."

In Tracy's tone I heard it, heard the reason we leave our feelings and emotions as far from a crime scene as possible. "Tracy? How you doing over there?" No answer. The camera activity quieted. I changed the topic. "Tell me, how long have you been taking pictures?"

"Since I was little. Mostly family, friends and pets," she said, her voice losing the punchiness I'd heard in it earlier. "But I never thought I'd be taking pictures of dead people."

"Well, at least you don't see them up and about," I joked. She kept her stare fixed on the male victim. There was a gruesome gash on his head, his eyes dead and a haunting expression frozen on his face. From my position I could see some of the defensive wounds. I could also see the damage done to the RV. There'd been a battle. The man had fought hard to live. Tracy remained silent. I joked, "*I see dead people*. You know, from the movie?"

She shook her head, answering, "I don't think I saw that one."

Her reply left me feeling old, but Tracy was talking, which was what I wanted. I got up and went to her, finding her eyes, a mix of emotion in them, tears puddling, her complexion pasty, sweaty. I urged her toward the door, afraid she was going to get sick and possibly compromise the crime scene. "Do you need to leave?"

"He—" She began, shaking her head. I put my hand on her back, her shirt damp. "He, he looks so much like my dad."

"But it's not your dad, is it?" I asked tersely, trying to break her away from herself. I could see her mind spinning in a whirlwind, her thoughts a storm like the hurricane lumbering up the coastline. What was happening to her an odd thing, the mind working its funny magic, a gift for some and a curse for others. Imagination has a way of inserting us into the crime scenes, placing us there—placing us as the victim. And when it's bad, we might even see a loved one as the victim, and then play the whole morbid scene from beginning to end. I'm not sure if that's normal, but for me, I let it happen. It's in the playback where I will sometimes find the questions and answers I failed to see with my eyes.

I nudged Tracy's arm, asking again, "Is it?"

"No."

"Then don't think of him as your dad," I told her, my voice short. I needed to snap her back to why we were here. "Can we get back to work now?"

"Yes," she agreed, swiping at her eyes. "You're right. I don't know why I let myself do that."

I gripped her arm, turning her. "It's perfectly natural," I said, telling her what felt right, but having no idea if it was or wasn't natural. "Use it. It'll let you see what most can't see—"

"Or won't see," she added, an understanding coming to her.

"Exactly." A band of light caught Tracy's face, the age in her voice deceiving. She had one of those forever-young faces, and looked as if she was still in high school. "How long have you been on the job?"

"Not too long," she said, fiddling nervously with her camera's settings. "I've had my certification a few months."

"If you don't mind my saying, you hardly look old enough to be in college."

"I am in college," she answered, correcting me. "I jumped ahead a few years in high school and the certification for this job was separate while I work on my degree."

"Is that so? Impressive."

An expression of calm settled in her eyes, the earlier reservation passing with the change of subject.

"I aced all my exams," she added with a smile, the shallow dimples I'd seen earlier appearing at the edges of her mask.

I saw a brief likeness to my daughter that took my breath for a moment. I realized then, Tracy looked a lot like Hannah—even with her hair pinned back, a cap on her head, and the rest of her garbed in crime-scene gear. It might have been her eyes, or mouth, or the constant dimples when she spoke. I couldn't put my finger on what it was. In the back of my mind, I could have been playing out a fantasy, seeing what I wanted to see. I was a cop, but a mother first, and I never stopped chasing my baby. From the moment she was lured into a stranger's car, I'd chased Hannah, including when I saw her in the resemblance of others.

"Detective? Are you okay?"

A flash of heat rose on my face, Tracy catching me staring. I ignored it, answering, "I'm sure you did. But keep in mind, the training and the books, they are only a part of it," I warned. I tapped my head, adding, "The rest is up here. Listen to your instincts."

She nodded. "Understood, ma'am."

"Casey," I said. "Or, Detective White, if you're more comfortable with that."

I went to the husband's hands, his knuckles bruised and scraped raw as though the skin had been shaven with a sharp kitchen utensil. "You're right about the fight. He looks to have put up a good one. His hands look like he'd been hitting a wall. However, punching someone, a face or body, even when it's repeated, it won't do this kind of damage. The attacker had protection."

"Body armor?" Tracy suggested.

I gave her a shrug, taking a note of it, setting up a question for our medical examiner.

The husband's head and face were covered with contusions, some perfectly round and the size of a large coin, a quarter or half dollar maybe. There was a gash across his forehead, leaving a ragged skin flap to hang above his right eye. Along the left side of his head, his ear had been split into pieces, shredded from continuous blows.

"I believe we may have a different weapon," I exclaimed. "Look at this." I took to a knee and motioned toward the victim's chest, a large incision at the center.

"One large knife wound, but also beaten with the butt of the knife's handle?" said Tracy.

"Or a hammer," I suggested. "The knife wound is also postmortem."

"He was already dead?" Tracy placed a forensics ruler along the knife's incision. "Width is around one and a quarter inches."

"That's big. Assuming only some of the blade was used, it could be seven inches or more," I said, thinking through the variety of knives I'd seen. "A butcher's knife?"

"If it was that long, the wound could be deep enough to reach his heart."

"The medical examiner will tell us how deep. As for the report, we'll approach two weapons, or possibly the butt of the knife as well."

"How about two attackers?" she asked.

I made a note. "Also a possibility," I answered.

"Dinner for three," Tracy said, having moved to a dining table where there were three meals, three settings, and three plastic cups filled with water. Under her breath, I heard her joke, "Like the three bears."

It was good for her to put a buffer between the horrors and the job. It was insulation, which made good technicians great. Without the distraction, the great technician remembers every detail.

"Three?" I asked, joining her.

"Correct. All identical, and none of them touched." She glanced at the bodies on the floor, and then asked, "Where's the third?"

Before I could answer, a noise came from behind us. Tracy twirled around, searching with big panicked eyes. She backed into the table, a glass tipping, the water gushing with a splash onto the day-old food. I thought I'd heard a sound earlier but had dismissed it as a gust of wind buffeting the side of the RV.

There was silence then, a lone drip-drip sound of water falling to the floor. I pointed toward a narrow door, certain it was the source. Another sound then, softer, like someone leaning carefully against it. I lifted my hand, telling Tracy to remain still. I cradled my gun, sliding my finger onto the safety, pressing until I felt a pinch and the metal release. The pleated doors bulged. The center panel fell back into place suddenly, giving us a start.

"Police!" I shouted, drawing my gun, approaching with one foot leading, my body turned perpendicular so as to make myself less of a target. "Pol—"

A hard knock rattled the panels. Tracy screamed, "Oh shit!"

"Police!" I yelled again, trying to swallow, my mouth like cotton. Another knock, and a low growl. I traded confused glances with Tracy, the both of us understanding what we'd heard. When the growl turned to a whimper, I holstered my weapon. "That's a dog in there."

The whimpers became a cry and I braced myself, my hand on the door's handle. I'd never been attacked, but I'd seen the results. Most times, the dog won.

"Shouldn't we call animal control?" Tracy asked.

"There's no barking," I told her. When she didn't understand, I added, "I think I know why."

The whimpering grew louder. The door was stuck and the pleated folds shook as I jerked the handle and shoved hard to free it. From the edge of light inside, I could see a bathroom and, on the floor, a rather large dog, ears perked up, tail poker straight, and eyes like two buttons, each milky with age. A roll of tape was wrapped around its nose. I took a chance and lowered my mask to uncover my face, letting the dog see me, showing that I was friendly. The smell in the bathroom was bad too, there were puddles of urine and feces piled in one corner, the stench making me gag. A window above the toilet was closed, but on the sill, I saw what might have been blood.

"Make a note of the windowsill," I directed. "There appears to be some blood there."

"Got it."

"Well aren't you a sorry sight," I said, my attention shifting to the dog, bending over to do a cursory check. The dog was a male, and friendly. He cocked his head and wagged his tail sturdily—a good sign. He was also old and slow to move. I knew I'd be safe and kneeled to lure the dog out of the tight bathroom.

"Aww, why would they do that?" Tracy asked, doe-eyed with care as she kneeled to help. "I love German shepherds. So beautiful."

"The tape must have been to keep from getting bit," I answered, stating the obvious, but unconvinced myself if that really was the reason.

Her nose wrinkled with a question. She glanced at the victims and then the dog. "Why not kill the dog?" she asked, and then quickly shook her head, adding, "I mean, I know how horrible that sounds, but…"

I started to unravel the sticky tape and signaled to Tracy for some water. "And *why* does it sound so horrible? Because we wouldn't hurt an innocent animal. Who knows, maybe the killer felt the same," I told her. The tape slipped off easily on some parts, but remained tacky on the pads of his whiskers. I cringed when the dog whimpered, feeling his discomfort in my heart. "Sorry, old boy," I told him.

"The killer was an animal lover?"

"Animal lover might be a bit strong, but it does tell us something about who we're dealing with."

"What do you mean?" she asked, propping a glass in place and snapping a series of photographs, capturing the table's settings as they were when we'd arrived.

"They wouldn't, or couldn't, kill the dog," I explained. "We're not dealing with someone who completely lacks remorse or guilt, or who has predatory behaviors. They have a conscience."

"They recognized the animal's innocence," she said, her words profound. "They cared?"

"From the looks of it, yes."

When Tracy was satisfied she had made the recording, she grabbed a bowl from the table, dumped the stale rolls that were in it and filled it with water. The dog limped toward the bowl, showing no signs of aggression, only thirst, lapping voraciously. There was a gash on top of his head too, along with dried blood in the fur above his right eye. Another check, and from his collar I found a dog tag and a name, Tiny.

"Does the tag have a name?"

"Tiny," I said and smiled at the irony, the dog's size anything but small.

"Hello there, Tiny," we said in unison, his ears perking, but then flattening when he saw the bodies. A whimper came with a growl and a bark. I coaxed him to turn away, his snarls fading, his emotions juxtaposed, a reaction to seeing his owners deceased. "You saw what happened, didn't you?"

"I guess he's your first witness."

"Yeah, I suppose he is," I answered. "And I'm thinking he was rendered unconscious, muzzled with the tape, and then locked in the bathroom."

I was speculating, and I could tell Tracy was also considering the events that took place. Her eyes first took in the door, the splintered pieces strewn across the floor and the counter tops.

She shook her head. "I don't think that's the case." She lifted one of the victim's legs, the rigor mortis causing a pop. Tiny startled at the sound, his nails scurrying atop the floor tiles. Beneath the victim's leg, I saw remains from the door. "The killer wouldn't have been able to manage all this with a dog on him, old or young."

I liked how Tracy was walking the scene, talking through the events, her intellect surpassing her age and experience, or lack of as the case would be. Investigating came naturally to her, she was thinking like a detective. I challenged her, hoping it would help me understand as well. "How about this? A break-in. The door is shattered. The killer enters and attacks victim number one, the wife. Victim one collapses and the husband fights the attacker, but loses. After victim two dies, the killer does what? There's a third setting on the table we haven't accounted for."

Tracy winced, her brow creasing as she tried to come up with an answer. She shook her head. "A third person?"

"Three bears," I said beneath my breath, running my fingers through Tiny's fur. I scanned the RV, finding the rear sleeping area open, a curtain pulled aside, the bed made, clothes folded and stacked. The couch was a pull-out bed, with the cushions in place. I lifted one, finding a sheet and blanket tucked inside. That's when I saw the cell phones, three of them on the counter, all plugged in and charging. "Look at these."

"I guess it wasn't a robbery," she said, taking a picture, preserving the countertop in digital space. "These are high-end, expensive. If this was a robbery, they would have turned up at a pawn shop by now."

"That's good," I said, nodding my head. And then hinting, "But that's not the only thing I'm looking at."

Tracy lifted her chin in an *aha* moment as she observed the cell phones, one of them covered in a deep purple with a pattern of bright-green misshapen ovals. "The third cell phone, the cover, definitely from someone younger, a teenager maybe." She brought her camera to her chin, dialed a setting on the back and snapped a round of pictures. "It's a cool design. I'd definitely buy it."

"Right," I said, a burn waking in my gut, the troubling kind. Most kids live for their cell phone, feeding from the screen like it was a drug. They'd never be without it. Not by choice. "How many kids do you know who go anywhere without their phone?"

"None," she said. "Three place settings. The cells on chargers. Do you think the killer came for the child?"

"Officer!" I yelled toward the door, picking up a wallet from the counter. I fanned through the pictures, a faint smell of sweat and leather wafting. I found a school picture of a girl, a teenager, maybe younger, the year printed in the lower corner telling me it was current. "I think the parents guarded their child, and the child guarded her dog. But once the parents expired, and the dog was locked away, the killer took the girl."

"This *is* a kidnapping," Tracy said, as a patrol officer stepped aboard the RV, his weight causing it to shift. Larger than most, the officer dipped his head to enter. Tiny stepped toward the bathroom, pausing, unsure of what to do. I expected a growl, but the dog seemed content in our company.

"Ma'am," Officer Tom Monroe said with a deep voice. He held a mask over his mouth and nose, his gaze darting from corner to corner, steadying on the victims. His brow was flecked with sweat, his patrol shirt pouched and stained in the pits and the collar. From the looks of his babyface, he might have been in his first, or maybe second year.

"Take this," I instructed, handing him a picture of the girl, along with the rental slip carrying the names Carl and Peggy Pearson. "Find out the identification of their child and have an Amber Alert issued."

"Lisa," Tracy blurted, holding a box, a prescription label beneath her thumb. "Their girl's name is Lisa Pearson."

"That prescription is to use in an insulin pump," Tom interrupted, looking at the box. "Diabetes. Type 1. Carl, my little brother, he has one of these."

"How long does it last?" I asked, as worst-case scenarios played in my head.

Tom shrugged his large shoulders. "Few days, give or take," he answered.

"We believe Lisa Pearson was here at the time of the attack."

"She wouldn't leave without some of it," he said, holding up the box. "And this box is full."

"Add the details to the alert," I told him. But he was already writing notes, understanding the possibility of a medical emergency.

"I'm on it," he answered, slowing as he turned, taking care not to bump anything. Before leaving, he asked, "What about the dog?"

"Call Jericho Flynn," I told him, giving him my partner's name, not wanting to see the dog in a shelter. At his age, the last thing Tiny needed was a small cage with cold concrete beneath him. "He'll know what to do. You ready to continue, Tracy?"

She glanced behind her and then forward, a look of awe on her face. "I guess. You're not leaving anytime soon?"

"Nope," I told her, blowing the air from my lungs. While the RV was cramped, we'd spend much of the day scouring every inch of it, including the exterior. I glanced at my watch, knowing it'd be late afternoon by the time we made a dent. "Well, pick a corner and let's keep going."

"There's so much," she said to herself, eyeing every part of the trailer.

"Tracy," I said firmly. "You're good. You're really good."

"If you say so."

"I say so," I told her as a gusty breeze came through the door and lifted the victim's blouse, the fabric torn, the buttons missing, the woman's paunch belly exposed in a flash of morbid white skin and showing me something I'd missed. I did a double take, uncertain of what it was I'd seen.

"What?" Tracy said, alarm returning to her eyes. "What is it?"

"There's something beneath the woman's blouse," I said, and kneeled next to the body, pinching the paisley fabric. Tracy crouched next to me, her camera at the ready. She was breathing fast, anxious, which made me feel the same. "Let's see what we've got here."

I lifted and folded back the victim's blouse, exposing a wound the size of my palm. The air in my chest went still and Tracy's camera shutter rattled in rapid succession. The victim had been sliced open multiple times, the cuts forming what could be a pagan symbol.

"Oh shit," I heard Tracy say. "What do you suppose that is?"

I shook my head, uncertain, the shock of it still registering while I quickly searched my memories for anything like it. "Can't say I've seen this before."

"Was it some kind of devil worship ceremony?" Tracy asked, her voice pitchy with excitement.

I didn't answer her, holding back any comments. I turned my head sideways, changing my perspective on the carving, and asked, "Could it be a letter A?"

Tracy shook her head, paused, and then nodded. "I suppose. Maybe," she answered, and placed the forensic ruler next to the symbol, laying the metal along the side and below the wound, providing scale in the photographs for the crime-scene's documentation. A brilliant flash bounced off the ruler. "I've never seen anything like this before. Only read about these types of cases."

"That makes both of us," I said, continuing to think through my case history. Killers sometimes left marks such as a bite, or bodily fluids after a sexual crime. It was a way of branding their victim as property. It was also a type of control. I leaned to get a closer look. This was the first time I'd ever seen a symbol, and the sight of it was both ghastly and surreal. "Notice the clean edges."

"They took their time?" she asked.

"The killer didn't just take their time," I answered, noting how the carving had been completed with detail and care, the symbol in perfect form, the angles exact, the borders precise. "They *had* the time to do this."

"There's no blood?" she said, questioning, the wrinkle on her nose returning.

The victim's skin and the floor were also dry.

"Good catch," I told her. "Do you know why?"

"Because she was already dead."

CHAPTER FIVE

Lisa Pearson changed direction, stopping in the middle of a crossroads, the dirt intersection barren, the four corners edged by fields. One of the fields was set with corn, the stalks knee high, a surreally bright green for as far as she could see. The other fields were plowed with rows of tilled soil, the earth scored like the top of freshly baked bread. There was a fresh smell, a mix of soil and compost with a scant reminder of salt, the ocean not so many miles from where she stood.

The grocer at the tiny store she'd stopped at to ask for directions had said something about sunlight and heading east when he'd pointed her to the abandoned church. Her description for where she was headed had been vague, the address just a memory of the details on her cell phone, which she'd had to leave back in the RV. She'd kept everything on it—all the vlogs, the posts, even the emails from him, his talking directly to her. Lisa's heart skipped thinking about it. She'd read them so many times, she feared the letter to her would become worn, as though that were possible with anything digital.

"If that's the church, it was Presbyterian once," the grocer said, chewing on a toothpick. "But ain't no congregation. Not in years."

He'd grumbled some other words as he made change for her, a few dollars and some coins, the only money remaining from what she'd found in her pocket after escaping the RV and her parents' murderer. An image of Tiny came to her mind, the sight of him firmly in the killer's grip. She stopped walking entirely, the emotion overwhelming, a tightness in her gut causing her to double over and cry.

"He'll make it right," she said to nobody through her tears. Roadside crickets and trilling cicadas were her only company.

The grocer had told her to go east. "Follow the dirt road, follow the sunrise."

When she was able to stand again, Lisa faced the rising sunlight. A warm breeze rushed over her skin, the sun's heat chasing the chill of the night from her tired body. Her neck and back were stiff, but she'd managed to get some sleep, finding a farm shed, the doors unlocked, a pile of empty burlap sacks to lay on for a few hours.

"The gathering begins early, at eight," she said, having no idea of the time, only that it felt as though it'd been hours since she was at the corner store, the True cigarette clock's hands at six forty-five. She'd been walking ever since.

She recalled the invitation, the online message that had decided where the Pearsons' summer vacation would be spent. Only, her parents didn't know about it. Didn't have to know about it. The invitation was for her. She'd missed the evening's gathering, but couldn't miss this one.

"I'm here now," she said to herself as fine dirt cradled her toes, her blisters from the night's long walk becoming sore again.

She stripped her feet of the cheap sandals found at the grocer's store. Lisa chanced touching a blister, the big one bulging between her toes. The sac burst without warning, fluid plopping onto the road like a raindrop fleeing the sky.

"Ew. Gross!"

She sensed she was close. Felt it even. She stood and closed her eyes. The air shook with a low drone of distant music. His music. Her eyes flashed open. They'd started already, started without her.

A distant wind-chime rang, an angel whispering in her ear, telling her to move along faster.

"This way," she decided, taking the road directly in the sun's path. As she pressed forward, sandals in hand, sending small clouds of road dust from her feet, she spied the field to her right, the budding yellow flowers, the stalks as tall as she was. Cobwebs glistened, wet with morning dew, making it look as if teardrops were strung from flower to flower, their beauty a trap the spiders made each evening to catch anything crossing their path.

He'd catch me, she thought wildly. *I'll be there soon.*

A half mile passed, maybe more, the music's volume increasing, the bass thumping hard enough for her to feel, her heart matching the rhythm. The itch came again, an unavoidable interruption, the skin circling the port for her insulin pump reddened and raised.

"It's in my head," she said, trying to ignore it. But there was no denying how she felt—her throat was as hot and as dry as the road, the horizon blurred, and her head dizzy. "I don't need it. They just want me to think I do." Her voice reduced to a mumble. "It's just in my head."

She staggered on and climbed a shallow hill. A steeple rose before her, the church coming into view. There were cars of all shapes and models parked on one side. On the other were rattling generators, electrical lines snaking along the ground, pumping electricity into the old building. The grocer had warned the church was abandoned. The grocer didn't know *him* though. He'd made it right, just like he said he would.

The church windows were clean, but covered from the inside. She thought of the website, *his* stories and the blog posts about what they did to him. Surely the windows were covered because of his condition, the sunlight being a risk to his health. The church was freshly painted, pristine like his soul. Surrounding the church were lawns of bright grass, a nearby well had been tapped and sprinkler heads pitched a morning drink to every blade. The site was a heavenly gathering in the middle of nowhere. It was perfect.

Behind the church, there were trailers like the type her family had rented. Her heart skipped with the idea of him living in one of them. It was where he ate and where he slept, the utensils and sheets and pillows blessed by his touch. Her breathing quickened and her feet lifted into a dizzying run as she anticipated finally seeing him in person.

"Whoa," a stout man said when she reached the wooden steps at the front of the church, the tread smoothed by the years, the touch cool on the bottoms of her sore feet. The man was younger than her parents, the lines fresh at the corners of his warm brown eyes, early thirties maybe. She liked the way he was dressed, formal, official. He had thick wavy blond hair that was tucked behind his ears and on which perched a pair of round glasses. A lanyard and badge strung from his neck indicated he was in charge of security. On the badge, a name—D.J. Reynolds—and beneath it, an official title she'd never seen before, Security & Events Director. He flipped open the cover of an iPad and asked, "Name?"

"Is he here?" Lisa blurted, and swiped an errant lock of hair from her brow. She ran her fingers through the rest of her hair, and wet her lips, the taste of road dust still on them. "Sorry, just excited. I'm Lisa. Lisa Pearson. I got an invitation."

"Ms. Lisa Pearson," the man said, a frown forming, turning his chin into the rind of an orange while he searched his iPad. "Yup. Found you."

"I can go in?" she began, her foot on the second step, the music's beat running through the church floor and into her legs.

"Hey now, not so fast."

"But, I was invited."

He cocked an eyebrow and leaned over, the smell of aftershave strong. He pointed toward the sky. "We were all invited. It's what we choose to do with the bidding that makes a difference."

"Invited," she parroted excitedly. "Yes."

"Now," he continued, leaning into his original posture. "Your invitation code?"

At once, her heart sank, her smile flattened, the anticipation of seeing *him* doused, as muscle memory moved her hands in search of a cell phone that wasn't there. "I... I," she began, voice stammering, a tear stinging. "I don't have my phone. The code I got. It's on my phone."

"Hmm," he said gruffly. He closed one eye, tilted his head and asked, "You wouldn't be one of them pesky reporters? Not one of them police neither, trying to stir up trouble for Mr. Dowd?"

Lisa's brow rose as she shook her head with vigor. "Oh no! I'd never cause Mr. Dowd any trouble. He invited—"

"Invited you," the attendant finished for her. Without turning, the man plunged his hand into a large box, his eyes remaining on her as he shook his wrist. "Then, Ms. Pearson, this would be for you."

He handed her a lanyard and badge similar to his, with her name and face, confirming her invitation.

"But how did you—?"

"Got a little magic in me is all," he answered with a smile, and closed his iPad. "You can go on inside, they've already started."

Without another word, Lisa opened the church doors, the grandness of them extending nearly to the church's roof, each door steepled, their massive size leaving her in disbelief as they glided smoothly. She opened them wide, taking in the sight within as though she were entering the Emerald City of Oz. The inside of the church was awash with digital colors, the atmosphere electric, tall monitors lining the walls where once there must have been images of Christ and the stages of his crucifixion. The wooden pews where the congregation had kneeled and prayed had been removed and used as scaffolds to build a stage, surrounded by speakers and metal stands, stacked high with rotating spotlights. The church's vestibule was guarded by a band behind a sheet of plexiglass, a guitarist and a bass player singing into microphones, and a drummer, their music shaking the church.

Lisa saw *him* then. Richard Dowd, the man who spoke truth and wisdom and who would lead her generation. She'd made it. And she had to tell him about her parents. He would know what to do. He wore his signature black hair slicked back, and his skin shone white like a bright light's reflection, its purity like cotton—an allergy to the sun, he'd said once on his vlog. It was from when he'd been forced to hide away from the Lord's light, an unforgivable injustice, he'd called it. He raced back and forth across the makeshift stage, the microphone pressed to his lips, his voice like a song, preaching His word, delivering truths nobody else would dare speak. His suit was as white as his hair was black, the cloth's shine absorbing the colorful lights and turning him into a living rainbow.

"And what say you, those who come in *His* name?"

"Amen!" the crowd roared.

Lisa had to reach the stage, reach him, but the crowd was enormous, and she was tiny. He'd never see her from the back of the church. The congregation's area was alive with bodies, swaying along with his words, most of them her age, some older, some younger, and all with lanyards similar to hers, all invited like Lisa had been.

"It is the sins of your parents, and their parents! The plastics they've created, an abomination. The oil they suck from the earth's arteries, draining the life of this planet, spewing it into the air and choking us all. It is their sins!"

Cheers and shrieks peeled the air.

"It is *their* sins that will kill *our* earth!"

"Yes!" Lisa yelled with the others, slipping into the crowd, a sweaty body bumping her, knocking her to the ground. There were feet on her then, her arms pinned as someone stomped her gut with punishing force. The air jumped from her lungs. Stars raced and her lungs burned.

"The earth—" she heard distantly, Dowd continuing as she struggled to get up.

There were arms on her, fingers touching her skin. They lifted her body high above the crowd and carried her forward as if she were on a magic carpet ride. Her lungs pained her, but she could breathe again, and when the church came back into focus she saw she was being delivered to *him*.

Lisa was set down at the stage, Richard Dowd's face close to hers, his hand on her wet cheek.

He said, "Welcome my child. Tell us your name."

"I'm Lisa," she answered. Her heart swelled, the sudden silence deafening. But she only saw him, saw the wonder of his soul through his eyes, the same she'd dreamily memorized and visited every night in his videos before falling asleep. "I'm Lisa Pearson."

"Lisa Pearson," he crooned. The band thundered with another song as he raised his hand in a twirl, the congregation humming along. "What do you want to tell us? What do you want to tell Him?"

Richard Dowd eased closer, his face brilliant with spotlight colors. He placed the microphone close to her lips, her heavy breath coming from the speakers. She tried to swallow but couldn't. He gave her an approving nod.

"It's my parents," she finally said.

Dowd jumped to his feet and yelled into the microphone, "Her parents!"

"Amen!" the congregation boomed as the band played harder. The drummer slammed his drumsticks across the symbols, the metal crashing. The guitar player plucked and strummed a neverending riff as the bassist bounced his fingers against guitar strings as thick as yarn. A bellowing tone resonated through Lisa, shaking every cell in her body. When Dowd was satisfied with the spirited response, he raised his hand above the crowd and closed his fist and brought silence.

The astonishment of it was surreal and Lisa tried to contain her emotion. But it wasn't tears that came, it was joy. A giddiness rose like a wave, carrying her to an indescribable place, a transcendence, hers with his, together. The words in his letters to her had been more than an invitation. She had to be here. They had the world to save. He'd made it clear who was to blame. He'd show them the way.

Dowd went to Lisa again, kneeling close enough she could smell him, smell his holiness. He placed his hand atop her head and asked, "And what did your parents do to our beautiful earth?"

She had her chance. She could tell him what happened. He'd help. He'd help just as he was helping everyone.

"They—" she paused, suddenly afraid.

"It's okay, child. You're with friends now."

"They're dead," she answered, taking his hand in hers, squeezing and waiting for his guidance.

"They're dead," he repeated softly, his face close enough for her to breathe his air. He was on his feet again, releasing her hand, and screamed, "They're all dead! Aren't they?"

"Yes! They are!" the crowd cheered.

"Are they not guilty? Are they not the cause of the earth's woes?"

"No! That's not what—" Lisa yelled desperately. "That's not what I meant."

"Yes, Lisa," Dowd went on. "There are polar bears swimming into extinction, their corpses floating in an iceless sea. And there is a mountain made of plastic afloat in the oceans. A mountain!"

Lisa was overcome then, bumped and pushed and sucked back into the crowd. Followers rushed the stage, each eager to be picked next, to be touched by him. They chanted his words, recited his passages, all the while misunderstanding what it was Lisa had tried to tell him.

The tears came then. The distance from the stage increased until she was returned to the church's front doors. She touched sunlight—a sliver invading the darkness through the crack between the doors. The tears came for her parents. They came for Tiny as well. She'd failed to make him understand, and now she didn't know what to do.

CHAPTER SIX

For most of the day, Tracy Fields and I—along with a large team of technicians, forensic photographers, and the medical examiner staff—tagged every scuff mark on the floors and every divot found in the walls. We labeled every possible finger and footprint and inspected a sizable scatter of glass chunks across the floor. This was a particularly time-consuming effort, a hand magnifier held closely to our faces as we combed through the broken glass, our efforts rewarded with dried blood discovered on one of the larger chunks. We'd crossmatch the blood type with the victims', and if it wasn't a match, we could have a new clue, the killer's blood type. We did the same with hair fibers and fingerprints. The most telling of the evidence collected was the symbol carved in Peggy Pearson's body. While it resembled a letter A, it could also be interpreted as some kind of religious symbol, leading us to consider it a possible ritual killing. We found no markings or carvings on Carl Pearson's body, which raised even more questions.

Room in the RV was tight, and with the peak summer afternoon hours baking the Outer Banks, the interior had become a hot box. None of us could stay inside for more than ten minutes at a time. Complicating the scene were the challenges faced when transporting the victims into the medical-examiner wagons. The small space and the large sizes of the bodies meant that moving each victim required six people and a stiff back board, as well as minds made for geometry to figure out the best way to get through the RV and out the door.

By the time we were done our coveralls were damp and pitted with sweat stains, and the afternoon hours had become late, with the campground's colors shifting to a dusky yellow and orange. But against the backdrop of this beautiful place, two people had been brutally attacked, and their child possibly abducted.

I'd sent my team out to begin the questioning, starting with the campground manager. From there, they'd moved on to every campground visitor, collecting the names and numbers of each person who'd heard or seen anything unusual in the days leading up to the murders. We had hope one or more visitors to the campgrounds might have heard the attack, or any kind of commotion, and had noted the time.

While we'd finished processing the RV, and with the Amber Alert issued for Lisa Pearson, I knew we'd only just started investigating this gruesome case. As with every kidnapping, a special place in my heart had been touched: a place reserved for missing children, a place that came to be when Hannah was taken from me. I held Lisa Pearson there now, her safety and recovery foremost on my mind.

The next morning marked a special day. I woke with a memory I'd forever savor, and another that cramped my heart with sadness. Today was my Hannah's seventeenth birthday. And to celebrate it, I'd planned to do what I'd done nearly every year on this day for the last decade. I was going home to Philadelphia and meeting with Sharon Telly, a sketch artist. With a contribution of some family photographs, Sharon would create a new drawing of Hannah, showing her at the age of seventeen. There was something about going home, about keeping with the ritual and meeting with Sharon that felt right to me, and made it feel as if I could get Hannah back for good someday. I also had some newer pictures of her for Sharon for the first time, from a previous case, as well as from the husband and wife who'd kidnapped her. I'd come so close to getting my daughter back.

Before getting on the road, I'd made a number of calls, touching base with my team, setting directions for the day, ensuring not a moment passed without all efforts on the Pearson case. The campground manager and all the guests had been interviewed. Tracy was working the evidence collected and organizing the crime-scene photographs. Nichelle, our department's IT systems specialist, had begun the tedious task of background research, identifying details involving the RV rental company, the Pearsons' home, anything that could help. A pang of guilt came with my ending the calls, my insides in a tug-of-war between the Pearsons' case and my daughter's, but I knew that having directed my team, there was nothing more I could do to help Lisa right now but wait.

My car smelled of pastries and coffee, black coffee—breakfast of champions—it was like gold touching my tongue. I couldn't stomach the burned swill Jericho liked. He sat next to me, insisting the all-night quick mart had to be good coffee, *aged just enough*, whatever that was supposed to mean. A sip of coffee burned my tongue, stealing some of the flavor. I tried to hide it and lifted the cup in a mock cheers motion. Jericho met his with mine as we exited the parking lot and headed toward Wrights Memorial Bridge. Sunlight swept across his face, the rays striking his blue-green eyes while I turned the corner. I felt a smile on my face and a giddy flutter in my chest. It had been a long time since I'd brought someone to my home-station back in Philadelphia, where I'd worked my whole career before coming to the Outer Banks last year. I glanced at Jericho as if he was some fancy new toy for me to show off at school for Show & Tell. He caught me smiling and returned it, the giddiness rising in my throat. I brushed his shoulder, the touch warm, appreciating he was with me.

I'd been alone since my daughter's kidnapping over thirteen years ago. Her father, Ronald, had exited our marriage soon after, and my life became a solitary existence. The timing of meeting Jericho, of experiencing an over-the-moon relationship, was long past due. Like most, I'd wanted the excitement and mystery of romance. I'd wanted passion and butterflies in my belly. I'd wanted to ache for his company and long to be in his arms. The spark had been there, and it didn't take long before Jericho had swept me off my feet.

We'd stopped for breakfast in the car, the day still early with layers of dew on the lawns and a thick ribbon made of bright-yellow and hot-pink colors hugging the horizon. Jericho knew little of my annual ritual but had jumped at the chance for a few hours alone together. And since the case that brought us together last year had ultimately led us to my daughter's kidnappers, he had a professional interest too. He also confessed to his wanting to see my old station. Jericho was the ex-sheriff, and was now a lead in the marine patrol, and like most cops, he was curious. Cops are always curious, interested in seeing other stations and going to strange cities, checking them out, contemplating if the grass might be greener. The grass certainly wasn't greener. It didn't have the beaches and oceans and waves—although Philly had its charms too, its famous delights, and I'd make sure to introduce him to a few while we were there.

A family of four waved to us, standing on Segways, a flash of sunlight beaming from their helmets. One of them called to Jericho, referring to him as "Sheriff"—a moniker forever fixed with his image in this town, despite the fact it was a role he'd left behind. He answered them with a wave, but cringed sharply and gripped his shoulder, an operation from earlier in the year continuing to bother him.

"You okay there?" I asked as the family rolled past us, the traffic light stuck on red.

His eyes flicked in my direction before he shook his head and closed them. There was a smile pasted on his lips, but he shut his eyes, the corners creasing as a spasm from nerve damage peaked.

A stew of frustration and helplessness brewed as I wished I could do more. "Oh babe, I wish you'd fill that prescription and get the painkillers."

"Nah," he answered, shaking his head. He refused to take anything more than aspirin, no matter how many times I'd insisted. "I'm just getting old."

I slapped his chest. "Don't you say that. I know your birthday, and it's not far from mine."

He let out a laugh, covering his mouth. "Oops, forgot about that."

The spasm passed and he leaned in with a sly smile on his face, a twinkle in his eye. I recognized the look of a carnal urge stirring. "Been meaning to ask you, any plans later this evening after we get back?"

I groaned when his fingers grazed my thigh and his warm breath was in my ear. "None."

Resistance was impossible and I met his lips with mine, the romance I sought coming on strong, the urge to have him even stronger. The traffic light turned green and the fleeting romantic urge fizzled with a horn blaring from behind us. I stomped the gas, taking us onto the bridge, the bay quiet, the surface unusually still like pond water.

"There's Tiny though," I reminded him.

"Yes," he said. "Thank you for that."

Guilt tugged on the moment, completely ending the romantic interlude. "I couldn't leave him with animal control. He's so old."

"I don't really mind," he admitted. "Just giving you a hard time."

"Mind if we stop by later and pick him up?" I asked. "I was kind of looking forward to having him at my apartment."

"You sure?" he asked, the corner of his mouth turning. "Ryan has taken a real liking to Tiny."

"Well tell your son not to get too attached," I warned.

"You could always come home with me," he said. I slowed the car, the line for a toll giving us a few minutes. He brushed his fingertips across my arm, the subtleness of it enough for me to face him. "I love you," Jericho said, surprising me, his words taking my breath for a moment. "I never thought I'd be able to say that again. Not to anyone."

"I love you too," I returned, my voice breaking as a small wave of panic hit me. Thankfully, the anxiety was only fleeting—a kind of early-warning system about the dangers of letting myself feel content. I hated how the slightest hint of happiness could quickly stir my insides with panic.

"Consider it?" he asked, opening a previous discussion, a disagreement really, referring to his place, and our living together.

When I'd moved to the Outer Banks, he'd opened his home to me. Only, I hadn't been ready, and wanted a place of my own first. I'd wanted a fresh start. I'd wanted a place that was the polar opposite of my life before where four empty walls and a roadside apartment was all I could handle. I'd made a lot of progress since then. I had a lovely apartment and I was in love with him, but I still wasn't ready to move in together.

Jericho tensed when I didn't answer immediately, and began to play with the radio. The traffic was stuck, the line of cars shimmering with heat and a low-hanging smog from the exhaust. With his focus on the radio, he added, "At least think about it?"

"Jericho?" I said, bracing his shoulder, asking him to look at me. When he turned, I took his face in my hands and kissed him hard. "I love you, but I need a little more time."

"Time," he answered. "I get it. Time takes time."

Although Jericho had been with me for a few of my nightmares, he could only do so much—holding me, easing me from the dream's sweaty clutches. I sensed his frustration, a wedge forming between us when they were bad. But he also desperately wanted to help. I think he wanted to help me as much as I wanted to help with his shoulder pain. Maybe he was right. Maybe living together was the best thing for us to do. We were in love, so why waste any more time apart?

A cold dread stirred in me; an answer to my question. It wasn't time, or the waste of it that was stopping me. The reason was Hannah, and the pain of mending a wound that would never heal. It had become a part of me, a part that I could never share with anyone.

CHAPTER SEVEN

There was another wedge forming between me and Jericho—his snoring. I was strung out on coffee and sugar while he slept in the passenger seat, his hands clasped and cradling the side of his face. The sight of him was cute, but the noises he made rattled my nerves and had me rolling the dial on the radio more times than I could count.

The drive back to Philadelphia had been smooth, the marshes, the backwater channels, and the tall reedy grasses slowly disappearing to be replaced by office buildings, warehouses and data centers. The billboard signs had changed too, the familiar names of local restaurants replaced by fast-food logos and odd Twitter handles with lawyerly advertisements begging for a phone call if we'd been injured or exposed to anything dangerous. I knew I was close to my old home when the sea air was gone from my car, the salt leaving my nose and the taste of it disappearing from my tongue.

When we'd reached Philadelphia, I woke Jericho and parked my car at my old police station, a flutter in my belly waking at the sight of it. I could smell freshly cut grass and wet pavement, an earlier rain shower leaving behind a few puddles to dry in the afternoon sun. Like most of the east coast, the Philadelphia area was under siege by the same early-season heatwave, but the city was also blanketed with thick humidity that coated me in an uncomfortable sweat.

I peered over the cars and beyond the parking lot toward a red-brick building with black windows—the place I'd started my career in law enforcement. The nerves hit me stronger with the idea of crossing paths with anyone who'd recognize me, anyone who'd remember why it was I'd left. In a moment of madness, I'd pulled a gun on another cop. Not one of my better moments on the force.

Jericho came to my side, stretching and shaking the car ride out of his arms and legs. "I'll take the drive home," he offered, the warm touch of his hand on my back.

I made a choppy nod, but said nothing, overtaken by a sudden emotion.

"You okay?"

"Wasn't sure I'd see this place again," I answered, sucking in hot air and trying to give myself a break about the past.

"We can leave any time you like," Jericho said, jangling the car keys. "Tell you what, take me out for one of those famous Philly hoagies or cheese-steaks." Only, his pronunciation of the Philly favorite came out as *hoj-jeez*, and instantly made me laugh.

"It's *hoe-geez*, with a hard g."

"Hoagies," he said, mouthing it slowly. His manner shifted, and with a troubling look, he sighed and said, "Listen, you already have pictures of Hannah. Why—?"

"It's something I have to do," I told him, patting the outside of my bag. I appreciated the concern he showed, and didn't expect he'd understand entirely. I offered a smile, adding, "Hoagies afterward?"

He jokingly rubbed his belly. "Maybe some cheesecake too?"

"You're on."

"You made good time," Sharon Telly said, grinning and waving her arm, greeting us near the station's door. She had a wide smile, and her round face was thinner than I remembered. As a sketch artist working for the force, she'd come prepared with visitor badges in hand, and eagerly clipped it to my shirt. Her eyes went wide when they landed on Jericho. She flashed me a smile, before returning to him and said, "You must be Jericho."

"I am," he answered shyly. Without thought, she began to pin the badge on his shirt, but then handed it to him, the moment awkward. "Thank you, I think I can take care of that."

"I'm sure you can," she said, eagerly shaking his hand. "It's so good to meet you. I'm Sharon Telly, a forensic artist."

"I've seen your work," he said, quickly following with, "your age-progression technique is amazing."

Sharon's face went red and her eyelids fluttered with the praise. "Why thank you so much." She took my fingers in her hand. "I would never have found the practice if Casey hadn't asked. It really is a game changer in a lot of unsolved missing-persons cases."

"I'll catch up in a few?" I asked Jericho, having warned earlier I'd want to work with Sharon alone. "There's coffee and machines over there."

Jericho left us then, seemingly knowing his way around, like any cop knows any station. I'd seen my old captain in the vicinity of the coffee machine and expected the two of them to kick up a discussion, the captain being an Outer Banks resident when vacationing.

"What's with the badges?" I asked Sharon, cringing that I should care, but also wanting to move us along, the meeting always a difficult one.

"New rules," she said with a tone of annoyance. "Security here is above madness now." As we walked, window-light bled through her blouse and showed a new figure, showed she'd found a diet that had finally worked.

"Probably for the better," I commented, taking her arm and adding, "And by the way, you look amazing!"

"You think?" she asked, brow raised as she jokingly turned to her side and posed like a poster pin-up. "After Bob and I split, I wanted a change."

"Well, change has been good for you."

She glanced over her shoulder to where Jericho was headed, and then stepped back to give me a once-over. "And change has been really good for you."

My skin warmed with bashful embarrassment, but I liked that she'd noticed. Life at the shore was good for me. "It's the beaching, the sand, the sun, all of it."

"And?" she implored, dipping her chin. "I'd say having someone in your life did a lot for you too."

"Yeah. Also, he has a lot to do with it."

"I'm happy for you," she said while leading me to one of the interview rooms.

"For you too," I told her.

The interview room was the same room we'd used every year since Hannah's disappearance. Sharon took to a seat, placing her art supplies and a portfolio case on the table. I did similar, pulling out a chair, opening a folder with pictures, our places rehearsed like actors taking to a stage before a performance. I sat opposite her, the two of us like bookends. Spreading the pictures of Hannah across the tabletop, sadness and remorse filled me. Being in this room, visiting with Sharon, meant one thing. It meant my previous year's attempt to find my daughter had failed.

"You okay?" Sharon asked, sensing my disappointment.

For the moment, I couldn't speak and could only shake my head. She reached across the table to take my hand. Her grip was soft, chalky, and firm—much like the portraits she brought to life, seemingly delicate, yet powerful.

"I saw her," I said, finding my voice, reminding myself how very different this visit was. "I saw Hannah. Last summer."

A look of shock and wonder came to her face. "You did?" she asked, shaking her head as if she couldn't believe it. "I mean, I read about the kidnappers, about the trial, the sentencing. And the captain filled us in on some of the details the papers didn't cover."

My chin quivered, her grip on my fingers firm. "She was there." A sting in my eyes. "The Outer Banks. It's one of the reasons I've stayed. It's why I won't leave."

"And you're sure it was her?"

I told her everything then, everything that hadn't been on the news, the details still new and standing out like a fresh scar. A husband and wife had confessed to kidnapping my Hannah. They'd tragically lost their own child and the woman suffered a terrible breakdown. In a distraught state, she'd driven west and came across Hannah by sheer chance. Convinced Hannah was her daughter, that she'd been returned, the woman snatched her from the side of the road. When her husband had seen how happy his wife was and how much Hannah resembled their daughter, he blocked his conscience, and the two raised Hannah as their own. While they'd gotten their family back, they'd destroyed mine.

"Wow," Sharon mouthed. "It's like something I'd see in a Lifetime movie."

"Yeah, I suppose. It's different though when it's your child," I told her.

"Hannah is seventeen now?" Sharon asked, her voice soft, her eyes in a squint as she tried remembering my girl's age. "Is that right?"

"It is," I answered, barely able to believe it myself. "My girl turned seventeen years old today."

She focused on her art supplies, the tools she'd used every year to draw Hannah's picture, one year older, one new face, a picture I'd use in new searches. "Do you still want to do this?"

"Oh yes!" I blurted, a rise in my voice. While I'd seen Hannah, I needed the drawing as a means of beginning anew. "I brought some more to help."

"I see that," she said, a curl of black hair flopping into her eyes.

"Did you get what I sent? Everything I found during my move?"

She gave a nod and then rearranged the photographs, answering, "I took some liberty with them and already started." Sharon picked up my additional pictures. "These will help with the finer details."

I scanned the table, my eyes focusing on the pictures of me at sixteen, and the photos of my relatives, great aunts and uncles, some who I'd only heard about. It was surprisingly easy to get the pictures, despite my having cut ties from everything and everyone after Hannah's disappearance. When I lost Hannah, my parents had lost me. On a visit to their home—a first in years—I'd discovered a trunk in their attic, and inside, I found photo albums dating back fifty years. It was in the old images, the history, where Sharon found the family resemblances, using them to pick out the likely physical traits that carried across generations.

"I have these from the Outer Banks." I placed a picture of Hannah in front of Sharon, which was taken from a video, the image acquired as part of the investigation which had ultimately found her—and lost her again. Next to it, I put another picture, one taken at a boardwalk photo booth, along with an identification badge, the name Patricia Fitzgerald beneath the juvenile-detention-center photo. My girl had been taken away from me, and ended up inside that place, under another name. None of them were very good quality, some showing only part of her grainy face, and all at least a year old.

"Patricia Fitzgerald?" Sharon asked, tracing the neck tattoo, the swirls of yellow and purple, and edged with cerulean blue, a color I'd never known to have a name until I researched it. Her look turned to one of questioning, asking, "This is the girl you believe is Hannah?"

"That's Hannah," I said, sounding almost indignant. "Sorry, I get asked that a lot."

"I think I see it," Sharon said. She rearranged the photographs of one of my great aunts, placing the detention center badge next to it. "I mean, the recent pictures aren't great, but there might be some resemblance in the eyes."

"It's enough to work with?"

She picked up the picture of the video clip, answering, "From the work I've already done, I think I'm on track."

"Really?" I asked, thankful. "If not, I can dig up some more. For the next—" I stopped myself, not wanting to jinx the coming year.

Sharon took my hand again with a shake. "Next year will be a visit only."

"How does it look?" I asked, eager to see the latest drawing.

"It's coming along, but these new images will help," she explained. "I extrapolated all the features based on growth—"

"Can I see?" I asked impatiently.

She nodded and flipped her sketch pad's cover over the spiral binder, turning it for me to see. I gripped the chair and stood to take hold of the drawing. Hannah's hair was imagined the same as mine, borrowed from one of my high-school pictures. Her ears were the same too. I felt a warm flush and stirring emotion. I saw my ex-husband Ronald in our daughter's face too. The dimples, his lips, but only slightly as the smile was so subtle, so beautiful. This was more than a police sketch, it was art, and it took all words away.

"Casey?" Sharon asked as a knock came from the door. "You okay?"

I picked up the detention-center identification to compare it to Sharon's sketch. The differences were immediate and doused my hopes, adding doubt. But when I searched for the similarities, I found them, especially in the eyes, like Sharon had said. It was the hard look in the identification badge—my Hannah had become Patricia Fitzgerald, had lived on the streets, and then been put in jail where she'd been abused. My heart wrenched to think about it. A hard life changes a person. It changes them on the inside and outside. Beauty is said to be skin deep. I hoped that was the same for the hardness, her shell a barrier. If I could find her again, and if she learned who she really was, maybe it'd soften it some.

"I've seen this girl," I told Sharon with encouragement. My friend smiled. She had her validation in the pictures I'd forwarded, and I had mine. "I can definitely see it."

"I'm sure you'll see her soon," Sharon said, sounding positive.

"Close," I said, pinching the air. "I was this close. It was a trafficking case. Hannah ran, frightened the gang was after her."

"Maybe time will bring her back," Sharon offered.

I held up her picture, adding, "This will help."

As I drank in the image of my daughter, my mind flashed to Lisa Pearson. Her parents were dead, lying in the morgue, unable to search for their daughter. For them, I'd search. After all, in every missing girl, I saw Hannah. For them, I'd search as though Lisa were my own.

"Are you guys staying the night?" she asked.

I sensed the end of our meeting approaching. I shook my head, a hunger pang gnawing in my gut. "We're getting some lunch, but then back on the road. I've got a case I have to get back to."

Sharon encased Hannah's picture in a sleeve to protect it. Once the drawing was complete, she'd make a second copy for me (it was part of our arrangement that Sharon could keep the original for her portfolio) and I'd make copies of that, distribute it, take it digital and spread it wide in the equivalent of putting her picture on the side of a milk carton.

"It's beautiful," I told Sharon, and then surprised her with a hug, the suddenness of it surprising me too.

"Okay, we're hugging," Sharon said jokingly and returned the gesture. "It's been great seeing you again."

"It has." I held her long enough to slip a couple of hundred-dollar bills into her bag. Later in the evening she'd find the crisply folded bills and curse me under her breath. We hugged until a pang of awkwardness pulled us apart.

"Oh shit, I completely forgot!" she blurted, her voice loud, taking me off guard. "My aging brain is slipping. When I've finished the copy you can pick it up at my brother's place, in the Outer Banks."

"What?" I asked, confused and excited.

"I'll be at my brother's place all next week. Near the beach. I'll have everything prepped and with me."

"Your brother lives there?"

"We grew up there," she told me, adding another surprise. "I'm leaving in the morning."

"Wait. How is it I didn't already know that?" I asked, amused by the news.

"Well…" she began, her expression telling me all I needed to know.

I dropped my chin briefly as if to hide in shame. I should have known. But I hadn't been the type of person to know or remember those sorts of things about others. Truth is, I should have been a better friend.

"Doesn't matter," I said, heat on my neck and face, ashamed.

She tilted her head, confirming. "I'll meet you at my brother's place?"

"Text me the address," I said, excited by the idea. "We'll grab a drink."

"That'd be dreamy. I can't wait."

I motioned for her to hold the drawing so I could take a picture with my phone. "May I? I know it's not finished, but I'd love a photo."

As expected, Jericho and the captain had hit it off and I had to pry him from the station, the double murder investigation waiting for us sticking in my thoughts like a stubborn splinter. Early results on the tire tracks had failed to turn up anything useful, the treads all matching vehicles on scene. This meant the killer may have parked elsewhere and then entered the campground. I'd left Tracy and the team working through the findings from the RV. The workload was heavy and would coincide with the medical examiner's work, Dr. Swales and the examinations of the two victims. The only preliminary findings she'd been able to offer was to confirm the blood found on the glass fragments were B positive, a match to the husband's.

For now, I couldn't do more than wait. We had a six-hour drive ahead of us, so I obliged Jericho's one request—a big, Philly-style meal beneath Billy Penn's statue, topped off with a cold bottle of sweet black cherry Wishniak for the trek back home.

CHAPTER EIGHT

Ben Hill flipped a pancake just as the batter pocked with air bubbles and the edges browned. Smoke reached his face and he lowered the heat, fumbling and cursing with the knobs, the size and placement of them awkward. The RV's kitchen was tiny, the range barely fitting a regular sized pan for grilling. But Ben made the kitchen work. He checked the time, urgency sparking his need to finish before her return. He wiped a scant batter spill from an index card, carefully cleaning the penciled recipe, the cursive handwriting dear to him.

This wasn't just any stack of pancakes. Ben was using Peter's recipe, cooking them exactly the way his husband had taught him. He brought the index card to his lips as though he could connect with him, lost nearly a year now. He grieved less these days, but had his moments when it was just as painful as the night he left the hospital alone, carrying a plastic bag of Peter's belongings. He wiped his eyes and poured two more pancakes. Andrea would be back soon, and this was one of their daughter's favorite meals.

"Pancakes with whipped cream," he spoke with a sigh before putting the index card away. "If that's what our girl wants, then that's what she'll get."

He added strawberries to the plate next, sprinkling sugar on the ripe fruit and topping them with a dash of heavy cream—another favorite to celebrate her fourteenth birthday. He opened a bottle of wine for himself, rocking the cork back and forth before tipping the neck toward a picture of his partner. They'd lived a decade together and made a home for them and for Andrea. Ben held Peter's picture and wished they'd had more time, then whispered promises to do his best to raise their daughter.

In his moment of distraction, smoke filled the cramped space, the grill too hot and the butter burning in the pan. The burn caught his eyes with a sting as he lowered the heat. A knock on the RV's door startled him, strong enough to rattle the thin walls. A visitor was unexpected, since they were strangers to the Outer Banks. They'd only been on vacation a few days. Andrea had insisted they come here, rent an RV, and stay at the campground.

"Why the Outer Banks?" he'd asked her, showing her a map, wanting them to travel west to Yellowstone Park instead.

"It's different," she'd said. "We've never been to the ocean before. Let's give it a try."

"We haven't," he agreed, slightly amused at her insistence but willing to go anywhere that would make her happy.

Another knock at the door, this time hard enough to feel it in his feet.

"Hold on a minute!" he yelled with a cough, waving toward the window, smoke hugging the ceiling. Ben made his way to the RV's door and opened it, the narrow steps leading outside forcing him into a lean. A man stood there, silent, the campground lights putting him in silhouette.

An unsettling notion hit Ben, a warning of danger he'd learned early as a child when people first noticed he was different. Ben backed into the RV, the man approaching, the kitchenette's light showing the odd safety gear covering the stranger's chest and shoulders and legs. But it was the black mask, like something out of a horror movie, which struck the greatest fear in Ben.

His voice shaky, he tried to believe this was some kind of sick joke, and asked cautiously, "Can I help you?"

Ben Hill never heard an answer. The figure charged into the RV, booted feet stomping the metal treads, an animal growl sounding from beneath the mask. Ben sucked in a breath and braced himself, his size no match against the attacker. Immediately, he was in the air with the first strike, his feet leaving the floor as air bled from his lungs in a violent gush. The driver's console appeared sideways as the back of his head crashed into a wall. Ben tumbled onto his side and rolled onto his back, a massive weight crushing him as he flailed like a dying fish on dry land. He swung and punched, connecting with the attacker, striking nothing but heavy plastic, his knuckles becoming bloodied.

"Why?" he pleaded, catching a breath, a sip of air stolen when the attacker shifted his knee. The man clutched Ben's neck, his gloved fingers squeezing as he pinned him again. Stars were in Ben's eyes, the strength zapped from his arms while he continued punching feverishly. "Please."

A moment of hope came when Ben's attacker released his stranglehold, freeing him to breathe. But the moment of reprieve soon ended as Ben felt a blade running across the side of his neck. The intense pulse pounding in his brain and the immense pressure behind his eyes were instantly relieved like a damn collapsing, a river's pent-up energy flooding a waiting valley. The attacker jumped clear of Ben as his life bled away.

"Andrea," Ben mouthed, terrified for her, terrified she'd walk in at any moment. The sight of his attacker blurred with a mix of tears, his breathing stiff and cut with bubbles filling his throat and mouth.

The RV was gone in a moment. The horrific scene had gone too. There was nothing. Ben's mind cleared, the terrifying anguish of pain forgotten. He saw the light then, and waited to see Peter emerge, to see an arm extended, feel their fingers touching, his lost love guiding him home.

The light was a lie. It was sharp and dangerous like the blade it glinted from. Cold air rushed over Ben's bare skin, the killer ripping his shirt like a hunter tearing the flesh from a fresh kill. Ben felt the blade again as he lay motionless, alive but unable to fight.

The killer hummed a gospel tune while he worked, using Ben's chest like a canvas, taking a moment to admire the work, and then carving some more. Dying thoughts rained in Ben's mind, filling it with the horrors of the terrible names he'd been called while growing up. He was different and had been chastised for it, tortured nearly daily by the bullies of his small town. And now he'd go to his grave branded forever.

"Please," he begged, trying once more to speak. "Please don't."

His plea went unanswered.

The cutting ended, the killer sounding satisfied. In the kitchen's oven door, a faint reflection showed his handy work. Bleary, Ben's vision almost gone, he saw the figure eight, the number meaningless. Ben's last breath came. On a most obscure level, he felt grateful. He'd die knowing he hadn't been branded with some terrible homophobic slur. He'd die knowing this wasn't a hate crime. As light exited his eyes, he'd also die never knowing why.

CHAPTER NINE

Jericho and I spent the evening driving to the Outer Banks, leaving Philadelphia behind with our bellies full and our souls rested. We timed the drive just right so we'd miss Philly traffic's smoggy congestion, while also reaching Wright's Memorial Bridge early enough for me to catch up on the Pearson case and to pick up Lisa Pearson's dog, Tiny. My annual meeting with Sharon finished, my sense of obligation to do right by my daughter in advancing her case—no matter how small the step—had been completed.

Jericho stayed the night, the two of us slipping into bed where sleep found me soon after I closed my eyelids. Rest didn't last long though. My dreams were haunted by Hannah's face, which was always just out of reach. I woke with a jolt, my pillow and sheets damp, ocean waves tumbling yards beyond my windows, a subtle glint of daybreak on the horizon. I'd stifled a cry into my pillow and discovered we weren't alone. Tiny had come into my bed, crawling between us, a soft whimper answering me, his wet nose nuzzling my neck. Almost instantly, I fell in love with Tiny, for his ability to sense something was wrong and try to comfort me.

Unable to sleep, I checked my phone, seeing a text message alert blinking. Dr. Swales was ready to offer a preliminary review on the Pearsons' case, with a meeting scheduled for seven that morning. The message I'd hoped to see was one about Lisa Pearson. Sadly, there wasn't a single word, the girl remained missing. Her disappearance stuck in my head the way terrible news never truly leaves. I was also certain it was what spurred my nightmares about Hannah. I sent a few text messages of my own, asking about sightings, reports, anything. The night patrol was quick to respond, but offered nothing hopeful. Lisa Pearson was still missing, and there were no leads.

The clock told me it was early, before five in the morning, but my mind told me to get up. The air was cold, a chill deep enough to set goosebumps on my arms as I swung my legs out from beneath the sheets and sat on the edge of the bed.

"A hot shower," I said in a convincing tone to Tiny, an attempt to motivate myself. His ears perked as I shifted to get up. "And coffee."

I'd make it an early day, a study of Lisa Pearson and where she could possibly be consuming my mind. I'd meet with Dr. Swales to discuss Lisa's parents, and then join the search for her.

A hand. Jericho's comforting touch on the small of my back. I leaned back in, resting against the crook of his warm body, his weight shifting so we'd fit. I found his hand and fit my fingers with his. The bedroom's ceiling fan paddled the air, its soft kisses touching my bare shoulders. Jericho propped onto an elbow, his hand touching my cheek to wipe the drying tears that came with the dreams.

"I think we have company," he said, his voice gravelly and dry.

"We do."

"Another nightmare?" he asked. He peered through tired eyes, mostly closed, his face appearing closer to mine in the early day's gray light. "Was it bad?"

"They're always bad," I said flatly, pressing my face against his, stubble scratching my chin. "Hold me."

I joined him then, laying on the side of the bed left empty most of the time, but not by his choice. It was mine. I wanted to save him from the nightmares, save him from the tortured evenings that woke me three, sometimes four times before dawn. With his arm hugging my middle, our bodies slipped silently into a rhythm of deep breaths.

With Jericho, I found sleep again. And it was a peaceful sleep. It was there I'd see Hannah as I wanted to see her. I'd see her father Ronald too, the three of us a family again, playing together on the lawn. But beyond the end of our street, high in the sky, black clouds swirled and bellowed a haunting cry. It was a warning of what would come.

Carvings. A knife to the skin after death. Of the husband and wife found dead in their rented RV, only the wife had been marked. These were the thoughts on my mind as I braced the thick resin doors, the chill of refrigeration seeping through the latex covering my palm.

Nichelle Wilkinson stood close to me, towering over Dr. Swales, the two with frizzy buns atop their heads as though in competition. But in Nichelle's big brown eyes, I saw the apprehension, her being unsure if this was an area of the job she was interested in seeing. She was young, a few years out of college, an expert with technology and wanting to explore more, possibly move into crime-scene investigation. I told her the only way to know was to try, to see it all and then assess.

"Follow my lead," I said, raising my brow. Her normally light-brown skin had turned pale, leading me to wonder if she could stomach the meeting. I fixed her a look of sharp concern, adding, "Nichelle, if you need to leave, you do so. Okay?"

"Uh-huh," she answered, snapping a latex glove on her hand. "I'll be fine."

Inside the morgue, we followed Dr. Swales to the wall of body refrigerators and I took my place on one side as she opened a door. A puff of cold air tumbled out, showing the feet of Carl Pearson, a pale toe-tag dangling, blue ink noting the victim's name and other details I found myself fixated on memorizing. Without thought, I grabbed the body tray handles, my motions mirroring the medical examiner's, the two of us sliding the victim into the open. Carl Pearson's body was covered by what was referred to as an evidence sheet, his hands and legs and face hidden until Dr. Swales removed the sheet with a swift motion.

"Quite the battle?" she said, a southern lilt in her voice, pointing to the abrasions on the victim's knuckles.

"Dr. Swales, I'm seeing more than expected," Nichelle answered gruffly, the gore too much, her gloved fingers working rapidly against her phone's screen, and her eyes as big as teacup saucers.

"Not quite the same as debugging code or searching the darknet, is it?" Dr. Swales asked, crisp lines at the corners of her eyes when she smiled. She glanced to me, adding, "This is a great idea, rotating team members across cases. They'll see every bit of detail, gory and otherwise, and get exposed to the entirety of a case."

"Nichelle is our first. She's our test, having asked to see more. If it works out, maybe you'd like to spend a day in IT with her?"

With that, Dr. Swales stopped and shook her head, her glasses slipping to the end of her nose, "Trust me, I'm the last person you'd want in front of a computer. I swear those things hate me."

"Help me out here?" I asked, wanting to get back to the case. I leaned closer, cold air drifting from Carl Pearson's body, his skin as white as the sheet that had covered him. The injuries to his body were significant, but I concentrated on his head and face and the defensive wounds. A sturdy flap of skin sat askew above his right eyebrow, the blow to his forehead deep enough to show skull. There were wide lacerations covering his forearms, possible knife wounds, the edges cleanly opened without signs of tearing. The knuckles on his right hand were torn to the cartilage, showing him to be right-handed, and that he'd assaulted the attacker with his fist. The fatal injury was a crushing blow to the back of the victim's skull, the instrument suspected to be a hammer, the end of it driven nearly an inch deep into the brain. I carefully lifted the victim's fingers, waved my hand to the ridge of damaged knuckles and asked, "Have you ever seen a fight between two people result in this much damage?"

Dr. Swales came to the edge of the drawer and joined my side, trading places with Nichelle. She tilted her glasses, magnifying the lens for a closer study. "A wall," she answered. "As in drunken brawls, fists thrown and missed, landing against a brick wall."

"I have the crime-scene photos," Nichelle offered, holding up her phone. "The RV's interior does show a lot of damage, but nothing to explain the marks on his fists. The wall surfaces are all smooth."

Swales left briefly, running to her counter full of equipment, coming back breathing fast. "Look closely," she said excitedly, holding a focused light with a large magnifying glass. We closed the space around the victim's hand. The magnifier showed the exposed knuckles, their rawness, along with a hundred cuts and abrasions. "These are from multiple blows against a single surface, rough, textured."

"The attacker could have been wearing protective gear. Like body armor," I suggested. "Meaning they were prepared."

"Prepared? So the killer knew what they were doing? And why only one carving?" Nichelle asked, rattling off questions, the bug of investigation driving her.

Dr. Swales jerked a tray from the next body refrigerator. We shifted focus to Peggy Pearson, the woman's skin as white as her husband's, save for the puddle of purple and black settled at the lowest points. The sheet was placed at the waistline. On the victim's torso was the carved figure we'd studied since first discovering it. The significance of it remained unknown.

"The letter A?" Nichelle asked.

"Could be," I answered, holding onto my first impression of it possibly being some kind of pagan symbol. "Or could be something entirely different."

"Too exact to be anything other than an A," Nichelle commented, taking a picture and typing on her phone.

"That's just one mystery," Dr. Swales said, her tone steady. "But I'd say you have multiple mysteries."

I nodded. "For now, let's assume it's a letter A. Perfectly formed, the edges clean, and the wound is superficial, the blade only cutting the first layers of skin."

"What does that mean?" Nichelle asked, a blue flash coming from her phone. "Knowing might help me with the image search I'll perform. I've got darknet searches in a queue, and scans across social media. If this was posted online somewhere, I'll find it."

"It's a shallow wound, inflicted post-mortem as well," Dr. Swales explained.

"Any reason why?" I asked her.

"Being post-mortem, the body is unable to heal, leaving the victim forever mutilated."

"Hate for the victim?" I proposed. "Enough of it that the killer wanted the victim to go to their grave wearing the mark?"

Nichelle's hands hovered over the victim, carefully framing another photo. Without looking at us, she answered, "Or the marking wasn't meant for the victim at all. It was meant for us to see."

Dr. Swales and I exchanged a look, the idea surprisingly profound. Nichelle sensed she'd said something of meaning, but wasn't sure what it was.

I urged her, "Go on."

Her focus nervously darted to the corners of the room while she collected her words. "I think this was made to be shown—you know, like in *The Scarlet Letter*."

"The victim branded," Dr. Swales commented.

"In the book, Hester Prynne was made to wear the letter A, which was a symbol—"

"—of Adultery," I continued, an idea stirring about a lover's quarrel, a mistress and jealousy as a motive. I stepped back from the victims, eyeballing both, and countered. "The scarlet letter A for all to see. But in this case, the obvious meaning is the first letter of the alphabet, indicating there would be more to come."

I caught a faint look of disappointment on Nichelle's face at my dismissing her theory. "All theories are good theories," I assured her. "It's the only way of exploring the possibilities of what happened."

Dr. Swales turned to face Peggy's husband. Over her shoulder, she said, "But we still don't have an understanding of why this victim was left without a marking."

Nichelle joined Dr. Swales, adding, "It makes sense if it was for adultery, shaming the wife for all to see."

I shook my head. "It's a good theory, but it doesn't work if the husband is dead too."

Nichelle lifted her chin, her focus remaining on her phone as she took notes. "Then why leave only one letter? Why mark just one victim."

I glanced back at Carl Pearson's face, the flap of thick skin. I went to him, lifting his hand, and circled the raw beating on his knuckles, imagining the fight he'd endured. "It could be that the killer didn't know him."

"Didn't know him?" Dr. Swales asked.

"Right. Look at these," I instructed, showing the wounds on the victim's hands again. "He fought the attacker, defended himself and his wife. From these wounds and the damage in the RV, the fight was brutal. Yet, the killer only marked one of them."

"The killer marked the person they'd gone there to kill," Dr. Swales said. She hung her finger in the air, continuing, "The only reason Carl Pearson died was because he *was* there."

I motioned to Peggy Pearson. "This wasn't random. The killer knew her."

CHAPTER TEN

My team greeted me in a meeting room that I'd commandeered for this case's investigation. Nichelle arrived with me and took a seat, her fingers clutching the tallest cup of coffee I'd ever seen, steam spewing over its porcelain lip, the face showing a cat cartoon with the words *Paws Off* beneath it. Tracy, the crime-scene technician, sat nearby with a pad and pencil in hand, eagerness pasted on her face. She'd taken me up on an offer to sit in on the investigation, her wanting to experience this side of what we did, and possibly consider it for her career. Cheryl Smithson, a third-year detective with fiery red hair and an attitude to go with it, gave me a courtesy wave, her eyes glued to her phone. Last to join the team was Emanuel Wilson, a popular basketball player who'd gone on to become a cop and had been recently promoted to a rookie detective. Emanuel was assigned to my team by the captain, after a request by Mayor Ashtole to advance the investigation by throwing more bodies at it—like that ever worked successfully. But I could always hope. I sensed there were frustrations already building on the lack of progress.

"Glad to see everyone," I said, gathering my thoughts as I wrote on the conference room's whiteboard.

Nichelle set up an old projector to display a map of the Outer Banks. Mid-morning sun beamed through the windows. Cheryl lowered the blinds until dust shimmered in the light's path, Nichelle twisting the lens into focus, sharpening the image on the wall.

"This thing is a dinosaur," she complained over a fan whirring. I'd asked for a big display, bigger than the monitor screens, and she'd found the projector buried in a supply closet. When it was focused, the map filled the whiteboard and some of the front wall. The map's overlay was dimly lit but we'd easily be able to identify locations. "But you were right about the detail."

"This is perfect," I told her.

The Amber Alert raised for Lisa Pearson had produced zero hits. And Nichelle's network tap into the town's camera surveillance system had also produced zero hits. At this point, we had two dead adults and a missing child who was presumed to have been kidnapped.

During my trek to Philadelphia, Emanuel and Cheryl had canvased the campground, working with the manager, meeting and interviewing the families vacationing there.

"Of the twenty-two campsites, we interviewed roughly thirty-five people," Emanuel said in a baritone voice deep enough to rattle windows.

"That's quite a number," I said, sounding hopeful. "And?"

Cheryl held up her hand, showing the team a count of one, her hand pale in the project's light, her skin pocked with bright freckles. She swiped her phone, searching her notes, answering, "There was a group of teens, out-of-towners. They reported seeing a car parked on Glebe Road, and the driver enter the woods adjacent to the campground around eight p.m."

Emanuel raised his hand. "They'd also reported the individual was dressed in black." He motioned to his head and shoulders, saying, "The person's head and face were covered as well."

"It would have still been daylight," Tracy commented, voice wavering, unsure of herself or her position with the team.

"Go on," I said, encouraging her.

"Well, sunset for this time of year is around twenty minutes past the reported time… give or take." She glanced around the room, and added, "There was ample light for at least another hour. Kicking in the RV door in daylight would be risky."

"Is it possible the killer waited in the woods?" I asked. Some motion, a partial agreement. "We have one individual. Any tire tracks, or other clues about the vehicle?"

Emanuel and Cheryl both shook their heads. Cheryl answering, "Glebe Road is asphalt and the kids could only guess it was a sedan."

"Glebe Road," Nichelle said, typing, the glow of her laptop screen in her eyes.

"Video surveillance?" I asked, thinking it possible we had a recording.

"Maybe," Nichelle answered. "I'll reconcile any video feeds leading into and out of the location during the time the vehicle was seen parked."

"Good," I said and motioned to Tracy, the end of her pencil twirling as she tried to keep up with the exchange. I made a mental note to procure her a laptop. "Tracy, I'd like you to join Nichelle, pair up, she'll show you some of the technical side to the investigation."

"Partners," Nichelle said warmly. Tracy gave her a bashful smile in return.

"Okay. For Lisa Pearson's search, beyond the campground…" I began, finding a cluster of buildings on the map. "What about here?" With a whiteboard marker, I underlined a block of stores and a gas station north of the kidnapping. "Have we questioned here also?"

"All of these," Cheryl answered, joining me, the smell of coconut moisturizer following her. She scratched a line through a gas station south of the kidnapping and one further east, the orange dry-erase marker screeching. She stretched onto her toes and added a second line through a row of businesses.

I stepped back to review where the search had progressed, where Lisa Pearson's photograph had been delivered, the sheets of eight-by-eleven-inch missing-person flyer handed out again and again to passers-by and store clerks. All to no avail. I picked up one of them, studied the photograph I'd found in her father's wallet, a hopeful likeness, but teenagers can change seemingly overnight. Lisa Pearson may have aged some since, but it was all we had while waiting for school records and contact from a relative.

From Nichelle's work, we'd learned Lisa Pearson was thirteen and diagnosed with type 1 diabetes at a very young age. The prescription that Officer Tom Monroe found in the RV told us that Lisa was apt to become sicker and weaker with the passing days, and not likely to survive more than a week without it.

"Anything on social media?" I asked Nichelle.

"I haven't found anything yet." She gave me a grim shake, and eyed the room, not wanting to disappoint. "It might be that her parents didn't let her online, or have any social-media accounts?"

"What about her phone?" I asked. "We have it, and at her age, they live on their phones."

Nichelle pinched her lips with another grim look. "I'm still trying to unlock it."

There were answers on the girl's phone, I was sure of it. "Don't be afraid to ask for help," I warned.

"I won't," Nichelle answered. "I just need a little more time."

With her words, I spoke to the room, "It's time we were fighting," I said, my tone dire. "Lisa Pearson is running out of time."

"These," Cheryl continued, circling a section of the map. "We haven't been here yet."

I recognized the location as having gas stations and convenience stores on the other side of Dare Memorial Bridge, which crossed the bay to Manns Harbor and the mainland. "If the kidnapper went west on Route 64, it is likely they stopped here first. There's nothing but highway afterward, billboards and farms for a hundred miles."

"There's south too," Tom Monroe said, joining late, picking up a green dry-erase and marking the southern tips. "They could have taken the split from Route 64 to 264, headed toward South Carolina."

"You lead that one," I told him, my sights on the west, checking my watch, itching to pound the pavement and knock on some doors. "Are we set?"

The small group traded looks and head nods, each stopping at the whiteboard to take notes, each with a direction to go along with a handful of Lisa Pearson's missing-person flyers.

We had no luck at the first of the stores, dodging vacationers, annoying the staff with questions and showing Lisa Pearson's pictures. My hopes of progress were quickly falling short as we crossed Dare Memorial Bridge. The sun was high in the sky, half the day already burned behind us when I came upon the smallest of convenience stores. It looked as if it was out of an old western movie; planks of ash-colored lumber made up the walls and it had a roof of chapped and split cedar shingles, years of weather turning handfuls of them green and black. There was a porch with a bench and a rocking chair, along with a screened door and ancient windows with thin sheets of glass. Only the rusting ice machine and flickering neon signs indicated the store was open for business.

The screen door creaked and clapped shut as I entered, the inside every bit as dated as the outside. There was a strong musty smell mixed with wood and ocean, and dust drifted in the front window's sunlight. Wooden shelves made up the aisles, with the surrounding walls lined by glass-front refrigerators, moisture clouding them. Strings of tacky fly tape hung from the ceiling, draping the corners with a season of fly carcasses forever stuck, the legs of one still moving. If not for the likes of the popular energy drinks and bags of Funyuns, I would have thought I'd stepped back in time.

That's when I saw hope, in the form of a short ATM next to a pair of old arcade games and a pinball machine. And above them, a security camera in the ceiling corner, a tiny blue light on its top, blinking with life. If anyone suspicious had stopped by, there would be a record.

I noticed the store clerk studying me as I'd studied his store. An older man, his bronze skin heavily creased like slats of wood flooring, his hair as white as the clouds, a toothpick stirring in the corner of his mouth. He was dressed like a farmer, but his front was wrapped in a clerk's apron. His eyes were carried by heavy bags, the whites of them dim with a hint of yellow, bleary, a faint stench of alcohol telling me he might be hungover. When I pulled out a missing-person flyer and revealed my badge, his attention shifted, and I could see his interest wane as he understood there was no sale to be made. From the looks of his disappointment, I might have been the only customer of the day.

"You looking for someone?" he asked, his voice low and soft over the faint sounds of the radio behind him, playing a Bee Gees tune from the seventies.

I placed the sheet on the counter and made it a point to look in his eyes as I asked, "We're looking for this girl—may have come in with someone, or could have been in a car?"

The clerk thumped the flyer with his fingers, strumming the counter as he studied the picture. He began to nod his head, igniting a spark of hope. "Yeah," he answered.

"When?" I asked without waiting. "Was she with someone?"

"I seen her on the news," he told me, which put my hope on hold. "Can't say for sure it was her though."

"Alone?"

He continued to nod, but then stopped. "Could be there was someone outside." He picked up the flyer and gave it another study. "It sure looks like her. The girl I seen was older."

"That's possible," I answered. I motioned to the security camera. "How about videos? Do you keep the recordings?"

The clerk's face lightened, a smile revealing surprisingly white teeth. "That thing?"

From the tone, I knew instantly it was a fake—a good fake. "It sure looks real."

The toothpick shifted to the other corner of his mouth and began stirring again. "Bought it few years back when I was robbed."

"Does it work?"

He let out another laugh, shaking his head. "Nah. Got robbed again a month later."

"Dangerous business," I told him. "Especially being one of the last stops west."

"The church," he said, thumping the flyer, recognition on his face. "The girl who come in here, she was looking for the old church."

"A church?" I asked, confused. "And she was alone?"

"All by herself," he said, motioning to a rack of cheap plastic sandals. "Came in barefoot. She bought a pair of those."

"Alone?" I asked again, beginning to understand Lisa Pearson might not have been kidnapped at all. "Where is this church?"

The clerk shifted the toothpick to the other side, swirling it as he hung his thumb over his shoulder and answered, "Drive another two miles, pass some fields. You'll come up on a hill and just on the other side, there she'll be."

Before leaving, I grabbed a bag of chips and a diet soda, plunking ten dollars on the counter. "Keep the change," I told him, shoving the flyer closer to him. "And if you think of anything else, any more details, be sure to give the number a call. That girl's life is at stake."

"Sure thing," he answered, ringing up the sale. He picked up the missing-person flyer and tacked it to the shelf behind him.

As the screen door slammed shut and the sun glared hot on my face, the questions about Lisa Pearson rose like a stiff wind. If she was alone, why didn't she call the police, or ask for help? And why would she visit a church?

CHAPTER ELEVEN

As I followed the store clerk's directions I entered a different part of North Carolina. *Coastal Plains,* Jericho had once mentioned, *heavy on the farming.* The wonder of it wasn't just the shift though. It was the dichotomy of this farmland and the vacation hotspots in the Outer Banks. It was also the sheer distance Lisa Pearson had traveled from the site of her parents' murder. The store clerk mentioned she'd been walking. What had driven the girl across a bridge, and then to the convenience store, and onwards to the church, all on foot?

I stopped at a crossroads, uncertain the church actually existed. With his bleary eyes and the evening's drink still on his breath, I had no idea of what to expect from the witness. The intersection was surrounded by fields, young sprouts, incredibly green, the air filled with the smell of plant life and earth. I heard music coming from up the road where the dirt lip met the horizon.

"A few more miles," I told myself, desperate to find the church. I followed the music like a rat following the Pied Piper out of Hamelin. And then I saw it.

The steeple rose above the road like a rocket ascending. From the peak of the hill, the building stood alone, surrounded by fields. The music became louder as I approached, the church beating like a white heart floating in a sea of endless gold and green. Cast against a cloudless afternoon, dusky blue, the image was surreal and like something I might have seen on a wall calendar.

The church looked to have once been a single room, old, country building, expanded later with a larger room in the rear. But the front had kept the original look, staying true to the architecture, genuine for these parts. I parked along the road's edge, taking to the fresh lawn leading up to the doors.

A line of people was waiting to go inside, the end of it wrapping around the side and toward the back where there were trailers and RVs with wood blocks shoved against the tires. The RVs naturally caught my eye, but with every new case, I was apt to find connections everywhere I looked. The insides of some RVs had ballooned, the walls expanded for sitting and sleeping. They looked permanent. I jotted down license-plate numbers, careful not to be noticed.

Electrical generators sat on the other side of the church, one puffing like a chain smoker, the others idle. The smell of spent fuel was thick, but the distant storm carried it away with a steady breeze. Around the church, I found others, mostly teenagers, all busily attending to its upkeep. A few worked the lawn, cropped short and fresh and as green as holiday trees. Others painted the building's outside, the whiteness blinding in the sunlight and making me shield my eyes. With the shade, I saw some of them were actually children, swimming in oversized coveralls, perched precariously on ladders, and standing on makeshift scaffolds, buckets and brushes in hand.

My attention shifted to the line of those waiting to enter. It was made up of young and old, middle-aged with babies and children, more teenagers. All were wearing expressions of anticipation and want, their faces plastered with smiles and eyes wide with excitement. Beyond the porch, two large doors, their grandness matched by their height, along with a slightly round man sitting on a stool, dressed in a fine suit, blond hair slicked back, some curls hanging in front, his face surprisingly free of sweat as he fanned himself with a leaflet.

"Afternoon," I said, greeting him from the lawn, taking care to dress my badge and lanyard. "I'm Detective White. I'd like to ask you some questions."

"D.J. Reynolds," he answered, his eyes never meeting mine.

I climbed the steps, the paint worn, wood showing through from years of wear. The attendant stopped fanning the air and pulled an identification badge and lanyard from a box, handing it to a teen who'd been waiting in line, the boy's face pocked with adolescence, his cheeks rosy and forehead shiny.

"I can see him?" the boy said excitedly, his voice cracking.

"Of course," the attendant answered. "You were invited."

As the doors opened, a mix of rock and soul music spilled out. I peered through the crack, curious. Colorful lights swung wildly. A preacher's voice boomed with evangelical fervor, the congregation responding to each passage in uniformed chorus. I craned my neck to see more, trying to understand who it was Lisa Pearson had come to see. I looked for a sign, anything with the preacher's name, but saw none.

With the man was a foldable table, the type used to play card games. On top, a box with the identification badges and next to it, a stack of leaflets held down by a red brick, the corners curled by a gusty breeze.

I cleared my throat, loud enough to get the attendant's attention. "I'll trade," I offered, freeing the top leaflet from beneath the brick, the name *Richard Dowd* printed in bold letters. I handed him a copy of the missing-person flyer, a warped reflection of Lisa Pearson's face shown in his round glasses. "This girl is missing. A witness directed her to this church."

"Lisa Pearson," the attendant said, handing it back to me. He closed his eyes slowly, his lips moving in silent prayer, parroting the words I heard beyond the church doors. The preacher was leading the congregation with a prayer I hadn't heard since attending weekend bible classes as a child. When he was finished, the attendant continued, "Lisa Pearson was here to see *him*."

My heart sank at his use of the past tense. "She *was* here?" I asked, glancing at the box of identification badges, and then to the line of people waiting to go inside.

"She was," he answered and resumed his work of handing out lanyards with passes.

I stepped between him and the next in line, annoyed by the struggle to keep his attention. *No cuts*, I heard from behind me. The attendant shot me a dirty look as I shook my head, pleading, "Would you mind helping with a few more questions?"

"Look, the girl left, and she hasn't been back," he answered, a scowl plastered on his face.

"Was she alone?"

No answer. I locked eyes with him. A sudden flush of adrenaline was pumping through me. Lisa Pearson had been seen, and I wondered if her parents' killer might have brought her to the church, brought her to this gathering. Theories danced in my mind as I thought of the carving in Lisa's mother's skin: could the killer have believed in some cult-like sacrifice?

"Was there anyone with her, and did she appear to be in danger?"

The attendant shook his head, his frown softening. "Not at all," he answered. He smiled then, appearing elated and said, "Lisa Pearson was invited."

"Invited?" I asked, suddenly confused, and scanned the church and the grounds and the people. "How do you get invited—?"

The attendant raised his hands above his head, "From *him* of course." As I pondered the idea of an invitation, he continued handing out the lanyards, the face of the doors swinging open and then closing.

"And was the girl hurt? Did she appear to be sick?" I asked, interrupting again. *Come on*, someone shouted.

His frown returned as he shook his face again. "Not that I could see. She was here to see *him*."

I made room for the line to proceed. With my experience, I suspected a kidnapper had brought Lisa Pearson here. But now there was doubt. I texted Nichelle, updating her and the team, our lead on the child's kidnapping possibly wrong. I checked pictures on my phone, pictures of the RV's bathroom window, the sill and the traces of blood. What if Lisa Pearson escaped through the window? Escaped the killer, and then came here alone?

I went to the church doors, my hands nearly on the handles. In a single motion, the attendant was in front of me, his height deceiving, the top of my head barely reaching his chin. He squared his shoulders and lowered his face close to mine.

"Listen, there's a medical urgency. We need to find Lisa. I'll have to check inside, ask around."

In a soft voice, he said, "You were not invited."

"I understand I wasn't invited," I said, masking a smile, bemused by the absurdity. When he refused to move, I raised my voice and held up my badge. "But I'm with the police, there's a medical emergency, and if the child was here—"

He shook his head, a clump of curls falling across his glasses. I read the identification badge hanging from his neck, his name, D.J. Reynolds as he'd said, and beneath it a title, Security & Events Director.

Reynolds combed his fingers through his hair, tucking it behind his ears. "Lisa Pearson was here, but she's no longer with us."

"Then, do you know where she went?" I said insistently.

"I don't," he answered, his gaze falling beyond me to the next couple in line. He handed them badges, the doors opening. An older man exited, a cane in hand and his face glowing. The couple approached, pushing in front of me to enter. As they slipped into the dark, they became alive with dancing colors. Frustrated, I tried to follow, but as I stepped across the threshold I found myself suddenly facing the doors again, the attendant closing them abruptly with a rush of air.

"You weren't invited."

Disappointment came with a wafting church smell. Reynolds took to his seat again and picked up an iPad and flicked the screen. He darted an eye toward me, waiting for my next move.

I held my badge again, and demanded, "For the safety of the child, I need to search the premises!"

"The right of the people to be secure in their persons, houses, papers, and effects, against unreasonable searches and seizures, shall not be violated—"

I raised my hand, livid. "Yeah, I know the fourth amendment." Reynolds filled his chest with air, pride on his face as he continued swiping the iPad's screen. "As an officer of the law, I have the right to enter when evidence, or suspicions of a crime are visible."

"You can try," he answered with a snarky smile. He waved his hand, adding, "We both know there's no evidence of any crimes visible here."

I gritted my teeth. "You've stated seeing this child, she is missing, and a crime has been committed."

"I'm happy to meet you at your office and provide a statement," he answered.

I broke eye contact, knowing he'd make a scene if I tried to enter, and that anything I discovered inside would be unusable in court. I couldn't risk it, and listened for something I could use to justify a search—a yell or a scream perhaps, but only heard music and the preacher spouting spiritual Tic Tacs to a hungry crowd.

"Then you have a nice day," I told the man, offering a fake smile.

"You do the same," he answered, his expression unchanged.

"Call the number on the flyer if you remember anything else," I told him. "We *will* be in touch with more questions."

If Lisa Pearson had left the church, I needed to move on to the next stop, follow the map as we'd outlined in the meeting. She'd been here, which meant someone possibly brought her, or someone inside had seen her, or spoken to her, or even knew her.

From the car, I sent Nichelle a picture of the leaflet, framing the name Richard Dowd. I also sent the church address, asking her to pull all the paperwork. I was sure they had a lease, but there might have been a county permit needed for the generators, or to park the RVs and trailers in a makeshift camp. It was a weak idea, but if it got me in the door, got me to where Lisa Pearson had been, it could save the child's life.

CHAPTER TWELVE

He'd made Lisa feel different, made her feel normal and whole. She'd found him online, a chance happening, a search result she'd clicked one desperate afternoon when she'd fought with her mother. That little link was a miracle. From it, Lisa had found his videos, his talks, and discovered how open he was about what he'd gone through.

Flashes of horror returned and ravaged her. She'd insisted they come to this place. And for what? To see him? She did see Dowd, heeding to his invitation. But he didn't see her, not the way she needed. Now her parents were dead. An errant giggle escaped her lips, mixed with a forlorn cry. A wave of hysteria for Dowd and the surreal situation she found herself in. Crushing sadness for her parents. With miles between her and the church, her parents' murders struck fully. She felt what death was, understood it, and she loathed the mourning that came with it. Unable to stop, Lisa wept. Teardrop blooms puddled in the road's dirt.

Lisa's mind was scattered. Her skin was hot with sweat that came with a relenting shiver. She was getting sick. Not as sick as before, not like the time she stayed in the hospital. But soon. There were bubbles in the tube leading from her insulin pump, the chamber in the device near empty, or maybe already empty. The doctor had told her what could happen if she didn't change it in time. She needed the medicine. Without it, her life was disappearing. She gently flicked the tube, careful not to damage the part burrowing into her skin. The bubbles jiggled with a slight tease, the medicine moving. It might have been a drop, might have been more. And it might have been enough. Or maybe there was none at all. But she knew where to get some.

Her head was light and the dizziness made her stop, the world in a strange lean. She dropped to the road, sitting squat, teetering on the edge of a blackout. She wavered and tried bracing for it, her toes and fingers tingling and covered in road dust as she gripped the last of her consciousness. A heaving breath came, wings batting the air with birds taking flight. She wasn't alone, and was being watched. The distraction helped, and the threat of passing out faded.

Corn stalks bordered the road like green statues, their budding ears like rungs on a ladder, the kernel prizes spied by the crows perched atop a power line. They glanced at her with beady rat-eyes, fluffing their heavy black coats, a flare of iridescence gleaming in the sunlight. Laughter broke abruptly from her lips, sounding manic and confused, a silly joke her father liked to tell suddenly remembered.

"If a group of crows is called a murder, what do you call just two crows?" he'd ask, his face red, his lips pinched, barely able to hold it in.

"I dunno," she'd answer, playing along. "What do you call just two crows?"

"Attempted murder," he'd roar.

He'd laugh so hard, tears would spring from the corners of his eyes. She'd laugh with him too, even though she'd heard the joke a hundred times. But today, the laughter was struck dead just like her father had been. She glanced at the crows, their glare fixed as though seeing the morbid image of him lying in the RV, half of his face torn from his skull.

"You shut it!" she yelled, gripping stones from the roadside, throwing them tearfully, her cries zapping what little strength she had. As if on cue, the birds took flight, leaving a pair behind in her company. Lisa's laughter returned on seeing the remaining two crows. It was sad, but it was for her dad. "See, Dad, attempted murder."

In the stilled air, the sun bore down, a never-ending heat making the top of her head feel on fire. She picked at her lips, the skin on them chapped and peeling. Drops of blood oozed, leaving the taste of a penny on her tongue. She slipped out of the cheap sandals on her feet, the straps tattered and coming apart, the front breaking from the miles spent. The air soothed where pink skin showed beneath torn scabs.

Type 1 diabetes. Lisa heard in her head, an echo of having heard it daily for as long as she could remember. For her, the world seemed to revolve around *her diabetes*. That's the way her mother would say it—*her diabetes*. Lisa cringed. *My daughter needs short-acting insulin all day long*, she'd say, describing it as though it was Lisa's fault, like she'd gotten the disease on purpose. Her mother didn't get it, didn't understand how those words were like bee stings, painful little bites nipping at her.

"The insulin, it's my medicine," Lisa told the remaining crows and scratched the itch on her belly. It was the insulin pump's needle, the portal. She dared a look, her fingers on the part that felt the hottest, her skin red and ballooning. She'd have to change the needle too, clean the infected area and make a new one. *Subcutaneous*, the doctor explained. *Just beneath the skin.* There was only one place she knew where she could get more supplies. The idea was dreadful, but her need was dire.

Through the confusion, a foggy image of the trailer's counter appeared. She saw her prescription. Saw the month's supply she and her mother had picked up from the drugstore. She'd have to trace her steps, have to remember which roads and which turns taken, carefully crossing every intersection if she had any chance. Once she had her medication and changed the insulin pump, she'd go to the police, she'd tell them everything that happened. Panic rushed over her as another sickly chill caused a shiver. What if they questioned why she'd left her parents dead in the RV? And why she'd gone to the church instead of to the police straight away? She clutched her hands nervously, gripping the air, unable to decipher the jumble of confused thoughts. *Insulin*, she heard in her mind, the word rising above the noise. *First.* She'd get the insulin, knowing that without her medicine, nothing else mattered.

"The bridge," she blurted with a spell of fresh enthusiasm, recalling the crossing over the bay and realizing she'd been on its path since leaving Dowd's church. "Cross the bridge and then to the boardwalk."

Heat rose from the pavement, shimmering. *A highway mirage,* her father had told her once. Lisa started when a car flew past, a flood of hot air buffeting her body, the sight of it a blur as it chased the road's mirage. The horn blared, and then faded, bending the way sound does when passing.

A few more miles, the top of the bridge showing over the fields. She stood, brushed her hair behind her ears, and set forth for her medicine. She grimaced putting the sandals back on, the blisters rubbing the broken plastic and firing tiny lightning strikes into her legs. But she slogged the steps, fighting every part of her that demanded she lay down and end this.

"Come along then," she said to the crows, wondering if one might follow, their curiosity in her continuing. She didn't wait and turned to face the hot road, the air wavering with dangerous invitation. Wings batted the air again, the caw of one answering, following. "Just a few more miles."

CHAPTER THIRTEEN

As I returned from the church, a report came in with news we'd all silently been dreading: another murder; another campground; and this time, a single victim. Worry weighed on my heart as I read the alert and the scant details. I told myself to breathe, told myself that I didn't know what I didn't know.

Thanks to the time of year, we had a full afternoon of daylight remaining. If this was anything like the first RV murder, we'd need every minute before the day got away from us. I drove directly to the scene, having delivered every copy of the Lisa Pearson missing-person flyer. I arrived early to the scene, as police tape was being strung and a few people gathering, curiosity on their faces. I studied each person, but saw nothing that raised suspicion.

Paper booties covered my shoes, a pair of blue-latex gloves were ready for wear in my hands, and my clothes stuck to my skin as sweat coated the back of my neck. From the outside, the RV showed no damage, the door being intact. I cautiously stepped inside, apprehensive about what I was about to see. I'd seen many crime scenes, but would never get used to that initial shock of seeing a victim for the first time—and deep in my heart, I hoped I never would.

The scene was as horrific as the first RV murders—a victim sprawled across the floor, a likely fatal wound in their neck area. As I'd feared, the similarities to Carl and Peggy Pearson's murders were there: most strikingly, a figure carved into the victim's skin. At once, my mind filled with thoughts of this being a repeat killer, possibly a serial killer. But I knew I'd have to hold my tongue until I had more evidence to support the idea.

"This is concerning," I commented as Tracy Fields stepped around me. "Have any of the details about the first RV murder been released?"

"I haven't heard or read anything," she answered, her focus darting from the RV's front to the back, her camera swinging on thin straps hanging taut from her shoulders. Tracy held her technician's kit in hand, using it as a balance while making her way into the RV.

"I haven't read or seen anything either. Dr. Swales still hasn't released the first victims."

"Do you think this could be a copycat?" she asked, recognizing the likeness to the Pearson case.

I gave Tracy an uncommitted nod. I'd seen back-to-back murders before. "I can't say just yet, so we'll have to go with the evidence we collect."

"I noticed the victim is from out of town. Maybe the RVs in both cases are rentals. Could be the same rental company."

Tracy's comment was spot-on and I had to hold back a smile, biting my lip, warm admiration rising. On the Pearson case, Tracy had had a rocky start, but once she'd settled and got comfortable, the questions came naturally to her. I'd taken a liking to her almost immediately, and believed she'd make a great investigator.

From the counter, a rental slip sat with a pile of vacation pamphlets—highlights of the Outer Banks, tours for Kitty Hawk and the Wright Brothers, fishing guides and piers. I held up my phone, checking the details for the other RV. "You're right. This RV and the Pearsons' are both registered to Trenton RV Rentals."

"A home away from home," she said, her voice in song, her pitch surprisingly good. "I've seen the commercials. But it might not mean anything. The company is huge, they rent nationally."

I shook my head. "Everything means something, so we take nothing for granted. As of now, all victims are from out of town. We have two RVs from the same rental company. That's a thread we'll investigate."

"A thread," she said, repeating, the idea seeded in her mind to work. She went to the body then, and kneeled. "Have you looked at him yet? Ben Hill is the name on the campground lease."

I joined her, taking in the victim's gray complexion, a grimacing expression frozen on his face. He was an older man, mid fifties, his hair silver and thinning on top, combed back, kept tidy. His hands were clean, fingernails trimmed and showing signs of a recent manicure. It was his chest that gave me pause, his faded purple shirt shredded, torn from his body. Beneath the ripped fabric was a symbol carved into his skin.

"Post-mortem?" she asked, taking pictures of the figure.

"No," I answered, sleeving my fingers and hand with blue latex, a breath of dry powder rising with a snap. "See these drops? They're signs of bleeding. Signs that he was alive."

"They look like tears," Tracy said sullenly.

"What do you make of the shape?" I asked, holding back my thoughts, curious to hear hers.

"A capital letter B," she answered without hesitating.

"Or it could be the number 8," I said. "A capital B would have a much harder edge, right?"

Tracy pit her head to the side and tucked her chin in her hand as she studied it. Tracing the figure, she answered, "I can see that."

"Plus, A and B?" I began. "There's not much significance if the killer is using the alphabet as a sequence."

"Infinity symbol?" she said with a question in her tone. She focused the camera lens. The size, shape, and style matched to the figure carved into Peggy Pearson. The camera's strobe flashed in quick successions, the electronics whining with a battery recharge. "If the national rental isn't enough to connect the cases, this certainly will."

I stood up, encouraging Tracy to stand next to me, changing her perspective. She followed, refocusing the lens and snapped the shutter twice more.

"Now look," I said. "Not the symbol for infinity."

She frowned and kneeled again. "Okay, I see the number," she agreed, her focus concentrated on the wound. "Look at this. It's uninterrupted, precise, the curves uniform, a single stroke." She stood again, saying, "A lot of attention went into this."

"The curves?" I asked, seeing what she meant, one stroke used to create the figure. "So, like the carving on Peggy Pearson, the killer took their time with this. Could mean we're looking for someone who knows how to cut."

"A doctor?" Tracy asked.

"It's just an idea. One of many we'll come up with," I told her. "We'll have the medical examiner help verify the figure 8 as well."

As I spoke, a framed picture caught my eye, the photograph sitting face down on the kitchenette's counter. I wouldn't have expected to see it in a rental RV, not these days, not with every video and photo as close as a finger tap on a phone or tablet. I lifted the frame to find a family portrait, recognizing the victim's face, sitting with another man, each of them wearing wedding bands. A girl sat between them, her skin dark, a daughter, possibly adopted. The idea of a hate crime occurred to me, but I hadn't seen or heard of the kind since arriving in the Outer Banks. It was possible though—hate knows no boundaries.

Blood rushed into my head with the possibility of another victim, and another kidnapping too. I narrowed my eyes and scanned the back of the RV, searching the floor for a protruding leg or arm, any sign. I opened the bathroom's door, shoving the pleated folds. The bathroom was empty, the tiny square window closed and latched securely.

"You found something?" Tracy asked before jumping out of my way. I raced to the rear and searched the sleeping quarters, which were also empty, one side of the bed unused, the covers tucked neatly, the pillow square and fluffed, while the other side lay mussed.

"I don't know yet," I answered, breathless.

"The picture?" she asked, sensing the tension and urgency, raising her arms in front of her chest, guarded, fear registering on her face.

I picked up the frame, showing her. "We may have another body," I said, sitting the family portrait on the counter. "And another kidnapping victim."

CHAPTER FOURTEEN

A second Amber Alert was issued. A second possible kidnapping. The child's name was Andrea Hill, her identification determined from her father's wallet. The victim's name was Ben Hill. My suspicions of a second victim were disproved, the remainder of the RV found to be empty. The unidentified man in the family portrait led us to issue an all-points bulletin with a description of his likeness. Until there was more, all possibilities had to remain open. While the murder and the carving in the victim's skin held similarities to the first RV case, this murder could be the result of the unidentified man copying the details before kidnapping Andrea Hill. I'd seen it before. In our law-enforcement careers, most of us had.

I stepped out of the RV, cleared my feet and hands of the booties and gloves, and was surprised to see Jericho stood on the other side of our crime-scene tape.

Sunlight stretched through the heavy campground evergreens, the sharp light dancing on his shoulders. With the increasing shade, the tree frogs had begun their songs and the lamp posts had flicked on, with moths darting errantly in and out of their orange glow.

"What've you got there?" I asked.

He was holding two bags, both white with paper handles, the name *Angelo's* printed in big, bold red letters on them. He'd brought a meal from one of my favorite restaurants.

I escaped the scent of murder by shoving my face in one of the bags, the smell of dough and cheese and red sauce filling my nose. "Did you bring me some Stromboli?"

"I heard you'd be working all day," he answered. "I thought I'd bring you some food."

"Aren't you the thoughtful one," I said, checking my phone, a message taking my attention.

"Bad one?" he asked, his gaze following the commotion in and out of the trailer.

"Bad," I said, looking over my shoulder, following Jericho's stare.

We were done with the crime scene for now. It had been processed and locked. With the victim's body safely removed, the RV would remain untouched until we released it. A bio-cleanup company had already been contacted, their twenty-four-hour service one of a few we called regularly in the Outer Banks. The same was true for the Pearsons' trailer, but the text message I'd just received indicated there'd been a possible break-in.

"Listen, I have to check the other RV."

"Follow up?" he asked.

"Kind of," I told him, starting us toward my car. I snatched one of the bags, popping a doughy garlic ball into my mouth. "I'm ravenous. Would you mind coming with me? We can eat in the car."

He put on a comical scowl, answering, "Not exactly the romantic interlude I was going for."

"Sure it is," I joked with black humor. "I'm a police detective. I've got you, and food, and a murder scene."

Jericho accepted the way I'd found to spend time together, and slid into the passenger side. I hopped onto the main road that led us back to the other RV campground and the Pearsons' case.

"There's a report of some motion in the RV."

"Cleanup service?" he asked.

"We released the RV this afternoon," I answered, my being the one responsible and having signed off on it. "The service is scheduled, and it's due to be moved, but not until later tonight or tomorrow."

Jericho wore a concerned look and checked my glove compartment, finding my badge and gun. "Was a patrol called?"

"Just us," I answered. "It could be someone from the campground staff. I sent a text to the manager."

"Or it could be more," he said, one brow cocked, his hands balled into fists. I hated when he was nervous. He was almost always level-headed, but when he was nervous, it was usually because he was right.

My car's headlights came on, shining against the road's surface, the sun dropping on the horizon. It was going to be dark at the Pearsons' RV and, on Jericho's concerns, I called in a patrol car to meet us at the crime scene. At a minimum it was added security, ensuring our safety and the safety of anyone inside.

We arrived at the campsite to find the RV had been opened. The police tape that cordoned off the door had been torn and hung limp, the yellow-and-black design looking electric in the dim light. With Jericho close behind, I wore my badge and held my gun, peering through the windows and the spaces between the drawn curtains. But the inside was too dark. We'd cut the power after the crime scene was secured and the bodies removed.

"Flashlights," Jericho said, handing me one and holding the other. "I'll open the door and wait until you clear it."

"What have you got in there?" I heard Cheryl Smithson's voice.

"Cheryl?" I asked.

Cheryl joined us, taking the space between Jericho and me, her flashlight beaming and her hand perched on her gun holster. "I was driving by when I heard the call. Thought I'd join the party," she said trying to joke, but I could hear the nerves in her voice. "Let's hope nobody is in there."

Tension seemed to stir up from nowhere, my muscles tight with nerves. "On three," I said, eyeing Jericho's hand cradling the door handle as Cheryl swallowed dryly. "One, two... and three."

Jericho swung the RV's door, the broken frame clacking where the metal was bent, the clamoring alerting anyone inside. Flashlights beamed ahead of me, brightening the dark interior, showing the dried pools of blood. The air remained stiff with death along with an undertone of rotting food. I had to cover my mouth and nose with each step. Flies buzzed around my head, the closed quarters having become a breeding ground for the pests. The RV's front was empty, the area covered in fingerprint dust, much of it looking like a jigsaw puzzle where tape had been used to lift the prints of all who'd been inside the RV.

"Nothing here," I said hoarsely, my hand cramped as I gripped my gun, a nervous flutter gnawing on my gut. There was blood spattering on the walls and floor and counter. It was hard to imagine it being cleaned and restored, even used again, another family unaware of the darkness it had seen. I motioned forward with my free hand. "Entering."

I moved in further, going beyond the areas of where the bodies had been, and approached the dining table, flies marching over whatever scraps of food remained. Adjacent to the table, the built-in sofa had been opened, the bed pulled out, the still lump of a body beneath a comforter.

"We got someone here," Cheryl said from behind me, her radio clicking as she pressed the receiver and called in a report to dispatch.

I lifted enough of the cover to see a face and knew immediately who it was. I yelled over my shoulder, "Cheryl, call an ambulance!" On the counter, I found an empty vial, the insulin prescription we'd identified when first arriving at the crime scene. I revealed more of the child's face, her hair pressed wet against her scalp. "We've found Lisa Pearson."

On my words, Jericho entered the RV, coughing and gagging until he could catch his breath. He was familiar with the case, and being in the marine patrol, he was also certified as a paramedic. He made it to my side, picking up the prescription vial while I eased the comforter from Lisa's body.

"She must have come back for her medicine," he said, lifting her arm to access the insulin pump. "Casey, she's burning up."

There were signs of vomiting and Lisa Pearson's face was sweaty and bright red with flushed cheeks. She was unconscious, her breathing rapid, a sickening sweet smell on her breath.

"An ambulance is on the way," Cheryl told us. "Tell me what I can do to help."

"Sweating and fast breathing could be ketoacidosis," Jericho said, trying to assess. He carefully lifted the child's shirt, the insulin pump soundless, the tube empty. It was the portal where the tube entered her body that told us more of what was wrong—her skin swollen red and oozing puss, the smell like rotting flesh. "Her blood sugar is too high. Also, tell them there's signs of significant infection."

Lisa's limbs were limp and I checked her pulse, eager to stay busy, the look of her tugging at my heart. Beneath my fingers, the child's pulse raced. I laid my palm on her chest next, her heartbeat faint, making me scared. "Jericho—" I began, shaking my head.

"Let's try and wake her," he instructed, removing the comforter to expose her arms and legs.

I pinched the girl's cheek, shaking her chin. "Lisa! Lisa Pearson! I need you to wake up!"

To my surprise, Lisa's eyelids fluttered, her blue eyes peering upward and swimming from side to side as she registered the sight of us. Her lips were chapped, the skin peeling and blotted by dried blood. She opened her mouth and asked, "Tiny?"

"Yes," I said, relieved to hear her voice. "Your dog misses you very much."

"Tiny," she said again, eyes half-lidded and suddenly rolling upward until they disappeared. Red-and-blue lights flashed from between the drapes, cutting sharp edges onto the walls, the lights bouncing while we tucked the comforter around the girl's body.

"It's cooler outside," Cheryl suggested.

"Let's carry her," Jericho struggled to say, his voice raspy.

He took hold of Lisa's shoulders while I picked her up from behind her knees. The comforter slipped and exposed the girl's feet, bare and covered with open sores and bloodied blisters, her heels worn to a red rash. In my career, I'd seen the likeness of such damage only one other time. On the floor next to the bed, a pair of sandals—the plastic shredded, the straps broken and then tied back together.

"Jericho, look at this! She must have walked."

"Walked to the church you visited?" he asked. I gave him a nod, shocked by the idea of it. "How far is that?"

"It's got to be thirty miles each way." I motioned to the sandals. "She walked sixty miles. In those."

"Why?" he asked, disbelief on his face.

I glanced back at the blood spatters and how they'd silhouetted the bodies of Lisa Pearsons' parents. They'd been brutally murdered, and her mother mutilated. And while her parents lay dead, still warm, Lisa Pearson trudged thirty miles to a church. "We need to find out."

CHAPTER FIFTEEN

Lisa Pearson was taken to the hospital's emergency room. From there, she was moved to the intensive care unit, her blood sugar dangerously high, and an infection from the portal causing sepsis complicating her path to recovery. In the ambulance, she'd opened her eyes once, asking again about her dog. It would be some time before we could interview her. But I thought this with hope for Lisa Pearson, hope for her recovery. With her parents murdered, the prospect of losing Lisa too was beyond tragic.

"Lisa will be with you soon," I told Tiny, his head cocking to the side, his ears pricking straight and his gray eyes locking on me when I changed my tone.

I leaned into my patio chair, ocean waves crashing nearby. Beach living suited me. Picking a place away from congestion, suited me even more. I'd always been a city person, but easily fell in love with the sand and surf, the sun warming me in the mornings, dolphins skipping across the horizon, and endless waves breaking on the lip of the world. The evenings were reserved for my patio, my feet up, western sunlight beaming, and the sunsets turning the shoreline electric, a mural of living color.

But this evening, the day weighed heavy, every part of me feeling as though I'd run an emotional marathon. Knowing my team were investigating every angle to find Andrea Hill—questioning the same grocery-store clerk as I had, questioning witnesses at the campground—I could briefly take a breather.

"An evening without work," I told Jericho as Tiny nuzzled my hand, his nose cold. "Don't forget, we're stopping by my friend's place." With thoughts of my daughter never far from my mind, especially with the RV murders and the missing girls stirring old memories, the recent trip to Philadelphia to work with Sharon Telly had stirred the emotions even more. We had a date planned to meet up with Sharon, her finishing Hannah's picture and giving me a copy to use. But now it looked like I might be going alone.

"I did forget," Jericho said.

"It'll be short," I promised.

Tiny pawed at my leg, begging for attention. I kneeled to scratch him behind the ears, his expression turning, grinning the way dogs do. Tracy was right, Shepherds are beautiful dogs. With the sunlight, Tiny's fir was tipped in gold, sparkling, his mane a deep black and bronze, his shape slightly rounded from age. And that smile, I loved it. Lisa Pearson would heal, I was sure of it, and Tiny would be returned to her. It saddened me to think about losing him, but at the same time, I was overjoyed for Lisa.

"Look, he's smiling," I said, my voice emotional.

Jericho laughed. "Not sure dogs can smile."

"Well, in my book, I say Tiny is smiling."

Jericho picked up a tennis ball and tossed it. Tiny watched the ball roll away, his brow raised, Jericho urging him to play chase. "I'm glad you brought him here."

"I am too," I agreed.

"Lisa Pearson will be happy you did this."

"I'll check with the doctors in the morning," I said. "She's in a dire state, between the IVs and the strong meds, I'm unsure when, or if she'll be able to talk to us, and tell us more."

"About the church?" Jericho asked, taking a wedge of Stromboli. I joined him, stealing a bite. "Lisa Pearson walked more than thirty miles to a church in the middle of cornfields."

"I know," I said, nodding. "It doesn't add up." I thought of the man in front of the church, the one barring the entrance, and added, "I called the number a few times now, putting in requests to answer more questions."

"And?"

"No answers," I told him. "I'll have to go back, talk to him directly."

"Enough for a warrant?" he asked.

I'd mulled it over, did the legwork, and came to realize we didn't have grounds for one. "No warrant," I answered. "Not yet, anyway."

"Well, if you do go back, take someone with you."

"*I wasn't invited*," I said sarcastically, my focus on Tiny as he pawed the tennis ball. "When I visited the church, the guy said, I wasn't invited."

"Has Nichelle come up with anything yet on Andrea Hill?" he asked. I shook my head. "There must be a connection. Now that Lisa Pearson has been found, I'm sure of it."

I checked my phone, showing Jericho the time. "A half hour should be enough with Sharon."

"Half hour?" Jericho asked, his hand on the small of my back as he pulled me into him, his breath warm on my neck as he spoke softly, "Any chance we could postpone?"

I kissed him, longing to take him into my bedroom, but Sharon was only in the area one more night and I wanted to pick up the drawing. I playfully wet his lips with mine, and answered, "All good things come to those who wait."

He backed away, and helped me clean up. "Till then, I suppose," he said.

"Sorry, but she's leaving tomorrow morning."

"It's fine," he said, kissing my cheek.

"I need the pic—"

"The picture of Hannah," he said.

I frowned, my fingers on my lips as I backed away from him. The interruption was hurtful. He'd used a tone that reminded me of how Ronald sounded when I'd mention Hannah's case, like he was tired of hearing about it. Jericho didn't notice my reaction.

I joined in the cleaning, swallowing my hurt feelings and telling him, "We'll be quick. I promise."

Jericho took my hand in his, seemingly realizing how he must have sounded. He bowed his head, his charm showing. "I'll drive."

The deep smell of fire hit us before we reached the address of Sharon's brother and sister-in-law. There was no mistaking the pungent hot soot or the glooming orange glow against the dark sky. The night came alive with the commotion of red-and-blue lights, patrol cars, ambulances, rescue vehicles, and the blur of uniforms and fire suits, the bustling chaos speaking without words, telling me something terrible had happened.

When we turned into the street, we faced the flames straight on—fire as bright as the sun, billowing thick smoke rising into the darkness, and sparks fluttering like a swarm of fireflies. We slowed the car as I scanned the house numbers and the gawking faces as a sudden hot breath swallowed my car like a dragon.

"Do you see her?" Jericho asked, choking, his voice tense.

"Keep driving," I answered with a gasp, trying not to get upset, telling myself the misfortune had to be a neighbor's home, insisting in my mind that Sharon was okay.

I slipped my badge's lanyard on my neck and opened the car door, jumping to my feet with Jericho objecting as he tried to park the car. The heat raged, burning my face and neck while I sought to get close enough to read the numbers on the mailbox.

A firefighter held my shoulders, his hand clad in thick protective gloves, his face dirtied and wet like a coal miner's, but his eyes alive with flames dancing in them. "I can't let you get any closer," he said, forcing me back, leading me to safety.

"Jesus, your hair," Jericho said, pinching my bangs, the smell of burnt hair faint compared to the burning home.

Glass exploded, shattering, the windows blowing out with fire spilling like a volcanic eruption. From the street, every window came alive with flames, every opening an inferno. Sirens screamed into our ears, deafening as two more firetrucks arrived. But there was no more help to give. The game of chess the fire played had put the firefighters into check, its flames were stronger, and winning this evening.

Flames crawled along the roofline and climbed the walls—a monster growing, consuming everything in its path. Firefighters evacuated the house, taking to a safe position along the street, their last hopes in the sturdy fire hoses they held. Spouts gushed a powerful spray, the water hissing and turning to steam on contact. I cried then, seeing Sharon's car in the driveway.

"Jericho, it's the address. This is where Sharon was staying."

Sharon's car was the next thing to catch fire, airbags exploding and causing the crowd to startle and voice collective *oohs* and *ahs* as though watching a show. The fireman who'd stopped me came again, pushing us back, the entire block becoming a danger. But I couldn't turn away, couldn't leave. I was certain my friend was inside. Jericho held me while I watched as the property burned to the ground.

The fire squads would work into the next day. Unable to do anything, we went home with a million unanswered questions, the stench of fire set in our clothes, a coat of soot on our skin. Jericho stayed, and comforted me through the nightly ritual of tossing and turning, the nightmares chasing me from my sleep. I woke the next morning to the red butter light of sunrise appearing through my patio doors and wondering what had happened to my friend and her family. Selfishness mixed with guilt too. I'd lost Hannah's picture, and although my friend had lost her life, I couldn't help but think about it.

The next morning, we were silent on the drive to the fire, the daylight bringing completely new horrors. What remained of the home was a shell, a pile of smoldering ruins, firefighters scattered amongst the debris, their fire hoses dousing hotspots. The air reeked of charred lumber and burning plastic, the odors of disaster filling my nose and watering my eyes.

With our badges showing, we entered the scene. This was out of both of our jurisdictions. I was leveraging my position to gain access and felt a guilt-filled twinge for doing so. The feeling was brief, my needing to know what happened overwhelming and consuming like the evening's flames.

"Put these on," a firefighter told us. She was wearing a cloth mask, her fingers clutching two. Jericho and I worked the masks, covering our nose and mouth. They didn't help.

"Any survivors?" I asked, deciding to stay in the street with one foot on the curb, a snake pit of fire hoses acting as a natural barrier.

The firefighter gave our badges a cursory look, recognizing we weren't with the fire department. "Sorry, thought you guys were arson investigators."

"Arson is suspected?" I asked. Then I remembered that all fires, particularly with this level of destruction, had to be investigated. I reframed the question as Jericho stepped behind me. "I'm Detective White, I work homicide."

Soot covered the firefighter's brow, her face gleaming with sweat, a lock of hair pasted to her skin. She removed her helmet, offering it to me. I took hold and was immediately surprised by the weight.

The firefighter swept her hair back, answering, "I can't say if this was homicide or not. The victims are already at the morgue. We're putting out any hotspots and waiting for the investigators."

My stomach was in my throat as Jericho's hand touched my back. A visit to Dr. Swales came to my mind. "You said victims?"

"At least three," the firefighter answered, taking back her helmet.

"Thank you," Jericho answered for me, my voice lost. He held my arm. "I'm sorry."

"I am too," I told him, glancing inside Sharon's car, the metal roof charred and pitted with a dusting of orange rust. In the back seat I saw the remains of her portfolio case, the size of it telling me exactly what it was. It had burned too. The leather was gnarled like burnt flesh, and the once bright brass zipper turned white by the heat. Beyond that, parts of the portfolio case remained intact. That meant the drawing of Hannah might have been saved too. I was tempted to take it, but held back, knowing the logistics of a possible crime scene, the necessary notification and then disbursement of any victim's belongings. I also knew my friend was dead. And if it was arson, then it was homicide.

CHAPTER SIXTEEN

Sharon Telly was one of the first people to help after Hannah was taken from my life. I'd never forget that, and I'd never forget her. Even while I knew the firefighter had said at least three people were taken to the morgue, I held onto the faintest sliver of hope she would not be among those positively identified. I texted her, my mind reaching for the hopeful miracle that she'd somehow not been in the house at the time of the fire.

I'd met Sharon in the days after Hannah's kidnapping. When my home had become a place I didn't recognize. One room had been taken over by the police with phone equipment and recorders, us waiting for a possible ransom call, and another room was filled with gray and black suits, detectives flashing badges and speaking with smoky voices and coffee on their breath, unfamiliar faces asking me and Ronald the same questions over and over.

Sharon had been with them in her role as a sketch artist, pad and pencils in hand, and her portfolio case slung from her shoulder—the same one I'd seen every year since. She asked the only questions I really remember. I gave her a description of the woman in the car, the faint image behind the windshield mostly ghost-like with little detail. It was her sketch of the woman and the vehicle, along with a recent photograph of Hannah, that went out with the alerts and then were plastered on the evening news. Like the ransom call that never came, there were only a few leads from the sketches, which also dried up.

The days had blurred as hope of finding Hannah dimmed. On one particular day, I thought I'd explode after a new lead had died. A low mumble and the sound of equipment being packed up filled our house, the ransom operation was shut down. I had taken to a chair near the front door, my hands tucked in my lap, a constant blur of shoes leaving my home and taking my hope. Hannah's case had officially shifted to the next stage. I'd been assured they were following the response plan to the letter and was told to stay positive. I was a cop. I knew the score.

When the house had emptied, it was no longer my home, no longer the safe place I'd made for me and Ronald and Hannah. There was furniture moved out of place, half-emptied notepads and crumpled balls of paper lying around, and the carpets looked as if they'd been trampled by elephants. The air was riddled with an overwhelming smell of people.

I had to move, had to do something, or risk tearing off my flesh to escape myself. I emptied a closet of all its cleaning supplies, brushes and dust pans and a portable vacuum cleaner with its million attachments scattering across the kitchen floor. I dropped to my knees, tearful, a bout of mourning hitting me hard. I knew the importance of kidnapping recovery in the first days, and the dread when the days became weeks. I let my head fill with the graphs and charts I'd studied, each showing a tragic statistical drop like a steep cliff where hope leaped to its death.

At that time Sharon came by with an updated sketch, asking for additional input from me. And she must have sensed that it was right then that I needed someone. She said little to me. In fact, I think she might have said nothing at all. Instead, she took a dustpan and broom and together we cleaned every inch of that house. Before leaving, she took my hand in hers, and told me, "When you're ready, tell me how I can help."

Later, when much of Hannah's kidnapping investigation had slowed to a crawl, I knew what I'd need. Other drawings of Sharon's had shown up on a news story, a rapist captured after she drew his likeness using a description from the victim. Once it was released to the public, they'd had their suspect within a day's time. It was a great shot for her career, the upper brass taking notice, adding funds to expand her department. Sometime soon after, I'd come across an article about aging techniques for lost children, using pictures of relatives, producing a likeness of what the child would look like. So began our annual ritual, meeting to age Hannah and refresh her circulated pictures. And now it was over.

Crisp air chilled my bones. Jericho's hand was warm, though, cradling my arm as he led me into the cinder-block room where rows of refrigeration units were stacked along the far wall. We'd changed into disposable fabric coveralls and cloth booties, satisfying Dr. Swales' *clean house* rules. The heavy rubber doors clapped shut, the air redolent with death and a putrid mix of burnt clothes and hair and skin. I went to a gurney wondering if it was Sharon, the body and face mercifully covered. Two other gurneys sat next to it, both dressed the same.

"I am so sorry to see you under such circumstances," Dr. Swales said, greeting me, tipping upward onto her toes to hug me. Her hair was combed back today, tightly packed and kept flat with clips pressing against her scalp. "We don't normally allow for this kind of visit given your relationship, but today I can make an exception."

"I appreciate it," I told her. "Honestly, I'm not really sure why I insisted on coming here."

Dr. Swales tilted her head, a frown on her face, and said, "I don't know if you are aware, but we don't have any identification yet. In fact, given the state of the decedents, it will take time before we confirm identities."

"It's that bad?" I asked, understanding what the fire must have done to them. The evidence sheets covering the bodies would remain in place. I felt relief but didn't show it. I wasn't sure if I would have been able to stomach seeing Sharon like that. At once I thought of the suffering, of Sharon burning alive. My chest felt like a knife had been run through it, and I had to ask, "Was it the fire that killed them? Or the smoke?"

Dr. Swales went to the other side the gurney. The victim's body was smaller than the other two, shorter than I was, and possibly the same height as Sharon. "With the autopsy, we'll confirm their cause of death. But I've seen enough house fires to suspect a combination of heat shock and carbon monoxide as cause."

"So how will you identify them?" I asked. This was a first for me. I'd worked cases with victims decomposed beyond recognition, in which we'd rely on DNA from hair or skin, but that didn't sound like it would be an option.

"For two of the victims, we're hoping to use dental records, possibly extract tooth pulp and form the necessary DNA markers."

"And this one?"

Without waiting, Dr. Swales donned a pair of latex gloves and revealed the victim's left hand. The stench of burned skin hit me. Jericho covered his nose and mouth, but I moved closer, recognizing the woman's hand, the fingernails painted a familiar beige color, her skin free of the fire's rapture. Dr. Swales inched the sheet back, exposing just enough of the forearm to show where the fire had bit into the victim and wasted the flesh until there was nothing left. "Does the ring look familiar?"

"It does," I said, nodding, my legs weak. It was Sharon's wedding band and her engagement ring, the two clasped to form a single gold ring, jeweled with small diamonds and a single marquise stone at the center. I'd gone to the jeweler with her one winter afternoon to pick it up after it had been damaged.

"That's Sharon," I said, noticing her fingertips then. On them, I saw charcoal smudges, colored pencil, the remnants of her being an artist. I couldn't help but wonder if she'd tried covering her hand, protecting it from the fire, never knowing the level of devastation awaiting her.

My throat was tight with emotion, my head clouding with Sharon's face, her years of helpfulness, of being with me no matter how crazy my investigation into Hannah's kidnapping had gotten. I gave Dr. Swales another curt nod, urging her to cover Sharon's arm as I leaned against Jericho, the mix of emotion and the smell making me feel unsteady and dizzy.

I couldn't shake the idea of Sharon suffering, and put Dr. Swales on the spot, "You're sure about the carbon monoxide?"

Dr. Swales understood what troubled me, her thick glasses sliding to the tip of her nose. She removed her gloves and took my hands. "I know this is horrible. I can only share with you my experience. The reports of the fire indicate it was fast moving. I'd expect they all succumbed to heat shock and carbon monoxide first."

"My friend didn't suffer?" I asked stubbornly.

She lowered her head and pushed her glasses back into place and focused on me and gave me a nod, answering, "Casey, I can't know for sure, but in my experience none of them would have been conscious."

My eyes dried and my insides calmed, deciding to believe they were already dead before the flames touched their bodies. As a detective, the questions stirred abruptly, investigatory, my needing to ingest and assimilate every detail into a beginning, middle, and end to identify if this was accidental or if my friend had been killed.

I motioned to the gurneys, and asked, "In this state, would you be able to identify any other injuries?"

Swales cocked her head, curious. "I suppose, depending on the depth of the burns, we'll identify other injuries."

"I'll want to see the reports as soon as they're ready."

CHAPTER SEVENTEEN

I could do nothing to help with Sharon's death, or the death of her brother and sister-in-law. For now, the investigation was in Dr. Swales' hands, along with the arson investigators. A cup of station coffee, black, would help me get moving. I thought of Sharon's car, realizing it would also be some time before I had an opportunity to see Hannah's drawing again, that is if it had survived the fire. But I did have one image, the picture on my phone Sharon let me snap before we'd parted.

"And now if I could only get this damn app to work," I said angrily, frustrated by the layout of the photo app, a new addition installed on my station's computer. With Sharon's drawing, I also had a small picture from an identification badge, taken while Hannah was incarcerated at a juvenile detention center. The image was grainy, the size of a postage stamp, and also a copy of a copy, the real identification badge remaining in custody. The photograph was older, with Hannah looking younger, but it showed her neck tattoo. I wanted to add it to Sharon's drawing to get the most accurate image possible of Hannah now. I watched a tutorial on how to make a mask, then selected the tattoo, parroting every word, "Add a new layer and change the blend options… but where's the blend—?"

"On the right, above the well with the other layers," I heard from behind me.

I turned around, my chair creaking, and found Nichelle propped like a scarecrow with her arms hung over my cubical wall. She perched her chin in one hand and gave me a wave with the other.

"You know this app?"

"Guilty," she said grinning. "I originally studied graphic arts."

I grinned back, a favor perched on my lips. "I'd think a job in graphic arts would be a heck of a lot more glamorous than IT."

"Maybe," she said, cocking her head. "But this is far from your average IT shop."

I glanced at my screen, thinking of the variety of cases, the growing touches on technology, especially on the deep web and the frightening escalation of cases there. If not for a few on the IT staff, we would be in the dark. "It's all about the mission, isn't it?" I said without looking up.

"Exactly," Nichelle answered, dragging round her office chair until it bumped with mine. She took hold of my mouse, her fingers brushing against mine, soft and perfect like a hand model's. "May I?"

"Yes, please," I said, keeping the favor, holding it for another time. "The quality is bad, but I'm only trying to get a likeness, merging the neck tattoo on this photo to the drawing."

"Is this a new case?" she asked, the question catching me off guard. By now, I was sure everyone in the Outer Banks knew of me, and Hannah's story. There was no harm in telling one more person.

"The girl I'm looking for is my daughter," I replied.

Nichelle turned to me with her big brown eyes, her forehead creased, a familiar look of surprise I'd seen a thousand times. She began to shake her head. "I... I didn't know—"

I felt a laugh of surprise slip from my mouth and rested my hand on her shoulder. "Honestly, I thought everyone in town knew by now. There's been enough press covering the case to produce a few books and movies."

Understanding cleared her eyes, an *ah-ha* expression coming to her face. "That's why you're working these pictures."

"Yup, that's why," I said, turning back to the monitors. "That drawing. That's an approximation of Hannah's current age. I want to pull the neck tattoo from the—"

As I spoke, Nichelle's eyes flickered with the screen's reflection, the mouse cursor a blur. Before I knew it, the neck tattoo floated from one window to the next, appearing on Sharon's drawing as though it had always been there.

"There you go," she said, saving the image to a new file. "I can print it up on photographic paper too if you'd like."

"Please," I said, gazing at the screen, seeing Hannah as I'd seen her briefly months earlier, a visit to a grave, her standing afar at a safe distance. "I update the image every year, hoping each will be my last. Maybe this one will be."

"Can I ask you a question about her?"

"Certainly," I told her, old nerves stirring awake. There was no knowing what people might ask. "What is it?"

"The case last year, I know she was nearly found—" Nichelle began, curly fronds on her hairline swaying as she reached over the cubical wall to retrieve the printed photo. "Why wouldn't she come forward?"

"She's afraid," I told her, wondering how much to say. The press had covered most of the case, but the finer details involving why Hannah remained in hiding had not been made public. "There was a guard at the detention center who was murdered. He'd discovered what the people running the detention center were doing. He and Hannah were also together."

"You're talking about the crime family up north?"

"Hannah is sure they're after her."

"Should she be?" Nichelle asked. "I mean, isn't the case over?" she asked, furrowing her brow.

"It's over," I said, my voice flat. "I'm sure elements of the crime family remain, but not here."

"Might be she'll come to you when she's ready."

I took the photo between my fingers and looked at Hannah's face. "Might be," I said. "For now, I want her to know I'm still looking."

"Well, I hope this helps," she said, handing me the picture. She looked at me again, her hand on mine, a gentle squeeze, a gesture I'd come to know. "If there's anything I can do to help you, don't hesitate."

"Thanks," I said, emotion in my voice, the offer unexpected and reminding me of Sharon. "Anything turn up on the Pearson case or Ben Hill? Their backgrounds?" I could spend every waking moment working Hannah's case, but the Pearsons and Ben Hill remained a priority.

"Backend jobs are still running," she said, a look of disappointment on her face.

"Keep me posted."

I heard the reporters first. Then the screech of chairs moving and doors opening, and next the sound of the gate separating our desks from the front of the station latching shut. There was a growing commotion, a shuffling of feet, and more voices, becoming louder, the pace of questions faster.

"No questions," I heard a patrolman say as Nichelle leaned her head outside of her cube, checking on the sudden activity.

"Isn't that the girl from the latest Amber Alert?" she asked.

I stood up to see a child of about fourteen, a patrolman guiding her in my direction. I recognized the girl. It was Andrea Hill, the daughter of murder victim Ben Hill. I'd learned earlier that Ben Hill and his husband had adopted Andrea five years before.

"Ma'am," the patrolman said, greeting me.

"Officer," I acknowledged, taking his hand.

"We found her wandering on the boardwalk," he told me, explaining she'd been walking along a section of the boardwalk I knew to be bordered by confectioners and games of chance. "Other than the injury to her arm, she appears to be okay. We determined there was no need for a hospital and brought her here."

"You're okay?" I asked.

The girl nodded and shifted her feet, uncomfortable with the station.

The officer leaned toward me so only I could hear him. "Couldn't get a word out of her."

"Thank you, officer," I said.

I tried to assess what happened. Andrea Hill had a pretty face, and was taller than expected, nearly my height, which at fourteen years old meant she must have towered over most of her classmates. There was money in what she wore, and she knew it, and she sized me up as I took to my chair.

"What happens now?" she asked, fear mounting on the girl's face.

"Can I take a look?" I asked her as I lifted her arm, a pile of gauzy wrap unwinding from it—loose and sagging, the ends frayed with medical tape hanging, having lost its tackiness. "Is this your handiwork?"

"No, ma'am," Andrea answered. "I got someone to help me with it."

I checked the bottom of her forearm, finding no blood, the injury stable. "Not seeing anything urgent. Did you get a cut? Is it deep?"

"No, ma'am," she answered again, lifting her hand to show the oozy side, the bandaging having yellowed and become stiff. "It's a burn... the kind that gets bubbly."

"Blisters," I said beneath my breath, my mind immediately flooding with images of the fire that killed my friend, a ridiculous idea floating as my brain went into overdrive. I put on a smile, a pretend one that I used when comforting younger children. "Tell me how that happened."

She shrugged, her focus shifting to the right of me, her gaze locked on the floor where there was nothing except the notion of guilt. "It kinda just happened."

"What just happened?"

She returned my look with a quick reply, "I was cooking pancakes with my dad."

CHAPTER EIGHTEEN

We attended to the burn on Andrea Hill's arm, having assessed the injury to be superficial, the skin blistered with some of them having opened and wet the gauze. An Emergency Technician happened to be in the station to fill out a report and offered a few minutes of their time. No hospital was required, just some burn ointment and a fresh bandage.

Andrea Hill had not been kidnapped from the RV. Like Lisa Pearson, she'd disappeared at the time of the murder. This time, Andrea had been found, and she was safe. The patrolman's report stated she was found alone. After some initial questions, we'd determined there had been no abduction or physical harm involved either. So where had she gone?

Time was sensitive, and the girl needed to be questioned. But I hated the idea of using an interview room, believing it would scare her terribly. For the time being, I brought Andrea to Sheriff Petro's office, inviting Nichelle to join us, and closed the door. I'd contacted child services who would take custody of Andrea once they arrived. Without a representative from them present, a single adult alone with a child for questioning was not customary—Nichelle understood and would help with the notes. I also made sure Andrea sat in a chair closer to the door and the window too, in an attempt to ease her nerves. I decided to keep any questions light, gathering timelines and whereabouts, that sort of thing. Anything deeper, I would be more comfortable with someone from child services in attendance.

"Is here okay?" Andrea asked politely.

I nodded as she took to the seat. "I thought you might like a snack," I said, placing soft drinks on the sheriff's desk.

She shook her head, but wet her lips at the same time. "Dad doesn't usually—" she began to say, but then stopped.

"It's okay," I told her.

Andrea grabbed a can of sweetened green tea, popping the top and eagerly slurping it. Next to the drinks, I made a pile of snacks. The vending machine forfeited most of them with a few thumps to its side, which sometimes made it spit two for every selection. I nudged a bag of cheese puffs, adding, "Help yourself."

Andrea opened the bag, hungry, and chomped on an orange puff treat, the satisfaction on her face quickly souring. "My other dad is dead too."

"Andrea, I'm so sorry for your loss," I told her and picked up the picture frame from the RV, pointing to the family portrait. After the frame was processed for fingerprints, I'd brought it with me. We'd need to collect Andrea's fingerprints as well for elimination purposes. "These are your dads?"

She didn't answer, but cast her eyes toward the door, keeping them there, deciding to shut our conversation down. Andrea didn't want to talk, leaving me in the difficult position of trying to get her to open up.

"I lost someone," I told her, shifting my chair just enough to put me between the windows and her gaze. "It still hurts too."

With that, she gave me a brief look, her mind working, trying to decide what to do. "Who?" she asked, opening up enough for us to continue.

"My daughter," I answered, and followed with, "she'd be a little older than you are."

"She's dead?" Andrea asked casually, the tone a surprise.

"Kidnapped."

"I think that would be worse," she said, chewing on a cheese puff as she considered the differences of a kidnapping and death. "I think I'd hate not knowing."

"I do," I told her. She caught the emotion on my voice and focused on the family portrait. I said, "Tell me about your other dad."

"Peter Murray," she answered. "He died last year. Got hit by a car while on his morning bike ride."

"He was a biker?" I asked.

"Used to be. Rode every day." Andrea took a shuddering breath, a sob coming, an orange puff perched from the corner of her mouth. The years with her adopted parents clearly had been normal, happy, until now. Her family was gone, and now her whole world had been completely blown up.

"That must have been terrible for you," I said, trying to console. I opened a bag of chips, joining her, encouraging the conversation.

"Now I don't have any dads." Andrea pinched a tear, her face scrunched. She masked it with renewed interest in the bag of cheese puffs, acting as though everything was okay. It wasn't. And I hated knowing what was coming for her. Her voice shaking, she quickly added, "Mm. These are good."

"I am so sorry for your loss," I said again.

Her stare shifted to the window and into the station. Andrea sat up as a man in handcuffs was led into one of the interview rooms.

"Is that the man who killed my dad?" she asked tearfully, voice shaky.

I shook my head. She eased back into her chair, sipping from the can of tea. "I was hoping you could tell me about your trip to the Outer Banks. Was it your dad's idea? Did he know someone here?"

"Uh-uh," she answered, clearing her eyes, her lower lip continuing to tremble. "It was my fault."

With those words, I paused a moment, waiting for her to add more. Andrea chewed slowly, interest fading. I asked, "What do you think is your fault?" She side-eyed the station's activity again, swinging her feet, eager to look elsewhere and stay busy, anything to keep whatever it was she meant to herself. I reframed the question. "Listen, you might believe you did something, but this was not your fault."

With that, Andrea's eyes fixed on mine, wide open, the whites of them like shining lights, almost frightful. She crumpled the bag of cheese puffs, her sadness turning to anger. "We wouldn't have been here if it wasn't for me."

"The Outer Banks?"

She nodded. "Dad wanted to go to Yellowstone, but I needed to come here."

"Needed?" I asked, picking up on her choice of words.

"I was invited."

I sat up, thinking of the church Lisa Pearson had visited. "Andrea, you were invited? By who?"

"Richard Dowd."

There was unrest in Andrea Hill's voice. Her stating Richard Dowd's name wasn't spoken casually. She'd said it with a struggle and immediately shutdown after, as though she'd revealed a truth nobody should have ever heard.

A woman from North Carolina's child services division opened the station doors, her hair lumped in strayed curls as if blown out in a hurry. She wore a gray business suit, which looked stifling hot for the time of year, her legs covered in a rose-colored sheer pantyhose that reminded me of the kind my mother wore when her and my father went out for Saturday night cocktails. I led her to Andrea, introducing her, and left them together in Petro's office. I hated to leave the girl, hated that she had no immediate family, nobody to come for her.

The burn on Andrea's arm bugged me, but I had seen evidence of cooking in the RV, and a best guess from the pitcher of batter and the stove suggested pancakes. The mention of Richard Dowd had gotten my detective's radar pinging like mad. There was a clear connection forming across the cases with both Lisa Pearson and Andrea Hill having been invited to Dowd's church. What were the odds? Two homicide cases, back to back, the victims' children invited by him to come to the Outer Banks.

Invited, I mouthed. What did that mean exactly? Amidst all the noise in my head about the peculiarity of Dowd's church, his linking the two cases, a sense of foreboding creeped over me. *He was targeting the victim's older children, the teens.*

"Nichelle," I said, deciding on her help again. I found her at her desk, her face aglow by the monitors she stared at. Without acknowledgment, I instructed her, "That request about Dowd's place, that church I texted you about. When you pull permits, research anything online about invitations being sent."

"Invitations?" she questioned. "Invitations to what?"

"The church," I answered, knowing it sounded off. I thought of the parked cars along the road in front of the church, the license plates reading from states up and down the east coast. "When I went there, I saw a lot of folks from out of state. There's got to be a web page."

"What was inside the church?"

"That's just it, they wouldn't let me in. I wasn't *invited*."

"Like Andrea was?" she questioned.

I nodded, asking, "Anything on the permitting?" I wanted news I could use for leverage.

"I was just about to email you." She turned to one of the monitors and pointed to the screen. "These are the permits we pulled for the location and activity. All of them check out."

"That's unfortunate." Dowd was legal, souring my earlier idea, leaving me empty-handed to do more on a second site visit. It could be the guy was on the up and up, and actually legitimate. This might be a real church that Lisa Pearson and Andrea Hill's families belonged to, the killer a member of the congregation and hiding among them like a wolf in sheep's clothing.

"Can't we get a warrant?" Nichelle asked. "I mean, have they even returned any of your calls?"

I shook my head, frustration mounting. "Unfortunately, just because they refuse to talk to us doesn't mean we can get a warrant and force them to."

"This is more than refusal," she exclaimed.

I picked up my phone and fished Ashtole's new business card from my desk drawer, adding his personal number to my contacts and then dialing it. As I waited for him to answer I said to Nichelle, "The mayor did say to contact him if we needed anything. Let's hope he's good to his word."

CHAPTER NINETEEN

The next morning, I was back in the station before the sun poked its round face above the ocean's lip. I'd taken Tiny to the beach, our morning walk completed in the dark, the moon easing down the other side of the world as cool sand squished between my toes and the old dog hurried us along the breaking surf. I'd rushed the day into being, leaving my bed and the nightmare that was haunting me there.

My call to Ashtole didn't exactly make the progress I'd hoped it would. He'd been a district attorney a long time and I trusted if there was one person who could figure out how to get a warrant issued for Dowd it would be Daniel Ashtole. While he agreed to the invitations being suspicious, he'd also said they could have easily been a part of a mail campaign, that I had no evidence the children had been targeted. His main concern was the lack of probable cause at this stage of the case to issue a warrant. His only other suggestion was to continue pestering with phone calls and even return to the church to ask questions. It all left me feeling discouraged. I knew something was off, but I didn't have enough to prove it yet.

The station was busy, surprisingly so. But that had more to do with the season than it did the neighborhood. Schools up and down the east coast had let out for the summer and the shores from New Jersey to Florida were being flooded with adolescents. Drunken bodies filled the small holding cell, boys and girls sat on the benches, half asleep and leaning on each other like books on a shelf. I gave a nod to an older patrolman processing them, his face telling me he'd give up his pension if he could end his shift early.

My team greeted me at my desk, catching me before I could finish my fist cup of coffee, the taste of it warm on my tongue as we readied ourselves for the day.

"Morning all," I said, a pinch of nervousness stealing my words—I usually liked to be prepared in advance of our meetings. Uncertain of where to begin, I ran through the case in my mind filtering through what I knew and what I wanted to know. Another mouthful of coffee as a round of morning greetings were returned, and I knew exactly how I wanted to drive. "Where are we?"

"Nothing from Dr. Swales on the Ben Hill case," Emanuel said, starting things off. He twirled a pen between his fingers while reading from a notepad. "But she's finished with the Pearsons' report, the findings to come later this morning."

"Good. Some morning reading to set up the afternoon," I said. Curious, I asked, "Was there reference to anything outstanding? Did the medical examiner address anything beyond the initial findings?"

He shook his head. "The causes of death match the initial report."

"How about the letter A and the number 8?" I asked. "Any change to what we determined in the field?"

"No change. The first carving is still believed to be the letter A, ruling out other symbols, and the second, a number 8."

"Nichelle, anything on A and 8? Anything online, possible similarities across the victims' account numbers, any type of sequence connecting them?"

She raised her shoulders in a shrug. "If I didn't know any better, the symbols look to be completely random. It's not enough to spot a pattern."

"Who are the victims?" I asked the team. "And why the markings on some and not others? Were they the intended targets?" I turned back to Nichelle, saying, "Starting with the victims marked, let's build a background profile."

"How far back?" she asked, already typing.

"As far back as you can. I want to know where they grew up. What schools they attended. Where their first jobs were. Even who they went to the prom with."

"And then look for any correlations?"

"Any connection at all," I said, agreeing. "I don't care how small. There's a reason for them being targeted, and I don't think it's random." I thought a moment, adding, "And include Dowd and his church too."

"Dowd," Nichelle said, repeating the instruction. "I'll find out if the Pearsons and Ben Hill had ever attended Dowd's church."

"Any findings on the symbols possibly being pagan, or anything other than what we believe?" I asked. Cheryl shifted, her having been assigned the research to rule out, or to include, pagan symbols and the like. "Cheryl?"

"I'm still researching," she answered, pushing a pencil through her bright hair. "Tracy offered to help."

With mention of her name, Tracy wheeled her chair from her cubical, a new place at the station I'd been able to get assigned. I found Cheryl's answer discouraging, having expected we should have closed that aspect of the case by now. "Continue with—" I began.

"A and 8," Tracy said abruptly, her gaze wide, catching herself interrupting.

"It's okay," I said. "Go on."

Her focus shifted from person to person, then back to me. "Two victims. A and 8. The letter A could indicate *first*, as in first days of summer," she said, bouncing in her seat. Her eyes were big with excitement, like I'd seen in the RV. Without the usual technician's garb, Tracy looked older, her hair flowing past her shoulders, her outfit a business suit, a little over the top for the station, but perfectly professional. I motioned to bring the excitement down a notch. Tracy acknowledged, lips round, mouthing, "Okay." She then added, "The number 8, rather the figure, it could be a symbol representing the solstice."

"The solstice?" I asked, the idea catching my interest. I indicated for her to continue.

"Well," she said tilting her head toward her tablet, her confidence wavering, "it's not a straight-forward theory, but the carving might be about the cycle of the sun."

"Shit," Emanuel muttered.

"Something to add?" I asked him. He glanced over to Tracy's tablet, reluctant. I urged him to continue, "The meeting is an open share, we're throwing everything on the table."

Emanuel straightened, and said, "It could be about the festival of the solstice."

The team shared a look, the term unfamiliar.

"Yeah!" Tracy said excitedly. "Celebrating the summer solstice!"

"Correct," he said. "When I was on the beat, summer solstice was the week when we'd get the nuts. I mean, I know that's an awful way to describe them, but—"

"Above average," I offered, getting the gist.

"Way above," he joked. "They usually crowd the beaches in celebration of summer solstice, believing there was a power to be had when the earth was at maximum tilt with the sun."

"That's it?" I asked.

"I wish," he said, a look of disgust on his face. "It was also the week we'd get the sacrifices."

"Sacrifices," Cheryl said with a nod. "I saw a few when I was in uniform—black cats were popular. I hated those calls."

"The dogs," Emanuel commented.

"Got it," I said, raising my voice, reigning in the side discussion. "Cheryl, start pulling old cases. Animal sacrifices."

"How far back?" she asked, her nose crinkled, disgusted by the order.

"All of them," I answered. "If this theory has some wings, our killer may have promoted himself. Emanuel, what's your confidence level with the figure 8 found on the body being connected to the solstice?"

He raised a brow, answering, "History is filled with similar, and it only takes one murder to validate."

"Okay, I'll give you that. Is the proposed theory for us to explore a killer who believes they're empowered to kill as a means of sacrifice to the coming summer solstice?" I said, half asking. We were early in the investigation so every bit of it sounded plausible. But inside, it felt naive and amateur, leaving me heavy with doubt. I was convinced the carving on Ben Hill was a number 8. To infer anything else was a leap.

"And their power comes to a peak on the day of the solstice," Tracy added, trading a look with Emanuel as she bought into the idea. "Specifically, at noon."

Regardless of how I felt, I refrained from voicing my opinion, knowing the theory had to be spoken, had to be played out for all of us to hear. I'd learned early in my career to never discount anything, no matter how far-fetched or massive a leap it might be. More than once, it was the strangest of ideas and theories that led to finding an overlooked clue hiding in the open. "What do we have on the calendar? A week before this maximum tilt you mentioned?"

"Eight days," Tracy answered, checking her phone, her eyes bugging. "Eight days!" She was enjoying this.

"That leaves the letter A, and what it might mean," I said. Tracy was on her toes again, eager to answer. "Continue."

"Throughout history, A is the most used letter. It is literally the beginning of just about every alphabet." She searched the room for approval, our attention hers. Swiping her tablet, she added, "And from Egyptian hieroglyphics it meant the beginning of the solar heat of the day. But more broadly, it meant the beginning of all things."

"The beginning," I said, my chin in hand, the theories we proposed beginning to sound more credible, especially if the killer had once been involved in ritual sacrifice.

"Peggy Pearson was first to die, the beginning, the letter A," Nichelle said, in a logical tone, eyes steady. "As to why the killer only marked Peggy Pearson and not her husband, maybe the killings aren't about the individuals murdered, but about the act of murder, each crime scene signifying a single act."

"A second victim at the crime scene was irrelevant to the intended message," I commented.

Silence came to the group as each of us considered what was becoming our working theory. If this was only starting, and he was intent on delivering more, the question of when had to be answered.

"What is the next symbol?" Emanuel asked.

"I think that's for you guys to find out," I began, pointing to Tracy, Emanuel and Cheryl. I motioned to Nichelle. "Also, work with Nichelle on the profiles. Try to identify why these individuals were selected, what it is they might have in common, if anything."

"We could start with researching the last ten summer-solstice events, scour the arrest records, see what's what?" Cheryl suggested. "I'll be elbow deep into animal sacrifices anyway."

"Paperwork?" Emanuel asked, his enthusiasm lost.

"Research," Cheryl corrected him.

"It's all part of the experience," I told him. "You'll get out in the field soon enough."

"We'll get on it," Cheryl answered.

I shuffled through my own paperwork, thinking about Dowd, my gut telling me to continue with the church as a possible lead. Nichelle approached.

"What have you got?" I asked.

She handed me a folded sheet of paper as if presenting an award. "Your invitation, ma'am."

"No way! You got an invite to the church?" I asked, shocked and impressed. Ashtole had said to continue pestering, now I had a pass to do so.

"Dowd's church website was rinky-dink. I mean, there was nothing to it. I was able to create an account, and then I posted a form with a script hidden in one of the fields which got me onto the server. Once there, I elevated my privileges and created an invitation for you. No vetting. No waiting. It's all yours as though you've been a faithful member since the early days of their website."

"*Created* an invitation?" I asked, questioning, hesitation in my voice, wondering how much I really wanted to know about what she'd done.

"Actually, I think it was already there," Nichelle said, rewording her comments.

"This is good," I told her. I only wanted to get my foot in the door. With an invitation in hand, I snatched my bag and turned off my computer, eager to get on the road. "You said 'early days'. Can you find out how early? And also find out where this church was before, especially Dowd. I want to know the history."

"Where are you headed?"

"I'm going to church."

Nichelle grabbed a laptop and bag, holding her phone. "I'm completely portable," she said, motioning to the exit. "Mind if I join you?"

"I guess you're going to church too."

CHAPTER TWENTY

The cornfields were greener than they'd been, the height of the stalks seeming to have grown since my initial trek west in search of Lisa Pearson. An aunt and uncle had come forward for the girl and had been a welcome constant at the hospital by her bedside. They were working with child services to take custody of Lisa, but there was still a question over returning Lisa's dog to her. It'd break my heart to see Tiny go, but he should have been with the child. However, the couple's home was filled with cats and they'd suggested surrendering him to the dog pound, citing age and incompatible living conditions. I couldn't let that happen and had offered to keep him until we found a more suitable arrangement.

With an invitation in hand and Nichelle at my side, we'd driven across Wright's Memorial Bridge and past the small market where Lisa Pearson had bought the jelly sandals. Fields bordered the road's edge, passing my window in a blur of green and yellow before opening to empty fields of tilled soil and workers hunched over, the sun beaming on their oversized hats, the brim like a canopy, hiding their faces in shadow.

"I've never been through this part of the Outer Banks," Nichelle said, resting her fingers on her keyboard. She gazed at the endless rows and big machines, a question on her face I already knew. "There's a church, way out here?"

"I don't believe this is the Outer Banks anymore. But I know there's a church," I told her, the car rising to the top of a hill, the church's steeple doing the same from the other side. The sun had climbed near to mid morning, leaving behind its blanket of soft orange and pink, plunking itself atop a sheet of denim blue. Recently painted, the church steeple glowed, even in the pale-blue sky, it was bright. "And there it is."

"I found some videos," Nichelle said, holding her laptop so I could see the screen. "They look like old sermons."

"From the church's website?"

She shook her head. "These are from other sources, mostly video-sharing sites." She spoke with her hands, as she did often, animated. "They look to be mostly cell phone videos, nothing official."

"Looks like a crowd," I said, dipping my head enough to see through the passenger window. There were rows of cars parked along an empty field, their license plates showing states from up and down the coast. The front of the church was teeming with people waiting to go inside, the same attendant in position, checking his iPad and slinging lanyards with badges, allowing entrance. "Can you feel that?"

Nichelle splayed her fingers on the window. The church music was strong enough to resonate through the car, the bass thumping into my legs and chest.

"It's like a rock concert," she said.

"I'm going in." I parked and opened the door, but then closed it immediately, an old couple catching a glimpse of my badge, the sunlight skipping off the metal and into the woman's face. I took my badge and gun, held them in my lap, staring, trying to decide if I should leave them or not. *Keep*, I told myself, wanting the security in case something went wrong. I tucked my badge out of sight, though, and would only show it if needed.

Nichelle packed her laptop, her hand perched on the door's handle. "I'll go with you?"

"But you weren't invited," I said, jokingly. "Unless you *found* an invitation for you too?"

She shook her head. "I didn't even think to look."

"Tell you what, I need you to wander the grounds, do so unnoticed. And get as many plate numbers as you can, especially from the trailers and the RVs parked in the back. I'm sure they're legit, but it can't hurt to look."

"That won't take very long."

I tapped her laptop, adding, "Watch the videos you found. See what you see." She shifted focus between me and the laptop, and I sensed the disappointment. "I know it's not glamorous, but it's every bit as important as the field work."

"I'll see what I see," she said. Then turned to me, asking, "You have your invitation?"

"I do," I answered, handing her the car keys. "Lock up when you leave."

I was eager to go inside, the detective in me wanting to claw at the walls that guarded the truth. Lisa Pearson and Andrea Hill had been here. I had to know why. I had to *see* why, and to understand how it was that Richard Dowd might be involved with the girls. Carefully, I approached the back of the line, not wanting to chance any missteps. I did my best to fit in, to look like the others already in line, but their dress and postures were all very different, Dowd's attraction diverse. There was young and old, poor and rich, white and black and every color in between. I saw nothing consistent, not even in the clothing, no signs of cult-like symbols, racial supremacies or politically charged subcultures. The diversity let me relax. I didn't have to be anyone else, and I didn't have to pull any weight or use my position to jump ahead. So, I waited.

An old couple stood with me, the woman's orange hair jittering in the breeze, her gaze reading me from head to toe and then back. I gave her a smile. The woman's lips were painted in the same color as her hair, a smile appearing, some of the teeth smeared orange. My grin must have been enough to pass her evaluation. Her husband greeted me before the two turned to face the church steps, and the line advanced.

When it was my turn to enter, I met the attendant, stepping softly and quietly, handing him my invitation, avoiding his eyes while trying to show eagerness to enter. By now the music was strong enough to feel across my entire body, the beat matching my heart.

"Casey White," the attendant said, waiting for me to meet his gaze. I looked into his round face, a curly lock of his hair draped in front of his eyes, a sheen of sweat on his plump cheeks. He held his iPad, showing me the website, only with a different view than I'd seen on Nichelle's laptop, rows of names and dates and dollar figures, the figures highlighted with different colors. His eyes grew as a smile appeared. "Why didn't you say something before? When you were searching for the girl?" he said. He snapped his fingers, adding, "What was her name?"

"Lisa Pearson," I answered. I followed the screen as he spoke, the tablet moving about. When I caught the word donations, I understood the surprisingly warm reception. Turns out, I was a huge donor. I'd have to thank Nichelle later. She'd done more than arrange an invitation. If I was understanding the donation tiers, the color scheme, Nichelle had made me one of Dowd's biggest financial supporters. "That was official business. I've been a fan for a long time." I cringed hearing myself use the word fan, thinking it was incorrect.

His lips thinned and he leaned toward me, eyes focusing toward the sky. "Isn't everything official business in *his* eyes?"

"Yes, *his* eyes," I said, remembering to put emphasis on the wording.

"His eyes," I heard repeated from behind me, rippling through the line. At the furthest corner of the property, Nichelle walked amongst the parked cars, making like she was talking on her cell phone, but secretly taking pictures of the license plates. The attendant caught the activity, his brow narrowing, a crease forming between his eyes. I was certain he'd seen Nichelle.

"My ride," I told him. "But she's not invited."

"That's right," he said with a nod. He reached behind and plunged his hand into a large box, pulling out ID badges by the handful, searching them, scanning impatiently until he found the one with my name, making the invitation Nichelle *found* for me official. Nichelle had really come through. "Printed fresh the last hour. Ms. White, this one is yours."

As I took hold of the lanyard and badge, the attendant's hands were on mine, his fingers like sausages, his grip moist. "For myself, and so many here, I want to thank you for helping make all this possible. Without your donations, we'd still be working beneath a tent, hoping for decent weather."

"My pleasure—" I began, playing the role, but not understanding. I raised a brow, adding, "*He* deserves it."

The attendant replied, "Mr. Dowd deserves it!"

I went to the doors, eager to move on and wanting to go inside, wanting to see for myself why Lisa Pearson and Andrea Hill had to be here. And I wanted to see this Richard Dowd in the flesh, determine exactly how it was he could garner such a following. I was sure he was no more genuine than any other snake-oil salesman, their only real magic being stiffing dollars from people who didn't know they'd been taken.

As I stepped inside the church, my eyes tried to adjust to the darkness punctuated by colorful lights. The music clutched my body like a giant hand. The doors shut behind me, and the church came into focus as the daylight was blocked. A crowd swayed with their arms in the air, their hands rising and falling like ocean swells as a man ran across a makeshift stage. Heads and bodies turned to follow the man, his voice booming and inviting me to listen.

CHAPTER TWENTY-ONE

Richard Dowd stopped abruptly at mid stage, focused beams of light centered on him, his face and hands white like snow, but his hair jet black. His eyes were fixed in my direction, his arms in the air as he demanded silence from the congregation. When satisfied, he posed a question, "What is it that is yours to keep?"

"What is it that is yours to keep?" The crowd roared around me.

I worked my way deeper into the gathering, eyeing the congregation, taking mental notes, seeing if there were any teenaged kids around the same ages as the victims' children. When I was closer to the stage, I glanced at Dowd, swinging his arms wildly, throwing his fists while running to the side where a band played. The stage shook as each member hammered their instruments in concert with Dowd's voice.

A body bumped mine and I raised my hands above my head to slip between a couple, her voice chanting, his voice cracking with shouts. Another bump and I was closer to the makeshift stage, side-stepping an older woman dancing, her hair thinning, her face heavily made up. She pinched my arm, insisting I move with her. I shook my head as she pirouetted around me and took my hand, leading me closer to the stage.

"We'd lost what was never ours to keep." Dowd stopped mid stage again, gauging the crowd's reaction. His words had me thinking of Hannah. I was bumped again, the same woman twirling clumsily, the crowd rushing toward the stage, and throwing my balance.

Dowd shouted, "And what was it that wasn't yours to keep?"

I planted my feet, my back against the stage, spotlights in my eyes. I turned and found Dowd, his question intended for me, his face suddenly in mine.

"Sorry," I said, "I'm not here to—"

"We are all here," he said. His face gleamed with sweat and was absent of color. His eyes were green, surrounded by a pale blue. His skin was smooth and without a single wrinkle or blemish or speck of razor stubble. That's when I noticed he was wearing a wig. Dowd had no hair at all, no growth of beard, nothing, not even eyebrows or eyelashes. It was a condition, but the moment stole my memory and the name, his voice insistent as he asked again, "What was it that wasn't yours to keep?"

"My baby," I heard myself say, a sympathetic moan coming from the crowd.

"Her baby," Dowd spoke into the microphone, his fingers on my shoulder, his touch delicate and soft. He jumped into the air, swinging his arms.

The band played hard again, shaking the church, the crowd chanting in song. I stood there stunned, but remained cautious. I glanced to my left and right, gauging the congregation's reaction. Dowd had a following, a strong one. But his questions to them, his answers for them, were general and could apply to anything and any situation.

Dowd kneeled again, his soft touch on my cheek, his focus with me. He put the microphone down and moved close enough so only I could hear him. He told me, "You can let the guilt go now."

Guilt? I questioned. He was trying to sway me as if I was one of his followers. I immediately thought of Ashtole and his suggestion. I had my chance. "What can you tell me about Lisa Pearson?" Dowd shook his head, unable to register the name. He glanced to the left of the stage, nodding to a broad-shouldered man with a tight shirt—a security detail. I had seconds and asked, "What about Andrea Hill?"

Dowd stood, yelling into the crowd, "Guilt was never yours to keep!" He ran to the band, urging them to play harder. The security guard took my arm, squeezing hard as he led me away from the stage.

"Reporters," the guard gruffed, tightening his hold as I peered over my shoulder in time to see Dowd back to jumping and shouting and preaching. He was feeding the crowd, telling them what they wanted to hear, what they needed to hear just as he'd tried to do with me.

CHAPTER TWENTY-TWO

I made my way back to my car, having shot off two questions, and made Dowd aware of me. I couldn't get them to come to me, so I'd gone to them. A small part of me couldn't help but think about his message. Yes, what he was delivering was broad, but it was helpful to some. I spied the security guard on the porch with the attendant as I went back to my car. There was a moment when Dowd had my ear, had me thinking of Hannah and the guilt I've carried for her. But I wasn't there to be saved or to save the world. I wasn't there to make friends either. I was there to solve three murders, and there was nothing I saw inside that had me excluding Dowd or his church just yet.

Nichelle was back in the car, her eyes wide as videos of Dowd's sermons played on her laptop's screen. When I plopped into the driver's seat, she said, "I was about to send in a search party."

"Was I gone that long?"

"Almost half an hour." There was a tone of disapproval, the formalities of police procedure broken.

"Sorry, I guess I got caught up in it," I told her. "I did get some questions asked."

"Anything usable?"

I brushed hair from my face. "Nothing usable, but I definitely got his attention."

"I can see that," she agreed, her eyes fixed on the security guard.

"It's not like we didn't ask them for an interview," I said. I turned her laptop to face me. "What's this?"

"Some videos I found online," she answered, her stare fixed on the church. She asked, "Is it really like a rock concert in there?"

"Yep," I answered. "I can't say it's all smoke and mirrors, but the crowd definitely love it."

"I do have a video to show you."

"What is it you found?"

Nichelle remained silent, a video playing with Dowd on stage preaching, the camera swinging toward the crowd, the focus shifting in and out, a spotlight bleeding into the lens and burning the pixels until everything turned white. She flicked the spacebar, pausing the playback.

"I'm going to advance the frames past the light, watch." She tapped the arrow keys, the video frames jumping ahead until I saw Andrea Hill at the center of the screen, wearing the same clothes she'd been found in, her arm without any bandaging.

"Save that," I told her.

"Already did," she answered. She pointed toward the bottom of the screen, saying, "Notice the time?"

The video's date and time showed the gathering taking place the night of the fire, the night my friend was killed.

"This is good work. It gives us confirmation Andrea Hill was there and there are no burns on her arm."

Nichelle did a double take and rolled back the video frames until Andrea Hill's arm was clearly shown. "I didn't notice that. Do you think she could have been involved?"

I shook my head. "I'm not sure. And I'd hate to think it even possible."

*

Nichelle drove my car while I watched the video with Andrea Hill in it, rewinding and forwarding it, taking stills of the people she was with. There were four, possibly five, kids her age she'd interacted with during the brief footage. In the process of analyzing the video, I felt sick to my stomach due to the thought of children being involved in these terrible crimes along with watching video in a moving car. I gripped my mouth and shut my eyes.

"Are you okay?" Nichelle asked, easing her foot from the gas pedal. "Do you need me to pull off the road?"

I shook my head, not sure how I was feeling. "It's good," I managed, closing the laptop. "I should know better than watch videos while we're driving."

"There's a possibility the date and time are wrong," Nichelle said, frowning, disappointment in her voice.

"What do you mean?" I asked, already making a case to work with child services to question Andrea Hill.

"Well, the date and time in the video aren't confirmed. We don't know if it was the time the video was taken, or posted—"

"Confirm it," I told her, daring another look at the video, unsure how she could do so.

"I'll get on it."

In the video's background I watched Dowd on stage, his jet-black hair gleaming, his face bathed in bright light, washing out the features and making it impossible to recognize him. If not for the suit and the hair, I'd think it could be anybody.

"This guy, Dowd—" I began, but never finished as our station came into view, Nichelle pulling into a parking space, as a man approached the car, waving at us. He wasted no time, stepping down from the curb and coming to my side of the car. The air was suddenly thick with heat, making my lungs cramp and my body sweat.

"Casey?" I heard Nichelle ask, her hand on my arm. "What's the matter?"

"It's fine," I said, lying easily enough, a garbage pail of hurt and disappointment about to spill from my mouth.

"Who is he?"

The muscles in my face were stony and frozen like ice. Empty. "He's my husband."

CHAPTER TWENTY-THREE

It was Ronald. My first love. We met, fell in love, and married in less than a year. He was my world. And for years, we were amazing together, we were the dream everyone else wanted to be. Until our Hannah was taken away, and everything crumbled.

It had been almost ten years since I'd seen him last. There were new wrinkles on his face, and he wore a thin beard, a gray scruff specked like salt and pepper, giving him a ruggedly handsome look. His hair had stayed thick and wavy, sharing the grays. Underneath it all, he still looked the same. Ronald tapped my window, showing me a smile, which brought the deepest dimples I'd ever seen. They were the same as Hannah's, a pair of charms he'd passed down to our daughter.

"Damn it," I said under my breath, finding his eyes and their light-blue color—another of his gifts to Hannah. A part of me had hoped the years had turned him enormously ugly. They hadn't. I reached for the door handle, my legs stuck like lead balloons. His smile was like a bright spotlight, blinding me to what had happened between us. I took a moment, refusing to reciprocate. Instead, I sought the pain of our past, the scars on my broken heart, and the healing that never was. When I found it, I gripped it like a weapon to defend myself. I was ready for him and opened the car door.

With a growl in my throat, I demanded, "What are you doing here?"

Ronald's smile disappeared. He raised his hands, backing up, tripping on the curb and taking to the sidewalk to give me space.

Nichelle heard the trouble in my tone and came to the front of the car. "Is everything okay here?"

"Yes, officer," Ronald said, adding the formality, believing Nichelle was a cop like me.

"Officer?" Nichelle answered.

"It's okay," I assured her. She searched my face until I gave her a nod, softening my voice. "I'm okay."

"Alright then," she said, turning to enter the station.

When we were alone, I joined him on the curb. The years had been cruelly kind to him. It was his smell that hit me; the same I'd remembered from when we'd first dated. I asked him again, "Ronald, you're a long way from Philadelphia. What are you doing here?"

He glanced toward the station's door and then back at me, a steady flow of patrol officers coming and going, the traffic making him nervous. "Is there somewhere private we can talk?"

In my head, I heard a memory of those same words. Words I'd spoken the day we'd ended our marriage. He'd ended it long before that day, I just hadn't known. Two days after he hadn't come home, I'd gone to his office, finding him there, showered and clean and dressed in clothes I'd never seen before. For two days I'd thought he'd been hit by a bus. But that wasn't it at all. He'd left me. And he'd done so in the most cowardly way. He'd left in utter silence, picking up his life and moving it someplace new.

"Talk?" I asked, brow cocked, pitching my toe into the sidewalk. "Like we did at your office ten years ago?"

I was glad to see the memory hurt him as it had me. "Yeah, that's a part of it."

"What else?" I asked, hating a stir of emotions that rose within me, some part of me still missing the couple we had been.

"Casey, I owe you an apology," he began, daring a step closer, his bearded chin at eye level, making me look up. The brush of his fingers on my hand came next, but I eased a step away. His tone had changed. He wanted to do more than apologize. "There's a lot I need to say to you. But really, I need to tell you that I was wrong for how I left. If you'd allow it, I want to know you again."

Know me again? I was stuck for words, cotton filling my mouth—stuffy and dry and choking the spit from my throat and tongue. How dare he. Why now? Images of Jericho came to me, along with what we had.

"Well, I'd say you're quite a few years—"

"Please, don't finish what you're about to say," he interrupted, shaking his head and stealing the space between us, again bringing himself close enough so I had to look up. My heart swelled and nerves stirred in the pit of my stomach. He put a sliver of paper in my hand, a phone number written in his terribly rabbled handwriting, along with a local address I knew to be a nearby hotel. "I'm in town for a while." He cocked his head, showing his dimples again. "I'm here for a podcast being produced about Hannah's kidnapping. A father's perspective—"

I shook my hand and raised my voice, "Don't you say her name to me!" A patrol officer slowed before entering the station, Ronald's gaze finding the ground while shifting uncomfortably. I motioned we were okay, giving the officer a nod.

"Casey, she's my daughter too," Ronald said with a bark, the tone of his voice bringing back memories with an emotional force.

"There it is," I said, locking eyes. "Ronald, you weren't even around. And when you were, you didn't help search for her."

"Listen, I'm only telling you this as a courtesy. But I'm also telling you that I might be moving to the Outer Banks. There's a job waiting for me and if Ha—" I glared at him again, daring him to say her name. "If our daughter is here, in the Outer Banks, then I want to be here too."

"Uh-huh," I said. For a brief moment, I wanted to show him the pictures I'd made, show him Hannah with the neck tattoo and the piercings. When Hannah's kidnappers were taken into custody, I'd informed him of everything, but nothing afterward. And I wasn't about to start. "Best of luck with the interview." I crumpled the paper, having heard enough. Nichelle appeared at the door. "I've got somewhere else to be."

"I'll be in touch," he added as I turned my back, thankful to use Nichelle as an excuse. I wouldn't have been able to hold it together another minute. Ronald had set off a storm inside me—memories of love and hate and a mountain of woeful hurt, all combining in a caustic stew of misery. "I'd still like to talk to you. Maybe over coffee?"

"What is it, Ronald?" I asked, frustrated, spitting the words over my shoulder. I stopped long enough to turn and face him, raising my arms, adding, "What do you want?"

"Us," he answered with steadying eyes. "It's about us."

There could have been an earthquake, a tidal wave, a volcano blowing up in my ears, but I wouldn't have noticed. I couldn't break the stare of my ex-husband, his telling me what I wanted to hear ten years earlier. I tried not to show any emotion and said, "Ronald, you broke *us* years ago."

CHAPTER TWENTY-FOUR

I couldn't bring myself to stay outside another minute. The last thing I wanted was my ex-husband to see any emotion from me. I'd already given him too much of me for one lifetime. I went into the station, eager to get back onto grounds that felt comfortable, felt at home, a place where I could breathe.

I found Nichelle and Tracy at their desks, and immediately caught a look from the both of them.

"I'm fine," I said, clutching the back of my chair, rolling it between the cubes.

"If you don't mind my saying, you don't look fine," Tracy said, her brow raised with worry. She handed me a cup of coffee, adding, "A fresh cup, black."

"Thank you," I said, my voice shaky as I tried to stave my emotions. I shook my head. "It's been a long time, I guess you never really get over someone. Good or bad."

"It's a shame it can't all be *good*," Nichelle commented.

"Definitely," I agreed with a curt nod, recalling the *bad*, and how it made me feel sour.

"Was he here about your daughter?" Nichelle asked.

"Partially," I said. Their eyes grew wide as they passed a look. "Hold on now, before you two start rumoring about me, I'm happily involved."

"No rumors," Nichelle joked. "Got to say, your ex is a looker."

"He's all yours," I told her. "Now, can we get to some work?"

"Nichelle was just showing me the Dowd videos," Tracy said, turning her screen, which showed a listing of them while one was playing. "I've been searching to get a catalogue of all of them."

"See how far back they go," I said. "I want to map a complete timeline."

I went to the small whiteboard hanging from Nichelle's cubical wall, motioning to Tracy to follow. Next to the whiteboard, was a cat calendar, the month showing an orange, black and white cat sunbathing, the words *purrr-fect beach season* beneath the picture. I drew a thick horizontal line on the whiteboard, and vertical marks intersecting at even intervals.

"I get it," Tracy said. "You want a journal of the videos we've identified."

The cat sunbathing caught my eye again, the calendar's day-to-day boxes empty. "May I?" I asked Nichelle. She nodded. "Forget the timeline. Instead, how about filling the empty boxes?"

"Yes, this is better," Tracy said. "I can add the times too."

"Are there a lot?"

Nichelle answered, "I've been seeing multiple videos per day."

"Okay. Then if Dowd skips a day or large spans of time, we'll have it recorded."

"If you have another minute, I was able to unlock Ben Hill's laptop," Nichelle offered, surprising me with the news.

"I thought that was a lost cause." I said. We'd found the laptop in the trailer, but had been unable to open any of the accounts, including the one for Andrea Hill.

"Ben Hill's password was easy enough, predictable. Once I had his account open, I was able to open Andrea's."

"And?" I asked. Although she'd already told us about going to Dowd, I needed hard evidence, anything that'd sway the judge to deem *probable cause* and to issue us a warrant.

"Well, I've found some email exchanges," Nichelle answered, her screen filled with a handful, the oldest of them showing an invitation to the Outer Banks from Richard Dowd. "Do you think that will be enough?"

"I think it is certainly persuasive," I said, my hopes lifting.

"Guys?" Tracy asked, her face close to her monitor. "We may have a problem. The Hill murder. That was about seventy-two hours ago?"

"Around then," I said, concern growing. "Why?"

Tracy shook her head. "I think Dowd has an alibi. Look at the date and time."

I watched the video playback on her screen, the sound off, but Dowd working the band, the congregation waving their hands in the air.

"We don't have an exact time of death yet for Ben Hill," I said.

She shook her head, answering, "Dowd has been a machine—holding services in three hour stretches, four, sometimes five times a day."

"That many?"

"It's like he's making up for lost time," Nichelle answered, joining my side. "And the church is always full."

"There's no way Dowd could have been at the campground," I said, my voice a whisper. "There's no way he was at Ben Hill's RV."

"If we go back further," Tracy began, the mouse clicking past a dozen videos. "We'll find a few videos around when the Pearsons were murdered."

"There goes our warrant," I said. "It'd be tough to get cause if Dowd has an alibi."

"Do you still want the calendar filled?" Tracy asked, holding it up, another month showing a cat wearing a red knitted, holiday sweater, and a Santa hat on its head.

"Yes. We'll definitely need it," I told her. "Here's an idea for us to explore. What if we look for someone else from the church, someone instead of Dowd?"

"From the congregation?"

I nodded. "If Dowd has an alibi, which he clearly does, and there's a connection to his church, which there clearly is, then we need to be thinking about the possibility of a church member, or even someone working for Dowd, committing these murders."

"Someone with IT skills or familiar enough with the technology that they can target the victims' children?" Nichelle asked, taking the words from my mouth.

"Exactly," I said. "The killer lured their victims to the Outer Banks through the children."

CHAPTER TWENTY-FIVE

My team reconvened at the station in the last hours of the day, blades of orange and pink sunlight touching the photos from the two crime scenes, the conference-room table covered by the morbid images. Emanuel's face wore a grimace as he picked up each, reviewed it, and went on to the next. Cheryl leafed through a stack of old cases, three piles towering from the tabletop and reaching her chin. She was scouring them, searching for anyone who'd participated in ritualistic sacrifices, or was arrested during a previous summer solstice, the charges unimportant, we were casting a wide net. Once she had a list, I wanted to find out if anyone on it had ever been to Dowd's church. Tracy took to the whiteboard, battling dead dry-erase markers, finding new ones and filling the room with the chemical odor. Nichelle worked a pair of monitors, having brought in the large second on my request, an intention to steer the discussion toward Dowd and the online videos Nichelle and Tracy found.

"Summer solstice," I said flatly, seeking out the attention of the team, expecting a share of their research, but secretly believing it was a dead end. I turned to Cheryl, asking, "The days are winding down, anyone we want to look at?"

She peered up from behind the stack of cases as I opened the top folder, the paper yellow with age and smelling musty. She shook her head, saying, "There isn't one that stands out. Most were first-time offenders."

"Let's get a list. Find out who's still in the area," I told her. I thought of Dowd's church, the group of people waiting to go inside.

There was an opportunity there. "Get their mugshots too, create a contact sheet, labeling each photograph."

"How many?" she asked, tapping the tallest of the piles. There was an objection in her tone, but I ignored it.

I closed the case folder, answering, "We'll need them all."

Cheryl rolled her eyes just enough to take notice. She crossed her arms, and said, "That'll take all—"

"I can help you," Tracy offered. She looked to me, adding, "If that's okay."

"That's fine," I told her. "Cheryl, does that work?"

"Thanks," Cheryl said. "We should have a list of names and pictures by tomorrow."

"Back to the summer solstice, and our earlier assessment for the letter A and number 8."

Tracy jotted down the symbols, labeling each: A as the beginning of all things, and the number 8 as the solstice, the cycle of the sun.

Emanuel raised his hand, asking to speak. I shook my head, motioned for him to lower his arm. "No need to ask," I said. "What do you have?"

He stood and went to Tracy's side. He was taller than the whiteboard, his hand swallowing the dry-erase marker. "From the research," he began, writing the date of the solstice on the board, "we have seven days before the summer solstice." He drew lines to the date, the image looking much like a wall of photographs, notes and strung yarn. Above the lines, he wrote the number 7.

"Seven days for what?" I heard from behind me. Mayor Ashtole entered the room, the team standing to greet him. He approached, his hand on my arm. "Afternoon. I hope it's okay if I sit in?"

The mayor's office seemed to be keeping him busy. His eyes were puffy and his skin even paler than usual. His suit hung loose from his shoulders, his face narrow with the loss of a few pounds he couldn't afford to lose. I gripped his hand, offering a smile. "You're always welcome."

"Seven days?" he asked again, going to the conference table, picking through the photographs until he found the crime-scene pictures featuring Ben Hill and the Pearsons. "I thought the name was familiar. The Hill brothers, they were from this area."

"Did you know the victim?" Cheryl asked, the usual confidence in her voice lacking. She was nervous. The entire team was nervous. He was the mayor, but I still knew him as Ashtole—the not so politically correct ex district attorney.

"Only by name," he answered and approached the table, giving the stack of case files in front of her a once-over, opening and closing the top folder as I had done. I couldn't guess what the stack of files told him, but from the frown forming on his face, it wasn't good. "Ben Hill was a few years ahead of me at high school."

"We're following multiple leads," I said.

"I see," he said and went to the whiteboard as Tracy continued with her notes, Emanuel joining them. "Summer solstice?"

"That's one of the leads," I said, thumping the stack of old cases. "These could be ritual sacrifices, the killer escalating their practice."

"Tell me more," he asked, intrigued, his focus on Tracy. She went on to the symbols morbidly carved into the victims' skin and the possibly connection to a countdown to the solstice, while I went to Nichelle and turned on the large monitor, preparing to present our second lead.

"Bring up one of the Dowd videos," I told her, speaking quietly while Tracy and Emanuel completed their review with Ashtole.

Ashtole laughed, a harsh snort through his nose. "Please tell me your second lead is better than this," he said, hanging his thumb over his shoulder, skepticism on his face. He made his way to the other side of the conference table, dropping the photos of Ben Hill.

He shook his head, hands raised, adding, "Look, no offense to the work done, but it's like something out of a low-budget slasher movie. Don't you think?"

There was immediate disappointment on the faces of my team. Tracy's shoulders slumped and Emanuel stepped forward, a hand in the air, ready to explain and defend their position. In my experience, it indicated we were trying too hard, justifying the theory, forcing it to work rather than letting it work. We were on the wrong path, and fighting it every inch. I shook my head, telling Emanuel to stand down.

"Believable isn't the question," I said. Ashtole pushed the wireframe glasses on his nose, a puzzled look forming, and lawyerly objections at the ready. "It was what we had at the time, given the evidence. It was also one of two." I signaled to Nichelle to play the video. The monitor came alive with an image of Dowd holding his fist above his head and racing across the stage, the church band blaring over the speaker.

Ashtole jumped from the sudden noise. Nichelle jabbed the keyboard, turning down the volume, a smirk hidden beneath her hand.

"The traveling preacher?" Ashtole asked. He nudged his chin toward the monitor. "I already know about the warrant. But is this the guy you also pulled the permits for? That old abandoned church on Route 13?"

"I did," I answered, surprised he knew. "You saw that?"

Ashtole tipped his head, looking at me over his glasses, and answered, "I'm making it a point to watch everything."

"Points for you then. And yes, we pulled the permits, but there wasn't anything to shake from them. All the permits were in order."

"Have you gotten anything concrete we can take to Judge Howell?" he asked, pointing to the photographs and then to the monitor. "What's the connection to this Reverend Dowd, or whatever he calls himself?"

Tracy and Emanuel closed in around Ashtole, the center of focus falling on the monitor, Dowd's face like ingot silver, his black hair swept to the side as he yelled into the microphone. I motioned to Nichelle to turn up the volume, recognizing where the video footage was.

"Whales, *his* masterpiece of the sea, roamed the oceans since the creation of time, they were already old when we were young. And now they're dying!" Dowd preached, cheeks glistening with tears as he picked up an empty water bottle and crushed it slowly. The plastic crumpling echoed over the speakers. "Inside their bellies, a hundred pounds of plastic. A hundred pounds. Their flesh starved. Their—"

Ashtole slid his fingers across his throat, telling Nichelle to cut the feed. She paused the playback. "And?" he asked, his focus shifting to each of us, but without waiting for an answer. "He's a preacher. I'm not following the connection."

Nichelle continued the video playback.

"Your parents and your parents' parents. They did this. In less than a few generations, they've filled the oceans with their spent convenience, their filth."

I flicked the keyboard, stopping the playback, and tacked pictures of the victims' children onto the wall, their faces filled with innocence, but their secrets revealed through the activities discovered on their phones and tablets and laptops.

Ashtole went back to Ben Hill's picture, tapping it, then pointed to the wall. "That's Andrea Hill?"

"It is," I confirmed. "And the church is the connection to the teenagers."

"The victims' children have been in contact with Dowd," Nichelle said, throwing email exchanges onto the monitor. Ashtole's lips moved as he read to himself, the emails showing the invitation from Dowd.

Nichelle showed text messages and more email exchanges next, one from Lisa Pearson and the other from Andrea Hill.

"Where is this from?" Ashtole asked, caution in his voice.

Nichelle dragged the email to Andrea Hill, bringing it to the foreground. "This is from Ben Hill's laptop, there was an account for his daughter," she explained.

"And there are others like this? From the victims' daughters?" he asked. Nichelle gave him a nod. He stared at the team as he adjusted his glasses. "Do you think the girls are involved?"

"Not directly," I assured him, but I spoke with uncertainty, wondering if the children could have been coerced to participate. The idea of it was sickening, but there was the burn on Andrea Hill's arm that kept the idea seated heavily in my mind.

"What about the warrant for Dowd?" he asked.

"Alibi," I answered, pointing to the video timestamps. "Nichelle and Tracy have identified ample video footage of Dowd at the times the murders took place."

"So Dowd isn't our killer," Ashtole said, and removed his glasses, cleaning them with his tie. "That leaves the invitations to the children. Any more of them?"

"I've found these, but don't ask where from," Nichelle said, warning the mayor. She'd retrieved the emails from the church server, eliminating any possibility of our using them for legal purposes. What we could do is identify potential victims and secure their safety.

"I don't follow," Ashtole said.

I raised my eyebrows, answering, "These are unofficial, off-the-record, so to speak."

"Understood," he said.

Nichelle then listed ten email addresses, two of which corresponded to the victims' children. All the emails had the same wording and a thorough set of instructions, including RV rentals, names of campgrounds, and times and dates of Dowd's appearances.

"One question," said Ashtole. "This is a church, which could have thousands, maybe tens of thousands of correspondences. Why these ten?"

"Great question," Nichelle said. "Initially, I'd recovered two invitations, each from the victims' children's devices. I used the wording, the times, and dates, and included campgrounds and RV rentals, to perform my search. That's when I found eight more."

"This is the other working theory, and it involves Dowd, or someone in his organization, sending tailored invitations, and targeting the parents," I said.

"These ten so far?" Ashtole asked, standing closer to the monitor, reading each of them. Nichelle had highlighted two invitations with red, showing a status of death. "Ben Hill, I never thought I'd see him again. Not like this anyway. The Hills haven't been residents in years."

"So he's local," I said, catching on to an idea. "Nichelle, step up the research on the Pearsons, where they grew up, went to high school, college, their entire background."

"I'll confirm," Nichelle said.

"Three dead so far. Two teens receiving emailed invitations. The possibility of eight additional invitations," Ashtole recited aloud. I could tell he could see the implications.

"This is our list of potential future victims," I said, turning to the team.

Nichelle's fingers were in motion, Tracy was working her laptop too. Nichelle updated the display, showing only the email addresses.

"Two identified," Ashtole commented, his hands back on his hips, studying the remaining eight entries, email addresses only. "Can we get a phone number? An address for the others?"

"That's the problem," Nichelle answered, her head tilted. "There's nothing concrete on the other side, no names, no phone numbers or any physical addresses."

"All we have to identify possible victims are the email addresses the invitations were sent to," I explained.

Ashtole turned to me, his face pinched. "Do you believe we have a serial killer?"

The formal definition of a serial killer ran through my mind, but with the targeting being this precise, I couldn't say with certainty. I shook my head, unsure how to answer him. "There is a type here, which I believe the press will identify soon enough—affluent parents, vacationing in the Outer Banks. By the basic definition, some might call it serial."

"But that's not what you're thinking?"

"These murders are very targeted, and the list is so specific."

"It also looks like the church may have reached out to them first," Nichelle offered. "I had to double-check, but in the case of Andrea Hill and Lisa Pearson, someone from the church contacted them first."

"*They* reached out to them?" Ashtole asked. "You mean someone in Dowd's organization approached the children?"

"I used the email addresses from our list and searched the server's mailing lists. I found account connections for Andrea Hill and Lisa Pearson, including their social-media details. Turns out, the email was only used to exchange the invitation—"

"Not another word!" Ashtole said, raising his hands. "I don't need to know how you got the list." He faced us then, adding, "But you need to find them."

"Their parents' lives are in danger," I agreed. "We're working on some ideas to identify who the children are."

"What about him?" Ashtole asked, pointing to the video frame with Dowd on stage. "What do we know about him?"

"Tracy and Emanuel will continue researching Dowd," I said, giving them their next task.

"He might have an alibi, but something at that church stinks," Ashtole said, his hands on his hips. He waved toward the whiteboard, the summer solstice theory. He went to Cheryl and the stack of case files, saying, "These. I know I was quick to dismiss them, but there's always that what if."

"We're not dropping that one," I assured him.

"I didn't think you would."

"But the list, it's priority," I warned. "If we have it, that means the killer already has the information. We have to find him."

CHAPTER TWENTY-SIX

It was arson. Those were the words I heard, my gaze dipping as I considered Sharon's death. Ashtole stood next to me, his voice a whisper as he went on to question Dr. Swales' findings. The doctor had joined us to deliver the news, and when I'd seen her enter the station, I think I already knew. She was aware of today's meeting to cover the other cases since I'd included her in the invite. I'd done so before as a formality, but this was the first time she'd attended. That meant she'd found a connection between Sharon's death and the RV murders. And the idea of there being one made me sick to my stomach, especially if Andrea Hill had lied about the burn on her arm.

"Any ideas on motive?" I asked her, talking over Ashtole. He gestured for her to continue, making room for me, aware of my friendship with Sharon Telly.

Dr. Swales held up the report from the fire investigation, her eyes steady as she gave me a nod. "In all likelihood, the fire was a very poor attempt to cover up the cause of death."

"You said they probably died from heat shock and carbon monoxide."

Her frizzy hair swayed with uncertainty. "In my experience, the number of fires I've seen, the cause of death is consistently heat shock and carbon monoxide. But in this case, the autopsy showed the victims dead well before there was a single flame. This is a case of murder. The arson investigation will continue, but the case of their murders is under your jurisdiction."

I didn't bat an eye or swallow my breath. "How?" I asked as Tracy and Emanuel took to the conference table seats. Ashtole followed, giving Dr. Swales the monitor.

She went to Nichelle, asking permission to use the laptop.

"Want me to drive?" Nichelle asked.

"Yes, thank you," Dr. Swales answered. "I sent the link in a reply to the meeting invite."

Nichelle opened the autopsy reports, a brief flash of charred bodies showing before the screen settled on forms and diagrams, the doctor's handwritten notes familiar to me. "In the case of both Darren and Caroline Telly, I was able to identify a wound severing the vessels in the neck."

"But their skin," Ashtole said, referring to the state of the bodies. "Even with all that?"

"Yes, Daniel, even with all that," she answered, reaching over Nichelle's shoulder and tapping on the keyboard. The screen changed to show a pair of X-rays. "We used X-rays to determine if the assault reached bone." She pointed to areas on the X-ray, showing us sharp voids in a bone, breaking the uniformity. "There is injury to the cervical spine, indicating a very deep laceration, and causing death within minutes."

"A stab wound to the neck. It's the same as the RV murders," I said. "Is there enough—" I paused, swallowing dryly. "Enough flesh to match the knife wounds to the victims?"

Dr. Swales shook her head. "I needed X-rays to know there was a knife wound. There is too much damage to the victims' flesh."

"And Sharon?" I asked, afraid to hear the truth, seeing a pattern of bludgeoning to those victims without a mark carved into their skin. It was as if use of a blade was reserved only for some, a hammer or bat or other blunt instrument used for the others. "Was she beaten to death?"

Without a word, Dr. Swales tapped the keyboard, opening a third X-ray image, a picture of a skull, portions of it broken free and floating in a mass of gray matter. "Severely," she answered flatly.

"Where were the bodies found?" I asked, picking up the arson report, hiding my face as I leafed through the pages until reaching a diagram of the house showing each floor and room. "They weren't together. Were they?"

"It's in there," Swales said. "In separate rooms."

"What are you thinking?" Ashtole asked, his focus stuck on the monitor and Sharon Telly's broken skull.

"A single assailant could only accomplish this if each victim was alone," I said.

"If they were together, they would've fought back," he said, finishing for me.

I held up my arms, asking, "Were any defensive wounds identified?"

"Some. There were additional lacerations, a few deep enough to strike bone."

"At least they fought," Tracy added. "What about carvings, any markings?"

"If this is related to our other cases, there'd be markings," Cheryl exclaimed.

"That's why you're here," I said to Dr. Swales, my stomach turning again.

She tapped the keyboard. The screen filled with images of the burnt remains of two of the victims, side by side, the charred skin surprisingly intact, somehow protected from the blaze. I thought of Sharon's drawing hand, the lack of burns and asked, "Stomach area? The victims found face down?"

"Yes. Exactly," Dr. Swales answered with big eyes, her glasses at the end of her nose. "How did—?"

I stood abruptly, chair legs scraping the floor, a pencil and paper in hand and went to the monitor, answering, "Because the killer wanted us to see the marks. He set their bodies face down to preserve his work."

"But why torch the place?" Emanuel asked.

I shook my head, answering, "I don't know. It doesn't match the profile." I didn't share what I suspected though, my thinking of Andrea Hill. "Or maybe they're playing a game, testing how good we might be. Just a theory."

"Go on with what you were going to show us," Swales said.

I carefully placed a sheet of paper over the screen, asking, "Turn the brightness to the maximum."

Nichelle did as I asked, the burned flesh bleeding through the paper. Dr. Swales held the paper in place as I traced what remained of a shape, the carving made by the killer. When we'd completed the second figure, we laid the sheets of paper on the conference-room table and huddled around them.

"A letter F?" Emanuel asked, spinning the first sheet.

"Or is it an E?" Nichelle challenged.

I flipped the paper in the other direction. "It could also be a number 3."

"Agreed. It's a three," Ashtole said, tracing the curves of the figure.

We debated for five minutes more, but collectively came to an agreement. The figure carved into Darren Telly was the number 3.

"Any significance to anyone?" Ashtole asked.

We searched each other's faces, questions abundant, shaking our heads.

"Okay, then, we'll settle on the number 3. How about the next one?" I said, shifting the papers.

For Caroline Telly, the debate lasted much longer with us rotating the paper in every direction, flipping it again and again, the fire damage to the woman's skin stealing too much of what the killer had left for us to find. We made a best guess, determining the figure to possibly be the number 7 or the letter L.

"A three and seven," Ashtole said. "Or the letter L."

I went to the other whiteboard, returning to the discussion on the summer solstice, ignoring Ashtole's eye-roll, and asked, "Keeping all ideas open, is there anything at all in our research involving L, 7 or 3 relating to the solstice?"

Emanuel and Tracy exchanged glances. "Nothing," Tracy answered.

Ashtole punched his hip, hitching his suit jacket up, a look of resolve on his face. "Good. Then let's continue with the latest markings. We have to figure them out."

I gave the whiteboard a slap, fingers splayed, saying, "As for summer solstice, I think we can all agree this theory is baked."

"Baked," Emanuel agreed.

"Baked," Cheryl and Tracy said in unison.

"Sharon Telly?" I asked Dr. Swales, needing to hear it for myself. "No carvings? No markings?"

"Nothing identifiable," Swales answered.

"She was a friend?" Ashtole asked.

"She was," I said. "We worked together back in Philly."

"But no connection to the church or Dowd that you know of?" Emanuel asked.

"None," I answered, emotion teasing my voice. "She was just visiting. And as far as I know, her brother Darren and wife Caroline had no children."

"This doesn't add up," Ashtole said, a finger tapping against his chin. "All these victims, in such a short span of time."

"And all the murders occurring soon after Dowd set up shop in that church," Emanuel said.

"Sharon's brother and sister-in-law," I began. "They were already here. They lived here."

"That is something," Swales commented.

"What we know is the victims were selected," I continued, taking to the seat next to Nichelle, shaking out the emotions. The killer wasn't there for Sharon. But the killer had gone there for Sharon's brother and sister-in-law. "We have four victims with symbols—an A, 8, 3 and an L or number 7. There's also the potential of eight more victims, eight invitations from Dowd's church. We need to find what is common, make the connection if we have any hopes of finding them."

"If it's someone in the preacher's congregation, can't we bring them all in for questioning?" Cheryl asked, voice pitched high.

"There are thousands," Nichelle answered. "We've no idea who is coming or going. What we see is just a taste, part of a roadshow, a tour."

Ashtole let out a guffaw, rolling his eyes. "Like the guy is some kind of rock star."

"Basically, yes," Nichelle said. "He is, and he's got thousands of fans."

"Eight more potential victims," I repeated, reigning in the conversation.

A text message stole my attention, my phone vibrating on the table with a phone number I didn't recognize. As if on cue, Jericho entered the station. We had plans to meet. I gave him a wave and picked up my phone, seeing the text message had come from Ronald:

Hope you don't mind my texting. Are you available for a coffee or a drink so we can talk?

I tucked my phone in my pants without responding. I took Jericho's hand. "You ready?"

Jericho's eyes followed my phone, but he said nothing about it. "Sure," he answered.

Before leaving, I told the team, "Good work everyone. Nichelle, continue to research the invitations. Tracy, keep looking into the letters and numbers, make sure we're not overlooking anything."

"Continue with these?" Cheryl asked, the corners of her mouth curling down with disappointment before I could answer. I took half the pile of old case files from in front of her, an idea in mind. Jericho offered a hand as I said, "I'll join in. As you go through them, send me names and faces. Emanuel will work with you too."

"Understood," Emanuel answered.

"Okay, we all have our actions to follow up. There are eight more families in danger." I took a moment to make eye contact with each of my team before adding, "Their lives depend on us."

CHAPTER TWENTY-SEVEN

The setting was about as romantic as I could have imagined it to be. I wore a sleek dress, sleeveless and with a low dip in front to show just enough. Jericho was in pleated slacks and a pressed dress shirt with a suit jacket that might have been cashmere. The night was ours, having planned it weeks in advance. It was also our first opportunity to spend the evening together since we'd driven to Philadelphia. And even with the circumstances of the RV cases, my friend Sharon and her family, Jericho was every bit of what I needed to shake off the bad days.

My belly warmed with some wine and my appetite was satisfied by the rich foods and the sweets we indulged in. Jericho brought me to his place at the end of daylight and the evening's beginning—sunshine just a memory on the horizon as the first stars showed through the night's curtain. A tree frog's song guided our walk along the edge of the bay, cool sand squishing between my toes, Jericho holding my waist, and the moonlight shimmering like diamond dust on the water's surface.

When Jericho brought me into him, my chest against his and our lips touching, I wanted him, but I also needed to be somewhere else. While our date was everything I wanted it to be, I was about to break it. My body stiffened as I leaned away from him. Jericho sensed it, paused to look at me. I backed away, my heels slung from my fingers, my motives switching between what I wanted and what I needed. I pinched his fingers in mine, but glanced at the time, a box of case files sitting in wait for me in the trunk of my car.

"Sorry," I said, finding a bitter smile on Jericho's face.

"It's about your ex isn't it?" he asked, his question shocking me.

I shook my head, answering, "What?"

He said nothing.

"I've got a box of old files to get through... Wait, how did you know Ronald was in town?"

"A producer contacted me," he said. "She's working a podcast and vlog. She mentioned the interviews."

"The podcast," I said, hearing Ronald's voice in my head, his working with a producer. Since arresting Hannah's kidnappers, I'd received a hundred requests for book deals, blog tours and interviews, but I'd ignored them all. "They contacted you too?"

Jericho nodded, moonlight glinting in his eyes, his hands remaining firm on my sides. "They got my name from the arrest records."

"Hannah's kidnappers," I mentioned, the memory a patchy blur the way they are when too painful to recall. But Jericho had been there. He'd been in the barn when I'd arrested the couple. I couldn't think of what to say, whispering, "The producers are thorough."

"They'd also mentioned who else they were interviewing and asked if I had any statements to provide. Said it was for an investigative view."

"Did you?"

"Nah," he said, shaking his head, moonlight swaying in his eyes. "It's not my place."

A hot sting flushed over me, the wine making my head spin a little. I wanted to say, *Damn right*, believing nobody had that place except for me.

"I appreciate that," I said, an urge coming next, my need to explain Ronald's surprise visit. With his face in my hands, his stubble scratchy on my fingertips, I planted another kiss, but was careful about the sensuality, backing off and turning it into a hug. "Ronald did contact me."

I waited for a response, but Jericho didn't react, didn't flinch. Instead, he stared hard at the bay, the tree frogs singing, the moment lasting uncomfortably long.

"He met me outside the station."

"What did he want?" he asked, his voice flat.

"Jericho? You're not the jealous type, are you?" I asked, playfully slapping his chest, trying to make light of the moment.

He smiled, but by now I recognized when it was forced. "I can't help but be cautious," he answered. He pulled away then, my chest turning cold where his body had been. He turned to face his house, intent on ending our evening.

My heart skipped painfully as if he had reached inside me and squeezed it. "What do you mean cautious? Aren't we past that?"

"Maybe not," he answered. "Maybe. I don't know."

"Which is it?" I asked sharply, my emotions a sudden jumble, the threads pulled into a knot. "Just so I know where we are."

He shook his head. "Forget I said that," he answered, ignoring my question. "What did your ex want?"

"Does it matter?" I asked, the hurt shifting to annoyance. I held my breath and stifled the emotion.

"It matters to me," he insisted. "He wouldn't have met you at the station if it was just about your daughter and some producers."

"You're right," I said. "Ronald wanted to talk to me, catch up over coffee or something."

"Why didn't you mention it?" he asked. Regret consumed the place where his words had hurt me. I probably should have mentioned it earlier.

"Why didn't *you* tell me about the election?" I asked, raising my voice, and changing the subject.

Soon after we'd finished our meal that evening—a steaming espresso in Jericho's hand, black coffee in mine—an acquaintance of Jericho's had interrupted and handed him a business card, telling him to contact him for details about the upcoming election. Jericho glanced over at me during the brief encounter, wondering if I had understood their conversation. I did. He was considering a run for the sheriff's office again.

I was ready to yell when a neighbor's light flicked on. I lowered my voice, saying, "Sheriff. Another term?"

"It was just a conversation. Something we're exploring," he answered, his nose wrinkled, his face perplexed. "We don't know if the numbers will support another campaign."

"Flirting with the past?" I asked. "You could have told me."

"Maybe Ronald is flirting with the past too," he said, the heat in his voice softer. He came to me then. "Sorry, if I seem insecure."

I took his hand, and went to the water's edge, him following until we were deep enough to cover our feet. A chill raced up my spine and I found a star, brighter than the others, twinkling, and wished Ronald hadn't said anything to me, had never visited the Outer Banks.

"Jericho—" I began, and held him tight, feeling the insecurities of his past catching up with him, understanding how the loss of his wife two years earlier could strain any new relationship. "There's no competition here. Nothing between me and Ronald. Nothing except our daughter."

"Are you sure?" he asked, brow curled, eyes round like saucers.

I answered with a kiss, but tempered the heat, knowing the evening would run away from us if I gave into what I wanted to do. "I'm sure."

"Then how can I help tonight?" he asked, putting space between us. "I know this is important. These are the cases from your meeting, right? Are they in your car?"

"The trunk, but—"

"I'll meet you inside," he said, interrupting, and raced out of the water, kicking a shallow splash before making his way around the house, and disappearing into the dark. The evening's romance, along with what might have been our first argument, was over.

We'd filled Jericho's kitchen table and his counters with open case files, spreading them from corner to corner and leaving none of the surface exposed. The aged-paper smell and the fraying folders tickled my nose and made my eyes water, threats of a sneeze imminent. A pot of coffee brewed in the background, a steady drip filling the room with a sweet aroma.

In preparation for the evening's work, I'd changed into something more casual: sweatpants, sneakers, and a loose cotton top. Jericho had done the same, changing out of his slacks and dress shirt, and slipping into sweats and an oversized rock-concert shirt from Def Leppard's *Pour Some Sugar On Me* concert tour.

"And these too?" he asked, spreading ten or more folders across the counter, opening them so we could review. "All of them are animal sacrifices?"

"They are." There was a look of disgust on his face. "Yeah, I know. Really gross stuff."

"Cheryl didn't finish going through the files?"

I hesitated to answer, the progress she'd made had been a disappointment. "I think maybe there are too many." We gazed at the number of files, my saying, "Definitely a lot more than I would have guessed."

"You still believe there's a connection with the summer solstice?"

I'd shut down most of the work activities on the solstice lead, but there was some credibility in our earlier theory of a serial killer having started at an early age, sacrificing animals, using the solstice as part of a ritual. I held up a mugshot, a teenager, charged with killing a puppy. Older now, any one of these perps may have escalated to human sacrifice. I couldn't shut down the lead entirely. Not yet.

"It's possible. What I want to do is make a contact sheet—include each perpetrator's mugshot, their name and the court docket number for reference."

Jericho held up a blank sheet. "How big?"

I gauged the size of the mugshots, and the amount of information I wanted. "Let's say eight per page, two columns of four." He went to his computer, an older iMac stuffed in a wall nook, an ancient printer on a shelf above it.

"What do you plan to do with your little mugshot book?" Jericho asked, opening a ream of paper, fanning the pages before filling the printer's trays.

"I'm going back to Dowd's church."

"To do what?" he asked, slapping the keyboard, trying to wake the computer. "You've already been there. Doubtful you'll get anywhere doubling back."

I'd already thought into the next day and who it was I wanted to show the pictures to. Dowd had an alibi. A strong alibi. Yet I couldn't shake the timing of his church's arrival, and it coinciding with the murders. The murderer could be a member of the church, but we already knew that with thousands of potential murders, combing them would be nearly impossible.

"Entirely different purpose," I answered, taking a picture of a mug shot, adding it to a note, and typing the name and court docket number. "When I was there, a lot of people were hanging around outside the church." I picked up five folders from my pile. "If one of these perps returned to the Outer Banks with Dowd's congregation, there's a good chance someone may have seen them."

Jericho tapped the keyboard again, the printer whirred and thunked, the lights blinking, the smell of toner mixing with the brewing coffee. "Okay, we've got life here." He stood, considered my explanation, brow furrowed with sharp concern. "Casey, just don't go alone."

I couldn't promise him, but answered, "I'll do my best."

CHAPTER TWENTY-EIGHT

Heather Doyle was roused awake, the motion on her bed jarring her. She expected the usual snoring of her husband Charley, but a sound like hitting a softball slipped into her dream, a memory from when she was on a team. The swoosh of the bat, the hard thud, the ball launching over the infield.

She stirred again, expecting to hear the ocean. They were spending the weekend on the water, parked in the marina, visiting the beaches and shopping. The crack of a bat, the abrupt motion jarring. This wasn't a game. Heather opened her eyes with a start. The shadow of a dark figure was in bed with them, arms raised above Charley. She tried to move. The face of the person was masked, their body in darkness, but there was a glint of piercing light in the eyes. The intruder saw that she was awake and winked before swinging downward with a violent force, hammer in hand.

A warm spray struck her arm, turning cold like an evening chill, her eyes popping open with alarm. There was a full moon, the first in the new cycle, showing through the port side windows. And from the moon's light, Heather saw their attacker reset and ready the hammer for another strike.

"Please, no," she begged. The attacker reeled upward and struck her husband again, bones breaking, crushing. Silent screams. Frantic, her bare legs slamming against the mattress, an arm caught beneath her husband's bloodied neck and shoulders, his misshapen face near hers. Heather's voice was stuck in her throat as she scrambled to get away. The killer lurched like a coiled snake, a blade running across the side of her neck.

Her mind filled with disbelief, the understanding of what had happened coming after the metal's touch—cold and frightful and oddly without any pain. Heather clutched her neck, the attempt on her life missed, blood running between her fingers and down her front. Her thoughts raced crazily like moths in and out of a flame—an idea of calling the police, her cell phone in reach, her children in the other room, their lives in danger.

Heather fell toward the nightstand, her upper body wet, the screen on her cell phone showing the time as three thirteen in the morning. She gasped, her breathing ragged, her heart beating heavy. She became faint, light-headed, her chest blood-soaked and cold.

Charley groaned. She turned to see that he was still alive. Tears cut her cheeks as she reached for his hand, touching his fingers. A rush of air whooshed past her face, landing against the side of his head with a densely sickening thwack.

He has to be dead, she thought painfully, and begged it to be, knowing she'd be dead soon too. *Please be dead.*

There was a rhyme in her ears, a song, maybe a hymn she hadn't heard since Sunday school. The killer spoke a few words, a man's voice. She remembered a prayer too, taught to her by nuns who'd insisted it was a sin if she couldn't memorize it. He was talking to her about death. Violent shakes erupted across Heather's body, the shivering uncontrollable as fear dripped from every pore.

Moonlight glinted from the wet blade as the killer left their bed and came around to the nightstand, tapping the wall with each step. When he reached her, a gloved hand appeared, pushing the cell phone just out of reach of her fingertips. Her head was jerked back, the roots of her hair breaking, yanking her scalp from her head with a terrible force, and hoisting her upward, her neck and front exposed. Heather gagged, jaw dropping as the blade went deeper, ending all thoughts of survival.

Her vision turned gray and her thoughts became disparate and disconnected. She fell face first into the growing pool, sticky, wet, and as black as night. She had a faint awareness the killer was turning her over. She tried to scream, but her voice was like a drowning person, her throat closing, gurgling sounds, bubbles forming on her lips.

Rape, she thought with fright and disgust, understanding she'd be dead before he finished, understanding that a monster had come onto their yacht and into their home and lives. She could see the killer, his body kneeling next to her, the bed sagging. He removed the mask. A sliver of light showed his face, his sneer.

In that moment, Heather realized she knew him, or knew him once upon a time. It had to have been more than twelve years since she'd seen him last. A breath bubbled from between her wet lips. She hadn't forgotten him. They'd never forget him. It wasn't rape he sought. No, it wasn't that at all.

The sound of clothes being torn and the hymn filled her ears. The killer cleaned her skin as gooseflesh and other odd sensations both hot and cold rushed over her while her brain misfired messages. She winced when the blade cut into her skin, but faintly knew her face must have remained blank, the ability to move at all ending while he sang. The last thought Heather had wasn't for her husband. It wasn't for her children. And it wasn't for the freshly carved figure on her belly. With stirring guilt, she questioned, *What if they'd been wrong?*

CHAPTER TWENTY-NINE

Jericho had helped me review two dozen cases of animal sacrifice that had taken place during the summer solstice. The case files dated back ten years, and each contained a small treasure of information: perpetrator's name, court docket number, crime details, and the perpetrator's mugshots. From the files we worked, and a steady stream of data coming from Cheryl and Emanuel, we created a *booklet of mugshots*, as Jericho called it, fighting with the printer most of the night, his son helping and saving the effort, twice. The booklets made, they would be distributed to my team so they could use them in canvasing crowds.

The team would canvas areas around where the killings took place, the RV campgrounds, neighboring shopping centers, the nearby beaches, and boardwalk. Everywhere so we could exhaust this detail and determine if the lead had any teeth. My plan was to question the crowd around Dowd's church, those standing in wait and those working the property.

Raindrops ran down my car windows, the view twisted and pulled into unusual shapes, a steady patter against the roof. While we'd worked into the early hours of the day, thick clouds had moved in and opened over the Outer Banks, bringing with them a heavy rain. Headlamps from the oncoming traffic bounced across the road's wet surface, their light sharp. The rain was torrential at times, blurring the road no matter how high I'd set the wiper's speed. Bad weather or not, the tiny back-country church would be crowded, packed, standing-room only.

The heavy traffic split after I'd crossed Dare Memorial Bridge, the cornfields coming soon after the country store, rows of green, golden silk tassels sprouting from the husks, their color paled in the dim weather. The uphill ascent came and went next, the church's spire on the other side, a sea of umbrellas sprouting across the church grounds like colorful mushroom caps.

I wasted no time, finding a parking spot and my invitation, tucking it in my pocket just in case questioning led me to someone inside. I stowed my gun in the glove compartment, choosing to keep my badge on me, the lanyard draped around my neck. The line to enter the church was long, the doors opened to their widest.

By my count, more than four dozen umbrella tops idled around the church property. On the church stoop was the attendant I'd mixed words with, a bundle of lanyards and badges slung from his arm, handing them out, collecting invitations, a steady flow filing around him.

I made my way into the crowd of umbrellas, noticing a bright-yellow one like the petals of a buttercup, a woman beneath, her aged face sallow, her eyes round and set deep, the corners drooping. She held a picture frame with a man dressed in a military uniform, his hair cropped short, the corners of his eyes sharing the same droopiness, leading me to believe it was her son.

"Ma'am, my name is Detective White," I said, introducing myself. I understood why she was here, her search for closure bringing her to Dowd. I couldn't help but wonder how many churches she'd visited before reaching this one. "I am sorry for your loss."

"Thank you," she answered, her clutch tightening on the glass-and-wood frame. "I miss him so."

"If I could take a minute," I said, showing her the pages. "Could you tell me if anyone in these pictures looks familiar to you?" I asked, flipping through the photographs, showing the mug shots, the woman mouthing the word no with each page turn. When I reached the end, I thanked her for her time and moved on.

The next umbrella was a faded paisley green, a middle-aged man and woman inviting me beneath it, the size large enough for the three of us. The couple wore clear plastic ponchos, their clothes telling me they worked a farm. A thunderclap threatened my questioning and I hurried, flipping through my booklet, their eyes darting from mugshot to mugshot, up and down the pages. The couple shook their head, the rain ponchos making crumpling sounds like plastic bags.

I repeated the same questions a few more times, the crowd thinning as thunder roared and lightning blades streaked across the western sky. I made my way to the side of the church and a row of tall flowers, their petals drooping in the rain, where a group of young men and women worked at landscaping. Before I could ask any questions, the team retreated inside, a few glancing at my badge.

The rear of the church was thick with mud and absent of people, the RVs parked and empty, the windows blocked with drawn curtains. I went to the grandest of them: tall with maroon-and-silver colored panels, dark tinted glass, wood blocks seated against the tires, and the trim adorned in shiny chrome. In the chrome's wet reflection I saw a group coming toward me, children, the same ages as Lisa Pearson and Andrea Hill. Before I could turn around, I was blindsided, a mind-numbing punch clobbering me from behind, filling my sight with a blinding flash, the bright shine turning black, the sound of rain becoming a deafening ring. And then there was nothing.

When I opened my eyes, the rains and fog had begun to burn off, the daylight brighter, the sun a steel penny tucked behind cloud cover. I was alone and surrounded by stalks of corn, a breeze bending them in a steady sway. I must have been knocked unconscious, struck hard enough to black out, the kids dragging me into the cornfields bordering the church property. I got to my knees and checked myself for injury. Somehow, I'd escaped it—body fine, head fine, even where I'd been hit was without signs of an assault. But my head, it was heavy, dull, and sleepy.

A red blur caught my eye, one of the attackers passing through the corn, circling around me. The sight set a flame in my belly, a warning of danger. I heard footsteps and the breaking of cornstalks, the sound closer. Through the tall stalks, a figure lurked, the definition of them ghostly. I moved enough to see a flash of color on their neck, a swirl of yellow and purple and blue—a cerulean blue. My heart leaped into my throat. I cleared my eyes and made out the figure of a girl, her hair color the same as mine and a tattoo like the one in Hannah's photos.

"Hannah?" I asked, my voice sounding like an echo, reverberating and dreamlike.

As her expression registered who I was, my heart walloped painfully. I bolted onto my feet, Hannah disappearing into the corn. I reached the place where my daughter had been standing, panting, a steady rain beginning again, dripping into my eyes as thunder rolled in the distance. I saw the different colors of her shirts, two or more layered, torn and ragged. She stood ten feet from me. I leaped into another row, my feet crunching vegetation as she disappeared again, turning the reunion with my daughter into a nightmare. Was this one of my nightmares? I ignored a nagging truth, ignored that I might still be unconscious, lying face down in mud, surrounded by children beating on my body. Hannah was near me and I intended to find her.

I stopped to listen, crouching, the smell of farm dirt and fresh corn rich. A flurry of footsteps came from my left. I took off in that direction, swinging my arms, continuing the blind search.

"Hannah!" I yelled, tears stinging my eyes, my lungs burning. When she didn't respond, I went into a flat run, my feet pounding, the loose ground twisting my ankles. I tripped and tumbled into the soil. The nightmare continuing.

"Stop," I heard from through the corn, her tone imploring.

I pulled myself onto my knees, the wet ground soaking into my pants, my arms stinging with a hundred cuts. "Hannah?" I dared to call again.

"I want to be left alone," she said, footsteps sounding from my left.

"Can I talk to you?" I asked, trying not to cry. The years of waiting, of wanting to be with my daughter became too much. "Please?"

The rain showers opened into a hard pour, plump drops ticking against my head, and paddling the cornstalks. "Hannah? Please let me see you."

"I thought I was ready. But I'm not," I heard in my ear, her voice like a breeze, the light touch of fingers on my shoulder.

I spun around, arms stretched to embrace my girl. She was gone. "Hannah?"

"Not now," she told me, the distant great again, her footsteps leading away, too far for me to follow.

"Get up!" A voice shouted, my ears ringing again, muddling the sounds. With the return of consciousness, pain knifed my side, the feel of a kick stealing my breath, the taste of blood and mud in my mouth. I reeled to my left, rolling, and got onto my knees, the RV's large balloon tires next to me, the smell of rubber mixed with dirt. A crowd of shoes surrounded me, twelve or more, all shapes and sizes and colors. I'd dreamed of my daughter again, the sight of Hannah adding another crack in my soul, a drop of grace spilled for the brief moment of her company. Thunder shuddered the air, rattling the ground with a boom.

A child's voice screeched, "Hit her again!"

My faculties began to return, dulled and unreliable, a battery of fists struck my back and shoved me into the mud, my lungs burning, muck plugging my nose and mouth. I gagged and spat and stole a breath, swiping at my eyes. My focus returned, showing me a single light bulb above the church's rear door, rain dripping from it, a group of five, maybe six, hovering around me, their faces a blur. I'd awoken from a nightmare, finding myself in a real-life one.

The children yelled louder, cheering one another on, their voices pitched high and too garbled to decipher what they were saying. I spat grit and tasted blood, a cut on my lip telling me I had to have been struck when I'd fallen unconscious. A blood-curdling fright washed over me. These were children, and they were going to kill me.

"I'm a cop," I shouted with a choking breath while trying show my badge. Fear drove my muscles, their function disorderly, but enough for me get to my knees, raising my arms, wobbly, but guarding. I blinked, but their faces remained unclear, fleshy blobs shouting in angry voices.

"Don't believe her!" one of them hollered.

I shook my head, desperate to clear the persistent fog. Their shoes closed in around me. Instinctively I took guard. "Listen, I'm a—" I doubled over with a kick to my side. I kissed the mud, planting my face in it again. I had to move, had to get out of there, and swung wildly to make room as I stood and retreated.

"What if she is a cop?" one of them asked.

"She's a reporter nosing around for a story!" another answered sharply.

"I'm not a report—" I began. A brilliant flash stole my words, my view gone, a searing pain in my right eye, another of the children coming out of nowhere. I rocked to one side, scuttling on all fours, spying muddied sneakers and flip-flops as they followed me like a pack of savage wolves ready to finish their kill.

"Hit her again!" a voice shouted, high-pitched and excited. They wanted blood. A sneaker plugged into the pit of my chest and shoved the air from my lungs in a wheezing breath. I fell over like a struck farm animal, gasping, muddy rainwater dripping into my nose and mouth.

"Break it up!" I heard someone grunt. I heard the scatter of feet splattering against the mud, my attackers fleeing. "Seems you got on the wrong end of an overzealous bunch."

"What's that?" I coughed, finding a hand in mine, hoisting me onto my knees and then cradling my arm as I worked my way back to my feet. "Listen, I'm a cop."

The man was tall and round, and his voice familiar. "When they get worked up like that, you could've told them you were the Pope and they still wouldn't have believed you."

I made my way to one of the RVs, clearing my eyes and catching my breath. When I could see again, I found the attendant, the one I'd met when I first found the church and asked about Lisa Pearson.

"Ms. White?"

"Detective," I corrected him.

He shook his head, searching the back of the church, his round face specked with raindrops, his glasses fogged by the humidity. "What are you doing back here?" he asked, offering a handkerchief from his suit jacket. I took it and pressed the soft cloth to my eyebrow, finding it was split open, bleeding profusely, the rainwater masking the flow.

"Who attacked me?"

He shoved his fingers into his wiry beard, scratching, and answered, "Hard to say. Not to mention, this area is off limits. Anyone questioned is going to tell you they'd been guarding Mr. Dowd's RV. We've had some burglary issues."

"Is that right?" I asked, a touch of sarcasm in my tone, knowing the direction we were headed. Without names it'd be nearly impossible to press charges, even if I wanted to. The cut above my eye wouldn't stop bleeding, the heavy flow stinging as I tried to keep it dry, pinching the wound.

"Mr. Dowd is extremely popular. We often find fans inside his RV, rummaging through his personal quarters, stealing hairbrushes, clothes. Even had them steal a washcloth and towel set once," the attendant said. He pitched his hands against his hips and shifted as rain dripped from his glasses and nose. His expression changed, a familiar look to me, like a cop eyeing a suspect. He stepped closer. "Why exactly were you back here again?"

I glanced at the RV nearest us, Dowd's name in bold print on the inside of the windshield, the attendant's excuse for guarding against burglary a sound one. "Part of an ongoing investigation." I picked up my pages, cleaning the mud, the paper wet and crumpled and torn. "I've been asking if any of these people have been to your church."

The attendant eyed the soiled pages, and shook his round face, his thick fingers on my arm, strongly guiding me toward the side of the building. I felt woozy and followed him as we trudged into the heavy rain to the generators, a cloud of smog and diesel hanging at my shoulders and clouding my face. With his arm stretched and pointing toward the front of the property, he said, "You'll want to go that way." He motioned to his brow, adding, "And you should also get that checked."

"I will," I answered, folding the remains of my mugshot booklet.

"Oh, and Ms. White," he said, painfully tightening his grip on my arm until I was forced to jerk it free of him. He shook his head. "Don't come back. Consider your invitation officially rescinded." He went back the way we came, walking briskly, leaving me alone with the generators, fear striking me again in the isolation.

Wasting no time, I made my way to my car, the cut on my eye continuing to bleed. I searched the faces of the crowd waiting to go inside the church and found my attackers.

While I'd no idea who in the group had struck me first, or who'd participated with the kicks to my body, there were six pairs of eyes following me. And like the pack of wolves they'd become, they were watching their kill scramble to safety. But what struck me most was a sneer pasted on one of the girl's faces—fifteen or so, with dirty-blonde hair and thick freckles on her cheeks and the bridge of her nose. The sneer turned into a laugh and her eyes were as cold as ice.

These kids weren't guarding Dowd's RV. They weren't guarding anything. I'd been spotted in the crowd, and they'd been sent to attack me. Jericho warned me not to come alone. My identity had been made the moment I entered the church property.

When the freckled girl moved in my direction, I picked up the pace, jumping in my car, my hands clammy, a pulse beating in my split eyebrow. The attack had left me afraid. It also left me wondering if there could be more than one murderer. I threw the muddied mugshot booklet to the floor of the passenger seat, disgusted with the weak lead. What if it wasn't one individual in Dowd's congregation? What if the true murderer *was* Dowd's congregation—the children?

Dowd's attendant was hiding something, and my invitation had been rescinded. The killer was here. Or was it *killers*? The online videos gave Dowd a strong alibi and, until now, our strongest feeling had us believing a member of Dowd's congregation was the killer. But could Dowd be influential enough to solicit children to perform murder?

Flashes of death came to me, cult leaders and their devout followers slain. Was that a possibility? I thought of Branch Davidians, the Peoples Temple and Jonestown. I thought of criminal cult leaders like Charles Manson and Marshall Applewhite, their influences having tragic consequences and impact on the once innocent, turning them vicious, turning them into monsters. There were a dozen other famous cult cases to prove the possibility, but I'd never expected to see one in my career.

Suddenly, this case was feeling big and overwhelming, the weight of it gargantuan. There was pressure from Ashtole to push us, to show progress and ease the voting public's concerns. I put my car in drive, wolves' eyes fixed on me, their threat vicious, head throbbing and making me wince. I'd have to call the mayor, update him on this latest theory. Maybe it was time to bring in federal help, get their experts working. They'd know how to handle a dangerous cult, if that's what this was.

CHAPTER THIRTY

My phone buzzed with a text message as I drove over Dare Memorial Bridge. I followed the white-and-blue signs with the letter H until I'd made it to the emergency room. I checked my phone, my stomach clenching as I read another text message from Ronald, asking again if we could meet.

The emergency-room doors opened with a swoosh. As I saw a man with a severely broken leg lying on a gurney, the fractures pushing bone through his thigh, his hands covering his face, at once I thought my injuries superficial. I thought of going back to the church, finding my courage, and then dragging the children who attacked me into the station. If only I could identify them with certainty, I could make a case.

The man screamed with a hoarse voice, making me flinch. A woman sat next to him, her eyes glazed and unfocused, both red and bruised, abrasions on her chin and cheek from an airbag. A patrol officer stood over them, asking questions as a nurse hovered busily nearby. Opposite the man and woman, similar carnage, more remnants of airbag deployments, a woman holding her arm, the forearm bent at an awkward angle, a man next to her clutching his chest and wheezing.

"Car accident?" I asked a patrol officer guarding the entrance. Her position told me they were guarding against them leaving. She recognized my face from the station, her eyes going to the cut on my brow with a grimace. "Looks like a bad one."

"Real bad. One of the kids is in surgery. Might not make it," she answered, motioning toward her eye. "Did'ya get that on the job?"

"Sort of," I answered. "But looks like I'll be waiting a while."

"Wish I could do something about that." She gripped her belt, the leather creaking. "If you need anything, let me know."

"I will," I told her and headed to the desk, finding the necessary forms on the counter, prepared to fill them out and wait.

I received a text:

You there?

I replied:

Busy at the emergency room. Will be here a while.

I glanced at a row of empty seats. I filled out the forms, turned them in and took to a row near the television, the evening news broadcast on the monitors. Was it that late already? As I watched the television, a call to sleep hit me, weighing on my head, turning it into a thousand-pound anchor that was impossible to keep straight on my shoulders. I closed my eyes, warning myself to rest them only a moment. But the warnings about concussions and staying awake came and went. I had to answer sleep's call.

I tried staying awake by concentrating on Dowd, the church congregation, and the children. They were all strong suspects, yet with each, there was a conundrum, a strong alibi for Dowd, and a lack of evidence for the others. We were coming up short and I knew, with a cold dread, that it meant someone else would die soon. The more I concentrated, the more my thoughts became a jumble of disconnected ends, their meaning escaping me, my grasp on them slipping the way lyrics of a song can become lost. Sleep found me, and then there was nothing after that.

*

"Casey?" I heard and stirred, half-lidded, a warm hand on my shoulder, the voice familiar, welcome. "Wake up."

I opened my eyes, my hands in my lap, holding the bloodied handkerchief. An ache in my head made me wince, my right eye throbbing, the overhead lights piercing. When I was able to focus, I saw Ronald's face next to mine.

"What?"

"You were dead to the world," he said, the smell of his aftershave rousing me. "I was worried."

I pushed back on the chair's rest, sitting up, my fingers tacky with a mix of dried blood and sweat. Swelling had closed my right eye enough for me to see a gray orb hovering. It blocked some of my sight. Instant regret at not having asked for an icepack came. When I moved, I coughed, choked on my breath, bruises rising from the kicks to my left side.

"What... what are you doing here?" I asked, checking my phone, seeing I'd only been asleep a short spell. I checked behind me and saw the folks from the car accident were missing, the woman with the unfocused gaze remaining, an officer continuing to take statements. I turned back to Ronald. "You... you really shouldn't be here."

"I was concerned," he said, flashing his dimples briefly.

I shook my head, the egg on my eye moving at a different speed. "But how did you know I was here?"

"You texted *emergency room*," he answered, holding his phone for me to see. Curious, I checked my phone.

"It was Jericho—" I began and checked the text message I thought I'd sent to Jericho. But the text I answered was a reply to Ronald. "Huh. So, I did."

"I brought you some coffee," he said, offering me a cup. "I saw you waiting and found a machine. I didn't know you were asleep until I came over."

"Thanks," I said grudgingly, taking the warm cup and bringing the steam to my nose.

"Black," he continued. "The way you like it."

"Sometimes I take cream and sugar too," I said, not wanting him to get comfortable in his memories of me.

"I can get some," he offered, beginning to stand.

I took a mouthful and shook my head. "This is fine." And I thought it was fine, his being here, the moment catching me, putting me in a place I hadn't been in a very long time. "Ronald," I said, sitting back. "What do you want?"

"Hannah was my daughter too," he said, his voice breaking. "Do you really think she's here?"

Without a word, I brought up the latest pictures, flipping through until I had the one from Sharon, the drawing Nichelle helped me update to include the neck tattoo. "This is her," I said, zooming in. "This is our daughter."

Ronald's hands met mine, his brow raised, asking for the phone without words. I nodded, letting go as he brought the screen close to his face, Hannah's image reflecting in his glassy eyes. "She's beautiful."

"If you swipe left, you'll see the years before." There was an unexpected tug of emotion in my chest. "That's our girl."

"She looks so much like you," he said, flashing his dimples again, his eyes beaming. He eagerly swiped to look at the pictures Sharon had put together over the years.

I couldn't help but return the smile. "I have the originals—" I began, not knowing where I was going. "They'd been taken last year, but I got them back. Some are damaged, but not too bad. I can show them to you."

"I think I'd like that," he said, unable to stop smiling. He looked up, adding, "I picked up the apartment I mentioned, and accepted the job."

Uncertainty came with his words. I wanted to warn him about getting his hopes up, tell him the dangers of what could come as a result. "She's here," I said. "I'm sure of it. But—"

"There's a but?" he asked, hearing my tone.

"I've been close," I said, slumping in my seat, unsure of how to explain the disappointment of never having got close enough. I shook my head. "But I could never make that final connection with her."

His gaze fell to my phone again, his expression emptying. "It could be, she doesn't want to be found."

Ronald's words pained me, the idea of what he'd said like a curse. Maybe it was because it came from him, our past filled with him telling me to give up. I snatched my phone from his hands, snapping, "What do you know?"

He shot straight up, hands raised. "Whoa, Casey," he said, frowning. "It was only a comment. Some reasoning to understand why Hannah hasn't tried to find you or me."

"Reasoning?" I blurted, feeling hot, my entire body pulsing from the attack.

"It was the news stories that brought me here. They're everywhere," he continued, trying to explain. "I mean, Hannah had to have seen them."

"There's also the possibility she hasn't seen any of them," I argued.

Ronald stared, saying nothing, avoiding a repeat of past arguments, the fights similar. He let out a sigh, and said, "And it's also you."

He put his hand on mine, the two of us holding my phone, pictures of Hannah showing through our fingers. "Casey," he said, dipping his face. There was a look in his eyes as though a sudden connection had sparked like lost souls suddenly remembered. "I came here for you."

I backed away, answering with a head shake, "Ronald, it's not—"

"Casey?" Jericho asked, his voice behind us. I let go of Ronald's hand, my phone dropping to the floor. I twisted around to find

Jericho standing behind me. He hitched his thumb toward the patrol officer working the car accident. "I got a radio call about your being here."

I braced my head, a knifing pain in my eye. "Of course you did," I said, annoyed with myself for the situation I'd created. I made a short introduction. "Jericho, Ronald. Ronald, Jericho."

Ronald stood, facing Jericho, their bodies separated by a row of plastic chairs and me sitting in the middle. Jericho's face was empty, blank, his lips thin. He reluctantly extended an arm. Ronald forced a smile which disappeared when he took hold of Jericho's hand. The two said nothing, their contact brief but civil as a doctor approached with a well-timed interruption. I stood and immediately felt woozy, the waiting room shifting as I clutched the arms of both men until I could regain my balance.

"I'll be back in a few," I said, offering nothing more, their eyes fixed on me. I was eager to leave, realizing just how messy I'd made things with my accidental text message. But one thought bothered me more, as a pair of wide doors swung open and then closed behind me. What if Ronald was right? What if Hannah didn't want to be found? I'm not sure how I'd be able to live knowing that.

CHAPTER THIRTY-ONE

The day's rain never slowed. The downpour stayed heavy, the sky thick with dark storm clouds, the sunlight a faint memory. My clothes had dried some since reaching the hospital, but felt damp and uncomfortable. I needed a hot shower to help shake the chill. I reached my home, surprising Tiny with an unexpected early-afternoon break, and also finding Jericho standing on my patio, his gaze fixed on the fog rolling onto the beach, breaking waves beneath it.

I said nothing, emptying my mind, and let instinct take over. It was instinct that was sometimes right, and had me warm next to him, chasing the shiver from my bones. The beach was nearly bare, save for a group of souls braving the weather, wearing colorful wind breakers, the fabric flattened against their bodies as a strong wind batted them. In the ocean break, a few surfers dared the waves, mounting the storm's heights like riders on wild horses.

Jericho didn't feel cold or distant. He didn't revolt or feel angry or resentful. A sense of relief pulled me closer to him. He felt good. "How's the eye?" he said, holding me.

"It's okay," I answered. I closed my eyes and found the look on his face when he saw me with Ronald. "How are we?"

"That's Ronald?" he asked.

"Yeah, that's Ronald."

"I could take him," he said, joking. I peered up, his smile warming me as much as any hot shower. "Not much of a threat."

"He was never a threat," I reminded him. "His being at the hospital was an accident. I replied to the wrong text."

"Still texting you?"

"He is," I answered, deciding to limit it there. "At some point I'll have to have that coffee with him, tell him about his daughter, her history here."

"I'm sure the podcast producer has filled him in."

"You're probably right."

His fingers were on my chin, his wanting to see my face, his focus moving to the stitches and bruising. "Casey, what happened?"

We went inside and I filled him in about the church, the possible connection to the children and the open cases. As I spoke, his phone went off with a text message from work; Marine Patrol.

"I have to reply to this," he said, rubbing my back affectionately. He gave me a much-needed smile then, saying, "You should get out of those wet clothes before a cold catches you."

"You read my mind," I said, leaving him to his call. In the bathroom I turned on the hot water, steam rolling across the ceiling. I stripped naked and jumped in, my face turned up toward the shower head. When I heard Jericho enter the bathroom, I knew what else would help chase away the chill too.

"I've got to go," he said, the shape of his body marbled by the shower curtain. I pulled the curtain aside, disappointed, his phone pressed against his ear. "Two bodies discovered on a yacht. We've secured the vessel, but the team is at a stop until the scene is processed."

I twisted the shower handles, hurrying with the news. "Accidental?" I asked, toweling my body. "Any other details?"

"Nothing yet," he said, disappearing into my bedroom, Tiny following. I heard the sound of drawers opening and closing, Jericho helping to get an outfit together for me.

"But two," I said. "What was the state of the yacht?"

"It looks to have come loose from its slip and drifted. A worker at the marina secured it. He knew the family was on board and investigated, discovering the bodies."

"A family," I said. *Children were involved.* I took my clothes and dressed fast, sleeving wet legs in pants and cringing at the feeling on my skin. "Does that happen? I mean, do yachts just come loose?"

Jericho held my shirt open so I could duck my head inside. "Not usually. Not unless human error is involved. Even then—" he shook his head.

When I popped my head through the shirt, I took advantage of the closeness and wrapped myself around him, my arms draped from his neck. "About Ronald," I began. His body went rigid, uncomfortable with the topic. I gripped his shoulders, his muscles taut. "I am sorry about his showing up at the hospital like that."

"Putting myself in his place, I think if it was my daughter, I'd be where he was too," he said, cocking his head. "And with all the news, the podcasts, it was bound to happen."

I brushed my fingers against his cheek, pinching playfully until I saw him smile. "That's why I'm sorry. I love where we are going, and I love you."

"I love you," he said, touching his lips to mine, a gentle kiss my consolation prize for the missed opportunity. He stared then as though he wanted to say more, but text messages blew up my phone. "Is that the station?"

My phone's screen filled, texts rolling from the bottom to the top—one from Ashtole, another from the station. Both messages about a double murder on a yacht.

*

The Innocent Girls

Nichelle was first to arrive at the crime scene and followed the directions I texted. We needed to determine if there were, or had been, any children on board the yacht. If so, she would identify their phones, tablets, and any computers, then secure the electronics as part of the investigation. While it was impossible to know yet if there was a connection to the other cases, one radio message had included a description of a neck wound on a victim, and the likelihood of it being fatal.

The marina was on the bayside of the Outer Banks—an exclusive club, expensive, with fewer than one-hundred slips. We made our way past the typical club amenities, the tennis courts, a driving range, and beaches edging the bay and peppered with chairs and umbrellas, games and a lifeguard. The yacht had already been cordoned off by a female police officer in her early twenties, and a young-looking marine patrol officer, possibly a rookie, their bodies clad in clear rain ponchos, the two chatting it up while guarding the entrance. A crime-scene technician worked with Tracy, their booties on, their hands gloved, camera flashes bouncing off a boat cleat and a mooring pier, the yacht's rope securely in place.

"Damn rain," Tracy said, a scowl on her face and hand on her hip. She held the yacht's rail and shoved her wet hair behind her ear, adding, "Unlikely we'll be able to determine if the yacht was intentionally unmoored."

"Why's that?"

"Too wet. Makes it tough to lift any prints."

"How about after it rains, when it dries out?" I asked.

She gave half a nod, saying to the other technician, "We need any prints we can find. Let's get this covered, get it dry."

We took cover under the yacht's awning, rainwater racing to the edges of the navy-blue fabric, plump drops pelting the surface. Tracy handed me a pair of booties and gloves, and held my arm for balance while I put them on. She followed me inside and down the stairs leading to the gut of the boat.

The space opened up to a small galley and a living area. Bloody footprints covered the space—not a single print, or one set of prints, but dozens. There were two, possibly three, sizes present—children's, toddlers or slightly older. I followed the prints like breadcrumbs as they led in and out of the galley, into the small television room and through a hallway entrance where I expected we'd find the bodies. In the room where I stood was a small white couch, stained with bloodied handprints, a throw rug in front of it along with a coffee table. Across from both was a large television, the screen locked on a message about the satellite signal being lost. Opened bags of potato chips, cookies and other snacks were spread across the table, a mess of bloody footprints where the children had stood while they ate.

"This is a sight," I commented, my voice caught in my throat. "Where are the children?"

"Child services have them," a patrol officer answered.

There was no question that this was murder. I took a deep breath, replying to Ashtole's latest text, answering one of his dozen questions.

"What do we know?" I asked, growing anxious.

A patrol officer handed me a pair of ID badges, a driver's license identifying Charley Doyle, and a hospital badge with the picture and name of Dr. Heather Doyle. "We did a check. A married couple. Mr. Doyle owns a venture capital firm, and came up as a big name in the tech field when we googled him. The female victim is the chief of surgery at a children's hospital on the mainland."

"Out of town," I said, checking the booties covering my shoes, and the gloves on my hands. I went to the bedroom where the bodies had been discovered.

There, a couple had been in bed, the husband on one side, brutally beaten, his face unrecognizable. Even the use of dental records would be questionable. Next to the bed, a woman's body lay on the floor, her throat cut and her clothes torn, leaving most of her body exposed. A single carving was made on her toned belly, just below the ribs. Yellow markers lined the carpeted floor, identifying footprints, most of them young children's. A bright-yellow measuring stick was placed next to the carving on the woman's belly, Tracy working her camera, the flash firing and the battery recycling its electrical charge.

"We'll want to get this too," I told her, the clamshell paint on the high wall behind the bed's backboard stained by blood spatters. Presumably the husband's. I wasn't a forensics expert on blood spatter, but the multiple sharp markings, the differing angles and the spattering's shape indicated the victim was struck repeatedly. This also offered us a possible direction. With the victim's position on the bed, I motioned a batter's swing relative to the blood spatter, and added, "We may be able to determine if the attacker was left or right-handed."

"I'll get photos from each angle," she said, kneeling carefully, her lens focused at an angle and path the weapon would have traveled.

I studied the victim's head, the deformities inflicted, and guessed the murder weapon likely being a hammer, having seen similar in a murder case on my second year as detective. The sight was just as gruesome then as it was now. I turned away, adding, "And all of that too."

"He wasn't the target," Tracy said.

"He wasn't," I agreed. I moved my focus to the character carved into the woman's torso, the shape looking like a letter O but it could have been the letter beta from the Greek alphabet. I leaned toward Tracy, instructing, "Have Nichelle begin a search on the victims, determine if either were originally from the Outer Banks area."

"Yacht is secure," I heard Jericho's voice. I went to the doorway, finding him stopped at the mouth of the stairwell, his gaze on the floor. "Are these children's footprints?"

I gave him a nod, the strong smell in the bedroom giving me pause. "Kids should never have seen their parents like this."

"There's three," Tracy said, stepping carefully around me. "These prints were made by the couples' four-year-old twins, a boy and a girl. Thankfully, the children were found unharmed."

I couldn't look away from the baby feet, the outline of toes and heel and high arches perfectly preserved in their parents' blood. "I wonder how much they'll remember?"

"None of it, I hope," Nichelle said, peering from the galley counter. She held up a laptop.

"And the third child?" I asked.

"The older daughter. Aged fourteen. Already confirmed there's an invitation to visit Dowd's church." Her eyes went to the footprints.

"Nichelle," I said, getting her attention. "Find the daughter's email address and reconcile it against the list of remaining invitations."

Nichelle shook her head. "I'm on it." she said, clapping her hand to her chest. "Do you think someone from Dowd's church wanted the family here?"

"Appears so." I shifted carefully, avoiding one of the footprints. "A member of the church congregation befriends the adolescent, the teens, and convinces them to visit the Outer Banks."

"And now we have the figure O," Tracy said, her booties swishing with papery kisses. She captured a picture of the coffee table and the prints on the floor, saying, "Another number to add."

"We'll leave this to you," Jericho said, narrowing his broad shoulders to turn around. "If you need us, we'll be in the wheelhouse gathering the nautical data for our reports."

I followed more of the toddlers' footprints into the galley, the two pairs leading to an opened drawer where the prints had amassed and smudged into a single dried glob. The drawer was filled with bags of cookies and pastry snacks. "At least they ate," I muttered under my breath. "Where was the older sister at the time of the attack?" I asked, already suspecting what the answer would be. It was pure speculation, but the teen must have been at Dowd's church. The pattern fit. Until we knew more, there was a practice to follow, a process, and I turned to the patrol officer with the next request. "Let's issue an Amber Alert for the daughter."

"I found some selfies if it helps," Nichelle said, lifting the girl's laptop and turning it around. On the screen, I saw one of my attackers, the cropped dirty-blonde hair and freckled nose a dead ringer for the one who'd sneered at me. A throb came to my eye, reminding me that danger comes in all sizes and ages. "Her name is Wendy Doyle."

"Wendy Doyle. She's one of them," I said.

"One of who?" Tracy asked, looking to Nichelle and then the patrol officer.

I motioned to my eye, the stitches and the dried scabs itchy. "She's one of the teens from Dowd's congregation that gave me these parting gifts."

"Should we issue an APB?" the patrol officer asked.

I shook my head. "Let's go with the Amber Alert."

"But you were attacked," he said, insistent, his police radio squelching as he prepared to make the issuance.

"I'm not pressing charges," I answered. "Issue the Amber Alert."

A text message rang from my phone, a message from Ashtole repeating an earlier warning about the council requiring a progress report. I texted a reply, telling him there were two more victims, a prominent couple, Charley and Heather Doyle. I peered out the window, the daylight waning, the hours growing long. It would be late in the evening by the time we were finished processing the scene.

Ashtole replied:

Doyle?

Correct. We're processing the scene. Team meeting early morning.

Jesus. I went to school with them.

"Nichelle," I said, raising my voice. Her head popped up from behind the laptop, eyes huge. "The victims, they *were* from the Outer Banks."

"Just like Ben Hill and the Tellys," Tracy said.

"That leaves the Pearsons," I commented, a connection forming across some of the victims. "Dig deeper on them."

CHAPTER THIRTY-TWO

The morning spoke to me, telling me to get up, get dressed, get to the station and the meeting with my team. And with the mayor. He wanted to join, to discuss the Doyles and also discuss my thoughts on the possibility of the adolescent sons and daughters of the victims being involved. We had much to cover, especially with the hometown connection. Tiny nudged my leg, his telling me it was time for his morning walk. It'd give me a chance to put my thoughts in order and to comb the sea air through my hair.

I glanced in the bathroom mirror, a harried and wild reflection telling me I shouldn't leave my bedroom at all. Yesterday's attack had done a number to my eye, the stitches a prickly nylon nestled at the center of a puffy bruise. It wasn't my first shiner. I was sure it wouldn't be my last either. There were bruises along my ribs too, making me wince when attempting a deep breath.

Wendy Doyle's freckled face flashed in my head, her menacing grin filling me with dark terror. They were just kids, but they'd inflicted damage, one of them having kicked me hard enough to bruise ribs. What else might they be capable of? I'd already planned my return to the church the first moment I had. But my next trip wouldn't be made alone.

As I dressed, Tiny butted me with his wet nose, reminding me about his walk. While no date had been set, I was sure he'd be leaving soon, with Lisa Pearson's health slowly improving.

"Going home soon?" I asked Tiny, torn by the idea as I took to scratching him behind the ears. Tiny's brown eyes saw me, his paw in my hand, his tail wagging. "Go for a walk?"

*

Reporters had picked up on the recent murders, the possibility of there being a serial killer on the loose. My body tensed as I entered the station. It was only a matter of time before we'd see them regularly, their clothes and figures familiar, their places and postures along the benches the same.

One of them raced toward me. "Any comment on the recent campground murders?"

"The investigation is ongoing," I answered, recognizing the reporter's face from previous cases, the frizz gone from his hair.

"What about danger to other tourists?" another reporter asked, the microphone near my chin, her face new and her voice scratchy. I brushed past and took hold of the gate. "Was there an incident?" she asked, leaning against me, looking intently. "Were you attacked?"

"No comment," I answered, making my way into the station, the gate latching shut with a metal clank, turning off the voices and ending this round of questions and answers. "Till next time," I said with a wave, my focus set on the scheduled meeting.

The conference room was filled with the sweet pastry smell of donuts and aromatic coffee, hitting me as soon as I entered. Ashtole had beat me to the station, and was standing up a stack of paper cups next to the coffee and creamers, the sugar packets and narrow wooden stirrers.

"Donut?" he offered, tilting a box of glazed delights, tempting me. When he saw my face, his smile went flat. "What happened there?"

"Dowd," I answered. "The kids I called you about."

"I heard you got attacked," Emanuel said. He gulped half a donut in a single bite. His mouth full, he added, "Heard you'd made a possible identification, Wendy Doyle?"

"The Doyle's kid did that?" Ashtole asked.

"Possibly," I answered, unable to confirm. "I never saw who actually hit me."

"That's not like any of the Doyle family I knew," Ashtole commented. "Then again, that was a long time ago."

"You didn't see Wendy Doyle?" Cheryl asked.

"Not quite. They ran off into the cornfields before my vision cleared," I answered, pouring a coffee, the steam rolling off the top, an invitation to drink it fast. "She was there though. She was one of a bunch of kids from the church that I believe attacked me."

"How convinced are you the kids are involved?" Ashtole asked, hands bracing his hips. Before I could answer, he shook his head, adding, "I can't even imagine what the press coverage would be like if word of this got out. News Flash: *Children of the Corn* cult in the beautiful Outer Banks."

I shrugged, knowing we had leads, but none ringing true, none of them standing above the others. "I only know they're involved. How exactly? We still have to figure it out."

"Nightmare," he said beneath his breath, taking a seat.

"The eye does look better," Nichelle said, entering the meeting room, a laptop in one hand, power and video cords draped over the other like a hank of yarn. When she reached a seat, she asked, "No sprinkles?"

"Free is free," Ashtole commented, sliding the donuts across the table.

"I'll have another," Cheryl said, poking her hand through the stack of case folders, the animal sacrifices now accompanied by her copy of the mugshot booklet.

"Morning," Tracy said cheerily, her eyes big when she saw the coffee and donuts. She grabbed a coffee and sat down.

I stood at the head of the table, plunking the remains of my mugshot booklet down with a slap. Cheryl followed me, doing the same, as did Emanuel and then Tracy. Ashtole picked up one of them and flipped through the pages.

"First, let's thank Mayor Ashtole for the donuts and coffee, and the additional company," I said.

The team raised cups and half-eaten donuts in a breakfast toast.

"Eager to be of some help," he said, motioning with his coffee. A warning look came to his face. The mayor sat up, his suit jacket fanning wide as he perched his elbows on the table. "I'm fielding concerns from the council. Specifically, the lack of progress. They're suggesting outside help."

I felt the eyes of the team on me, my neck warming. Inside I questioned the idea of asking for the help. I picked up the mugshot booklet, stitches and a bruise the only things I had to show for the effort. "Let's review where we are, and then determine next steps."

"Just so you know their 'suggestion' for outside help is more of an insistence," said Ashtole.

"Trust me, the thought had already crossed my mind," I told him, gauging the team's reaction. They didn't know it yet, but we were close to losing this case, and a part of me wondered if maybe we should. At the same time, I also felt we were homing in on the right path to a breakthrough.

Ashtole dropped the mugshot book, swiping his phone's screen, saying, "Then if you thought it as well, let's not waste another minute." The team's eyes shifted to him. "We can have the FBI here within the hour."

"Wait." I said, raising my voice, bracing the table, the stress of making a decision clouding my head with pressure. Eyes shifted back to me. "Daniel. Just wait."

"Why?" he asked. The stares returned to him, his glasses sliding to the end of his nose.

"Give us a couple of days?" I asked, searching the team for agreement.

Daniel took a deep breath, lips pinched white. "I might be able to buy you another day."

I held up two fingers. "Two?" I pleaded.

"We need a suspect. Bring *someone* in for questioning. Anyone," Ashtole demanded, standing briefly to air his jacket before moving to the whiteboard. With his left hand, he scribbled large letters on the board, spelling the name, Dowd. "Bring *him* in."

"Dowd?" I asked. I gestured disagreement and motioned to Nichelle, who understood and displayed the church videos. "We know where Dowd has been. He's got a solid alibi—"

"Then invite him!" He raised his brow, borrowing from our last meeting, having learned about the invitations. "Send an invitation. If he's innocent, it's him and you having a conversation. But if he's guilty, he'll balk, lawyer up, tell you to get a warrant. His response will tell us plenty."

"We've already made the request," I answered, frustration building. "More than a few times now."

"Invite him again," Ashtole answered, hands raised as he returned to the table. "Pester him and his church until they file a complaint. I'll handle the noise."

"We can certainly do that," I said, calm returning to my voice.

Ashtole stretched his arms like a scarecrow, palms up. "Now was that so difficult?" he asked, but didn't wait for me to reply. "It'll get you the time."

"I don't think it's Dowd though." The throb on my brow watered my eye and I carefully wiped a tear from my cheek. "But there is more going on there than we know."

"You only need to *question* him," Ashtole answered, his focus on his phone as he texted. "It'll give the council what they're looking for. Capeesh?"

"Capeesh," I answered. "Now let's talk about the victims." From the whiteboard, I erased the scribbles about the summer solstice, but kept the list of email addresses and victims' names. I added Heather and Charley Doyle. "Nichelle, what do you have on the Pearsons' background?"

"I found this," she answered, displaying a picture of a much thinner Peggy Pearson, a high-school yearbook photo, the credits listing drama club president and debate team beneath the name Margaret Jenkins. "It turns out, Peggy Pearson was a local."

"I thought the Pearson couple was from out of town?" Ashtole asked.

"A married Carl and Peggy Pearson were from out of town," I said.

Nichelle changed the picture to show a DMV record for Margaret Jenkins, saying, "But Margaret Jenkins grew up in the Outer Banks, marrying at an early age, taking her husband's surname, and moving west."

I erased the name Peggy Pearson, replacing it on the whiteboard with Margaret Jenkins. "Sharon Telly often mentioned her family was from the Outer Banks," I said, underlining the hometown names with blue. "Her brother had always lived here. I suspect his wife was also from the Outer Banks."

"Why?" Ashtole asked, his focus jumping across the team. "What am I missing?"

"The markings," Tracy answered.

Ashtole regarded the reply and looked to me for clarification.

I ran the blue marker around the whiteboard, circling the names. "They are all from the Outer Banks."

"Is that so?" he answered, his posture shifting with understanding, the strength of the connection gaining strength. "That is something. But we need to confirm about Caroline Telly."

Nichelle held her hand in the air, answering, "I found their engagement notice. It's from a local paper." The large display flashed with a newspaper clipping, a picture of a young couple, smiling, the engagement announcement dating back twelve years. "Darren Telly and Caroline Jones, who later became Caroline Telly."

"Both went to the same high school," Ashtole read from the clip, mumbling the words, searching for anything vital. "And they met while serving on a jury."

"Jury," I exclaimed, biting into it. "They met while serving on a jury?"

"Can't say I've heard that one before," Emanuel commented.

"Nichelle, do we know what case it was?" I asked.

She shook her head. "I've only got the newspaper clipping." Donut glaze on her lips, she said, "I'll see what I can find."

"All three victims in the fire were originally from the Outer Banks," I said, and fished out the arson report. "But only Caroline and Darren Telly were marked."

"But your friend may have also been marked," Tracy said. "The burns, the fire. There's no knowing for sure."

"That's true too," I said. "What do we have on Ben Hill's school record?"

Nichelle opened another yearbook photograph, this one showing an adolescent Benjamin Hill, the credits beneath his name listing newspaper and yearbook photographer. "Like the mayor told us, Ben Hill was also from the Outer Banks."

"The family grew up in these parts, but later moved out of state," Ashtole said.

"What about your friends?" I asked him, referring to Heather and William Doyle. We were onto something. Some of the team was standing, others sat on the edge of their seats. "You'd mentioned also knowing them."

"Heather Doyle," Ashtole answered with a rasp. He swallowed dryly and tried to wet his lips. "Her maiden name was Richards. Heather Richards."

"Anything?" I asked Nichelle. She continued typing, the screen flashed, the reflection in Ashtole's glasses changing colors. Heather Richards's high-school picture appeared, beneath it credits such as photography club and debate club.

"I went to school with her brother. Heather was a few years behind us." With a look of gloom, Ashtole turned away from the display. "She's from my hometown. She's from here."

"Do you still think this is a cult?" Tracy asked me. "Should we continue to investigate that idea?"

"Yes. Continue," I told them, the pain in my eye and ribs urging the response. "We'll tackle this from both sides—the possible suspects, and the victims. If I'm right, we'll find what we're looking for. Someone they all knew. Someone who wanted them dead."

CHAPTER THIRTY-THREE

I passed the reporters, their positions at the station entrance the same as the previous morning. Only today, there were more of them. A lot more. They looked oddly like the crows from the cornfields—perched with feet together, shoulders squared and beady eyes fixed in a constant state of search. I ignored the questions tumbling from their mouths as I made my way through the gate, latching it securely behind me and hurried to my desk.

A day had passed since a new round of invitations had gone to Dowd, his church surprising us with a quick reply. Word had gotten out about the church, the reporters connecting the names of the teens in the Amber Alerts with the deceased victims of the campground murders. A blog post had gained momentum during the late afternoon, the report listing the murders and mentioning the odd coincidence of the victims' adolescent sons and daughters having attended Dowd's church.

The mention of the kids in the press was unexpected, but may have urged the preacher into accepting our invitation. Lisa Pearson was inaccessible, but I suspected that one or more reporters had questioned Andrea Hill. She was underage, but while there were ethical boundaries crossed, the reporters had broken no laws. The hammer I wanted to bring down on them was in temper only, my position on the force completely useless in these matters.

On cue, Richard Dowd entered the station, the reporters instantly clamoring and jockeying for position. The preacher appeared differently than I'd seen in the church. He wasn't as tall as the person racing across the stage had seemed, but then again, a stage gives presence, and he'd had plenty with the addition of lights and his booming voice. He did have his jet-black hair in place, the wig fixed and the only hair on his person. I'd come to learn his condition was called alopecia, his a particularly rare form affecting his entire body. Large patches of Dowd's skin was as white as snow, giving more than one patrol officer and reporter a double take as the man approached the gate. He'd dressed formally for our meeting, opting for a three-piece suit in a light blue, with a turquoise vest and a pale-blue shirt to limit the contrast of his pale complexion.

Dowd's expression remained unchanged as the reporters pounced and surrounded him, vying to get close, bombarding him with questions about the recent murders and the possibility of teenagers being involved. I even heard a few questions about the upcoming summer solstice, one of the reporters impressing me with their witted theory matching one of our own.

I glanced toward our conference room, which had been converted into a kind of war room, the campground cases and everything else related covering the walls and table and monitors. I craned my neck until my muscles warned with a sharp cramp. But I was certain no reporter's eyes could see that far into the station to pick up on our leads, and risk compromising one of them.

A patrol officer fixed me with a look, her asking if she should intervene, the reporters smothering Dowd. I gave a subtle shake of my head, wanting to see how Dowd responded, and to read him and his reaction. In the minute since Dowd's arrival, the air had become charged, electric. He seemed to feed off the attention, a faint smile on his lips as he approached the gate without hesitation or reserve. I found his manner interesting, having seen even the strongest-willed suspects easily shaken by the onslaught of microphones and cameras and lights. But Dowd never flinched, never lost focus or step, and proceeded through the gate without need for help from us.

"Mr. Dowd," I said, extending my hand, a courtesy.

"Ms. White," I heard from behind Dowd, D.J. Reynolds appearing, his hand in mine, curly locks of hair flopped over his brow, his round cheeks pink.

I shifted focus to the man I'd met at the church, and who I'd come to know as the attendant, a glorified security guard. He caught my confusion, cocked his head and lifted a briefcase for me to see. "I'll be joining Mr. Dowd today as his council."

"You're a lawyer?" I asked with surprise. *The right of the people to be secure in their persons, houses, papers, and effects, against unreasonable searches*, I heard in my head, Mr. Reynolds's voice reciting the fourth amendment when I'd first met him at the church. I reminded him of my title again. "And it's detective."

"Of course," he said with a smile. "And, yes, I am Mr. Dowd's attorney, and will be representing him today."

"Mr. Dowd," a reporter yelled. "What of the children in your church, the teenagers?"

D.J. Reynolds put his arm on Dowd's shoulder, leading him away from the reporters, but Dowd stopped and turned to face the question. He raised one hand, two fingers up like a boy-scout pledge. "Our most precious of creations," he answered.

"Did they have anything to do with the campground murders?" another reporter hollered.

"We have turned away from our home—" Dowd began, but with his lawyer urged him toward me.

"This way," I said quietly.

Dowd's focus shifted to me, his gaze steady and intimidating. My stomach knotted.

"Are you *him*?" a reporter mocked.

Dowd's lawyer jumped, a reproachful look on his face. He took guard in front of Dowd as though rocks were in hand and poised.

"A furtive response when there is truth to be heard and seen," Dowd answered, using his hands to mime covering his ears and then his eyes. "But only if you can accept *Him* into your heart."

"Let's get moving," I demanded, raising my voice, having heard enough of whatever biblical chess game Dowd was playing with the reporters.

He followed me, turning away, his sly grin never fading.

As I made my way toward an interview room, the two men followed me, praying, lips moving, words in whisper, their faint prose a memory from my early years at my parents' church. When I reached the interview room and opened the door, Dowd's smile broadened. He'd enjoyed the exchange with the reporters, leaving me to wonder how much of him was truly holy, and how much was pure narcissism. I followed them inside. Nichelle was already in the room, her laptop hooked into a monitor we'd positioned opposite from where Dowd would sit. I left my emotions in the hall, and motioned for her to present pictures of the decedents while Dowd and his attorney took to sitting. Dowd paused, his body stuck as a morbid image of Benjamin Hill flashed on the screen. We followed it quickly with crime-scene photos of the Pearsons' bodies and then Heather Doyle and her husband, Charley, a close-up of the injuries to his face.

"And the purpose of these?" Dowd's attorney asked. He waved his hands flamboyantly, adding, "I'm assuming this is an attempt to shock my client."

"Or determine his reaction," I answered flatly, gauging Dowd's response to the images of the victims. Dowd cringed, but it came a moment too late. "Something like that."

"I've seen worse," Dowd offered, his comment surprising me.

"Is that right?" I asked, opening a folder, a single sheet inside with Dowd's name and his previous addresses, dating back five years. I held it in the air. "Where was that exactly?" I shook my head and didn't wait for a response. "There's not exactly a lot of information about you out there. In fact, I can't find much of anything."

"Is that why we're here?" his attorney asked, his hand on Dowd's arm, indicating to his client to say nothing unless given the okay. "As you've seen for yourselves, we do have pressing matters with our church. We've come as a courtesy, and I'd expect you to oblige with questions on point and pertinent to the purpose of this meeting."

"I'm just curious where your client's been the last five years." I said plainly.

"Previous addresses?" he asked, checking his watch, taking a moment to show Dowd. "If that is all you wanted to ask about, I'll have a list compiled to satisfy the last *ten* years and send it to you. We have another meeting." The men began to stand.

"Fair enough," I answered. Dowd's past, or lack of it, was on point, but not relevant to our questioning. I'd leave that to Nichelle to uncover, and to cross reference with any supplied lists. I slid the file across the table, the men following it like cats watching birds skitter along a hedge. "Here is your church's website." Nichelle updated the display, showing a registration form. "We've come to learn the adolescent sons and daughters of all the victims we've shown you today have been to your church."

Dowd and his lawyer exchanged looks. Dowd gave a nod to his lawyer, his lips tight. "And?" the lawyer questioned.

I went to the monitor, Nichelle refreshing the screen to list each victim's name next to their child's registration. "The timing, and the invitations sent from your church, are suspect."

"Invitations?" Dowd asked, turning to his lawyer, as though he'd never heard of them.

"Invitations," I repeated.

Dowd squinted when he looked at me, the whites of his eyes red. But not from crying or lack of sleep. I suspected it was part of his condition, the interview room's lighting making him uncomfortable, which could work to our favor.

"We have a service emailing campaign," the lawyer said, explaining it. Dowd nodded with understanding.

"Well these are more than just spam in an inbox," Nichelle commented sharply, opening the invitation sent to Wendy Doyle. "In fact, they appear to be quite personal."

I motioned to the injury on my eye, catching the lawyer's attention. "And the girl you issued the invitation to is responsible for this."

"Like I told you that evening, the security for Mr. Dowd and his belongings are all volunteers."

"And the invitation?" Nichelle asked. Dowd's lawyer silently opened his iPad, his fingers brushing the screen. When he was ready, he showed us. "Wendy Doyle's parents," he said, showing the same styled invitation, the same wording, one with the name Charley Doyle and a second with the name, Heather Doyle. Nichelle shook her head, checking her laptop screen. "Wait, I didn't see those invitations—"

"Didn't see what?" Dowd's lawyer asked, lowering his tablet, turning his ear in Nichelle's direction. His eyes narrowed, the corner of his mouth curling. When we didn't answer, he said, "I'm sure you understand me when I say we maintain very strict privacy controls on our technical infrastructure. Our IT security is managed by one of the top cyber firms in the country." Nichelle backed into her seat. "Questions have surfaced about donations from Ms. White. We had records of the donations but were unable to reconcile them. We also have an extended retention period for all server activity in the event a forensics investigation is deemed necessary. Would you clarify for us what it was you did not see? As well as where?"

My mouth went dry as Nichelle lifted her fingers from her laptop like a child caught with their hand in the cookie jar. A look of satisfaction came to Mr. Reynolds as my questions evaporated. Dowd's lawyer knew we'd been on the church's servers, that we'd planted an invitation for me and researched the teen's invitations. And following Nichelle's lead, someone in his organization had created invitations for all the victims too, plugging up any holes we could have used to question Dowd. I traded glances with Nichelle as she cleared the screen, her face blank and like stone.

I reframed my question. "The issue still remains of how it is these families were invited to your church, and then murdered."

"They're with *Him* now," Dowd answered, his lawyer softly gripping his client's arm.

The lawyer swiped his tablet's screen again and showed us a new page with dates and times and the address and picture of the church. Beneath the photographs the name, Trenton RV Rentals with a phone number—the name of the rental company we'd found early in the investigation. He was showing us an advertisement, a flyer about as generic as any I'd seen on the hundreds of telephone poles across the Outer Banks.

"If it's this one," the lawyer began, swiping again. "It is part of a sizable email campaign. Last I looked, it went to over twenty thousand recipients on the east coast."

The men stared, waiting for me to say something. They'd done their homework, leaving nothing we'd discovered useful. Resigned to salvage whatever might be, I asked the men point blank, "Do either of you have any reason to believe, or to suspect, a member of your staff or congregation could be involved with these murders?"

Dowd was about to speak when the lawyer indicated for him to remain silent, an inkling of hope stirring.

"Is there someone?"

"There're thousands," the lawyer began. "I'm sure you can understand, we don't have any insights into our congregation beyond our church."

"Do you believe someone in my church could do such things?" Dowd asked, his voice like a boy's. Reynolds tugged Dowd's arm again.

"I do," I told him. An absent look appeared on his face, telling me he wasn't aware of what we were discussing. With nothing more to ask, I added, "I want to thank you both for the help in clearing this up with us."

Nichelle's expression shifted to one of glum defeat as the men collected their things and made their way through the door. Outside, I heard the reporters clamoring again, leaving their perches as strobe lights flashed on the walls and a rush of footfalls echoed into the room.

"That did not go well," Nichelle said when the hallway noise dissipated.

"It did not," I agreed. "Dowd doesn't seem to know anything beyond what he's preaching. That, or it's all an act."

"The lawyer does," she added. "I know the invitations were only to the kids." She flipped through server entries, showing me rows of data. "The backend data, it's been updated."

"It had to be my invitation. We tipped them off," I said. "I should have known the lawyer would look into it. The surprise on his face when I showed up with an invitation should have told me."

"He guessed we'd been on their servers," she said, paging through a screen not shared from her laptop. Her brow rose and her chin dipped. "Oh shit. Look at this."

"What?"

She updated the room's monitor with a news report about Dowd's visit to the station.

"You're kidding me. The reporters posted something already?"

"Well, everything is real-time. Live feeds deliver the most clicks."

Children of Dowd, one of the headlines read, the report updating every few seconds, the reporter likely sitting in the station. Another read, *Possible cult presence in the Outer Banks.*

While our interview connecting invitations to minors had been a failure, Dowd's visit to the station may have done much more than we could have ever expected. We had nothing on Dowd and his church, but that didn't stop the press from convicting him. I bit my lip, a feeling of guilt troubling me as I read through the headlines, the live blog with terrible comments from readers, people believing the Outer Banks had a cult leader, comparing Dowd to Jim Jones and Charles Manson. What if Dowd's church was genuine? Did my answering Ashtole and the council cause us to jump to a conclusion? What if we were wrong?

CHAPTER THIRTY-FOUR

It wasn't long before Ashtole was in our company again, my team assembling in the conference room. The air was humid, the day's heat growing, the air-conditioning system pumping stale air. The conference-room table was littered with the case files Cheryl could never finish, along with the printed booklets of mugshots Jericho and I had worked. The donuts and coffee had been replaced by water bottles, energy drinks, and soda pop, the containers sweating in the thick humidity.

"Well, this is one way to keep a meeting short," the mayor said, loosening his tie and unbuttoning his shirt. And for the first time since I'd met Daniel Ashtole, I watched him remove his jacket. "I might have to go home and put on my Bermuda shorts if we don't get the AC fixed."

"Please sir, no," Emanuel begged, the room laughing. "Just no."

"Hey now," Daniel said, lifting his knee, daring to show some leg. "Might be pasty, but Judy finds them sexy."

"TMI sir," Cheryl warned. "Too much information."

"Afraid I'm going to have to agree," I told him.

"Fine. Have it your way," he said, taking his seat again.

"Children of Dowd," I said, announcing the reason for our meeting. On the screen, Nichelle posted a headline in big bold print. Ashtole's smile faded, his sentiment shared around the table. "Yeah, I know. This wasn't what anyone expected from the interview."

"Not at all," he offered, and then shrugged. "But is there any truth to it? Anything?"

"There was the attack on me," I said, starting us off, placing credibility where it was deserved.

"We've hit a dead end on the background checks," Emanuel said. "Richard Dowd has no history beyond the five years with his church."

"But the victims do," I said, sounding confident, leading the meeting in the direction I wanted. "Who the victims are and, in some cases, who they were, is where the answers are."

The door opened, Jericho filling the frame, looking handsome in his Marine Patrol uniform. I tried hiding my smile, glad to have him join the meeting. Marine Patrol jurisdiction was limited, but due to the Doyles being found on their yacht, their involvement was enough for us to cross paths.

"Daniel," he said, tilting his cap and entering. The mayor replied with a nod. "I thought I'd stop by. Marine Patrol has closed the case on the loose yacht, shifting the murder investigation to your hands."

"You're welcome to stay," I offered, glancing at each of the team. Tracy's face told me she'd like the addition, as did Emanuel, his having worked with Jericho before. Cheryl's eyes never left her phone, while I knew Nichelle was open to everything.

"Sure. I can take a look," Jericho answered, eyeing the whiteboard and the monitor. He turned to Ashtole, asking, "If it's okay with the mayor."

"By all means," Ashtole said, his usually chalky skin tinged pink in the warming room.

"As you can see, we've got a puzzle to solve," I said, continuing to brief the room. I underlined the letters and numbers that had marked the victims, asking, "Where in their history will we find the numbers 3 and 7 for the Tellys, the letter A for Peggy Pearson, an 8 for Ben Hill, and a letter O for Heather Doyle?"

"It still looks like gibberish to me," Emanuel said.

"That's because it is," Cheryl commented.

"How so?" I asked, challenging her.

She put her phone down, my question unexpected, her cheeks warming to match her hair. "What if they're bullshit?"

"Fake?" Ashtole asked, eyeglasses in hand, cleaning the lenses with his tie.

"Yeah," Cheryl replied. "I mean, what if the killer is purposely spinning up the investigation in different directions?"

"It's a viable possibility," I said. "The killer could be masking their motive."

"The press do have a lot of ideas about the murders," Tracy said.

"They do. But regardless of what's been printed and posted online, the letters and numbers have not been published," I said. "The meaning of the sequence inscribed on the victims is unknown."

"I heard summer solstice was a going theory," Jericho said.

Ashtole laughed though his nose, Jericho twisting to face him. Ashtole explained, "It's been considered, and the press is still working that angle."

"It's the kind of story that sells papers and mouse clicks," Jericho said.

I shook my head. "It does, and solstice is a lead we've exhausted."

"What's your lead now?" Jericho asked. He went to the monitor, the yearbook photos of the victims on the screen, along with the names of their schools. "They were all local?"

"Do any of the names look familiar?" I asked, his having been born and raised in the Outer Banks. He shook his head. "How about the schools?"

"The schools? Sure," he answered. "I know all the schools. When I was sheriff, we'd visit once a month."

"The victims inscribed with the numbers and letters—"

"Mutilated is more like it," the mayor interrupted.

"—*were* locals. That is, they lived here at one time," I said ponderously, an idea forming. "Nichelle, did you finish the search on the Tellys' jury case, the one they'd served together?"

"Public records are a needle in a haystack," Ashtole said, paddling the air, his balding head gleaming.

"The mayor is right. I found courthouse records," Nichelle said. "But there's so many of them. I also hit a huge roadblock when I tried searching the names directly."

"A roadblock?" I asked. "Aren't the court records in a database?"

"Not necessarily," Ashtole answered. "There was a time when every piece of paper was kept in a document, legal forms and court records, all scanned and saved on one system."

"A document management system," Nichelle said, nodding. "That explains a lot."

"How so?" I asked.

"Take a look," Nichelle answered, clicking on a folder, a list of files displayed, their document names without meaning. She selected one at random to show an archived trial record, legal forms filled with names and numbers and handwritten notes. "Notice the pages? They're images, like photographs."

"Which means they're not directly searchable," I said, disappointed.

"Well, I am able to search them using character recognition," she said, her explanation without enthusiasm. "I've already started, but it's going to take a really long time."

"Unfortunately, time isn't what we have."

"What jury?" Jericho asked.

"It was my friend Sharon's brother and sister-in-law," I answered. "They met while serving on a jury. Those files Nichelle has up there are the trial documents. And in one of them, we should find their names and find out what case they served on."

Nichelle split the screen, the list of trial documents on one side, an open case on the other, displaying a perpetrator's name, their photograph, and trial dates.

"That sure looks familiar," Jericho said, picking up one of our mugshot booklets.

"It does, doesn't it," I said, the painful reminder coming with a throb in my eye. I swiped my muddied copy from the table, the paper crinkling, and read the entries, comparing the list we'd created to the one on the screen.

"There's got to be a thousand cases tried during that time," Ashtole said gruffly. "It'd take—"

"Wait!" I blurted, running to the whiteboard, my heart thumping with huge, walloping beats. The team's focus was on me, following me as I picked up a red whiteboard marker and hastily drew circles around the clues the killer gave us. The sudden excitement had me near tongue-tied, but I managed to call out the letters and numbers. "3, 7, A, 8, and O. What do these look like to you guys?"

The room exchanged glances, their lips moving as they recited them. A murmur, "A… O, 3."

"A little more?" Ashtole urged, making a come-along motion.

I jabbed the board then pointed at the screen. "Look at the documents," I said, not wanting to give away the answer. Eyes were wide, some empty, others squinting. I went to the screen my fingers beneath the files.

"The filenames *are* the docket numbers," Jericho said. "The letters and numbers are referring to a trial."

"But the nomenclature—" Ashtole began, stopping, his focus darting from the screen to the whiteboard and back. "Yeah, I guess it could work."

"It does work," I said adamantly. "When the court records were scanned to archive them, the trial's docket number was used to identify the document."

"I think you're right," Nichelle said, hopping in her seat and clicking through another list.

"Filter the list with the numbers and letters we have," I instructed, feeling strong about this.

The keyboard rattled with Nichelle's typing. "Ready?" she asked the room, her finger poised over the keyboard's Enter key.

We held our breaths as I signaled to go. The screen emptied with a flash of white, an hourglass cursor appearing at the center.

"Still could take—" Ashtole began, but never finished.

"It's done," Nichelle said, her voice hitched with excitement. "We've got around a hundred trials with docket numbers that include the letters and numbers supplied."

"Now, use the recognition you mentioned to search those results and include the Tellys' names along with Benjamin Hill," I said. "If I'm right, that'll get us to a single case."

Nichelle did as asked, keyboard rattling, reworking the query while we patiently waited. When her finger was poised over the Enter key, she asked, "Ready?"

"One case," I said, muttering to myself. I gave the signal, the screen flashing again, the hourglass appearing, the room waiting. A minute went by, the heat in the room ratcheting up, the query's execution showing nothing but a spinning hourglass.

"What happened?" Ashtole asked, his taking to a window, cracking it open.

"It'll take longer, I'm scraping fields, doing character recognition and a few regular expressions," Nichelle answered, justifying.

"One!" I announced when the results returned. I glanced warmly at Jericho and then the booklets, our efforts paying off after all. "If I'm right, this is the trial both Caroline and Darren Telly served as jurors."

"Open it," Ashtole asked, going over to the screen. Nichelle clicked on the document, court forms appeared, the name Caroline Jones in one of the fields. "I don't recognize that name."

"She got married. Her name changed to Caroline Telly, Darren's wife. Scroll down," I said. Nichelle scrolled until the name Benjamin Hill showed, followed by Heather Richards and Darren Telly. All the victims who were marked were listed. "Our victims."

Daniel jerked his glasses from his nose and wiped his eyes as he mumbled something under his breath. He was visibly shaken. Enough so that I was suddenly afraid for him, but didn't know why.

"What is it Daniel?" I asked.

"This was bound to happen," he said. "Eventually."

"What?"

"What case is this?" he asked, panic in his voice.

"Upper left," I told Nichelle, her fumbling with the mouse, zooming in and out, searching the form.

"Upper left corner, that's where the court details are," Daniel said, demand in his voice.

"There they are!" Nichelle answered, the numbers and letters exploding on the screen. "The file name *is* the docket number."

"The killer is marking each jury victim with part of the docket number, directly linking their murders to this case," I said, trying to contain my excitement over a lead with corroborating evidence.

"Jesus!" Ashtole said, returning to the table and plunking into his chair.

"That's one hell of a find," Emanuel said. "Nice job."

"Thanks," Nichelle said, a smile stretching from ear to ear. She highlighted the jury names. "We've got our list of men and women still in danger."

"Already on it," I said, urgently sending the names to get a security detail in place. "We'll have to find them first, but something tells me they're visiting the Outer Banks this summer."

"I'll do a reverse lookup against the church server," Nichelle said.

My focus shifted back to Daniel, his color gone, his skin clammy. "Mayor?" I asked, raising my voice with immediate concern for his health. He said nothing but acknowledged me, letting me know he was okay. "Do you know this case?"

"Look at the court date," Jericho said. "Daniel, when did you get sworn in as an assistant district attorney?"

"Thankless job," the mayor answered, sounding more like himself. He read the form on the screen. "That date sounds about right."

"Do you remember this one?" Tracy asked, the room's focus shifting to the mayor. "I mean this trial?"

"I think I do," he answered, his words soft, a near whisper. Ashtole twirled his hand above his head, asking, "Zoom out so we can see the entire document."

Nichelle did as he asked, the sides and top and bottom coming into focus.

"Who was the defendant?" I asked.

The court form blurred, shrank briefly, then bounced back and refocused. While the victims had been vacationers now, years earlier, they'd all met. I found Lisa Pearson's mother, Margaret Jenkins—she'd later go by the name Peggy Pearson. She was jury seat number two. Also on the list of names, Ben Hill, Heather Doyle, along with Darren Telly, Sharon's brother, and Caroline Jones, who would later become Caroline Telly, Darren's wife. They were jury seat numbers five and six. While the victims meeting in the past had been brief, they'd worked side by side on the trial and conviction of a man named Ethan Hughs.

"I got the name, give me a minute to bring up his record," Nichelle said.

"Scroll to the right," Jericho asked. Nichelle obliged, the prosecuting attorney's name appearing. "Daniel Ashtole."

"Mayor?" I asked, his gaze wandering to the open window, his eyes glazed and unfocused.

"Daniel?" Jericho asked.

"Would you guys give me a second," the mayor barked, gripping his forehead. "I'm trying to remember the details."

"Ten years for sexual misconduct with a minor," Nichelle said, refreshing the screen with additional court papers, along with a mugshot of the defendant, Ethan Hughs—barely an adult, light-colored hair, thick glasses, and a narrow face, his chin coming to a point. "He was released from prison seven years ago."

"Where is he now?" Jericho asked. He went to the whiteboard, putting the full docket number next to the inscribed numbers and letters. And at the top, in large print, he wrote: Ethan Hughs.

"Nowhere?" Nichelle answered with a question.

"There's got to be an address," I said, leaning over her shoulder, searching the multiple windows. "A DMV record, a work release or something?"

"Check the parole board," Emanuel offered. "If he's been released from prison, parole officer visits and all the details of a parolee will follow him."

"No parole," Nichelle said with surprise, the room's focus shifting to her. "It says here, Ethan Hughs was offered parole hearings, beginning with the fourth year of his term."

"He served his full term," Emanuel said, nodding his head. "He knew."

"Knew what?" Tracy asked.

"An ex-con isn't exactly free once they're released on parole," Emanuel explained. "There's the parole officer, the check-ins, the rules about where you work and who you're with. And most of your rights remain locked up until cleared of the parole agreement."

"And if you serve full term?" she asked.

"Then you've served your time," Ashtole answered glumly. "You're free with all rights afforded you under the constitution."

"What about registering as a sex offender?" I asked.

Ashtole's brow rose, "Any record of other offenses?"

The room quietened while Nichelle typed, the screen changing faster than I could follow. When the changes settled, she said, "No. Just the one. And the address is a dead end." She opened a screen with a map. "There's no other record of his registering except for the one time. The man is a ghost."

"Well, our ghost is now our prime suspect," I said, underlining his name on the whiteboard. "Best guess, he's a member of the church congregation, or possibly working in their organization. He knew these families would be in the Outer Banks. He knew they'd been issued with invitations."

"A ghost." Ashtole was as white as a sheet, fright plastered on his face. "Judge Malone's been deceased five years. District Attorney Johnson, my old boss, he's hanging his hat in the Florida these days. So that leaves me. I'm still here. My family is here. And so is Ethan Hughs."

CHAPTER THIRTY-FIVE

We stayed in the conference room until the station's ventilation belched a cold breath, making us all feel a bit more reasonable in the overwhelming heat. Ashtole only stayed an additional hour, his demeanor off, visibly shaken, sweating, and weary. He was afraid. It was a huge discovery—the archived court filing, the docket number, and the victims all being part of a jury that had put Ethan Hughs behind bars. Where would his revenge stop? The DA? The assistant DA? Today, that person was our mayor and a security detail was immediately dispatched for Daniel Ashtole and his family.

I thought of Sharon Telly's brother and sister-in-law, and their engagement announcement, the mention of their quirky meeting as jurors serving on the same panel. It hurt inside me, thinking about Sharon, but there was also resolution in our finding a puzzle piece that fit—the brother and sister-in-law marked with values from the case docket number.

Six jurors remained on the list. There were jury alternates as well. A quarter of the station was working to find them, notify them, and provide security details, wherever they were. And for the rest of us, we were searching for a ghost: Ethan Hughs. In our digital world of record keeping and personnel tracking, the man didn't exist after his release from prison. Maybe ghosts were real. And maybe they were sour with revenge, and capable of murder.

*

Of the remaining jurors, two were immediately identified through motor vehicle records, Nichelle using one of many of the state's databases to get us addresses, places of work, all the details to make contact. Justin Blake and Tina Sommers had remained in the Outer Banks and lived in close vicinity to the station. As the team researched the other jurors, and the alternates, I volunteered to visit Tina Sommers, who was now the proprietor of a shop on the boardwalk. It was a choice of convenience for me, my having a meeting there with Hannah's father. I'd avoided Ronald for as long as I possibly could, but his latest message said he urgently needed to meet, that it was time sensitive, and that it involved Hannah. I had to go.

I met Tina Sommers at her workplace, a nail and hair salon near the edge of town, a stone's throw off the boardwalk entrance and within walking distance of my apartment. Unlike in our conference room, the salon's air conditioning stirred the strong smells of shampoos, hairspray and nail polish. The narrow room was lined with wide mirrors and chairs that backed into low-hanging shampoo bowls, the walls plastered with pictures of models showing off fingernail designs and hairstyles, some outrageous, and one of them looking much like the kind Dr. Swales wore.

Tina met me at the door, her face round and smiling and heavily made up. Her hairstyle was tall and sculpted and unmoving. She greeted me warmly, handing me her card. I returned the gesture, handing her a picture of Ethan Hughs. Her smile faded at once as she recalled the details of the case, telling me it was the only time she'd served on a jury, and that she'd never forget it. She went on to explain how she'd voted a *not guilty*, but was eventually made to believe she needed to change her mind. We spoke for less than ten minutes, her shedding some light on what went on in the courtroom back then. A hair appointment cut our time short, but I assured her there would be a security detail assigned for her safety.

*

I made my way onto the boardwalk, entering the bustling foot traffic, instantly feeling out of place. I'd gone dressed for the station while everyone else had dressed for sun and surf and boardwalk fun. A man carrying a rack of cotton-candy clouds bumped me, his painted clown face putting on a frown when I cursed beneath my breath. He squeezed his red nose, the bulbous thing sounding a tiny horn. He mimed a smile, urging me to put on a happy face for him. I did, eager to see him move on, an air of carnival thick as though a traveling circus had come to town and spilled its cars. There was the smell of popcorn and roasting peanuts, of sweet confections and hotdogs. And the games, the bells and whistles and stuffed prizes handed to clutching fingers. It didn't matter what the calendar said, that it was early in the season, the Outer Banks was full today.

It was his dimples I saw first. It helped that Ronald was taller than most, a full head and neck above the flocks of tourists crowding the boardwalk. He waved toward me, but I wouldn't smile, not for him.

"Is it always like this?" he asked, his lips suddenly on mine. I pulled away in shock. Ronald gave me space, disappointed understanding in his expression. "It's good to see you."

"I'm here as a courtesy, for Hannah," I said. Jericho was on my mind, and I wanted to establish where I was before we continued. "We're clear?"

He nodded, then offered, "I got us a table," he said, pointing to a boardwalk cafe with tables and chairs in front.

"That's nice," I said, waving the heat from my face as we took to the chairs, him sitting across from me. "I have to tell you, I'm with someone."

Ronald fixed me with a look, his lips pinched, nodding slowly. "The guy from the hospital?"

"Yeah," I said, a sharp flick of sunlight catching my eyes, a reflection from a lens across the boardwalk. I shielded my face and moved my chair to avoid the light. "I want to be upfront with you. I want to set expectations."

"I was involved with someone too," Ronald told me, a suggestive look in his eyes.

Distant jealousy stirred deep in my gut, the uncomfortable gnaw a surprise emotion given how long we'd been apart. I guess in all the years alone, all the years of working Hannah's case, I'd never considered Ronald with anyone else.

His eyes became glassy, his breath choppy. "Her name was Renee. Renee Walsh. We never married, but we were together a long time."

I sensed the sadness, and noticed his fidgeting with his hands, pulling on his fingers, a tell whenever he was bothered.

"Ronald, what happened?" I asked, genuinely curious.

"Cancer." He swiped at his eye, his knee bouncing—another of his tells. His stare went to the passing crowd, a curtain of color and noise blocking the beaches and boardwalks. "It took five years, but she fought hard. Fought it every day—"

He couldn't finish. I cautiously took his hand, hurting for him. While we'd had a terrible break-up, it bothered me to see him so upset, as it would seeing anyone this upset. I squeezed his fingers until he looked at me. "Ronald, I'm so sorry for your loss."

The corner of his mouth lifted, a dimple playing peek-a-boo. "It's been a few years, but I still love her."

As I looked at him with sympathy, razor-sharp light cut into my eyes, blinding me again, the sun at the highest point in the day. "Sorry," I said, moving my chair again, positioning it so we were next to one another. It wasn't ideal, but it worked.

A waiter joined us, delivering iced coffees and mounds of ice cream, Ronald's a traditional fare of chocolate, vanilla, and strawberry, and mine a mountain of mint-chocolate chip with pralines and cream. I traded looks with Robert, awestruck by the unexpected delivery.

"I took the liberty of ordering ahead. Your favorite."

"You did, didn't you," I said, finding the gesture sweet. "You remembered."

"Of course," he said with a mouthful of ice cream, whipped topping bouncing on his upper lip. Without thought, a muscle memory perhaps, I swiped the topping with my finger. He caught my hand, adding, "Casey, I remember everything."

I didn't pull away from the touch, him being genuine, sincere. A moment passed, and I took my hand back to shovel a mouthful of mint-chocolate chip. "It's been years," I said, the cold striking between my eyes with a relenting brain freeze. I squinted at the pain, Ronald laughing.

"You still get those?"

"Yeah. I guess I do," I said, unable to recall the last time I'd had such a painful delight in the middle of the day. I shoveled two more mouthfuls, suddenly ravenous for more. "This tastes amazing," I said, vaguely aware of my wearing the stupidest grin with ice cream on my chin.

Ronald's smile remained, melting the apprehension I'd carried to our meeting, the moment warm and brief and a flashback from a better time. We blurted a laugh then, both of us finding a place that was comfortable. And it was good.

As much as I wanted to sit on the boardwalk and eat ice cream, I had a case to solve and rushed another bite. Ronald noticed, a worried look replacing the smile. "What's the matter?"

"Listen, I have to keep this short. What was it you wanted to talk about?"

"Tell me about her," he said, the sun melting the ice cream fast, sweat ticking on my scalp. "Did you see her?"

"Only briefly," I answered, the image of her fleeting. "In pictures involving a case last summer."

"I read about it," he said with a frown, more of the whipped topping on the whiskers of his chin. I lifted a napkin as he tilted his chin, the two of us carrying on a conversation and acting like an old married couple. It was easy to fall back into a groove with him. "Terrible thinking our daughter was a part of it."

Another flash of light struck my eyes, the sun catching glass from someone in the crowd. I shielded my face, and told him, "She—" I stopped then, looking up at him, a hearing aid in his ear, a curly cord snaking into the back of his shirt. I straightened, asking, "Is that a hearing aid?"

Ronald cupped his ear, a blade of light crossing his face. When the hearing aid popped out, the wire following, I saw the end connected to a clip on his shirt. "I have to wear it sometimes."

But I knew his words were a lie. I knew what I was looking at. "Are you recording this?" I demanded, confusion rushing through my head. "Who? Who is listening?"

"Detective Casey White," I heard as light pierced my eyes again, the sun's flare turning everything white. "Can you tell us more about your search for Hannah?"

"What the hell is this?" I shouted, jumping up from the table, green shadows in my sight. A blink, and I saw the faces of a man and woman on the other side of the table. My breath was hot, asking, "Who are you?"

"We're with a micro-blogging team, Foster and Kelly. We have half a million subscribers to our podcast, and we're ranked number three across the true crime genre."

I was silent, my whole body suddenly raging with anger. Ronald's interests were his own. He'd set me up.

"We're also recording video of this meeting for an upcoming true crime documentary to be streamed online."

I turned to Ronald, an animal reflex taking over, and toppled the table, the ice cream raining over the reporter, the cameraman's mouth gaping.

"How could you do this?" I spoke coldly to my ex-husband, his expression empty, vanilla and chocolate and strawberry dripping. "How dare you!"

"Maybe if Hannah sees us together," he said, pleading. "Then she'll want to talk."

"This is great footage," the cameraman said, escaping the mess, panning the camera while continuing to film us. "Especially the whipped topping. What a personal touch."

"You can't use any of it without my consent," I barked, knowing it was an empty threat. Revolted, I kicked the chair out of my way, leaving the three of them.

I shoved my way through the crowd, needing to get as far away as possible, tears stretching and pulling my view as deep sobs began. *How could he do that? How? He used me. He used us.*

And as I made my way across the boardwalk, deciding on the beach and a walk back to my place, I heard Ronald call to me. I refused to turn back and staggered down the wooden ramp until my feet hit the sand. It hurt to breathe, my lungs burning, my chest pounding. It felt as if something might break inside me.

A twisted thought entered my mind. Were they right? Would it help if Hannah saw us together? I shook my head, swiping the tears, the idea of it feeling wrong. Hannah's story was already out there, and it was a popular one. This wasn't the first-time reporters had cornered me, and I was sure it wouldn't be the last.

I reached the waves edging the beach, seawater breaking, the white foam racing toward me. A sandpiper landed near, mottled feathers, brown and black, eyeing me cautiously while it pecked the sand in search of food. I plunked onto my bottom, breath shuddering.

I'd let my guard down and allowed Ronald to hurt me again. I should have known better, and that hurt more than anything. The sandpiper skittered along, its yellowed legs reflecting in the wet sand, ignoring my mix of laughter and cries. As my tears dried, any old, sentimental feelings for Ronald were gone, replaced by my temper. I shook my head, the encounter a much-needed one. I'd been reminded of his true colors.

CHAPTER THIRTY-SIX

The rage toward Ronald steeped deep inside me like a cauldron of sour stew. As upset as I felt, I had the Hughs case to work, Nichelle texting me that she'd finished one of my asks. I could no longer call on Sharon Telly to age enhance photographs, and instead asked Nichelle to use some of her technical magic to do the same. She'd completed the work, printing aged pictures of Ethan Hughs, using the single mugshot we had from his case file. With his updated picture, and with hours remaining in the day, I wanted to go again to the church to determine if Hughs came to the Outer Banks with the church's congregation.

As I entered the station, I ducked the usual suspects, the reporters' questions erupting in chaos, asking about the Children of Dowd and the possibility of a connection to the campground murders. In the rear of the pack, a reporter asked about Hannah, and the latest news of her whereabouts. The question stopped me dead, the shift unexpected. I pinched my mouth shut, saying nothing, and continued forward with my head down, eager to reach Nichelle's desk. I shoved open the gate, the back of it slapping the rail with a clashing thump, hushing the reporters with an unintended message. I felt them disperse and recede into the shadows like crows returning to their perches to roost and await their next target.

"Got a minute?" Nichelle asked, her tone urgent and her face telling me it was important.

"I was just coming over to pick up the Hughs pictures," I answered. Her brow furrowed, a frown forming. I took a guess, asking, "Printer problem? Text me it instead. I can use my phone."

She shook her head. "That's not it. I've got the prints. I'll text the picture too."

"Wonderful," I said. She flashed a brief smile, her face returning to a scowl. She had bad news to tell me. I clenched my hands, nerves shook. "What is it?"

"Casey, I think you need to see this."

"From the looks of you, it can't be good," I said, trying not to show any emotion, slipping my gun and holster from my hip, along with my badge and locking them in my drawer. Nichelle didn't reply, didn't offer any clues to what the news was. When I was ready, we went to her desk, me dragging my chair behind me, one of the wheels spinning and sounding a screech. "What do you have?"

"First, the pictures," she said, handing me a stack of prints. The composite she'd made included the original mugshot of Hughs tucked in the upper left corner. The rest of the page showed the age-enhanced photograph, adding the years since his arrest, a slight sag in his jawline, pouchy eyes, his hair thinning and going gray. It was exceptional work.

"Nichelle, this is brilliant." I expected to see her pleased with the compliment, but she only gave me a nod. "You sent this out, got the APB issued?" Another nod. I lowered my head, encouraging her to talk to me.

"It's about your daughter—" she began but stopped and shook her head. She rolled herself into a soft ribbon of afternoon light, the orange and yellow turning her skin bronze and her eyes golden. She was nervous, which put me more on edge.

"It's okay," I assured her. "Whatever you have, I can take it."

It was a lie.

"I hope you don't mind, but I've been following your story... yours and your daughter's," Nichelle said, her fingers sweeping across the keys, a second monitor coming to life and showing lists of websites with my name, along with Hannah's and a few with Ronald's.

"What am I looking at?" I asked, the links seemingly endless, the list of them deep.

"They're mostly blogs, forums, and alerts to help track sightings. We also post theories and do a kind of an online sleuthing," she answered with a short laugh through her nose.

"Who's *we*?" I asked, feeling unnerved. "What have you found?"

She pulled up another page with posts and comments, discussions about Hannah, her sightings, a map near the top showing where she'd been, and a collection of video footage, security-camera closed-circuit television mostly, each showing a possible sighting.

"You and your daughter have quite the following."

I looked at her, feeling peculiar, uncertainty growing. "I see."

She tilted her head, asking, "You don't know about these?" I shook my head. "This is one of the bigger sleuth groups. We work cold cases together, identify clues, pick apart any public surveillance videos, find breadcrumbs, that sort of thing."

"You mean all these people... they're investigating me and Hannah and my ex-husband?" The idea of it felt invasive and left me put-off—an online community working my daughter's case, and there being so many eyes on my family's life. But extra eyes meant extra help and extra clues. I shouldn't have been quick to knock a gift when given.

Nichelle heard the concern in my tone, answering, "No. I mean, not directly. More what happened and your search for your daughter."

I shook my head. "You're right, I had no idea this existed." Bashfulness aside, I drank in the screen, the links, all of it. There was help in these pages, help I wish I'd known about.

"Power of social media." Nichelle flipped through a screen. "I should have mentioned my involvement earlier, but I was sure you knew about them."

I rubbed her arm, a sense of comfort coming to me about the idea. "It's fine," I said. I found her eyes, adding, "In the future, don't hesitate about sharing. We've no room for shyness here."

"I won't," she answered with a slight smile. "This isn't what I wanted to show you though."

"No?" I asked, concern returning.

"It's about a video that showed up. Posted in the last hour."

"Go ahead," I told her, nudging my chin toward the monitor.

She flicked the keyboard, and on her screen I saw the video—it was me laughing, cleaning whipped toppings from my ex-husband's face, the two of us looking like a cozy couple enjoying an afternoon on the boardwalk. My heart sank like a stone, the two of us appearing as if we were on a date.

"How?" I asked, gripping the arms of my chair, squeezing until my knuckles turned painfully white. "This was only a few hours ago."

"It's a newer podcast, along with a corresponding blogger."

Cotton filled my mouth and throat, stealing every drop of saliva. "I can't believe they posted it!" I said, my voice hushed and scratchy.

She took hold of my seat and jerked my chair, rolling it until it bumped hers. I didn't understand the movement until she lowered her monitor and angled it so only we could see the video. "Over there," she instructed, and motioned to the sheriff's office.

I sat up, my eyes breaching the cubical wall, and found Jericho with Sheriff Petro and Mayor Ashtole, the small office crowded. "Shit, I forgot he had a meeting. He might be running for sheriff again," I said under my breath. I glared at Nichelle, demanding, "But you didn't hear that from me."

"No worries," she told me, and returned to her monitor. "But what are you going to do about that?"

"Can you take it down?" I asked, knowing the answer, but feeling desperate.

She shook her head. "I would've by now if I could."

"What can I do?" I said in a heated whisper. I glanced at Jericho again. He didn't deserve to find the video, or have someone show it to him. "The best course is honesty. I'll have to tell him. I'll tell him exactly what happened."

"Is there more?" she asked, her tone implying guilt, as though I'd been having an affair.

"Of course not," I snapped. "We met to discuss Hannah. They're only showing a part that makes it appear completely different than what it was."

"Then that's all you tell him."

I searched the online post, my insides hurting, the video of me and Ronald together already showing over five thousand views. "There's that many people watching this stuff?"

Nichelle raised her brow. "You and your daughter are a very popular case."

"And how is this even relevant to Hannah's case?"

"They'll only show what works best for them, and garners views," she said. She pointed to the view count, the two of us watching as it bumped up again. "The highest click counts are in the timelines of the post."

"The timelines," I repeated, knowing how bad the timing actually was. I looked for Jericho again, cold dread making me feel weak. What was he going to think if he saw the video? The context of the snippet posted could be easily misconstrued. "I'd say the timeline downright sucks."

"I wish I had something better to tell you," she said, her hand on mine. "Maybe Jericho didn't see it yet."

"But nothing happened," I said, talking to myself, shaking my head, the video playback stuck on an image of me smiling at Ronald.

Nichelle jumped, flicking her keyboard, changing the screen to show a spreadsheet. "Sir," she said, looking behind me.

"I thought that was you," Jericho said, giving Nichelle a nod, his attention on me. "Afternoon plans?"

His gaze went to the Ethan Hughs sheets. I handed him one, my tongue feeling fat and clumsy. "The church to canvas the crowd, show them Hughs's picture. I stood and turned to Nichelle, adding, "We'll review more of the numbers later."

"I'm off the rest of the day if you can take a break?" Jericho asked, his fingers brushing against my hand, his touch warm and gentle.

"Are you up for a drive?" I asked, believing a car ride alone might be the best place to get ahead of the video's story. "We can grab a bite at the diner after, before your shift."

"Lead the way," he answered, my feet clumsy like my tongue as I struggled to roll my chair back into my cubical, bouncing the squeaky wheel against my toes.

"Thanks, Nichelle," I said without looking at her. I faced Jericho, asking, "I'll meet you outside?" I pitched my thumb toward the ladies' room. "I need a rest stop first."

"Sure. See you outside."

I didn't need the rest room. I couldn't have the two of us making our way through the flock of reporters and chance one or more of them having seen the micro blogger's story. Questions about Hannah's case were a constant. Adding Ronald, along with the posted video, would raise a circus of new ones. I didn't want to risk Jericho hearing a half truth. I needed to tell him myself.

CHAPTER THIRTY-SEVEN

"I saw the video," Jericho said, breaking our quiet drive, my mind collapsing on his words.

I took my eyes off the road, peering over to him, his face without expression, his gaze fixed on the cornfields as we approached the rundown convenience store.

"Wait! Stop here!"

I did as he asked, afraid to say anything. The single neon sign was on, and sitting beneath it one dungaree leg draped over the other, the clerk I'd questioned when first investigating Lisa Pearson's disappearance. "Listen, Jericho, I wanted to talk to you about the video. I wanted to tell you what really happened. They're only—"

"It's fine," he said, cutting me off, opening the car door and exiting without giving me a chance to explain. When it was closed, he perched his elbows on the window, stooping low enough for me to see him. "Do you want anything?"

I wanted to tell him what happened, but instead, I answered, "A cola?" I tried to gauge him, read him like I could read people when I was questioning them. But I couldn't do it, my nerves acting as a guard, and throwing my sense out of whack. I suppose it was because I was trying to gauge someone I was in love with, and if there was one thing that can blind, it's love. "A bag of chips too?"

He clapped his hand on the door frame. "Sure." He stood and strolled to the porch, dust kicking from the heels of his shoes. The clerk followed Jericho inside, leaving me to watch them through the store's front windows, the filth on the glass hiding all but the faintest of images, a shadow of Jericho moving from the front to the back and returning, his hands filling as he passed the shelves.

I rolled down my window, the afternoon's heat ballooning. It'd pop soon, angry storms marching from west to east, daring to strike in the next few hours. In the roadside silence, trilling cicadas came to life, along with a woodpecker hammering mercilessly against a nearby tree. Before long, batting wings flew above my car, the cornfield crows perching on the convenience store's rain gutters, the sheet metal sagging as they cawed to one another and hunched their feathered shoulders to follow Jericho exiting the store.

"That was quick," I said as he jumped in the car. He stayed quiet and avoided eye contact, handing me a cold soda bottle. I thought I was beginning to understand why we stopped. He needed to stop. He needed to get out, and to walk off whatever ill words were coming to him. "Look, just say it!"

"Say what?" he asked, raising his voice suddenly, gooseflesh rising as I was put on guard. I pushed back into the door, giving us space. In our time together, I'd never seen him outwardly angry. "What do you want me to tell you? That I'm upset? That I'm fucking embarrassed?"

Tears pricked my eyes, his expression like a boy's, my chest aching. I put my hands in the air. "Jericho, please. The video, it isn't showing everything."

"Well, thank God for that!" he shouted, assuming the worst, the snarky remark intentionally hurtful.

"That's not fair!" I argued, my voice matching his.

"Well..." he began, shoving his foot against the car floor, searching for another pithy response. "There's a lot that isn't fair."

I took his hand, daring the touch, squeezing it, insisting he look at me. The air was hot, both of us sweating. But I held his fingers tight and waited until he gave in, his eyes darting past me before finally settling steady with mine.

"That video, the whole thing was a setup," I said.

"What do you mean, a setup?"

"Ronald," I began, swallowing hard, the hurt from his betrayal paling compared to this. "He used me to improve the podcast ratings, to get more online views and clicks and whatever else they do to make money."

"It was the podcast?"

"That producer woman has a blog and that's the video they were making. They're producing some kind of docudrama. Only. I didn't know."

"But you were there."

"I met Ronald to discuss Hannah. He'd told me he had something urgent to tell me. Ronald set up the place, the ice cream, all of it. What the video doesn't show is the reporter and cameraman wearing the ice cream when I stormed out of there."

"Wearing it?" Jericho asked, a brow raised.

"I threw it at them," I answered, the words catching me funny, the tension easing. "Threw the whole table with it too."

"Good," he said, beginning to relax. He leaned over the center console, taking both of my hands in his. "Casey, you're the first person I've been with since my wife. I just want you to be honest with me."

"Same," I told him, running my fingers through his hair. He leaned into my touch, kissing my palm. "But you have to understand, Ronald is Hannah's father. I can't help that."

"I get it. I understand."

"And I'll do better to avoid any of his bullshit. Especially the bloggers. What a bunch of assholes—"

"You that cop!?" a loud voice hollered. I jumped at the sound, the store clerk in my window, his toothpick dangling from his gray lips. "Yeah, yeah. That's you. You was the one who'd asked me 'bout that missing girl."

"Yes, sir. I am," I answered. "She was found."

He waved a flabby arm, the skin limp and mottled with liver spots. "Yup. I seen that on the tube." He put his hands on the lip of the car door—nails yellowed and chipped, fingers browned with tobacco stains. "I wanted to ask about that church I gave directions to. Wanted to ask ya about that preacher I'd seen on the tube too. 'Children of Dowd' or whatever it is they saying."

"Richard Dowd?" I asked, wanting clarification. The old man's eyes swam slowly toward the direction of the church, the whites of them a faint yellow, matching the color of his skin. "What about him?"

"Well, when that news come on, the lot of them stocked up their campers and took off."

Dowd took off? The congregation? I started my car and thumped the gas pedal, revving the motor. "You saw this?" I asked, fearing we'd lost our chances of finding Ethan Hughs.

"Like they was some kind of circus. Folded up their tents, emptied my shelves, and whamo!" he answered, slapping his hands with a loud clap. "Damn near cleaned me out too."

"When?" I asked, raising my voice as I shoved the car's shifter into reverse. The car lurched backward, causing the old man to jump out of the way. I repeated with a yell, "When!?"

He scratched his chin, counting. "Gotta be near a day now."

"Thanks!" I shouted, not waiting to hear anything more. I floored the gas pedal, spinning the rear wheels until dirt and stones pelted the underside of the car.

"Take it easy!" Jericho hollered, bracing the dashboard, slipping sideways across the vinyl seat. He clutched a safety strap and buckled it, yelling out the passenger window, "Thank you!"

We had another few miles before the church, and reached the intersection with the plowed fields and farm workers. A blur of cornstalks flew by the car windows, the hills coming next, the tallest of them ahead of me, the words about the video and Ronald a memory as the car's engine squealed while climbing to the top, reaching the peak with the church's steeple appearing on the other side. "There it is!" I shouted, stomping the gas and racing down the backside. And as we closed the distance to the church, I saw the aftermath of Dowd's congregation, the remains of the crowds, *the circus*, the store clerk called them. They'd packed their things and left town. The church was abandoned.

"Park over there," Jericho instructed, my easing up on the gas pedal. "It looks like they left in a rush."

One of the church doors had been left open, the breeze moving it back and forth, swinging slowly. Church flyers littered the patio and steps and the front lawn. The manicured grass, the sod carefully placed when I'd first visited, had already begun to wilt and brown, the watering and tending by church members interrupted. I exited the car and ran to the steps, the table and chair where Mr. Reynolds had handed out the identification badges gone as well.

"They just up and left," I yelled, grappling with the idea of what to do next, where to go, who to show Hughs's pictures to. I snagged a loose flyer picked up by a breeze. The ink was faded, but on the page I saw the next stop for Dowd and his church. Over the hills, sharp lightning lit the dark clouds, a thunderclap following, the rumble rolling as the wind went cold and tried to pry the flyer from my fingers. I held it up, asking about the name, "Somerville?"

"About a hundred miles west," Jericho said, closing the car doors and joining me, his hands on his hips. "You okay?"

"I'm frustrated," I told him. "But as long as they stick to this, I know where Ethan Hughs might be."

"*Might* be," he repeated.

"It's our strongest lead." I motioned to the doors, opening them fully, and entered the church with Jericho following me.

Everything that had given the old church a modern technical feel was gone. The walls were back to their normal state, the progression of Jesus's life and demise playing out in wooden figurines. The church vestibule was visible again, its mahogany archway clear of any musical instruments and metal scaffolding used in mounting disco lights and sound equipment. And the stage was gone, the benches for the congregation returned, the church's original altar appearing as it had always been. Other than the door having been left open, the inside was immaculate.

"Got some history over here," Jericho said, his phone's light shining on an old bulletin board, aged cork with thumbtacks fastening pictures and paper postings to the wall. I stood next to him and read about upcoming yard sales that had occurred decades earlier. I saw listings for picnics and a book-club meeting with some of the dates going back twenty years. Jericho shined his light on a plaque and a picture next to the bulletin board, reading it aloud, "Robert Hughs, the church's pastor."

"Hughs?" I asked, the name striking a chord, its presence startling.

At once, Jericho began texting while I took a closer look at other pictures tacked onto the corkboard, finding a photo of the pastor's family. A tall and slender man, Robert Hughs stood on the church steps, a younger man by his side, adolescent, late teens, possibly early twenties. I held up the picture Nichelle made for me, the younger man's face changing little from his mug shot.

"Ethan Hughs."

"I'm already notifying Ashtole," Jericho warned.

My phone was out too. "Nichelle," I said when she picked up. "The permits pulled for the church, find out who owns this property."

"Yeah, sure," she answered. "But why?"

"If I'm right, it's Robert Hughs."

"Did you say *Robert* Hughs?"

I looked at Jericho as I spoke to Nichelle, a steady excitement building in me. "Yes. I did. I believe we've found where our ghost has been hiding."

"Ethan Hughs?" she confirmed.

"We were right to suspect Dowd's church. Hughs has been with the congregation this entire time."

CHAPTER THIRTY-EIGHT

Nichelle confirmed that Robert Hughs was the pastor of the First Presbyterian Church. He was also the owner of the land. We'd missed the connection when searching permits for Dowd's use of the old church. Although the Hughs name was on the paperwork, our attention had been concentrated on the county permits being legitimate. To our relief, the pastor was still alive. Nichelle tracked down his address, finding he lived in an assisted-living facility not far from the church, a few towns further west of the Outer Banks.

I was itching to get there and to ask the staff if Robert's son had been sighted on the premises. But an urgent message from Dr. Swales first had us travel east to her office and to where Sharon Telly's body was showing us more of her story.

A single sheet covered Sharon's remains, her body scheduled for the journey home to Philadelphia in less than a few hours, shipping overnight, her family to receive her in the morning. I bit my lip and then took a breath through my mouth, the icy snap of refrigeration and the burned flesh hitting me like a slap.

"Your face," Dr. Swales said as she approached. She eyed me cautiously, gauging my demeanor, and placed her hand on my arm. She eased up onto her toes, giving my stitches a cursory look. She wagged a finger, saying, "No ointments, leave it dry. That'll minimize the scarring."

"No ointments, check," I said, my voice shaky, my insides more so, memories of Sharon's burns affecting my emotions. Swales gripped my arm. "I'll be fine. Can't say I've adjusted to her being gone yet."

"Nobody should ever adjust," Swales said flatly. She raised her brow then, concerned. "No Jericho?"

"He had to go to the station," I told her.

"You know, there's a rumor going around," she said, a puff of white smoke on her breath.

A flash of embarrassment heated my chest as I thought of the video. It must have become more public than anticipated.

She raised a pointed blue-latex finger and continued. "It's about Jericho running for sheriff again."

"You know about that?" I said, heat dissipating.

"Many of us do." A hard look came to her face, making me question if this was a good thing or not.

"What should I know?" I asked.

"Jericho was an excellent sheriff. But it changed him. He seems to be so good where he is today, so much better than where he was." Swales stopped and thought about how to word her concerns. There was respect there.

"And?"

She waved her hands, unease waning. "Never mind the thoughts of an old woman. What will be, will be."

"Are you sure?" I asked, taking her concern as counsel.

"He is a good man," she said, and turned to face Sharon's body. "I asked you to come in to show you these."

I braced for the worst as Swales pulled back the white cloth, Sharon's ravaged skin showing. "What am I looking for?"

"Your friend had a secret," Swales said, and slowly rolled Sharon's arm to expose some of the morbid flesh, but also to reveal a handprint, the kind I'd seen in previous cases. "Post-mortem bruising."

Sharon's attacker had gripped her arm, in a struggle possibly, the firmness hard enough to leave a bruise. I could easily make out a thumbprint, and four fingers, even the heel of the palm had bruised her.

I looked on, my interest growing. "Tell me you can pull a fingerprint."

Swales nodded, but pointed her gloved finger in the air again. "The possibility is there. Latent fingerprints on skin can be lifted." She took hold of a metal tray and rolled it next to Sharon's corpse. On the tray, a glass box, the size of a doll house. "This is for what we call glue fuming."

"I've seen this before, but never in person," I said as she began the process. "Do you think it will work?"

"We have five distinct bruises, we only need one print to make a match." Swales flipped the switch on a hotplate, and began to clean the black rubber seals plugging the glass box, preparing them for the process. "I believe the odds are favorable." She held up her hand, the latex glove loose and wrinkled. "However, if the killer wore a glove…"

"Well, let's hope they didn't," I finished for her. I went to the glass enclosure and the hotplate. "You heat the glue?"

Swales gave a nod, continuing the preparation. "The glue gets heated, vaporized into the chamber, and, like magic, fingerprints can be lifted." She smiled, adding, "Although there's a lot more science to it than magic."

"How long?" I asked anxiously.

"That part is not an exact science. But in a day, maybe a few, if we lift a usable print."

"As soon as possible," I urged her.

"I'll do what I can." She paused in her work then, her stare fixed on my friend's arm, the sheet edged by the gruesome burns that took her life.

"What is it?"

"It's almost as if your friend protected the evidence from the fire," Swales answered, a look of disbelief forming. "But that's not possible. She never would have known."

"You didn't know Sharon," I said.

Swales faced me. "How so?"

"That's exactly what she would have done."

CHAPTER THIRTY-NINE

Daniel Ashtole fell into his evening routine with only a smidgen of consideration for what day it was: *summer solstice*. To him, the idea of the murders being linked to this day had always been far-fetched. But the news had sensationalized what the peak of the evening meant to a possible serial killer, and the council had regarded the theory as sound. They wanted it pursued. Who was he to stand in the way? Especially since they signed his paychecks.

Summer solstice, he thought, cringing at the absurdity of it. Even more so now that a ghost from his past offered what could truly be the motives behind the campground murders.

The evening was thick with humidity, lightning throwing soundless white flashes onto the corners of his home. Daniel stayed to his routine, pouring himself a single shot of whiskey, ice tumbling with a glassy clank that pleased him. He'd done the same to complete his day every evening since he took the position of assistant district attorney, seeing his first case through to its completion. He'd sent Ethan Hughs to prison for sexual misconduct with a minor, a jury of twelve deciding the man's fate.

He considered the man, although just a boy at the time, training to become a preacher at his father's church. Daniel had always harbored doubts about the case, questioning if there was even a crime. He remembered the victim's father the most, the man's rage, and his insistence that Ethan Hughs had molested his son. Daniel closed his eyes, wishing the memories away, the conflict coming up like an undigested meal. What if they'd been wrong all those years ago? Hadn't the victim said so himself? One afternoon, Daniel had found himself alone with the victim, when the boy's father was getting coffee. That's when the boy had told Daniel that it was all a misunderstanding, that Ethan hadn't done anything to him. It was already too late—as a new ADA, Daniel had to go with what the jury had found. But a part of him had always wondered.

"Jesus," Daniel muttered, a flash of light brightening the room, wishing he could rewind the clock and do it all over again. He drained the scotch into his mouth and poured another, the bottle remaining tipped longer the second time. It wasn't enough to get him drunk, but it'd give him a solid buzz so he could sleep, and stave off the creeping guilt and the needling ideas of having sent an innocent man to prison. "This isn't about the summer solstice. You're back, aren't you, Ethan Hughs?"

Daniel kicked off his shoes and gripped the carpet with his toes as he drank the scotch and questioned the warm idea of a third. He decided against it, the idea of revenge sticking with him, his step heavy, the staircase groaning. He stopped to check the shadows of his downstairs hall and the living room, peering into the darkness, searching for ghosts that weren't there. An image of a young Ethan Hughs came to him. The preacher boy had been meek, gentle, barely a man. Hughs hadn't just survived prison, he'd served a full sentence. *What happened to you in there?* Daniel wondered, shaking his head.

When he reached the upstairs landing, the scotch had touched his brain, numbing it. He poked his head into each bedroom, the hallway light throwing shadows on the walls, dark crisp lines, uninterrupted. When satisfied the rooms were empty after his cursory house check, he went to his bedroom, a single nightstand lamp throwing a yellow halo onto the ceiling, the sheets and blankets bulky on his wife's side of the bed, a pair of stocking feet dangling over the edge of the mattress.

"All is quiet," he said, and began undoing his tie. "Listen. About the council and their siding with this summer solstice theory—"

Daniel never finished. The sound of a kitchen dish crashing echoed against the walls and rifled up the stairs. His heart in his throat, he heard footsteps, porcelain crumpling with each step. Was it possible Detective White's team had been right about the threat to him?

"Stay with me," he heard a weak voice say from beneath the covers. But Daniel ignored the request, the whiskey giving him an edge. Nervous sweat riddled his back and beneath his arms as he rounded the bed and went to the hallway, the bedroom voice following him, "Wait!"

He could hear footsteps in the hall leading away from the kitchen. Daniel gripped the banister as he made his way downstairs, his feet sliding as he ran, an overwhelming urge to confront the intruder pushing him faster. But when he reached the bottom, when he saw who had come for him, terror stole every ounce of strength the whiskey had mustered. Standing before him was a figure dressed in black, their face covered with netting, a hammer in one hand, and in the other Daniel saw a knife, the blade as long as his thigh. Without warning, the blade swept the air, destined for his neck.

Daniel's heart beat double-time in his chest, he felt the strength of it in his throat and in his temples. He dodged the knife with a grunt, his attacker too anxious, swinging prematurely, and leaving an opening for him. For much of his life Daniel had avoided physical confrontation, knowing his strengths lay elsewhere. But he'd fight now that his home had been violated, his life in danger. He swung his arms wildly, connecting solidly with his attacker's shoulder, the feel of it punishing, sharp pain flying up his arm, the attacker shielded with heavy protective gear. Daniel reeled back, a bone in his hand broken, his feet sliding again on the hardwood floor. The attacker was wearing armor like a football player. Even their hands were covered with thick padded gloves, showing only the ends of their fingers, digits, like pale sausages.

The first hit came then, the butt of the hammer finding Daniel's stomach, invading the soft belly fat he'd so desperately tried to firm since landing on his fortieth year. His lungs raged with fire, burning as the air he held spewed like a fountain, leaving him doubled over and nearing a blackout. There was a laugh then, a viciousness, but there was no recognizing the voice as it said, "I'll have to make this one special."

His breath returning, Daniel screamed, "Now would be good!"

The team was already coming, footfalls pummeling throughout the house, wall pictures shaking, the overhead light fixtures rocking back and forth, glass bell shades jingling against their brass seats. There was safety in the ruckus.

"Hurry up!"

Daniel sucked in another breath and swung upward, but struck more of the protective gear, cutting his knuckles, peeling the skin, the sting of a broken bone rifling into his elbow. From the corner of his eye, he saw the knife swing toward him, the blade nicked his skin, the sharpness opening a shallow wound on his neck. He fell backward, saving himself just as the lights of his home became brilliant, shining like tiny suns in every room. The voices came like sirens then, yelling cannon-fire demands, screaming at his assailant, guns drawn from every direction.

Daniel clapped his hand over the cut on his neck, checked his palm and found blood. It was superficial, a puddle on the floor for him to clean later, and a shirt for him to take to the dry cleaner. He got to his feet. He was shaken and woozy and a flush of nausea had him clutching the stairwell banister. It wasn't due to blood loss, but rather adrenaline, a gushing flow of it racing through him with a burning mix of whiskey.

"Summer solstice," he said, a laugh erupting in a snort. "Who would've thought there was any merit in that theory?"

"We did," Detective White answered. "But probably not for the reasons behind summer solstice."

"How so?"

"Probably followed a lead from one of the newspaper stories," she said, joining his side, a facecloth in her hand. He looked up, finding her green eyes, soft light shining in them as she pressed the square towel gently across his neck. Her hair was pinned tightly at the back of her head into a small ponytail. The concerned expression on her face made him suddenly nervous. "They wanted you dead, and wanted to make it look like it was related to the summer solstice."

"Am I going to live?" he asked, joking, his nerves rattled.

She lifted the cloth to check the bleed, clamping it tight again and instructing him, "Hold this." She took his fingers and placed them on the cloth. "Paramedics will want to take a look. And at your hand too."

"Just a scratch," he told her, a respect for her work, her persistence filling him with gratefulness. The Outer Banks had struck lucky to get her. "Thank you, but I'm fine."

Detective White scowled, her brow furrowed, her lips tight. "You know you should have waited, Daniel. You should have stuck with the plans we made in this afternoon's meeting."

He shrugged, his confidence returning. "I got caught up in the moment."

"Upstairs is clear," Emanuel said, burying his gun in his holster.

"Detective Wilson," Daniel said, staring at the man's stocking feet. "You're a nice man, but I'll be glad to have my wife back in my bed with me."

"That goes for me too, sir," Emanuel answered.

Daniel sized up his attacker then, his first impression remaining. The man was big, too big to have been Ethan Hughs, who he remembered as a short boy.

"Who are you?" he asked.

The assailant said nothing, his face still hidden. Daniel fumed inside, a feeling of violation settling with an understanding this man had broken into his home to kill him. What if his wife had been home? What if his kids had been in their beds? What tragedy would have happened then?

"You'll all see," the man said, breaking his silence. "It will be *his* justice served."

Detective White's eyes widened in what looked like understanding. Daniel sensed she knew the words, or something in the assailant's voice registered with her.

"Detective?" Daniel said.

As patrol officers held the assailant, Casey tucked her fingers beneath the lip of the face netting, but the attacker squirmed against her touch. An officer shoved down on the assailant's shoulders, pushing with all his weight. At once the assailant went to his knees, a fighting cry coming from beneath the mask. Another officer joined the first and then a second, all three standing above and holding the assailant as he tried to stand and fight. Three on one proved no match, and Detective White yanked the netting free.

"Mr. Reynolds," she said, blinking rapidly, shooting glances at her team, their sharing a look of disbelief.

"You know him?" Daniel asked, vaguely recognizing the man's face, but unable to recall who he was.

"It's Dowd's lawyer," Emanuel answered from the steps.

"Lawyer?" Daniel repeated, speaking softly, circling his assailant, doubt ticking in his mind. His eyes met with his attacker's—the brown color seeming to become black with hate. Daniel backed away, afraid. "How do I know you?"

White crossed her arms then and tried to put on a stone face, the circumstances of their case changing abruptly. Nothing was said for a moment as Reynolds stared blankly, his lips moving without words. The revelation of who was behind the attacks was settled, but left Daniel uneasy, frightened even. Ethan Hughs was still out there.

Detective White leaned over Daniel's attacker, and gave Reynolds a slow nod, saying, "I believe we'll have that second interview now."

CHAPTER FORTY

We had D.J. Reynolds. But for the life of me, I couldn't make heads or tails of why or how or what his motives were. What was his relationship to Ethan Hughs? Early morning, a steaming cup of coffee, I watched Reynolds on a small black-and-white monitor, static interference racing up and down the screen. The interview room was outfitted with a single camera, along with a one-way mirror. We recorded everything on digital video and audio tape—a swarm of bits and bytes flying into a cloud somewhere where they'd live forever. The recordings kept everyone honest, leaving nothing to chance for when the defense attorneys got involved.

Reynolds tried laying his head on the metal table, his hands cuffed behind him. He'd been in the room since his arrest, and I'd insisted we leave the cuffs in place after his armor was removed. Reynolds had been stripped to his underwear with everything collected as evidence. In return, we gave him coveralls, a large size, long sleeved and bright yellow. The coveralls were jail issued, our station keeping a few dozen shapes and sizes stocked for such occasions.

It wasn't unusual to collect a suspect's clothing before interrogating them. It was our best opportunity to find surface evidence such as fibers, skin, blood, hair. I'd even recovered a piece of a victim's tooth once when a woman under attack bit the assailant's shoulder. While it had been just a chip, an orthodontist testified the victim's tooth as the source, getting us the conviction. Evidence is evidence, and having caught Reynolds in the middle of attacking Ashtole, we probably had more than we'd ever need to send him to prison. But I wasn't leaving anything to chance.

In my head, I saw the victims. I saw Carl and Peggy Pearson, and then I saw Ben Hill, and Heather Doyle, and the remains of Charley Doyle's face. I saw the charred remains of my friend Sharon Telly and her relatives.

The hammer and the knife were the first to be bagged and tagged, and then shipped immediately to the lab for forensic analysis. We expected they'd link Reynolds directly to the campground murders. But what linked him to a court case from seventeen years ago?

Reynolds was falling asleep—his head down, face turned to the side, moisture from his breath appearing on the metal table. I went to the interview room and kicked the bottom of the door hard enough to briefly shed light through the crack of it. The locks and door handle latches held, but anyone inside would have been jolted by the abrupt noise. I went back to the video monitor to find Reynolds sitting upright, his eyes wide, his hair standing up on one side. I didn't want him sleeping. I wanted him exhausted, so he'd answer every question. It seemed harsh, but considering what I believed he'd done—eight innocent people murdered, countless lives ruined—I was willing to push the law as far as it would go.

"Detective White," Ashtole said, joining me, his usual suit in place, clean shaven for the early day, a scent of aftershave following him. He carried two steaming cups of coffee, carefully pinching the lips with three fingers, his other fingers taped tightly around large popsicle sticks, broken bones in both. "Dump that station swill into the trashcan."

"This smells promising," I told him, doing as he said.

"I know you like your coffee as much as I do and thought to bring some from home." Daniel smiled at me as I took the cup. The gauze on his neck was three times larger than I thought it needed to be, the cut beneath oozing, although he wore the evening's injuries without complaint. "I roast my own beans."

"Is that right," I said, tipping the cup against his. "Thank you. This is a nice treat."

"How is he?" he asked, staring at the monitor as Reynolds tried standing, his posture clumsy. "Kept him cuffed?"

"And minimal rest," I said.

"Be careful with this," Daniel warned. "He's a lawyer and he knows his rights."

"I'm within the margins," I said, knowing I was treading a fine line. I only wanted him pliable, tired enough to make it easy for me to work with him.

"As long as you know where the line is," he said, tipping his head.

"Detective, we're ready when you are," Tracy said, arriving at our side, notepad in hand. From the station's pool of cubicles, Emanuel stood up, towering over the dividers. He gave us a wave. I'd requested both of them participate in the interview.

"I'll be there in a second," I told her.

As Tracy turned to leave, Ashtole called to her, "Tracy, would you do me a favor and tell my sister to pick up the phone."

"Seriously?" she asked, motioning toward the office, annoyed. "You promised."

"Yeah, I know," he answered. "But it's important." He jokingly clasped his hands together.

"Fine," she told him before returning to her desk.

"Sister?" I asked, curious. "You know Tracy?"

"All her life," he said, then checked himself as if adding numbers. "Well, almost all of her life."

"She's your niece?" I asked, deducing the relationship.

He nodded his head with a smile, and said, "You know, she really looks up to you. I mean, the admiration has me jealous." He glanced over his shoulders toward Tracy, said nothing for a moment, and added, "Not sure if you've figured it out yet, but she's special."

"She's certainly bright," I answered, having noticed her quick thinking already.

"She's a lot more than bright," he commented, but offered nothing more. His face turned sincere then. "You'll watch out for her?" he asked. "This world we're in... this job."

I touched his arm, his concern for her well-being noted. "Daniel, we all watch each other," I assured him.

"Good. That's good."

"Listen, I'm about to start. Would you like to join us?"

A look of reserve came to Daniel's face as he glanced at his hand and gently touched the wound on his neck. He'd shown a lot of guts going after Reynolds, but he'd done so in defense of his home and himself. We're different people when saving our own. But this morning, he was the mayor again, his position above the ceremony, the cadence, of interviewing a criminal suspect. At most, Daniel could only observe. He'd also been the subject of Reynold's attack, which in itself caused a conflict of interest that any defense attorney worth their salt would pick up on. I shouldn't have put him on the spot, and gave him an out.

"Actually, it's best if you hang back. I know you'll want to get in there, but let me and my team have a crack at him first."

"Sure, by all means," he answered, sounding relieved. "I'll watch from here."

"That'd be great. By the way, Jericho is stopping by to check on you."

"Shucks," he joked. "All this attention."

I smiled with him. While the case was tragic, even sickening, it had shown me a side of the Daniel Ashtole I'd only known about through Jericho's stories, the two having grown up together in the Outer Banks.

I opened the door and was immediately met with the strong odor of sweat. The evening had been humid with the station's air conditioning working only some of the time. Tonight it had been off, and while the rest of the station had large oscillating fans, the interview room's air was still and thick and smelled like a football team's locker room.

"Ms. White," Reynolds said, the neckline and pits of his yellow jumpsuit dark with sweat. His face was pink, his brow damp.

"Detective," I corrected him, and decided that'd be the last time I played that game. "But you can call me Casey."

His brow lifted, a grin on his lips. "Casey it is."

"Can I get you anything?" I asked as Tracy and Emanuel joined me, their faces cringing at the smell as they entered the room. Reynolds' eyes went to Emanuel, the sheer size of the man intimidating in such a cramped space. "Water? Cigarette?"

"I don't smoke."

"You drink water though?" Emanuel asked. He had good experience with questioning suspects.

Tracy took to a corner, observing, her eyes wide, drinking in every detail. I searched for any semblance to Daniel but couldn't see any. I'm sure Sharon would've been able to point out the details if she were there. Tracy had asked me if she could join the meeting, explaining it was the experience she needed to support a paper. I agreed, but explained that I'd run the interview and she'd remain silent like a shadow on the wall unless a request was directed to her. I needed my fingers on the pulse of this interview.

"Water?" I asked again, before Tracy took to her seat.

"Coffee?" Reynolds said, his eyes on my cup.

Tracy waited for my direction. I gave the nod, thinking the hot cup was more about Reynolds saying *fuck you and your hot-box tactics.*

As Tracy made her way toward the door, I asked him, "Where do you want to start?"

"Handcuffs would be a good place," he said, leaning forward, his chest against the table. I motioned to Emanuel, feeling safe with the two of us in the room. Emanuel released the cuffs. Reynolds rubbed his wrists, bruises and abrasions ringed around them. "Thank you."

Emanuel said nothing as he took to the seat across from me. Reynolds perched his elbows on the steel table, his fingers woven together, his eyes steady, his expression unchanged. We stayed like that until Tracy returned, steam hovering above the hot cup as she placed it in front of Reynolds. He gave her a casual nod, appreciative, as though we were sitting in a restaurant.

"Comfortable?" I asked.

"Much better." Reynolds's gaze fixed on the coffee, taking his time, slurping from the top. He cringed. "Bitter."

"I hear that a lot," I told him, making small talk as I opened a folder—information I'd thrown together that morning.

But what we'd learned of Reynolds overnight could have filled a small book. He came from wealth, an old family in the Outer Banks, original settlers, as Jericho had told me. And though his family was affluent, they weren't famous or in the news, which is likely why Reynolds went unrecognized until Nichelle pieced through his past. We also didn't have a motive for his crimes.

"Before we begin, are you seeking representation?" I asked, formally acknowledging for the camera that D.J. Reynolds had been offered counsel.

"Nah." He shook his head, waving his rights for representation. "I'll be representing myself."

"You've given us a significant amount of evidence," I said, not wasting any time. I pushed a photograph of the hammer across the table, the paper scraping the metal surface.

"Bought that one at a local hardware store," he said without looking at me. Another slurp of coffee, his lips wet as he made a kissing sound. "Imagine finding a local hardware store these days."

"Imagine," I parroted, then slid the photograph of the knife alongside it.

He gulped the coffee this time, saying, "I forget the name of the place, but they sold kitchen supplies, cutlery, stuff like that."

Reynolds wasn't making this difficult. But I suppose when caught red-handed, there wasn't much to say to defend yourself.

"And these?" I asked, sliding across a photograph of Ben Hill, showing the puncture wounds, the knife wound to the neck and the carving on his belly. "For the purpose of the audio and video recordings, I am showing the victim, Ben Hill. The picture shows the wounds inflicted, particularly a carving on the victim's torso."

Reynolds raised his brow, nodded, and answered, "Number five." He shot a glance in Tracy's direction then, her frame sinking into her chair. "You might want to write that one down." She did as he instructed, the top of her pen twirling as she made notes about his mention of the number five.

"Number five. What does that mean?"

"Does it matter?" he asked. He plunked his cup firmly on the table, hitting hard enough to bounce the coffee over the lip, spilling it. "Whatever confession you want me to sign, I'll sign. You have me dead to rights."

"Can I remind you that this is a death-penalty state?"

"I understand," he answered meekly. "Brother will betray brother to death, and a father his child; and children will rise up against parents and cause them to be put to death."

For the recordings, I asked for clarification, "Are you saying you are ready to accept the charges brought against you, accept whatever the court ruling is?"

"I am," he answered, eyes half-lidded as though expecting the punishment to strike in the moment.

"Detective Wilson," I said, giving a nod to Emanuel to continue.

Emanuel took pictures of the Pearsons from my folder, and placed them in front of Reynolds, sitting them side by side. "And the Pearsons? Carl and Peggy Pearson. Are you responsible for their murders?"

Reynolds flipped the picture of Carl Pearson over, his focus only on Peggy Pearson. "She was number two. She was a lot thinner back then though."

Emanuel caught the possible reference to time, Reynolds having known his victims before. Tracy's pen danced. Emanuel didn't wait for a response but flipped the picture of Carl Pearson back over. "And her husband, Carl Pearson?"

Reynolds stared for a long time, frozen. Finally, he shrugged. "He was just there."

"Just there?" I asked. "No other reason to kill him than that... *just there?*"

Reynolds belted a laugh, abrupt and loud. From the corner of my eye I saw Tracy jump in her seat, startled. "Well, I mean, come on, the guy was trying to *kill* me."

"In defense of his wife," Emanuel said, his voice rising to match Reynolds's.

"Yeah, well, there was that," Reynolds responded, shrugging again, turning to his coffee and taking a sip.

"The victims," I said, shifting the topic and thinking of the teens, wanting to know the details of how they'd been used, *if* they'd been used. "How did you select your victims and target them?"

"You and that other one." Reynolds wagged his finger. "I know you guys were on our servers."

"The victim's children?" I asked, eager to stay on topic. I also didn't want any defense attorneys scouring the recordings of this interview and raising questions about my fabricated church invitation.

"Oh, I get it," he said, understanding, glancing at the video camera. "Fine. Yeah. I befriended them, spoke on behalf of our church, targeting them with an overwhelming amount of email and text messages. All in an attempt to get them to come here."

He was giving us everything we'd need to secure a conviction. But it was too easy. I needed to know more. "Why?

With that he retreated, his shoulders slumping forward, the light in his eyes gone. He shook his head. "It doesn't matter."

Emanuel spoke up. "What do the numbers two and five mean to you?"

Reynolds came alive again, tapping his head, acknowledging. "Jury seats. It's amazing the amount of information you can find online."

"What is your relationship to Ethan Hughs?" I asked, showing him the only picture we had. The mugshot was old and Ethan Hughs had surely changed, but on Reynolds's face I saw immediate recognition of the man.

Reynolds turned the picture around, his expression softening. We had something. "I've said enough," he answered, pushing all the photographs to my side of the table. "You have my confession, and I'll sign whatever it is you need me to sign."

"Uh-uh," I told him and placed pictures of Darren and Caroline Telly in front of him. Emanuel turned his head at the sight of the charred bodies. But Reynolds didn't flinch, didn't cower, didn't show an ounce of disgust. "For the recordings, I am presenting the photographs of the victims, Darren and Caroline Telly. Mr. Reynolds, a number three was carved into Darren Telly. And the number 7 was carved into his wife. I want to know why you did that."

Picking up the photograph and spinning it around, he answered, "Their sin is like scarlet, to wear forever, for all to remember."

Tracy shifted, his mention of scarlet familiar, an earlier idea finding ground.

"Did you know the people in this photograph?" I asked.

"I knew them once, and I know what they did," he said, studying the pictures. "But I can't tell who is who. Not anymore. She was number six though, and he was number five."

"How did you know them?" Emanuel repeated. His face was blank but I could sense frustration.

Reynolds put the photograph down and braced his face with the palm of his hand. "I'm tired now."

"We'll take a break, leave these here for you to look at," I said, shuffling the pictures like pieces of a puzzle, because that's what they'd become to me, before shoving them under Reynolds's face.

"When you come back, bring the forms for me to sign. I'm ready."

I didn't look at Reynolds as I left the room, but shook off the feeling of him, shook off whatever it was that compelled him to commit the crimes, leaving it in the room. Tracy and Emanuel followed as I went to the surveillance monitor, curious to any reaction from Reynolds once he was alone again. As expected, he'd placed his head in his arms, ignoring the photographs left on the table, wanting to steal a nap while we took a break.

"What the hell was that?" Ashtole asked, his voice harsh, seeming to appear from nowhere. "He didn't tell you anything."

"He told us everything," Emanuel answered defiantly.

"But he never said why," Ashtole said.

"Reynolds did give us everything we'd need for a conviction. Open and shut," I countered, joining Emanuel. In my career, I'd never had anyone blatantly confess like that. "We don't have a motive. But as much as we want to know why, we don't need one for a conviction."

Daniel shook his head. "No motive. Maybe we don't need one."

I tapped the monitor glass, our answers sitting in the interview room. "You and the council wanted someone. Reynolds is ready to sign."

"You don't sound convinced," Ashtole said.

I wasn't. As much as I wanted to lock Reynolds away, this case felt unfinished. "As easy as he's made this for us, it isn't over. He's got to be hiding something."

"Hiding something?" Ashtole asked with a frown.

"Better yet, hiding someone," I muttered, watching Reynolds. As though he'd heard every word we said, Reynolds looked up from his power nap, peering into the camera, a smile plastered on his face. "I think he's hiding Ethan Hughs."

CHAPTER FORTY-ONE

The message from Ashtole and the council was clear—get a confession, get a conviction. This request was fulfilled easier than anyone could have thought. The interview with Reynolds produced all we would need to secure the conviction. So much so, the state wouldn't require a trial. With his signature confessing to each victim's murder, once the forensics teams completed marrying the murders to Reynolds and his knife the case would be over. Reynolds would never see daylight as a free man again.

What we didn't have was a motive. We only knew that Reynolds had carved the court docket number from Ethan Hughs's case into his victims—their having served on a jury that convicted the man. But why Ethan Hughs? Hughs's father was the owner of the church and the land which Reynolds had secured for Dowd's church, using it like a spiderweb, a trap to which he'd lured his victims to the Outer Banks. On paper, we needed nothing more for the courts, but I had to know if Hughs was involved. If he was, Reynolds was hiding him. With a motive we'd get the answers. I couldn't let this one go.

The crows were flying again this morning. Blades of sharp sunlight cut through the station's front windows as a rally erupted from the benches, the reporters leaving their perch in a rush. The cloud of noise and flashes spilled through the station doors and reconvened at the station's front steps.

"What's the commotion?" I asked one of the patrol officers.

"It's that reverend guy, the preacher," she said, rising onto her toes while she tried to listen to what he was saying.

"Dowd?" I asked, thinking him long gone, hours west of the Outer Banks.

"Yeah," she answered, gesturing toward her face. "The one with the patchy white skin."

Reynolds had returned to the Outer Banks, and we knew why. But what was Dowd doing back here? I stopped in front of the gate, staying where the reporters usually congregated. When I couldn't see the preacher, I stood on the bench lining the gate, but still only managed to catch the top of Dowd's wigged head.

"Let's turn on the televisions."

Another officer did as I asked, while the first helped me down from the bench. The station monitors flicked on, the picture fuzzy as Dowd's face came into focus, his voice coming over the speakers, a tinny sound, but audible. With the station set east to west, the sun beat on Dowd's figure, his skin appearing washed out, featureless, his eyes beady, his mouth just a sliver of bright pink. His black wig was a stark contrast. Shaped like a bowl, it didn't move while Dowd spoke.

"Turn it up!"

"—my brother, Mr. Reynolds, we pray for you. We pray for the victims and their families. I am deeply saddened, deeply touched and troubled by his acts. I've learned of their horror, the heinous crimes, the vile mutilations made upon the bodies—"

I texted the mayor.

Dowd is on television

Already watching

"—*I pray my friend finds his way*—"

I got the impression Dowd's speech was more about the press than it was about Reynolds. I texted Daniel back.

He came back to clear his name?

"It sounds like it," Daniel answered in person from behind me, surprising me as he appeared. "I was in with the sheriff."

Dowd ended his press conference and entered the station, his return to the Outer Banks becoming more than saying a few words for the camera. His skin glistened with sweat and his wig was askew, his suit a thick material even for the coolest of summer days.

"What's he up to?" I asked.

Dowd found me, his direction shifting, the flock of reporters following.

"I'd say you're about to find out."

Daniel retreated, trying to disappear behind me. I grabbed him by the arm. "Not so fast, I think Dowd is here for you."

"Mayor Ashtole," the reverend said, his hand extended.

The reporters were silent, their cameras and voice recorders hovering above us. The mayor saw the cameras, a floodlight popping and causing him to squint. On the station monitors, the news broadcast aired a live feed across the Outer Banks. Daniel responded to the courtesy, extending his hand, the popsicle sticks and white tape appearing on the television as a barrage of camera shutters snapped the moment when the men shook hands.

"On behalf of my church, I am sorry for the attack on you and your family, and on your home," Dowd continued.

"Thank you," Daniel said, noticeably uncomfortable, the handshake awkward.

"You and yours are in our prayers," Dowd said, abruptly gripping Daniel's broken hand, causing the mayor to wince. Dowd let go before it was noticed, and then turned to face the cameras again. "Thank you. I won't be taking any more questions at this time."

Dowd came back to us, leaving the reporters, his face in mine. The reporters took the cue and went to their perches, a few staying behind to sign off from their live broadcasts.

"Detective," Dowd said once we were alone.

"Mr. Dowd," I answered, watching the mayor enter the sheriff's officer, his gaze never leaving Dowd. "What can I do for you?"

He glanced at the reporters and the patrol officers, checking we were entirely alone. He adjusted his wig, setting it straight. His skin was wet with perspiration, drops of it on his upper lip and brow, and what looked to be a fresh rash of blisters on his cheek, the brief time in the sun causing the reaction. "A cup of water would be appreciated."

"Follow me," I asked. When we reached my desk, I showed Dowd the picture of Ethan Hughs, the printout updated by Nichelle to include a copy of the picture Jericho found in the church. "Sir, can you identify this man?"

Beads of sweat covered Dowd's upper lip, the patches of white skin edged with red. He brushed the back of his neck, wincing, and studied the pictures. "Yes. Yes, I can."

"Who is he?" I asked, grabbing my phone to enter a new note. "Was he in your congregation?"

"This picture," he said, tapping the photograph. "It's from the old church bulletin board."

"And the others? This one?" I asked, referring to the age-enhanced photograph, my hopes doused.

He shook his head, and then asked, "The water?"

I didn't answer immediately but saw that he was looking more peaked than he had moments earlier. "Sure," I told him, standing again and motioning for him to follow me down the hallway where our water cooler stood. I readied a cup of water, turning to find Dowd had walked past me to enter the hallway to our interview rooms.

"Mr. Dowd," I called after him, the cup of water sloshing. I caught up to the preacher standing at the surveillance monitor and touching the screen. "Mr. Dowd, you're not allowed to be back here."

"He confessed?" Dowd asked, ignoring my warning, his voice breaking with emotion and his eyes glistening. Reynolds sat quietly in the room, his hands folded in front of him, fingers laced as though in prayer.

For the moment, I ignored the rules and made a mental note to sign Dowd in as an official visitor later. "Why would he do this?" I asked, answering Dowd's question with a question, hoping for some idea to finding a motive.

"Why does anyone do such things?" Dowd answered, surprising me by not reciting a biblical verse as he usually did. He turned to me, his hand suddenly on mine, asking, "May I see him?"

"The man is in custody for committing multiple murders. You do understand the magnitude of his crimes?"

"I do. But please," Dowd implored, eyes wide, his touch soft, his fingers gentle like a child's, delicate even. "I might never see him again."

My insides squeezed with the idea of what I was about to do. "I'll have to ask Mr. Reynolds for permission first."

"He'll see me."

My stomach knotted, cramping with wanting to say no, but also wanting to say yes. "Fine. One minute," I told him, opening the door, knowing full well I was breaking policy. But in the back of my mind I had the idea Reynolds might crack when he saw his boss. He might tell Dowd everything, the way a child sometimes confesses to their mom or dad when confronted. "You have to make it quick," I warned.

The two said nothing as Dowd took a seat and leaned his head against Reynolds's, Dowd's hands on Reynolds's face, a silent prayer shared. I gave them a minute, snapping my fingers to hurry the time. As the men broke from prayer, their hands clasped tightly together, it occurred to me the two were much more than friends.

"Thank you," Dowd said, leaving the interview room and looking as if he'd just lost the love of his life. He did not turn back to see Reynolds.

I closed the door and secured it. When I went to ask Dowd more questions, he was already gone. He'd exited through the rear of the station, avoiding any additional questions by me and the reporters.

At my desk, I found Dr. Swales waiting. I almost told her what I'd seen, but thought twice about sharing, thinking it better for me to keep my policy slip to myself. "Anything on the fingerprints?"

Her hair stood higher than usual, the bun somehow fluffier, adding a few inches to her height. Swales caught me staring, and said in a perfectly adorable southern twang, "Everyone has a bad hair day now and again."

"That we do," Nichelle said, joining us.

"And no. I've got zero fingerprints matched from Sharon Telly's arm," she said, her lips askew and pinched.

"Reynolds?" I asked, having forwarded his fingerprint card from his arrest.

"He was a definite no," she answered surprising us. "Of the five latent prints, three are partial and two are complete. While that's more than enough, I knew immediately they wouldn't match with D.J. Reynolds's fingerprints."

"Why's that?" I asked.

She held up her hand, fingers splayed. "His hands are bigger than the hands which produced the post-mortem bruising."

I stood to wave the mayor toward us, hearing his voice over the cubical walls. He saw the impromptu meeting and joined me by my side. "Just about to leave. Do you guys have something?"

"A problem," I told him.

He gripped his hips and shook his head, hesitating to speak. "Please tell me we're not letting Reynolds go on some stupid technicality."

"Nothing like that," I answered.

"It's the fingerprints from the victim, Sharon Telly," Dr. Swales told him. "They're not a match. And if I didn't know any better, I'd think they could be adolescent."

"Adolescent?" Ashtole barked. He held up his hands. "Whoa. We've still got Reynolds for everything else?"

"We do. It's a solid case, and will be direct to sentencing with his confession signed," I assured him.

"And the arson?" he asked.

I had to shake my head. Reynolds hadn't hesitated to sign a confession for the murders, but had offered nothing about the fire. I thought of Andrea Hill and the bandaging and burns on her arm. Wishing desperately there were no kids involved, I had to check with Swales, "So it's possible the latent fingerprints could be from a teenager, say thirteen to fifteen years of age."

She tilted her head, her bun leaning as she thought about it. "It's possible. The size is right." She held up her hand again. "Could also be an adult, small in stature, like me."

"Do you have someone?" Ashtole asked me.

"I believe I do." As much as I hated the idea that Reynolds would have enlisted the help of a child to perform such acts, I had to follow up on the idea. I turned to Nichelle, "Let's find out the location of Andrea Hill. Tell child services we have some additional questions."

"I remember Ethan Hughs being small for his age," Ashtole said. "We could check his fingerprints."

"I need to ask you about that," Nichelle said. She turned her laptop for us to see, the court docket number and forms from the mayor's first case on her screen. She pointed to blocks of black rectangles, the words beneath hidden. "A lot of the details are redacted, which is blocking us from closing the investigation. We need to reconcile leads, corroborate stories with—"

"Yeah, I get it," Ashtole said, his gaze shifting toward the sheriff's office. "The case involved a minor, so any public records are redacted to protect their privacy."

"They aren't a minor anymore," I said, my tone insistent. "Could you help us find out who the victim was?"

"Ethan Hughs's fingerprint card is missing too," Nichelle added.

Ashtole scratched his chin, lips moving, a finger in the air as he counted. "The year of the arrest… yeah, his arrest was made before we went digital." He rolled his eyes, saying, "I'm old, it was a long time before digital." He pointed toward the basement steps where old case files and records were kept. "If we still have his original forms and fingerprints on file, that'd be the place. Lucky for us, I might also have a copy, including the court documents with nothing redacted. I'll get the victim's name for you."

"That would be very helpful," I said.

"It sounds like Reynolds had some help with the murder of your friend," Ashtole said to me, his voice sympathetic.

I nodded.

"Looks that way," Swales answered.

Ashtole brushed my arm, adding, "Well, we've got Reynolds for now. It's just a matter of time before we have any accomplices."

"I know," I told him, thankful. I saw Andrea Hill's face in my head and shuddered with the thought. "That's what I'm afraid of."

CHAPTER FORTY-TWO

There was another set of fingerprints we had to reconcile if we were going to close the case of the campground murders. Officially, the mayor, the council, and the press were satisfied with Reynolds's confession, the ink of his signature enough to close the investigation and move onto the next case. That was them. For me, if a string hung loose or errant from the hem of my shirt, I'd pull. It was in my nature, even knowing I'd risk unraveling the garment. This case was like that, loose ends, errant strings just begging to be pulled. Meeting Robert Hughs was one of those strings.

The biggest loose end was the fingerprints. On the evening of the fire, someone other than D.J. Reynolds had grabbed Sharon Telly's wrist with enough force to leave a bruise. We had two complete fingerprints and three partials. The first time I met Andrea Hill she'd passed off the burns on her arm as being made while cooking pancakes with her father. Coupled with her size, the burns made her my number-one suspect.

There was one other leading suspect, and that was our ghost, Ethan Hughs. He'd served a full sentence in maximum security. On his release from prison he'd checked in to register as a sex offender, and was never seen again. Although our painstaking searches through the records of Dowd's organization had given up nothing, and Dowd had denied knowledge of Ethan, we had a strong suspicion he was with Dowd's congregation. We suspected Ethan Hughs had befriended D.J. Reynolds, and that it was with Ethan's encouragement that Reynolds had committed murder. There was a connection between the men, and until we found Ethan Hughs we'd never know what it was.

I crossed Dare Memorial Bridge, Route 264 becoming Route 64, the traffic thinning for the mid afternoon as vacationers settled into the second half of their days. For the car ride, it was wrapped sandwiches, salt-and-vinegar chips and soda pop. The map app had me driving due east, crossing a few more bridges, the islands becoming fewer until we reached the little town of Dardens, North Carolina. It was where Robert Hughs, Ethan's father, lived in an assisted-living community.

"I don't understand why we can't just issue an APB for Ethan Hughs?" Nichelle asked, joining me on the drive. She picked chips from her bag and added them to her sandwich, layering them like lettuce and tomato. "Not that I mind lunch on the road, but if it's Ethan Hughs we want, why not arrest him?"

"It doesn't work that way," I told her, tapping the map application, the voice telling me to go an alternate route. "The only grounds on which we could have currently arrested Ethan Hughs was if he'd left North Carolina and had never registered. Every state has a sex-offender-registration law on its books."

We were on Warren Bridge by now, and the route was the only road into Dardens. I closed the map app, asking Nichelle, "Do you know where Dardens is?"

"Sure, it's not that far from where I grew up. Stay on this road, you'll know it when we get there." Nichelle took a bite of her sandwich, potato chips crunching, crumbs dropping onto her lap while I made do with one hand, eating quickly, eager to get there. "When you see the 'Entering Dardens' road sign, make the first right."

"Let's hope Ethan Hughs stayed in touch with his father," I said, following her directions, eating as fast as I could while steering. Within minutes we passed the sign Nichelle mentioned—a square panel of thick wood, freshly painted, the border edged with bright white and a solid burgundy interior with the name "Dardens" painted elaborately. "I'm turning right at the next light."

"At the end of the street, the assisted-living facility will be on the left."

"I see it," I said, and immediately took to canvasing the grounds, searching the depths of the heavily shaded benches and walking trails, the rows of electric carts, and a line of elderly men and women jockeying for a position in a line as they waited at a bus stop. "Shame."

"Shame?" she asked.

"Even at that age, we have to hurry up and wait."

When we entered the building the smells of antiseptic, stale air, and age hit me. The walls and floors were made up of a light-brown and beige, and the overhead lighting beamed yellow light, turning my skin a buttery color, and Nichelle's golden. The reception area was a round desk with an open pit in the middle, the counter lined with computers and paperwork covering every workable inch. A team of three made up the afternoon shift, two of the staff on the phone, a third eyeing us as we approached.

Four corridors surrounded the foyer and counters—each hallway clearly marked as living quarters that stretched the length of a football field. The area immediately to our left was the only open space, where wheelchairs were parked in front of a large-screen television, some chairs with green oxygen bottles, clear tubes threaded beneath the residents' noses.

"A, B, C, D, E, F—" an elderly woman sang, her verse hanging on the letter G. She stopped, took a rattily breath, her eyelids half shut, and then started over again. "A, B, C—"

There was a reading area next to the television room, chairs and couches lining the walls, along with card tables and shelves stacked with books and board games. A few residents sat near a pair of patio doors, daylight spilling onto a foldout table where a large jigsaw puzzle was being worked by an old couple, their hands shaky as they took turns pressing pieces into place.

"Can I help you?" one of the staff asked. Her hair was knitted into tight rows on her scalp, pulling on her eyes, the lids heavily shadowed with a turquoise color. She opened a register and placed it in front of us.

"We're here to see a Robert Hughs," I said.

The woman started singing her ABCs again, but more loudly.

"Gladys," one of the staff called. "Indoor voice. Please."

Nichelle's eyes were wide and she crinkled her nose as the chemical smell of the place set in. "Sign in here?" she asked.

"If you both could," the attendant asked politely. Nichelle hoisted her laptop as we both signed the page. The attendant added, "You're in luck, Mr. Hughs is in the sitting area. He's the one with all the hair."

I saw the man she referred to, a head of silver hair which stood out from the other men's, and some of the women's. "I see him, thank you."

Before leaving, I leafed through the pages of the registry, hoping to get a glance at a name and signature that'd tell me if Ethan Hughs had visited his father. The attendant closed the book, snapping it shut on my fingers. "Ma'am, this is a private facility," she said sternly. "I'll have to ask you see administration if you're seeking information about our residents."

"Understood," I told her, uncertain of the policy or privileges I carried, and sided with caution, thinking a warrant might be required, but only if Robert Hughs gave us a reason for one. "I'll visit with Mr. Hughs."

I didn't waste any time and went to the old man, Nichelle following, the two of us finding empty seats amidst the dozen wheelchairs occupied by residents. Most were asleep, a baseball game on the television over my shoulder. Mr. Hughs was awake, eyes lively, keeping score with a tiny pencil in his hand and a notebook in the other.

"Sir?" I asked, interrupting.

He glanced in our direction before his attention returned to the game. "Can I help you?" he asked in a bored voice.

"We're here to ask a few questions."

"Are you reporters?" he asked. Nichelle side-eyed me, the question unexpected. "If so, that was a long time ago."

"No sir," I answered, believing he was referring to his son's case. "But I am here about Ethan."

On hearing his son's name, Robert Hughs picked up the remote and hit the pause button. I spied the screen, the game stalling with the pitcher's arm telescoping like the hand of a clock stopped just past twelve.

"I'd appreciate a few minutes."

"Hey, I was watching that," a resident hollered. His face was round. Rolls of skin beneath his chin shook as he took to standing with a lean against a walker, the legs tipped with bright-green tennis balls. "You always take the remote."

"Stow it, Harold." Robert Hughs eased back, remote in hand, his eyes gray with red lines like rivers on a map. "Go change your bag or something."

"Would it be easier if we went somewhere else? Somewhere we can be alone?"

Harold nudged his chin defiantly. "This'll do. I don't plan to spend the day answering questions."

"About Ethan," I said.

Robert turned back to the television. Liver spots riddled much of his neck and cheeks, along with the tops of his hands. "Is he okay?" he asked.

I shook my head. "My name is Detective Casey White. This is my colleague Nichelle Wilkinson."

"We've been unable to locate your son," Nichelle said, opening her laptop. She showed him the only photograph we had of Ethan, his mugshot. "Can you confirm if this is him?"

Robert Hughs frowned. "Of course it is." He spoke with heat in his tone. He leaned forward, tapping his head and saying, "I'm not like these turnips in here."

"No sir," I said, the preacher's off-color remark surprising.

The elderly man scoffed at the picture. "My boy was handsome, and that's the only picture they'd show in the newspapers. Terrible."

Nichelle flipped screens to show the pastor's old church. Immediately, the senior Hughs softened, his hard expression melting. "Can you tell us about this place?"

"It's my church," he answered warmly. "I wasn't much of a pastor though, my flock strayed... and so did I."

"Strayed?" I asked.

"With the ladies," he answered. Shamefulness knows no age, turning the old man's face red. He bowed his head, shaking it. "I set a terrible example, terrible."

"The state shows you still own the land, sir."

"Sure," he answered, perking up. "It was my father's before me, and his father's before him. It'll be Ethan's when I'm gone."

"Can you tell us where Ethan is?" I asked, getting to the point of our visit.

The old man answered without hesitation. "He comes to visit. David does too."

"David?" Nichelle asked.

There was confusion in his eyes.

I said, "No sir, we're speaking about Ethan."

"Yes," he answered more clearly. "Ethan visits me."

"Your son visits?" Nichelle asked. "Recently?" She swung her laptop to show a newspaper clipping from Ethan's arrest, in case we had confused him. "This man?"

"A terrible business!" he scolded, a pout forming, his lower lip hanging wet like an angered bear's. "He was just a boy. What happened to him in prison was criminal!"

"What happened to him?" I asked, uncertain of what he was referring. Nichelle began typing, taking notes.

"A minor!" Robert yelled, agitated, catching the attention of the staff. "My boy was a minor."

"Sir?" I asked in a calm voice. "We're only trying to understand the truth."

"The truth!" he said, sounding more agitated. "He was just a boy, a gentle soul, frail like his mother. And he was put in a prison with men, with real criminals. Scum of the earth! What they did to him was horrible!"

"What happened?" Nichelle asked with hesitation in her voice.

Robert Hughs cried out, tears falling, his breathing heavy. I saw one of the staff get up to check on us.

I brushed Mr. Hughs's arm, taking his hand to try and calm him, his skin thin like paper. "Sir, tell us what happened."

The old man bolted upright, startling me, my stomach lurching. He slumped forward suddenly, his silver hair flopping into his face. For a dreadful moment I thought the man had died. He wiped his eyes a moment later, a woeful moan coming on a whisper. He raised his head as if in prayer and tearfully cried, "They raped my boy. They made him a slave in that place and traded him like he was… like he was currency."

Robert blurted a louder cry. My heart was breaking for the man, but I had to ask, "Sir, on multiple occasions, your son was offered the opportunity for parole. Instead, he remained incarcerated. Why?"

The old man gazed at us, his eyes weepy, the bags beneath them glistening and red. He stared until he caught his breath, his wiry silver brows rising as he answered, "To be free!" A shallow smile showed. It was pride for his son's decision, the kind of a pride a parent has for their child. "But being inside that place, it ruined him, it changed him forever."

"Changed him how, sir?" Nichelle asked.

Robert motioned to his hair and face. "Took the hair from him, turned his skin patchy white like he'd been rolled up and dunked in a barrel of bleach."

Nerves stabbed me with a jolt. "That sounds terrible, sir," I said sympathetically, encouraging him to go on, and leaned toward Nichelle, whispering, "Open the church's website."

"The prison's doctor said it was Ethan's nervous system… losing his hair was alopecia, they called it. The patches on his body they said was vitiligo. Nerves attacked him mercilessly. Made him allergic to the sun, to light. But my boy stayed inside that place. Hell on earth. He was hairless like a newborn, but free of the police and courts and the parole office when he finished serving his time."

"Do you recognize this man?" Nichelle asked, showing Dowd on stage, face shiny, a microphone to his lips, his suit lit up with colors, a giant crowd at the stage, their arms raised in a cheer.

Robert Hughs straightened his shoulders sitting at attention, his expression looking ten years younger. "*He* will not forget your work and the love you have shown him as you have helped his people and continue to help them," he said proudly, hands raised. When he was done, there was honor and love in the old man's eyes. "Look at my son giving back, being of service to others. He's more of a preacher than I ever was."

"Sir?" I asked, imploring, sitting on the edge of my seat. "Please, can you tell us this man's name."

Robert Hughs shook his head, frowning at me. "That's my boy, Ethan!" he said, raising his voice again. "Don't much like the wig on him. Looks like he's wearing a dead animal for a hat."

I looked at Nichelle, cold realization hitting us.

"And if you ask me," Robert continued, "it's that friend of his that should've gone to prison. Got away with murder, that one did!"

"And who was Ethan's friend, sir?" I asked, trying to keep calm as my heart pumped wildly.

"David!" Robert yelled, his temper reached, his face turning purple.

"Right, the one who visits you," I said, trying to wheedle the information from him. The preacher's shout had brought the staff to attention, a large round woman heading toward us. I held my finger up, asking her, "One more minute." Robert's focus had returned to the baseball game, resuming the play, our progress with him stifled. I dared another touch, taking his arm gingerly, the papery feel on my fingertips. "They visit you often?"

"They do," he answered, his voice calming.

"I'm going to have to ask you to please leave," the staff member said, insisting. By now, Gladys was rocking back and forth, and a strong smell of urine came from her as the tempo of her singing was a near shout. "We work hard to keep a quiet place for our residents."

"We understand," Nichelle said, finishing a note on her laptop and closing it.

"Sir?" I asked again, eager to confirm what was already on the tip of my tongue. "About Ethan's friend, David. Do you remember his last name?"

"Ma'am!?" the staff member insisted, bracing her hip with a tilt of her head. "Do I have to get security?"

"We're leaving." I stood, but kept my focus on Ethan's father, hoping for a reply.

As we made our way to the sliding doors, Robert Hughs finally said one more thing. "It was after my son went to prison, that friend of his killed his own father. I'll never forget it."

"Thank you, sir," I said, hastily leaving. While he hadn't told us who David was, I knew it had to be Reynolds.

On the return to the Outer Banks, Nichelle and I were chatty like birds, unable to keep still. *Dowd was Ethan Hughs.* Our ghost had been there the entire time.

"He must have legally changed his name," Nichelle said, opening her laptop. "I'm sure I can find the official records, now that I know what to look for."

"That explains why he served his full sentence."

"Why's that?"

"Like Emanuel mentioned, when on parole you're still without rights, which includes being able to legally change your name."

"So now we can bring him in?" Nichelle asked, her fingers running mercilessly across the keys, the laptop fan whirring with activity. She ducked her head to peer out the window as we passed a streetlight, the dome dimly lit, the light casting long shadows across the road. "Even out here, I've got a really good signal and can get any paperwork started."

"There is his alibi," I said. I drove east, the horizon like pleated folds of pink-and-red cloth in the dusky light, the clouds lumbering aimlessly. I thought of Dowd's visit to the station, his confidence in freely walking about without mind of where he was. "He has no idea we know who he is. We have to be careful, or risk losing him."

"Where does that leave us?"

"We need evidence, concrete, something that is counter to the videos you found. It has to place him where and when the murders occurred."

"I'm almost sorry I found those videos."

"Simple fact is, we still don't know if Dowd has done anything at all." From the corner of my eye, I caught Nichelle's stare. "Don't get me wrong, he has motive. But that is all we know for certain."

"What about the church? And the invitations to the victim's adolescent children?" she asked, looking perplexed and sounding frustrated.

"We have Reynolds' confession. The district attorney and Ashtole will never go for any change there. Reynolds has already confessed to orchestrating the work on the servers and targeting the jurors." I shared her frustration. With Reynolds' confession, he'd made it impossible to touch Dowd. I thought of the way Dowd and Reynolds had held hands, the affection between the men more than a strong friendship. "Let's take a closer look at everything gathered about Reynolds. Dig deeper, include his family's history."

"I'll start with the admissions exams, law schools, that sort of thing," Nichelle said, keyboard rattling. "I bet I can find his practice too."

Figuring out the connections, I repeated, "D.J. was a *friend*, a lawyer, and Ethan Hughs hired him to file all the paperwork for a legal name change and to incorporate his new church."

"I guess Reynolds was really taken with Hughs?" she asked.

"How so?"

"I mean, Reynolds left his legal practice to start a church. And then he took it upon himself to kill on behalf of Ethan Hughs and what happened to him in prison. Was this about revenge?"

"Revenge is a strong motive. But in the case of Reynolds, his act was retribution. We may never fully understand the details of his motives," I said, the disappointment in my voice. "But to get a conviction, we don't need to." As we drove, a hundred motives floated in my thoughts. I might never know for sure which of them held truest for Reynolds, but now I was focused on determining which of them was behind Ethan Hughs.

CHAPTER FORTY-THREE

A ghost. That's how Daniel Ashtole had referred to Ethan Hughs. And for a while, Ethan Hughs was a ghost. Now we knew he was Richard Dowd, and that he'd been here this entire time. I discussed bringing him in for questioning, even took the request directly to Daniel. But with a full confession from Reynolds, the council and their politics were satisfied, which limited my options. As Daniel explained it, there were no charges to bring against the preacher, and there was still bad press from the previous interview. I wasn't comfortable with the decisions, especially with loose ends that I couldn't pin to Reynolds. I went along with it though, for the time being. That left us with the evening free. And this evening was about celebrating what we did have.

Another round was called—the third already, the evening getting long, and the celebration getting rowdier. In my previous life, I had rarely gone to a team celebration, or any celebration for that matter. A row of shots was lined up on the bar, the oaky top as long as two conference tables, with my team occupying the corner furthest from the door. The bar had a tropical theme, bathing everyone in warm colors—red and yellow and orange. The music was a soulful beat we could feel from the tips of our toes to the tops of our heads. Everyone who'd helped with the campground murders was there, including our mayor. To my surprise, he'd become the life of the party, showing a side of him I never knew existed.

"One more round," I told the bartender, circling my hand above my head, indicating I was buying.

"A double," Daniel added, a soft slur in his words. The bartender held the bottle and searched my face for approval. Daniel nudged my arm, saying, "Don't hold out now… Just getting started."

"Sure," I told the bartender. I held up my glass to toast our success, holding it while Tracy, Emanuel and Nichelle joined in. "We may not have all the answers we want yet, but we do have D.J. Reynolds in custody, and if all goes as expected, he will be going straight to sentencing."

"Hear! Hear!" the mayor said, Tracy taking his arm when his balance fought him.

"A job well done," Jericho joined in, the sound of glasses clinking.

"One more round," I offered, waving toward the bartender. "But then it's coffee or water or tea or whatever, so that we're sharp for tomorrow."

"Another," Nichelle called, smile brimming.

"I should get a move on," Tracy said, placing a glass of soda on the bar. "I have a paper due by midnight. We get docked ten percent on lateness."

I blinked in surprise for a second. "I'd completely forgotten you're still studying," I said.

"Special," Daniel said, his arm on Tracy. "Jumped through high school and hurdled college like it was nothing."

"I had no idea," Nichelle commented, sharing in my awe.

"A regular Doogie Howser," Emanuel said, referencing a show I'd watched a million years ago about a boy who'd been a genius and became a doctor. Tracy's face went red, a bashful smile appearing. Emanuel commented, "By the time she's done, she'll—"

"She'll be running the FBI," Daniel interrupted. "Or maybe the country."

I glanced at Tracy's drink on the counter, a buzz circling in my head. "Now I'm intrigued," I said. "Tell me more."

"I like to study," she answered.

"Likes to study... Let's see," Daniel started. "Finished high school when she was twelve. First bachelor's degree when she was fourteen. A second when she was sixteen, and now she's a year into her studies for a master's degree." Daniel smiled proudly.

I was floored, at a loss for words. "And the certification?"

"Oh yeah, forgot that one," Daniel said. "Deciding on the law"—he held up his finger— "but not to be a lawyer, she also got her certification as a crime-scene technician." He leaned in and kissed her cheek. "I'm very proud of my niece."

"Impressive," I told her. "Definitely going to have to hold onto you as long as we can."

"Uncle Dan," she scolded, her cheeks color warming. "You're embarrassing me."

"What's next?" Jericho asked, his hand on the small of my back. I leaned into him, relaxing, with a feeling of becoming one with the music and the atmosphere. "Your uncle mentioned a master's."

"I'm working on forensic science," Tracy answered as she played with her hair, a smile appearing with the shallowest of dimples. "My other degrees are biology and criminology."

"You've definitely decided clearly on a path," I said, continuing to be impressed. "Wait, how old are you?"

"Doogie Howser," Emanuel joked, lifting his glass over our heads. "Tracy is a bonafide kid genius."

"I'll be eighteen soon," she answered shyly.

"I told you she was special," Daniel boasted.

"Well, to Tracy, who will soon be eighteen," I announced, lifting my glass to meet Emanuel's. We gestured another team toast. "To us, and a job well done."

*

"Want to head out soon?" Jericho asked after our toasts and obligatory speeches were complete and the team began to disband. "I have an early shift." His breath was strong with coffee, his days of drinking forever gone. When I'd once asked about it, he'd told me he drank a lifetime's rightful share soon after his wife's death, and that he'd never drink again.

"I think I'm going to hang back a few with Nichelle and Emanuel and Dr. Swales," I said. The three had already found a table, a pitcher of beer in the middle, surrounded by frosted mugs. I waved to them, telling them I'd be there in a minute.

"Ah," he said with an eye-roll. "You guys are still working, aren't you?"

I wrapped my arms around him and tucked my face into the crook of his neck, the smell of him inviting, the feel of his body against mine enticing. "Jericho, you know me so well."

"I do," he said with a squeeze and planted a kiss on my forehead. I peered up, finding his eyes, the bar's hanging amber lights making them shine. "You have someone in custody for murder. You guys did a great job."

"But we don't have all the answers," I told him. The latent fingerprints on Sharon's arm had gotten under my skin, and I wouldn't be able to rest until we'd identified whose they were.

"Did you speak to the girl with the burns?" he asked.

"Not yet," I said with a hint of frustration. "We're hoping to get another interview lined up tomorrow."

"Go on then," he said, a smile on his face. "Your friends are waiting."

"See you at my place?" I asked, uncertain where he was staying the night.

"Sure," he answered, raising a brow, a sly smile on his lips. He let out a sigh, the smile gone. "But first, I need to take care of that." We turned to find Daniel Ashtole at the bar, his voice louder than most while he cheered for a women's football game on the television. "I didn't even know he liked football."

I laughed and said, "Take care of him."

"Don't work too hard."

I started toward the table, the sting of not knowing all the facts needling my brain. I searched the faces of the team, thankful they'd obliged my asking them to stay behind to let me talk through the uncertainties about the case. I was determined to unveil the details, and the truths of them. I was determined, despite Ashtole telling me to consider the politics and that I needed to learn to let go. This case wasn't closed. I was certain if we identified the fingerprints, we'd find the motives too.

CHAPTER FORTY-FOUR

Daniel Ashtole checked the upstairs first, poking his head into each bedroom, flipping the wall switch, the ceiling light blinding him briefly before he flicked the switch again and returned the room to darkness. *This house is going to be too much for just us*, he'd told his wife, speaking of their oldest daughter approaching her final year of high school. Their son was already a junior in college, his sights on becoming a lawyer like his father. With both children soon to be out of the house, it was time to downsize.

"Empty-nesters," he laughed, mocking the name, feeling young, confident, even virile on his better days. He checked the master bedroom next, securing the windows, ice cubes clanking softly in the glass of scotch he carried while treading through the room, and ditching his shoes. He stopped to finish his drink, adding to his earlier take from the bar, the effects still wrangling in his head. He considered the talks they'd had about maybe fostering a child, using their home to do some good. They certainly had the room and the finances, and they had the time if he retired from state service after his one term as mayor. *This is a good house. It might be time to open it up.*

He made his way into the kitchen next, checking each of the windows on the way, the locks securely fastened. A breath of frigid air spilled from the freezer door as he fished out one of Judy's pre-made dinners. She'd made one for each day he thought they'd be apart. And God bless her heart, he loved her, but no amount of cooking classes were going to help. He plopped the Tupperware onto the counter, the contents dropping with a thud, a Post-it note on the top reminding him to take his cholesterol medicine. She'd penned hugs and kisses and a 'Luv u' for him too. He opened the container, the skinless chicken and mixed vegetables unappealing.

"Love you too," he said, her affections felt and appreciated, but with no interest in the meal. He put it back in the freezer. From their junk drawer Daniel found the menu of his favorite pizza place. Moments later, his order was on its way—a large pie with double cheese and double pepperoni, along with a large side of boardwalk fries drowning in cheese. He smiled, hanging up the phone, his gut gnawing with a hunger pang. *She won't mind what she doesn't see.*

In his study, Daniel spied the file cabinet, and rolled up his sleeves, pouring another scotch, lubricating his mind for a look at the case that had bothered him since the mention of Ethan Hughs. He found the key in his desk drawer, his knees popping as he kneeled. He jiggled the lock, a metal on metal argument, the key unmoving, the drawer refusing to budge. Daniel forced the stubbornness until the latch slid open.

He slipped his fingers toward the rear of the drawer, his having filed copies of every case he'd ever worked, ordering them from oldest to newest. As his very first, this should be at the back. Nearly elbow deep, the tips of his fingers touched the rear of the drawer where he felt the folder's outline, the edges a pulpy fray. He took hold and yanked it free, bringing into light a case which had sent a boy to prison and changed lives forever. *Let's get this over with.*

Daniel placed the folder and his phone on his desk, stripping his jacket and necktie. He glanced at his chair, but remained standing, his third scotch empty, another waiting on the narrow bar his wife gave him for his last birthday. He began paging through his phone's text messages, finding the one from Detective White, her requesting a copy of Ethan Hughs's fingerprint card and the name of the victim in the case. She'd texted him again later, requesting all the details that had been redacted in the court documents Nichelle recovered.

Well, first things first, Daniel thought to himself, opening the old file, a page from a legal pad filled with his personal notes, in cursive of course, because that's the only way he ever wrote anything. Adding case notes was a habit he'd formed early in his career for just such an occasion, knowing it was foolish to rely on memory alone.

When he saw the charges and the age of the defendant, Daniel took to his seat and read the words he'd crafted nearly two decades earlier. He read about Ethan Hughs having just turned eighteen, the charges of sexual misconduct, and the district attorney at that time deciding to charge the boy as an adult. Daniel stopped, a bad taste in his mouth. He got the other drink, his heart in his throat, his own words from seventeen years ago betraying what he'd believed was right, what he'd argued was right.

He read on about his meeting with the DA, and the decision to try Hughs as an adult. There were notes of an argument, even though the age difference between the victim and Ethan Hughs was only two years. Today, most cases like this would never exist. Today, there was the Romeo and Juliet law to protect minors. *Daniel, what were you thinking?*

Daniel flipped the pages, scanning the statements, his personal copies clean of any redacted marks. He came across the victim's name and stopped, a memory bubble exploding like a brain aneurism.

It was the victim's father who'd insisted on charging Ethan Hughs as an adult. Daniel flipped the pages, finding one of the witness statements, the father telling them he'd found Ethan Hughs sexually assaulting his son. The victim's father was also one of the district attorney's biggest donors, which had expedited the processing.

Daniel stopped reading then, the weight of what they'd done giving him pause. From the legal system's perspective, Ethan Hughs was guilty. He'd been found with a minor. However, he'd only turned eighteen a month prior to the incident. Without another moment, Daniel took to his phone, texting the name of the victim to Detective White. Killing the jurors wasn't just retribution by a sympathizer. It was pure revenge for having sent a boy to prison.

It was then the first strike came, knocking Daniel sideways in a single swift motion. The room went black and soundless. But then the ringing came and screamed at him, the room coming alive, tipping sideways in a blinding fog. He braced his desk, bringing himself upright, his head aching, his ear split into two. The sight of blood didn't register fully. He shook his head, staring down at the Ethan Hughs file, the white-and-black pages draped in red, beaded like a crimson rosary, along with his cell phone, which had gone tumbling beneath his desk, the *send* button never pressed. Daniel wasn't alone.

"Wait!" he managed to say, the figure to his left featureless, except for the eyes. The attacker's outfit was all black, fingers gloved, face masked. Daniel thanked God his family were still visiting Judy's sister, away for their safety. A sharp light glinted from a blade in the attacker's right hand, a holiday gift Daniel recognized, a butcher knife he'd given to his wife when she decided to enroll in a gourmet cooking class.

Daniel cupped his ear, a second strike hitting him like a hammer thrown into his gut—his attacker wielding a croquet mallet, the one with the blue stripes, the one his daughter always selected when they played the summertime game in the yard. They kept the croquet mallet in the garage—the only room he didn't check before finishing the day. "Jesus! Wait!"

The attacker didn't wait, but spun the mallet again, the mallet striking Daniel's face, his mouth suddenly destroyed.

"You've said enough," the attacker commented with a snicker.

"My family," Daniel tried saying, his words coming out as unfamiliar sounds, a moan filled with spittle, blood, and broken teeth.

"I had one once too," the attacker said, understanding enough, his voice soft and frighteningly calm.

"Who are—?" Daniel asked, needing to know. His insides were on fire, the mallet breaking more than ribs.

The featureless man lunged at him, burying Judy's knife into Daniel's belly, the impalement a pain beyond anything he could have ever imagined. He'd brought charges against hundreds for similar, sending them to prison, but had never imagined the physical assault, the feel of it, the punishments inflicted, the metal like lightning parting his insides.

Daniel reeled upward, fighting it, feeling as though boiling water had been poured into his throat and shot straight through him, splitting his body into pieces that could never be mended. He staggered to the file cabinet and clutched a handful of folders, flinging them at his attacker, filling the office with paperwork, the pages scattering and drifting like tree leaves spat on a windy day.

"I wanted to make this last," his attacker told him, standing above Daniel as he panted like a struck animal about to die while loose sheets rained around them. "But you'll be done soon."

Daniel yanked on the attacker's mask, seeing who it was. "You," he managed to say, his single response a raspy breath, his memories serving once more as he met the eyes that would watch him die. Without hesitation, Daniel lunged at his attacker, grabbing the back of their neck, and dug his fingernails, finding skin, clawing at it, his thoughts wildly focused on Dr. Swales and what she could do with the evidence he was giving her.

The attacker answered his attempt, plunging the butcher's knife deeper, burying it until it reached the knife's handle. Daniel fell back to the desk gasping, unable to breathe, his attacker poised to finish.

"For my love," the attacker said, jerking the knife free from Daniel's middle. Daniel's heart leaped, his blood spreading around him. Instantly, Daniel's hands and feet and brain went numb, a warm gush soaking his clothes. The attacker leafed through the desk's paperwork, taking hold of Ethan Hughs's case file before Daniel bled on to it more than he already had. He left Daniel alone then, a knock at the front door hastening the retreat.

The breathing was hard, but the pain became less, which he understood too well. His hands shaking and shock settling. Daniel closed his fist, tucking the tips of his fingernails into his palm, preserving what he was able to capture in his feeble attempt to fend off his attacker. *Phone*, he thought, grateful it was safe as the front door opened, the hinges creaking. His fingers wet, bloodied, he scrabbled a message on a sheet of paper.

A tear pricked Daniel's eye as he thought of his boy who would become a man soon and make his way into the world without a father's guiding hand. Another breath, harder this time, the faint smell of pizza and pepperoni, his thoughts shifting to his little girl and the father-and-daughter dance next week, her dress already fitted, his suit pressed and hung in the closet. Who would take her now? He gasped, a sharpness like the knife wound, a gush from his middle. It robbed a breath while thoughts of his wife came to him, her taking a step into their next chapter alone. *Judy*, he tried writing on the paper, his finger tipped with blood.

He didn't finish her name though and began parting from this life, the walls and ceiling and floor slipping from sight like displaced pieces of a jigsaw puzzle. His brain fired a feral mix of regrets and sadness for life's milestones he'd miss and the family he'd leave behind—the unfairness of losing them, and the parallel of Ethan Hughs's case a stray afterthought. In his dying breaths, there was one comfort, as he knew that retribution for his life would be found too.

CHAPTER FORTY-FIVE

The call waking me near midnight was like a bad dream, the previous evening's celebration a low-hanging fog in my head, the truth spoken outside my grasp as I slipped from the clutches of a deep sleep. I bolted upright, swinging my legs over the edge of my bed. I was awake now, asking the person on the phone to repeat what they'd said, to please have been misinformed, and be wrong. The words I heard were surreal, unimaginable, an impossibility I couldn't wrap my head around: Mayor Daniel Ashtole had been found murdered in his home.

I reached the mayor's house within a half hour, a steady rain filling the night, the moon covered with heavy cloud cover. Fat drops plunked onto my windshield, twisting the sharp red-and-blue lights from the cars parked along the streets and filling the mayor's driveway. A medical examiner's wagon was already on sight, as was Jericho's car, him leaving my apartment before me. I'd hoped to console him, to comfort him, the mayor having been one of his oldest friends. But Jericho had snatched up his things, pecked my cheek with a dry kiss, and then was gone. He'd made it though, and I was relieved to see him here.

I stood at the front door, the portico keeping me covered, a crime-scene technician offering booties and gloves for anyone entering. There were no signs of Tracy. She was off the next day, and I'd sent notices to the team to remove her from any notifications. News like this should come from her mother, Daniel's sister. My heart ached for Tracy, knowing the loss she was about to face.

The inside of the house was busy with forensics already on site, a concentration of camera flashes coming from the left, the mayor's home office, the room I'd been in when we set up a stakeout to catch Reynolds. I'd made a call to the station on the drive, requesting a visual confirmation of D.J. Reynolds, finding out he remained in the holding cell.

With the booties on my feet and my fingers sleeved in latex, I took a step inside and went to Daniel's office. There was an immediate smell of blood, reminding me of the first campground murder, the case of Carl and Peggy Pearson, her body drained like a pig at slaughter. Is that what this was? Another slaughter? On the office desk, I saw Daniel's body amidst a sea of papers, the folders and their guts thrown everywhere.

Jericho stood at the far wall, away from the body, a hand on his chin and his arm propped, his gaze locked on a picture. I met him there, the old photograph showing a group of friends in a boardwalk setting, a sepia-colored image, the background a saloon, the photo made to look like something from the old west—the men dressed as cowboys, and the ladies, workers of the brothel.

"I remember that day," he said, struggling to smile, his chin quivering. He tapped the glass where I saw an adolescent version of himself. "Believe it or not, that's Daniel next to me." He pointed to the young man, a full head of hair, his body lean and toned with muscle. And next to them, the girlfriends of the day, Jericho's wife, who I recognized from photographs in his home. The woman with Daniel, I would meet soon enough to deliver the dreadful news of her husband's death.

"I am so sorry," I said, knowing no words would help with the shock.

"This should never have happened," he said in a cold and chilling voice. He didn't take his eyes from the photograph. "Casey, find out who did this."

I gripped his arm, easing into him, his body stiff with remorse. "We will, Jericho," I told him. Richard Dowd was at the forefront of my mind, him being Ethan Hughs, the boy Daniel helped put in prison. That was enough to issue an APB, Dowd being a person of interest.

"He was my friend," Jericho said with pain in his voice. He leaned into me, his body weakened by the sadness. "I have to tell Judy."

"We can do that. We can tell his wife."

He shook his head, cheeks wet, a tear on the end of his chin. "I cleared it with the chief. It should be me."

"You sure?" I asked, nudging him to look at me. His eyes were red and glassy. Seeing him cry broke my heart. Catching his emotion was unexpected—feeling his pain, even more so. I buried my head in his shoulder, selfishly needing it to pass so I could do the job I'd come here to do.

"I'll meet with her," he answered. "I'll leave from here, get on the road. I have the address of where they're staying."

"Detective?" one of the technicians said. "You should see this."

"Go," Jericho said. "I'll hang back here."

I went to the mayor's desk, his body lying on top, his face in pieces, his mouth and nose a mess of pulpy tissue, his eyes lifeless and gray and wide open. The cause of death was apparent, a pool of blood beneath his body, a single wound in the middle of his torso. Next to him, a chef's blade, blood covering most of the steel. If I was right, I recognized it as being a butcher's knife. Leaning against the desk, there was a large mallet of some kind—entirely wooden, blue stripes at the end of it covered in blood.

"Tell me these are the murder weapons."

"They may be, but forensics will confirm," Dr. Swales said, appearing from behind the desk, her complexion pale, her eyes red-rimmed and wet like Jericho's.

"You don't—" I began.

"Nonsense!" she snapped. "I had to come. I've known Daniel all the years I've been here."

"I understand." I went to the desk, careful of where I stepped, the smell of blood an overwhelming odor, forcing me to cover my nose and mouth. By now, much of the pool had begun to turn dark, some of it almost black. Dr. Swales kneeled over the desk, Daniel's fingers on his left hand splayed on a medical examiner sheet.

"There's tissue and blood beneath his fingernails," she said, pushing a headlamp onto her forehead, the light beaming. "I'm doing the recovery before we move him."

I saw blood on Daniel's right hand, and asked, "You believe there's enough to identify someone through DNA?"

Swales looked up, the headlamp making me squint. She beamed her light on Daniel's face, the hole where his lips and mouth were, and then shifted to the stab wounds. "I hope so."

"Who discovered the body?" I asked the team around me.

"It was a pizza delivery boy," a technician answered, pointing toward the nearest wall. Lying on the floor, a pizza box was upright and opened, the guts spilled in a lump of dough and cheese and sauce. Next to it, a paper bag, the outside mottled by greasy patches.

"They just walked in?" I asked. "Are they being questioned?"

"Outside, ma'am," a patrol officer answered. "The delivery boy said he had instructions to enter when he arrived. He'd delivered to the residence before."

"Let's get a full statement," I commented, my focus shifting to the right side of the office desk where I saw a filing cabinet, the top drawer pulled open, some of the contents missing. It was the likely source of the paperwork littering the office floor and furniture. I turned one of the sheets over, finding a case number, recognizing them to be case files, copies the mayor had made when he worked as the district attorney. "So we suspect he fought back, possibly scratched the killer. Any other defensive wounds?"

"Possibly," Swales answered, carefully lifting Daniel's hand, the knuckles showing fresh abrasions. "I think the blood and tissues beneath his nails is his attempt to give us something. And Daniel also left this for us." She motioned to a sheet of paper beneath his other hand, a bloodied set of numbers scrawled along the page.

"Zero, six, one and one," I said. "What does it mean?"

"What was that?" Jericho asked, footsteps on the hardwood.

"Zero, six, one, one," I repeated. "Does it mean anything?"

"It's his wedding date," he answered, joining us, his eyes focused on the sheet of paper, avoiding the murder's gruesome sight.

"Possibly a message to his wife?" Swales said, unsure. "He was thinking of her in his final moments?"

I shook my head. "No, that's not it."

"We have his cell phone," a crime-scene technician offered. She held the evidence bag, showing the phone's screen, which was locked.

"Where was it?" I asked, seeing the edge of it covered in dried blood.

"We recovered it from beneath the desk." The technician handed me the phone.

"Wedding date," I said. "Is it possible he left us his code?"

"If he had something to say," Jericho answered, urging me to enter the PIN.

Through the plastic, I punched in Daniel and Judy's wedding date. The phone unlocked and the screen opened to the text messaging app, my name in bold print at the top. I looked up. "He was texting me before the attack."

"What did he say?" Swales asked, hitching up onto her toes to read the phone's screen.

I read out the text, "3, 7, A, 8, O. It's from the Ethan Hughs case." My mind raced when reading the next part. "The redacted parts, the missing names. Daniel named the victim. A minor, David Jonathon Reynolds." My mouth went dry, as I repeated to the room, "It's D.J. Reynolds."

CHAPTER FORTY-SIX

Daniel Ashtole's murder stayed with me through the night and into the early morning. The horrible truth was, his murder would stay with me for the rest of my life. As would the sound of his wife, Judy, her unexpectedly arriving at her home before Daniel's body was moved to the morgue.

I stole a restless catnap when I got back to my apartment, but it bordered on useless, letting me close my eyes just long enough to call it sleep. The evening made my stomach sour, the heartache and sadness overwhelming, the details at the forefront of my thoughts while I walked Tiny. The waves washed onto the shore, the sand packed hard and glistening, the sun climbing as early beachgoers greeted me with warm smiles. I couldn't muster so much as a grin though. Tiny pawed the sand, chasing air bubbles—preferring them over the ball I'd thrown. He made me laugh, showing a face full of comical curiosity, brows rising and falling, reminding me of a puppy. I went to my knee, his sensing something wrong, his thick fur flopping against my chest as I wrapped my arms around him. The sadness for Daniel's family had turned the laughter into a cry. Tiny groaned and nosed my chin, a thought of Tracy coming to mind, her having heard the terrible news by now, and making the hurt all the more painful.

As sad as I felt, a gnawing ache came with knowing how terrible Jericho must be feeling. I missed him too. Maybe I should have been with him? Instead, I'd worked the scene with Dr. Swales and the crime-scene technicians, while Jericho stayed with Judy Ashtole and worked with the station to secure her children.

On presenting the facts, we'd immediately had a warrant issued by Judge Howell for Richard Dowd. Questioning the preacher in the death of Daniel Ashtole was our strongest lead. With the paperwork in hand, we only needed to then find Dowd, his church having packed up again and on the move. Patrol cars sent to the next location listed on his flyer had found the place empty with no hint to where Dowd was going next. He had gone underground. And this morning, I called for another interview with D.J. Reynolds, the boy allegedly victimized by Ethan Hughs.

Blood ran from David Jonathon Reynolds's face when I placed pictures of Ethan Hughs and Richard Dowd on the table, straightening them so they were square and side by side. The pictures were of the same person, we knew that now, but to look at them, they could have been anybody.

"Have to say," I began, and slid the pictures back and forth, noting the impact of years with vitiligo and alopecia. "To look at them, I would never have guessed in a million years they were the same person."

"So, you know?" he half questioned, his focus shifting between the photographs and me. "I'm his lawyer. I helped him establish his church and establish a corporation. I also worked his name change."

"That was some impressive work," Nichelle commented.

"It was," he said. "I'm guessing you couldn't find any history. I made the name Ethan Hughs disappear like the wind too."

A ghost, I thought, hearing Daniel's voice in my head. "Let's talk about something else," I told Reynolds and flicked the keyboard on Nichelle's laptop, an image of his father appearing on the monitor.

"We know about his death," Nichelle said.

A look of disgust came to Reynolds's face. He eased back into his chair, saying, "I was only questioned about his murder, my whereabouts, the usual. Nothing else."

"The usual," I repeated and dropped a folder on the table. "Robert Hughs is convinced you killed your father. From the medical examiner's report, the cause of death was suffocation," I said, walking around the table until I was behind Reynolds. He tilted his head, his eyes steadily following me. "Fabric from your father's pillow was found deep in his throat." I moved into view, miming the motions of suffocating someone. "Do you know what kind of force it takes for pillow fibers to be found in the human throat?"

"A lot, I guess." Reynolds perched his elbows, lacing his fingers and cradled his chin. "Again, nothing proven. Can I get some coffee?"

"Your father had suffered from a stroke the year before his death," Nichelle said.

"Coffee?" he asked again, bartering his answers. I said nothing and waited. "Fine. Yeah, my father had a stroke a year earlier. It's how he ended up in the nursing home."

"Why kill him though?" I asked, continuing with the implication.

"I was only questioned!" he answered, pegging the table with the tip of his finger. "I filed a wrongful death suit against that place. The staff should have checked on him more often. He was found with his face in the pillow, the stroke leaving him incapable of turning. An accident that could have been prevented with the proper care."

I pegged the pictures on the table, asking, "How well did your father know Ethan Hughs?"

A look of disgust washed over his face, my reaching the edge of antagonism. "Straight to sentencing," he answered coolly, color returning to his face. "I've already confessed enough to serve a lifetime. Let's get me in front of a judge and get it over with!"

I shook my head, refusing to give him what he wanted. "I'm not satisfied."

"It's not up to you!" he shouted, his voice choking with emotion. "Where's my meeting with the district attorney?"

I slapped pictures of Daniel Ashtole on the table, picking the worst of them—the mayor's bloodied face, his skin gray, lifeless, and his eyes wide with fright as though he'd seen monsters in his dying moments. "What can you tell me about his murder?"

Reynolds covered his mouth, a shocked smile spreading across his face with a gasp escaping from between his fingers. "It is done. Complete."

"What's done?" I demanded. "What's complete?"

Reynolds stood to bring his face closer to mine. "I'm finished."

"Not until I am," I answered. "Your family, your mother and father, they were members of Pastor Hughs's church. It was there that you met Ethan Hughs."

Reynolds couldn't take his eyes from the pictures of Ashtole, a look of satisfaction radiating from him as he eased back into his chair. "It is finally over."

"What happened in that church?"

Reynolds acted as though he didn't hear me and picked up the photograph with Ashtole's terrifying stare and began to pray silently, his lips moving. I smacked the top of the table, jarring him, stealing his attention. When he focused on my face, I softened my voice, asking, "What happened to you and Ethan?"

His brow rose and his mouth fell open as he shook his head, answering, "We... we fell in love."

There's a moment in every case when it feels unknown, when every piece of evidence is wrong, every thread of detail loose and disconnected. And then, in a blink, that moment flips and there is clarity, the stray threads binding to form answers and the truth. This was that moment, and I could barely contain myself.

I sat down, asking, "And your father?"

"It was a Wednesday," he began. "Dad was out of town most of the week, and I was at the church. I told my parents it was service work, cleaning the floors, the windows, that sort of thing." He shook his head. "But it wasn't service work, it was to be with him. To be with Ethan."

"And on that last Wednesday?" I asked, taking a guess at what might have happened—the original case file showing an arrest made for Ethan Hughs on a Thursday morning.

Rage took Reynolds's face, his lips in a snarl, tears popping into his eyes. "They took him from me."

"Who took him?"

"My father!" Reynolds barked. "He'd come home early, stopping at the church so I wouldn't have to walk through the cornfields." Reynolds had to stop, his face in his hands. Nichelle took the moment and got him a coffee.

"Your father found you with Ethan?" Nichelle asked when she returned with a cup.

"Yeah," Reynolds said, his voice nasally. "He walked in on us, and we were... well..."

"I understand," I said, the details unnecessary.

"I thought Dad was going to kill Ethan. I thought he was going to kill us both."

"He didn't though."

"Wish he had," he answered, his tone flat. "Dad went to the police instead. Insisted an arrest be made." Reynolds shook his head, cringing at the taste of the coffee. "When they argued the charge, he made a few calls, being the fat cat he was. And then our lives... mine and Ethan's, our lives were over."

"Ethan Hughs was arrested the next morning," Nichelle commented.

"Do you know what happened to him inside prison?" The anger and rage returned to Reynolds. He punched the table, his fist on the pictures of Daniel. "*He* let that happen. I went to him, told him we were just kids, begged him to put a stop to what my father and the DA were doing. They were charging Ethan as an adult... we were teenagers. But your Mr. Ashtole said his hands were tied, that it was already a done deal." Reynolds rocked in his chair, the conversation uncomfortable. "I know it was my dad. It was his money. He threatened to starve the DA of campaign funding."

"And what happened after?" I asked, wanting to keep the momentum of questions going, wondering about the years without Ethan Hughs.

Reynolds waved his hand around his head, saying, "Dad had this crazy idea that there was a *cure*. He thought being gay could be cured like it was some kind of cancer."

Nichelle shook her head wordlessly.

"There were these camps that claimed to cure homosexuality," he continued, tilting his head. "They were rooted in brainwashing kids, convincing them what they were feeling was only a phase. When that didn't work, there was torture, justified in the name of God so they could beat the sin from our bodies."

"That had to be horrible for you," I said, trying to sympathize, trying not to cringe, knowing the man's true self.

He fixed a cold stare on me, and said, "I'd do it again. I'd do a hundred years of that religious punishment. What I went through was nothing compared to Ethan."

"Is that why you killed the jurors from Ethan's trial?"

"They stole our lives," Reynolds answered, his demeanor returning to the man I'd met at the church. "So, I decided to take theirs." A spark flicked in his eyes, coming alive with thoughts of what he'd done. "The best part was using their kids to get to them."

"Can you tell us how?" I asked, wanting him to explain it, to make things absolutely clear in the recording of this interview.

His eyes narrowed and scanned the room with understanding. "The brainwashing I went through. I'd learned a trick or two in those camps. I also learned about the psychology needed to get into someone's head. It wasn't hard," he said with a nod. "I got into their heads and used them like they were marionettes, pulled on the strings, convincing them they had to come to the Outer Banks. Like little puppets. Although some took a lot more work than others."

"Was Andrea Hill one of your puppets?" I asked, the burns on her needling an idea that wouldn't rest.

"She was," he answered, the brief enthusiasm waning.

"But why take the risk?" Nichelle asked, confused. "You and Ethan. Both free. You could have been together again."

His focus went to the coffee, his breathing heavy, the earlier spark doused. He remained like that a moment, swiping at tears. "The Ethan I knew died in that prison. He was never the same." He looked at us coldly, eyes red-rimmed, lips quivering. His voice broke. "I serve Richard Dowd, but I avenge Ethan Hughs."

CHAPTER FORTY-SEVEN

Straight to sentencing. That's what Reynolds requested. The moment he uttered those words, I was obligated to contact the district attorney, who was ecstatic to hear the news, her voice ringing over my phone, telling me about saving taxpayer dollars, along with time and resources. It was a win for her, and a win for us. But it wasn't a win for Daniel Ashtole.

I had Nichelle begin to review the latest Dowd church videos, logging the dates and times, hoping to find a window, a period of time where Dowd could have been anywhere, including Mayor Ashtole's home. We'd also created a timeline of Daniel's death using phone records; his order for pizza and boardwalk fries, and the delivery boy's call to 9-1-1 to report finding Daniel's body. Unless there was a video of Dowd's preaching during that exact timeframe, he was our number-one suspect.

"Any new videos?" I asked Nichelle, hoping she'd found none. I went to her desk as a river of blue, gray, and black suits supporting the district attorney entered the station, arriving to meet with Reynolds. The judicial train was already moving. David Jonathon Reynolds was going to get his moment in front of a judge and complete his straight to sentencing request. The press was going to eat it up.

"Dowd's church videos?" Nichelle replied.

I nodded, adding, "Tell me something helpful, like you can't find any videos from the evening of the mayor's murder."

She gave me a squirrelly look, wanting to say something. I raised my brow, encouraging her. "It's just... okay, this is going to sound terrible, but should we follow up about the girl?"

"Andrea Hill," I answered, knowing where she was going. I glanced at my phone and the time. "We finally got the meeting with child services. Emanuel and Tracy are there now."

"They're questioning the burns?"

"Correct," I answered. "They'll collect fingerprints as well, test them against the handprint on Sharon Telly."

"If Andrea Hill was enamored enough by Reynolds's story, is there any reason to believe she could have killed the mayor?"

I shook my head, grabbing the folder of Daniel's case, showing her pictures of what I'd come to learn was a croquet mallet. "I considered Andrea Hill as a possibility, but the damage inflicted with the mallet required a lot of strength." I held up three fingers, adding, "Three fractured ribs."

"Andrea Hill isn't a small child," Nichelle reminded me. "She's at least your height."

"You're right," I said, texting Emanuel, wanting them to also get Andrea Hill's whereabouts the evening of Daniel's murder. I had my doubts though, knowing the likelihood of the teenager leaving the protection of child services to get to the mayor's house being small at best. "Now, how about videos?"

"Oh, I've got that automated," she answered, a series of mouse clicks changing her screen. "I've set it up so they come in as alerts."

I nodded. They were not all that different from the alerts I continued to receive about dead teenage girls, my obsession to identify if they might be Hannah. "Any hits on the night of the mayor's death?"

She shook her head, scrolling a list, the dates and times appearing, but absent of the time when we believed the murder took place. "He was here for the press conference. So maybe he never left town?"

"That's the going theory. And the warrant is issued—"

"Casey," Nichelle interrupted. "There's an event going on right now. Someone is live-streaming it."

"Can you get a location?" I asked, voice raised, ready to get a patrol dispatched.

Nichelle's fingers blurred as she flooded a black screen with green text, networking, commands I'd seen her use before but didn't understand.

She shook her head, answering, "There's no metadata, nothing to determine a location."

"What about invitations or flyers? Like before, their publicizing the location?"

Nichelle switched computers, hammering another set of commands, a look of disappointment on her face. "Nothing."

"Word of mouth only. Underground," I suggested. "How about cell towers, tracing back to the source phone?" I asked, desperate. She shook her head. "Let's take screenshots then, capture images of the church, the walls, anything that we can use to identify the building they're in."

Tightness gripped my throat as Nichelle produced screenshot after screenshot, her desktop filling with untitled icons that we'd later sort through and print. "It's her," Nichelle said, pointing to a grainy figure in the foreground. The camera panned as though I'd willed it, the frame showing Wendy Doyle. My heart jumped into my throat as we grabbed another screenshot. The video swept left and then jerked back to the right, the live stream changing directions, moving to a new location in the crowd. "I lost her."

"Maybe you didn't," Nichelle exclaimed with big eyes. "It's live. It'll take time, but I can do image searches, figure out what church it is, where this is coming from."

My focus was stuck on Wendy Doyle's screenshot, the sight of her shooting phantom pains into the wounds she'd inflicted on me. I touched the stitches on my eye, the bruising still tender. "Call me the moment you have a location," I told Nichelle, her catching a tone, the sound of it demanding.

Heat climbed up my neck and face, my fingers tingled, frustration filled me. The video stream swept back to Richard Dowd. I couldn't stand seeing him on stage, his live-streaming while Daniel's body was tucked inside a cold storage locker, his life extinguished.

I put my hand on Nichelle's shoulder, assuring her the temperament was not meant for her. I trusted she'd weed through the puzzle of bits and bytes, and the digital veil Dowd was hiding behind. She'd reveal his location. A glint of hope warmed in my gut. We were coming for him. And with it, we'd bring retribution for Daniel's murder.

CHAPTER FORTY-EIGHT

I could only wait. The entire police force of the Outer Banks had pictures of Richard Dowd. Nichelle's server farm crunched videos, while the team and I assembled the locations of churches Dowd's latest videos might have come from. There was the potential of a massive failing on our part—an assumption Dowd was at a church. The screen captures hadn't matched on any building, nothing recognizable, making my glimpses of hope turn cold.

I grabbed the dog leash, Tiny knowing immediately it was time for our walk, a bark erupting, the hours in the day long, his patience worn. He'd become my fur-baby, my ever-present roommate, companion, and guardian. It was impossible not to love him. I dove my fingers deep into his fur, his cold nose nudging my hand, his eyes alive, telling me to skip the niceties and open the door.

"Eager to get outside?" I asked him, feeling guilty for having stayed at the station as long as I had. Tiny jumped, his excitement building, his bladder probably close to bursting, and I hoped he hadn't left me with a surprise on the carpet. He let out a soft cry and nosed his leg, the swelling in one of the joints noticeable. "Let me see that." I rubbed and kneaded, believing it'd help, a veterinary visit in mind. His gray stare remained fixed on the door, as did his attention.

I peered through the curtain, the sun falling in the west, the sky clear, the sunlight bending around the earth, a stew of gold and orange and red stirring on the ocean's surface. It was my favorite time of day for a walk, watching the sun set on one side and on the other, the ocean smoldering like fire.

When I pulled the curtain aside, Ronald appeared on my deck, Tiny shifting uneasily, tensing, his front legs steadied, his ears pointed, his teeth bared with a low growl forming somewhere deep inside his throat.

"Easy boy," I told him, petting the rise of thick fir on his neck and back. I faced Ronald but didn't open the door. "What are you doing here?"

"I have to talk to you," he said. Tiny barked in response, another growl coming. I bit my lip, swallowing the words I wanted to say, his presence unexpected and unwelcome. I shook my head. "Please, it's about Hannah."

Tiny barked again, his voice piercing in the small space. "Tiny," I begged, holding tight, fastening a leash and opening the door a little. At once, Tiny lunged toward Ronald, my grip on the leash tightening. For a moment, I wanted to let go, wanted to see if the old dog could learn new tricks—like how to neuter a man in a single bite. "Tiny, sit!"

The dog listened, obediently sitting, his tail wagging, his growl fading. His ears remained pointed, as did the hair on his neck and back. Ronald went white, terrified of the dog, a memory of his being chased by a neighbor's German shepherd coming to me. I was laughing inside, the look on his face sad, but utterly hysterical. It was beyond mean, but after what he did on the boardwalk, the look on his face was glorious.

"You have him?" he yelled, his voice rising an octave, his hands shaking badly.

"Yeah, I have him," I said, closing and locking the door behind us, leaving my arm loose, the leash swaying, providing a ten-foot buffer between me and Ronald. "Listen, I don't have time for you." I exited onto the beach, the sand dry and warmed by the day's sunlight, coating my toes, letting me sink until my feet were hot. Tiny took to doing what Tiny did when he first stepped outside, crouching on a spot of lawn Jericho helped me put together for the dog.

"I just want to explain—"

"It's a public beach," I told him, interrupting with a roll of my eyes. I stopped and tipped my head in his direction. "Before you ask, I haven't seen Hannah."

"Like I said, maybe she doesn't want to be found?" he said.

"Doesn't mean I won't stop looking," I told him. "I'm also not interested in whatever blog or podcast productions you're into."

"I only want to know she's safe," he answered, offended, raising his voice. Tiny shifted with a snarl, his teeth showing, taking guard in front of me. I raised my brow, warning Ronald. He quietened and calmly asked, "Do you think it's possible Hannah is with that nut I've been seeing on the news?"

"Why would you think that?" I asked, keeping a calm tone. He was clutching at straws and seeing Hannah whenever he saw youths gather. I knew, because there were times when I'd seen her everywhere too. He frowned, his face red, lips pressed with a fatherly concern. "I can tell you that we have eyes on the guy and I haven't seen any evidence of Hannah being involved."

"Thank God for that." He nodded his head, eyes fixed on Tiny. "Children of Dowd. The news has it sounding like every kid in the Outer Banks is part of his church."

"I know," I said, uncomfortable seeing him worry. I considered what I'd learned of my daughter since arriving in the Outer Banks to find her. "Hannah is too strong-willed."

"Gets that from her mother," he said, trying to smile.

"Probably," I agreed. "Is that why you're here? To ask about Hannah?"

"It's you," he answered, the words putting me on guard, my nerves ticking like a bomb. "I wanted to apologize about the podcast. That did not go well."

"You think?" I said, raising my voice. By now, Tiny's interest in Ronald was over. I recalled our past, our history, the painful memories, the harsh arguments, the looks, every spiteful word. It was twice now that Ronald had betrayed me.

"Any chance for a do over?" he asked, his voice soft, a sheepish look on his face.

"Why?" I asked. I thought of my life after Hannah's kidnapping. We'd both changed. But we hadn't changed together. It wasn't all his fault, and it wasn't mine either. Seemingly overnight, we'd become entirely different people, which was the beginning of the end for us. And if I wanted to be completely honest with myself, even if Hannah had been found, it would have been too late for me and Ronald.

"Does it matter? I came back for you," he said, daring a step, his arm raised, fearing Tiny.

"You should really put your arm down," I warned. Tiny's interest was in the waves now, and the children playing in the surf. He yelped, eager for our usual walk along the ocean so he could chase bubbles in the sand and retreating seawater. I motioned, making more of the act than it was. "You don't want to appear like you're going to strike."

"No," he said, his focus jumping between me and Tiny. "I wouldn't want to do that."

"Follow us this way if you want to talk," I told him, leading Tiny toward the waves. Ronald followed, shuffling clumsily through the deep sand. When we reached the ocean, I told him, "Ronald, there will always be our daughter. But there is no us."

He stopped short of the rushing sea foam, the tips of his shoes daring the lip of seawater. "Why not?"

"There can't be," I answered flatly. And though the sun was setting behind us, I had to shield my eyes. Tiny stepped into a wave, a stirring sea of sparkling diamonds, his legs steady, his nose in the foam while he pawed at a burrowing sand crab.

"Why, Casey?" Ronald asked again, his voice rising, fervent. "I never stopped loving you."

I squinted, his face appearing from a silhouette. Tiny's leash wrapped around my knees, him tugging playfully. "Ronald, didn't you hear me before? I'm in love with someone else."

"You're sure about that?" he asked, a hand on his hip, dismay on his face.

Jericho appeared on the deck, his timing impeccable. But of course, I knew he was coming. He gave me a cautious wave to see if I was okay. And I was. I was more than okay. "Be there in a few minutes," I yelled.

Ronald saw Jericho then, his posture changing at the sight of him in full uniform. When Ronald had seen enough, he asked, "This is what you want?"

"This is what I want," I told him, shutting my eyes, relief breaking something deep inside me. It wasn't painful or aching. Instead, it was freeing, as though the shackles Ronald put onto my heart years before were gone forever. "Yes. Jericho is who I want."

Ronald dipped his head, his mouth in a frown. He dared a step near the ocean again, letting his shoes get wet this time. He came to me, hands extended. Cautiously, I offered a hand, his fingers holding mine. "I have to tell you, I'm sad. I came here with a lot of hope, for you and me and Hannah again."

"I appreciate it," I said.

"But I do wish you the best, Casey." He kissed me then, a brush of his lips against my cheek. "You'll let me know if you hear from our Hannah?"

I nodded, answering, "You'll do the same?"

"Always."

A moment later, Ronald was gone. He would remain in my life for as long as I held a breath with Hannah's name on it. But as far as our being romantic, becoming a couple again, it was never going to happen.

CHAPTER FORTY-NINE

Stills from the videos littered the station's conference-room table, with the team and Jericho gathered round. Daniel's chair remained empty, a reminder of why we were there as the hours swept by. By the time we'd reached the gut of the night, we'd identified Dowd's new church, and we'd also identified its location.

Dowd's new church was a larger building than the one Robert Hughs had leased to D.J. Reynolds. Before taking on all the jurisdictional necessities, we'd learned it was an abandoned Lutheran church. A red-brick building with running water and electricity, it had fared better than the Presbyterian church, giving Dowd a quick startup time and the ability to hold masses almost immediately after finishing the move west.

I had patrol officers line the rear of the building where four large RVs were parked. They were also sprinkled throughout the grounds where massive plots of fields had been converted into a parking lot along with rows of porta-potties, the chemical smell sitting like a cloud over the entire property. There were no generators lining one side of the building, so the noise levels outside were quiet, save for the crickets in the fields, a hawk calling overhead. We were near radio silence, strict instructions for limited communications only. I didn't want to do anything that would muster a run, or a repeat of the attack I'd endured.

The open fields gleamed with morning dew, our shoes coated wet as we made our way to the front doors. When the people waiting to enter the church saw us, they dispersed like frightened mice in a dim cellar. I motioned to the team, telling a third to go one side, and for the remaining to go the other, blocking any windows. My gun drawn, I wanted the building secured, leaving no chance of Dowd escaping.

Tracy and Nichelle stayed back, standing with my car, along with Dr. Swales sitting in the front seat after she'd insisted on joining us. I glanced over, finding Jericho with them, keeping watch, his gun holstered but unbuckled in the event this arrest went south.

"Remember," I said calmly. "There are a lot of people inside."

"Copy," Emanuel responded, his standing next to me, dwarfing my height. "Nervous?"

"Never," I told Emanuel, a grin on my lips. "This is the part of the job I live for."

Two officers peeled open the doors, bracing them with cinder blocks, the colorful spotlights spilling onto us, the band playing loudly, the congregation stomping their feet. Through the crowd, I saw Dowd racing across the stage, his face wet, his suit bright, singing a hymn.

His heart beat heavy as he sang a verse and urged the congregation on. They did as he asked, singing and stomping and playing hard enough to make the church's overhead lights shimmer.

This new church came with a holy reinvigoration. The weight of resentment gone from his soul and from his heart. A cleansing, lifting him, lifting his given name of Ethan Hughs so that Richard Dowd's birth was final. Sweat poured over his face, his white skin bathed in *His* holiness, but like the slightest of nagging itches from his wig, a heartfelt pang came for the one he missed, his one true love, David.

The rear doors opened, slices of daylight cutting across the congregation. Dowd's heart swelled, his church growing and bursting at the seams, the word of mouth carrying his name far and wide. He pressed the microphone to his lips, the metallic mesh warmed with his breath, "Come, enter and pray with us," he yelled, the band's guitarist driving a riff as the crowd cheered.

The doors remained open and bodies filed through. He heard gasps and screams, the service abruptly ending. The overhead lights came on, the rear of the church lined with police, the congregation filing through doors. Dowd's excitement turned like a burning flame batted by the wind. "Wait! Where are you going! I haven't finished—" Fear took his words when he saw them, saw them standing in his church. It was Detective White, along with the one they called Emanuel, their guns drawn on him.

"You bring a gun into this holy place?" Dowd yelled at us, his small frame frozen on stage, the microphone pressed to his mouth.

"Richard Dowd!" I yelled, scanning the crowd, ensuring our safety as we made our way closer to the stage. I saw the girl who had attacked me, the smile from that evening replaced with shock and awe. "Her," I told one of the patrol officers. "Wendy Doyle. We'll want to talk to her too."

"Get your hands off me!" Wendy Doyle screamed as the officer took her by the arm. "Motherfucker!" A wad of spit smacked the side of my face.

"You okay?" Emanuel asked.

I holstered my gun, wiping at the warm gunk running down my cheek, sickened by it. There were lines forming to exit, faces of disappointed believers passing in silence. "I'm fine. Let's get on with it."

Behind Dowd, patrol officers appeared on the stage. The band members huddled closely, confusion on their faces. One by one, they placed their instruments on the stage as the colored spotlights stopped dancing. "You can go," I told them, tilting my head toward the exit. They hurried in a near run, single file, their backs to Dowd. As they exited the church, they never turned once.

"Richard Dowd, you are under arrest for the murder of Sharon Telly."

"Bullshit!" Dowd yelled, his voice booming over the speakers, his lips still pressed against the microphone. He'd broken character for the first time. I was speaking to Ethan Hughs. "You don't have a fucking thing on me!"

Dr. Swales appeared from behind Emanuel and me. I gave her a stern look, frowning, my instructions clear about her staying in the car. "I had to see," she said to me. In her hands was a copy of the fingerprint card from Ethan Hughs's case file. It was the evidence we needed. The partial fingerprints on my friend's arm were not Andrea Hill's after all. The fingerprints were from Ethan Hughs.

She handed me the card. I held it up. "We've confirmed your fingerprints."

Dowd jumped from the stage, the cordless microphone still in hand. He approached me, anger changing the shape of his face, his eyes never leaving mine. I sensed Emanuel's unrest, his posture shifting. I motioned it was okay, but inside a part of me was suddenly very afraid of Dowd, the sting above my eyes coming to life like some kind of warning signal.

It was the microphone that did it—breaking the proverbial camel's back, the last straw—when I reached for it, threatening to take his voice from him, Dowd swung at me. It was a gut reaction from a man who'd spent his early adult life in prison. He was defending what was his. He missed hitting me, a rush of air breezing across my face. The swing was wild, his wig falling askew, putting Dowd into a position that made it easy to restrain him. He squirmed like a child as Emanuel held his shoulders and I placed the handcuffs on his wrists.

"May I?" Dr. Swales asked. Dowd's height accommodated her small stature. She leaned up to check the back of Dowd's neck. "Detective, did you see these?"

"Bug bites," Dowd huffed, snarling. "I scratched myself while I was asleep.

"Funny," I said. "With your back turned, you knew what we were talking about? Oh, and by the way, love that press conference you gave the other day."

I walked around Dowd, his face contorted by fear and confusion and anger. "What about it?"

"You mentioned the victims and the mutilations. A particular detail we never released."

"Does it matter? I probably overheard it when I was in the station."

I shook my head, moving so my face was in his. "You didn't overhear anything. You knew what David Reynolds was doing. You knew he was killing the jurors."

"You'll never prove it," he said. I nodded at the patrol officers and watched Dowd as he was escorted from the church.

CHAPTER FIFTY

The surf pounded the beach, waves thundering and chasing Tiny and Lisa Pearson, the two reunited, melting years from the old dog as they frolicked in the foamy water. Lisa's aunt and uncle had had a change of heart about Tiny and had decided to bring him into their home. A smile was plastered from ear to ear on Lisa's face, and I could tell from the way she held Tiny, she must have had some say in convincing them.

"We want to thank you both," Lisa's aunt said, her husband taking my hand, and nodding to her words. A stout woman with a round pale face, she held a small yellow umbrella to shield her from the sunlight. Her husband was taller, bigger, the two resembling Carl and Peggy Pearson. But it was in Lisa's face where I saw the real resemblance to Peggy and also in her eyes.

Jericho dug the tip of his shoe into the hard sand, a quiet nod. "She looks better," he said, nudging his chin toward Lisa. "Have to admit, I'll miss Tiny."

Lisa's uncle swallowed hard, the reason for our meeting on the beach coming to the surface. He shook his head then took Jericho's hand. He took my hand again with his left, holding both of us and saying, "I can't tell you how grateful I am. The way you guys saved my niece's life. If it hadn't been for you—"

"I'm glad we were there for her," I told them as he choked up, his wife's arm wrapped with his. I peered over their shoulders, watching Tiny bow, his hind legs in the air, rump wiggling as he jumped and played with Lisa. I couldn't get over how much of a puppy he'd become in her company. And I couldn't get over how well Lisa had healed. She was a different person than the frail body we'd discovered inside the campground RV. "She looks amazing."

"Like nothing happened," Lisa's aunt replied. She tilted her head, eyes cast down. "Well, almost, but you know what I mean."

"They're in prison?" her uncle asked. "That preacher and the lawyer?"

"Jail," Jericho answered. "For now. Once the sentencing takes place, they'll be in prison."

"Good," Lisa's uncle said, his voice choppy as the rising tide sent a wave rushing across our feet.

Lisa's aunt cupped her hand and faced Lisa to yell, "Honey, we need to get on the road."

"Reynolds the lawyer, won't face a trial," I said, continuing to explain what would happen next. "But it's a good thing," I assured her as her eyes widened. "He's going in front of the judge tomorrow for sentencing, and then to prison from there."

She side-eyed her husband and brushed a lock of curly hair from her eyes. The day's heat and high sun had already started to turn her skin pink, her cheeks flushed while she fanned the sweat on her brow. "The sooner this is over with, the better."

"What about the preacher?" Lisa's uncle asked, a look of reserve on his face, the kind I'd seen before when toying with the idea of retribution.

"He'll face trial, but the evidence against him is strong. Rest assured, he'll be in prison the rest of his life."

"Lisa!" the woman yelled, beads of sweat on her upper lip. She gathered herself and tugged on her husband's arm.

"Thank you again," Lisa's uncle said as his niece and Tiny joined us.

Lisa surprised me with a hug. I kneeled to meet her, my knees in the wet sand, Tiny's nose on my face a last time. The suddenness of it came with a hitch in my chest and emotion tugging my heart. I was going to miss his company, but was happy to see him go with Lisa, where he belonged.

"You take care," I told them.

The family gathered themselves, leaving us alone on the beach, the waves mounting with a new storm in the Atlantic. We'd gone full circle since the first campground murders—a hurricane ending when the Pearsons were murdered, and a new one beginning as Lisa Pearson began her new life.

Like Lisa Pearson, Andrea Hill had found a new home too. Child services were contacted by a law firm, discovering that Ben Hill and his partner had made arrangements years earlier, giving specific instructions of granting guardianship to two gentlemen who'd been very active in Andrea's life. As for the burns on Andrea Hill's arm, she finally confessed to us after Dowd's arrest. Andrea told us she'd been with Dowd the night of the fire, his having talked her into helping him. Her confession was filled with regretful tears and pleas of forgiveness, and although I felt for how terribly misguided she was, I knew this case wasn't over for her. She was likely to spend a lot more time in the Outer Banks and its juvenile court system.

As I watched Lisa with her aunt and uncle, the last glimpse of them as they rounded the corner of my place, I couldn't help but sigh as I thought of Hannah. If one family could be reunited, a missing girl found, why not mine? I'd been plagued with the same cruel jealousies for as long as I'd searched for my daughter. I was happy for Lisa, her family, but inside, it killed me a little.

"Any news on Hannah? Any sightings from the sites Nichelle showed you?" Jericho asked, seeming to read my mind.

I shook my head and turned into the wind and the ocean. The horizon was a deep gray blue, the center of it turning black with dark-green edges and swirling with bright soundless flashes coming from the center. Nichelle hadn't found anything new. I gripped his arm. "She's still here though. I can feel it."

"If Nichelle is helping, you'll find your daughter," he said, sounding the way I needed to feel, more confident. He gave me a squeeze, his phone breaking our moment with text messages. His eyes went to the screen while I watched the ocean. Breaking sunlight shined into the surf's spray and threw rainbows into the air. "It's official."

"What's official?"

"The council is calling for an emergency election to fill the mayor's position."

"Really?" I asked, a sad weight in my chest, the news a reminder about Daniel Ashtole. "It's so soon. Don't you think?"

He shrugged, shallow pouches beneath his blue-green eyes evidence of the trying times we'd endured. "This place needs a mayor. It won't run itself."

Vote Flynn to Win, a memory spoke from out of nowhere, a reminder of Jericho's old campaign slogan. "Jericho?" I asked, my voice pensive.

There was hesitation, a salty breath batting against our bodies, the looming hurricane whispering in our ears. Jericho tucked his phone away, and said, "I've been asked if I'd consider running, fill the seat."

"You're talking about running for sheriff, right? And only if Sheriff Petro decides not to run next term?" I searched his eyes for clarification but saw there was more. This wasn't about being sheriff at all.

"I think maybe I'm ready to try something new, grow a little," he said with uncertainty in his tone, something I'd never heard before. "At first, I thought about running for sheriff, but I've already done that. Doing it again would be a step backward."

"Mayor?" I asked, a part of me excited by the idea, but cautiously so, even a little afraid for him. I cupped his face in my hands, kissing him again, and then said, "Let's hear how it sounds, *Mayor Jericho Flynn*."

"Not bad," he answered, a smile returning. With his brow raised, a sheepish look on his face, he asked, "Can I get your vote?"

"Always," I told him. He pulled me into his arms, a wave crashing against our legs, the tide rising fast. I yelled into the surf, "Vote Flynn to win!"

"It does mean a lot of changes though—campaign managers, some traveling, speeches, photo ops, and I'm sure there will be a few debates." I peered up into his face, anxious about the changes. "Do you think you're up to it?" he asked.

"I can handle it," I told him nervously, without understanding what was in store for us. But I trusted Jericho knew and that's all I needed. "I love you."

"I love you too," he said as I tucked my face into his chest, happy to have the issues with Ronald behind us—our living for the future rather than my living in the past.

We walked along the coastline for the next hour, the waves at high tide, cresting above my head and pummeling the beach. With their roar, I could feel the power in them, feel it in my feet. I kept my arm in Jericho's, his changing the subject about Hannah, and trying to cheer me up with talk about his upcoming campaign, his platform, and his plans to do all the things he knew Daniel wanted to do.

"Do you feel up to walking on the boardwalk?" he asked as we reached the entrance, sea spray hitting us, water droplets glistening from the stubble on his chin.

"How about some ice cream?" I asked with a laugh, spying the shop where I'd thrown a fit.

"Only if you promise to behave," he joked, following me up the ramp, the sand crunching beneath our shoes.

"You know I can't promise anything," I said, my spirits lifting with the jamboree smells of boardwalk fun along with the flashing sights and carnival sounds.

We wove through the foot traffic, the ice-cream shop within eyesight of the beach, passing couples young and old, and families hand in hand with their children. There was a new pair of clowns near the shop, dressed in ballooning blue-and-green polka-dot slacks, red-and-white striped shirts, and enormous yellow ties, all the colors clashing wondrously. They danced in circles, arms hooked, legs kicking as they balanced racks of cotton candy and apples on sticks, their candied coatings glistening with secret invitations to my sweet tooth.

"Rocky road," Jericho said when we reached the ice-cream shop, our bodies pressed against the counter like children waiting anxiously for that first sugary taste. The inside of the shop smelled frosty and sweet, the counter fronted with long refrigeration bins, glass covered and showing massive tubs of ice cream. "What do you want?"

I searched the dozens of flavors, deciding I'd try something new today. "Do you carry something with coffee?" I asked the attendant behind the counter.

"One second," she answered, standing on a stepstool and carefully pulling a carton of sugar-cones from a shelf. Like the others working the store, the attendant wore the colors of the shop, brown pants and a bright-yellow shirt, her head topped with a green baseball cap, her hair in a long braid that reached the middle of her back. "Be right there."

"No rush, I'm still—" I began, my heart stopping when I saw her, the girl stepping down, the carton in hand, a glimpse of her face and neck and a tattoo I knew.

Jericho sensed my reaction and came to my side, my weight shifting into his arms. She turned to face us, her eyes set on Jericho first while she handed the sugar-cones to a co-worker. I was breathless, unable to speak, my daughter standing on the other side of the counter, asking Jericho about his order.

When the girl I believed to be Hannah faced me, she hesitated a moment, turning briefly toward the exit, the neck tattoo identical to the pictures I had. For a horrible moment, my heart went cold with the thought she was going to run. She surprised me then with a wave, telling me she recognized me.

I offered my hand, debate clear on her face. Hannah took a step, locking eyes with mine, the moment taking me back to the morning she'd been kidnapped. Her smile appeared. It was faint and brief, but I saw her dimples and melted. My daughter was ready to see me.

"You're right," I told Jericho, finding the courage and strength to break our embrace, taking Hannah's hand in mine. "There's going to be a lot of changes."

A LETTER FROM B.R. SPANGLER

I want to say a huge thank you for choosing to read *The Innocent Girls*. If you enjoyed it, and want to keep up to date with all my latest releases, just sign up at the following link. Your email address will never be shared and you can unsubscribe at any time.

www.bookouture.com/br-spangler

I hope you loved *The Innocent Girls* and if you did I would be very grateful if you could write a review. I'd love to hear what you think, and it makes such a difference helping new readers to discover one of my books for the first time.

I love hearing from my readers—you can get in touch on my Facebook page, through Twitter, Goodreads or my website.

Thanks,
B.R. Spangler

authorbrianspangler
@BR_Spangler
brspangler.com

ACKNOWLEDGMENTS

I want to offer my immense gratitude and appreciation to a few who aided me with this novel.

To Ann Spangler for reading multiple drafts and for the keen eye in finding those nuisance mistakes I'll never see.

To Chris Cornely Razzi for the feedback on book two and for having allowed me to send her every book I've ever attempted over the years.

And to Monica for enduring multiple synopsis drafts and the earliest pages, and for her opinions and suggestions.

Also, a HUGE thank you to Ellen Gleeson for her amazing talent in recognizing the stories in the story and the help in pulling them to the surface for all to enjoy. Thank you to Peta Nightingale, Kim Nash, and the wonderful team at Bookouture.

Printed in Great Britain
by Amazon